"I marvel at the wisdom tucked away inside these pages, at the generosity and artistic grace on display here. This is a fine, fine book."

—STEVE YARBROUGH, author of *Prisoners of War* and *The Oxygen Man*

"Marshall is an extraordinary storyteller....[Her] greatest triumph is her ability to convey the humanity of all her characters." —*Publishers Weekly* (starred review)

"*Right as Rain* is a saga in the best sense of the word.... Marshall has put her heart and soul on the page for the reader and the result is a novel so haunting and beautiful that it will stay with me always. This book firmly establishes Bev Marshall as one of our most amazing and vivid American voices."

—SILAS HOUSE, author of *A Parchment of Leaves* and *Clay's Quilt*

"Bev Marshall has not so much written a novel as she has drawn back the curtain on a south-facing window, a view of Mississippi fifty years ago, of forty and thirty years ago.... They are not so much characters as people we have known; their stories not so much witnessed as shared. The shifting points of view—female and male, black and white—never shift away from honesty and authenticity."

—SONY BREWER, author of *Poet of Tolstoy Park*

Praise for Walking Through Shadows

MAIN

"This is a moving and beautifully written story that has the same authentic feel for a small southern town as Harper Lee's *To Kill a Mockingbird* and Olive Ann Burns's *Cold Sassy Tree*." —*Library Journal*

"Marshall's first novel is magnificently crafted with powerful characters that tug at the heart and create a spiral of emotions." —*Booklist*

"Bev Marshall's suspense-filled novel grabs you from the first paragraph. The voice is authentic and compelling, and the descriptive details are unusually vivid. You will have difficulty putting this one down until the mystery is solved."

—CASSANDRA KING, author of *The Sunday Wife*

ALSO BY BEV MARSHALL

Right as Rain

Walking Through Shadows

Hot Fudge Sundae Blues

Ballantine Books / New York

Hot Fudge Sundae Blues

a novel

Bev Marshall

A Ballantine Books Trade Paperback Original

Copyright © 2005 by Bev Marshall
Reading group guide copyright © 2005 by Random House, Inc.

Published in the United States by Ballantine Books, an
imprint of The Random House Publishing Group, a division of
Random House, Inc., New York.

BALLANTINE and colophon are registered trademarks of Random House, Inc.
READER'S CIRCLE and colophon are trademarks of Random House, Inc.

Library of Congress Cataloging-in-Publication Data
Marshall, Bev
Hot fudge sundae blues : a novel / Bev Marshall.
p.   cm.
ISBN 0-345-46843-0
1. Teenage girls—Fiction.   2. Children of alcoholics—Fiction.   3. Grandmothers—
Death—Fiction.   4. Child sexual abuse—Fiction.   5. Stepfathers—Fiction.   I. Title.
PS3613.A77H68 2005
813'.6—dc22
2005043571

Printed in the United States of America

www.thereaderscircle.com

2   4   6   8   9   7   5   3   1

Book design by Susan Turner

For the women who share my sundaes,
Shirley, Mandy, Tana, Jan, and Andreé,
with love and gratitude

In memory of my brother-in-law,
James B. Marshall,
who could eat sundaes faster than any of us

Acknowledgments

My heartfelt gratitude goes to Allison Dickens, my editor and friend. Her enthusiasm and sense of humor buoyed me through long days and problematic times, and her keen insights and incomparable editing skills made this novel far, far better than it might have been. My publicist, Cindy Murray, is just about perfect in every way, except for making her own reservations. And as if I weren't blessed enough, there is a warm support system for lucky Random House/Ballantine Books authors that includes Gina Centrello, Nancy Miller, Kim Hovey, Johanna Bowman, and Ingrid Powell. Thanks to all of you and to the staff members in various departments who work so hard to publish quality books.

And then there is Lisa Bankoff. If she liked chocolate, I'd send her a hot fudge sundae every day. She's my agent, my friend, my adviser, and the woman I most like to dream about. Thanks, Lisa. And thanks to Tina Dubois at ICM for graciously and promptly answering every SOS e-mail!

Working with gifted author Silas House was great fun and a true honor. Bless you, Silas.

The St. Tammany Writers Group are the most dedicated, loyal

group of writers in Louisiana, and I thank each of the members for their encouragement and sharp critiquing skills. Tracy Amond, Andreé Cosby, Lin Knutson, Karen Maceira, Mark Monk, and Katie Wainwright all read parts of this novel and contributed significantly to my revision. Special thanks and love to members Tana Bradley and Jan Chabreck, who read the entire first draft and made great critical and editorial suggestions.

My outstanding support system includes the board members of the Tennessee Williams New Orleans Literary Festival, especially Paul Willis, Jim Davis at the Jefferson Parish Library, Eric Johnson and cuz Dayne Sherman at Sims Library on Southeastern Louisiana University's campus, all the book sellers and reviewers I appreciate so much, and my wonderful and talented author friends. I wish I had space to name them all.

At Southeastern Louisiana University I am overjoyed to be the recipient of the warm support of Dr. Joan Faust, Dr. Tammy Bourg, Dr. Jeanne Dubino, and the English faculty, whose excellence is unequalled. Your friendship is sincerely appreciated, and I look forward to working with all of you in the coming months.

I am indebted to Rammie (Bubba) Gauchier for teaching me about molds and cement mixing and for sharing his life story with me one fine afternoon, and to Chris Forrest, who explained court procedures so well that, for the first time ever, I understood legalese jargon. I'm so lucky to be your aunt!

As always, my dear friends and wonderful family cheered me on and nourished me with their love. With my love in return, I thank Mandy and Joey Marshall, Shirley and Irvin Tate, Jim Forrest and Don Gouger, Zora Marshall, Cathy and Maria Marshall, David Acosta, Tana and George Bradley, Jan and Dickie Chabreck, Andreé Cosby, Emily Heckman, and the gang at Oak Knoll.

My heart belongs to Angela and Chess Acosta and to my dad, Ernest Forrest, who continues to bless me with his unconditional love, his wry sense of humor, and that incredible optimism he shares with everyone he meets.

Finally, to my husband, Butch, I appreciate you every day of my life for many reasons. For driving the bookmobile all those miles while patiently listening to me read my stories aloud. For turning my tears into laughter, for liking Piggly Wiggly takeout and cheap wine. For uncoiling the tangles in my mind with a dose of reality every now and then, and most of all, for loving me beyond belief on my empty days. I couldn't love you more.

Hot Fudge Sundae Blues

Chapter 1

THE YEAR I TURNED THIRTEEN I GOT RELIGION. OH, I'D BEEN going to church, praying like a sinner on her deathbed, but when the Holy Spirit flew over Mississippi, it never landed on me. All through the spring and summer of 1963, I sat beside Grandma on the sixth pew of Pisgah Methodist Church waiting for salvation, but the Lord never spoke one word to me. Grandma's shoulders drooped in disappointment when, Sunday after Sunday, I didn't join the other sinners who accepted Brother Thompson's invitation to "come on down and get wrapped in the bosom of the Lord." She was counting on me to lead a pious life because both her husband and her daughter were bent on sinning themselves straight into hell. Every Sunday, during the hour or so we sat on our hard wooden pew, breathing in the suffocating air of wilted gladiolas, Old Spice aftershave, and Mrs. Duncan's Midnight in Paris perfume, Papaw would be out riding across the pasture on Jim, a dappled gray that he claimed was the fastest in Lexie County. Mama slept late on Sundays.

So as Grandma's only grandchild and last hope for conversion, I felt a huge responsibility to get saved, but I hadn't been able to get my feet moving down the crimson carpeted aisle of Pisgah Methodist up until this Sunday. Brother Thompson hadn't enticed a sinner to come up and get saved for several weeks, and at the end of every service, he would wearily lift his hand for the benediction. Then, with his voice filled with disappointment, he would pray for us sinners to get washed in Jesus' blood and become whiter than snow.

So on this hot August morning, I pretended the Holy Spirit had finally lit on me because I wanted to please the preacher and Grandma, who had had a big fight with Mama the night before and seemed more down than usual, and because Jehu Albright, the cutest boy in the ninth grade, was sitting across the aisle on the fourth pew down from us. We always sat on the right-hand pews because the morning sun bore down on the other side of the church, making it hotter than Hades, and over there you could see forty or more cardboard fans flapping faster than a wasp could fly. I had thought that Jehu was a Baptist, but his mother told Grandma that they had been attending Centenary Methodist in town and didn't like their new pastor, who had posted on the bulletin board in the vestibule a list of the members who hadn't signed their pledge cards.

Today Brother Thompson's sermon was about Jesus feeding the multitudes with a few hunks of bread and a couple of little fish, and although I believed in miracles, I was having a hard time picturing the baskets filling up with loaves and fishes over and over like that. But then it occurred to me that, if what you couldn't imagine could be true, maybe Grandma wouldn't know that I was about to fake salvation. So when Miss Wilda banged out the first chords of "Just as I Am" on the old black upright piano, with heart racing like a galloping horse, I squeezed past Grandma's knees and stepped out into the aisle. My taffeta dress, the color of a grape Popsicle, rustled applause as I slowly made my way up to the altar. When I passed Jehu's pew, I paused, tucked a curl behind my ear, and glanced over at him with what I hoped was a beatific smile. After I reached the altar rail, Brother Thompson, trembling with joy, leaned over and placed his hand on the top of my head. "Do you accept Jesus Christ as your Lord and Savior?" he whispered.

His voice was filled with such happiness I thought he might burst out laughing, and quickly I answered, "Uh huh. Yessir."

I had been rehearsing this scene all summer on Saturdays, which was the day Grandma and I cleaned the church. Grandma had taken the job, refusing payment for her labors, avowing that menial tasks would keep us humble. She assured me that the reward of serving the Lord was compensation enough. I didn't want the Lord's rewards. I wanted cash to purchase a madras blouse and a wraparound skirt, but Grandma had refused even the paltry sum that Brother Thompson offered her from the collection of coins and bills that piled up in the silver pie plate we passed around every time the church doors opened.

After I finished my Saturday chores of dusting pews and straightening the song books, I enacted all the roles in the play I had written, entitled "Layla Jay Gets Saved and Wins a Young Boy's Heart." I pounded out hymns on the piano, switching my singing voice from soprano to alto, harmonizing with myself as perfectly as an entire choir inside my head. In the role of preacher, I gripped the lectern until sweat stung my eyes as I shouted out for the sinners to come down and be saved. I had also rehearsed the heroine's part I was playing now—that of repentant sinner tearfully asking for forgiveness. I was ready to testify, to admit to any and all sins, for what would it matter, the past? But before I could blurt out a single sin, Brother Thompson raised his hands and gave the benediction. My moment was over in less time than it took to close a hymnal. I stood beside the preacher, filled with disappointment as I accepted the first congratulatory hand, which belonged to old Mr. Stokes. "Bless you, child," he said, spraying small droplets of saliva on my new taffeta bodice, which I had stuffed with a pair of socks for Jehu Albright's perusal. Then came the others: Mr. Felder, Mr. and Mrs. Frank Utley, Doris Faye Wiggins, Joan Gail Martin, Mary Lynn Sutter, and Johnny Moore Jr. They shuffled past me with blessings and smiles, and suddenly there he was standing right in front of me. Blond crew cut pomaded with grease, rabbit-sized front teeth, a good strong jaw, my Ideal.

"Congratulations, Layla Jay," Jehu mumbled. "You staying for dinner on the ground?"

"Thank you. Yes, I am," I whispered in the reverent tone I had practiced. And then he was gone, and Mrs. Gabe Tucker was swinging her oversized purse into my stomach as she stretched out her fat fingers to pinch my arm. "Welcome, child. You're safe in the Lord's hands now."

After pumping the remaining hands of the Lord's disciples, I escaped outside and meandered around the church grounds, where I spotted

Jehu lobbing pinecones at my cousin James Louis, who was firing back with cones of his own. I have hated James Louis for as long as I can remember. He is meaner than a starving bulldog, but around grown-ups, he acts like a poodle puppy, all fuzzy and soft and eager to please. Like all older women, my grandma loves him. This is how I came to know that women can be easily fooled by men, and, since learning this fact, have resolved to never never be taken in by anyone of the opposite sex. I do not fear this happening with Jehu Albright. I will never believe that he is capable of the kind of duplicity my cousin James Louis demonstrates.

When Brother Thompson called for quiet so he could get another prayer going, I walked over to the folding tables set up between two oak trees that served as boundaries for the little kids. Waiting for us to assemble and quiet down, he stood at the head of the table, holding up both hands like he was signaling a touchdown for the Zebulon Cougars. Jehu was standing to my left with his head bowed and his hands crossed over a pinecone behind his back.

Although delirious with happiness over my conversion, Grandma frowned when I fished around in one of the fried chicken platters for the piece that held the pulley bone. I ignored her. I needed to make a wish and I figured a pulley bone that had been blessed by a preacher would be extra good luck if I broke it right. Jehu was already going back for seconds when I took my plate over to the brick steps that led to the back of the church. My best friend, June McCormick, had saved me a spot, and when I sat down beside her, she leaned over and bumped my arm with her plate. "How come you decided to get saved today?"

I bit off a piece of crunchy chicken. "Got filled up with the Spirit."

"You did not."

"Did so."

June patted her teased wheat-colored bubble hairdo that Mama said made her face look fat. "Well, I don't believe you. You just wanted to parade up to the altar to show off your new dress I'll bet."

Better to let her think vanity rather than seduction. "Well, okay. But I was planning on getting saved sometime soon anyway," I said, holding up my pinkie. "Secret pledge?"

June licked the fried chicken grease from her fingers and wrapped her little finger around mine. "Sure. I won't tell anyone. I'm your friend. You wouldn't tell on me."

Thinking that a subtle hint of blackmail was good insurance, I said, "No. I didn't tell anyone that you took a quarter out of the collection plate to buy nail polish that time." This prompted June to recite from memory all the new colors of polish sitting on her dresser, and after I offered my opinion that blue-based red polish, rather than orange-red, went with green outfits, I broached the subject I was most anxious to talk about. "Grandma said Jehu Albright's family is joining Pisgah. They switched over from Centenary."

"Yeah, I knew they were going to. My mother and his mother are in Beta Sigma Phi together. I think he's cool, looks a little like Steve McQueen, doesn't he?" I held my breath, hoping June didn't have a crush on him, too. She was far more popular than I and could get boyfriends as easily as you could catch chicken pox. She glanced over to where Jehu sat with his back against an oak tree. "But he's got big teeth and everybody knows crew cuts are passé." Breathing with a lighter heart, I tore the white meat away from the pulley bone and held it out to her. As we closed our eyes and pulled, I made my wish for Jehu Albright to love me and got the short bone.

After everyone had eaten all their stomachs could hold, they began to gather their empty bowls and say their good-byes. As I walked to Grandma's old green Plymouth, I saw Jehu and his family driving away in their big white Chrysler Imperial and vowed that someday I'd be cuddled up beside him on the backseat of that car.

As soon as Grandma parked the Plymouth under the carport, I ran into the house to find Mama. She was sitting at the dining room table in her green satin robe, smoking a Lucky Strike between sips of strong black coffee. I could tell by the straight lines between her brows that she had a hangover again.

When Grandma came in through the kitchen door, Mama blew two smoke circles over the table and then said, "So how was church?"

"Wonderful. Layla Jay got saved." Grandma drew the pearl hat pin from her pink pillbox and lifted it off her head. "It's a shame you weren't there, Frieda."

Mama ignored the last comment. She laid her cigarette on the ashtray and lifted her arms to hug me. "Honey, that's nice. I'm glad for you. And you look so pretty in your purple dress. Were many people there?"

"Regular crowd," I said, sliding onto the chair beside her. "Brother

Thompson gave me a New Testament." I drew out the small white leather-bound book from my patent purse.

Mama laughed, took up her cigarette again, and blew out another ring of smoke. "I didn't know you got a prize along with salvation."

Grandma ignored the joke, but I couldn't help smiling. Next to Papaw, Mama was the wittiest person I knew. Grandma pulled at the fingers of her white gloves until they flapped off the ends of her hands and fell onto the table. She looked down the hall. "Where's Claude? Did he feed the chickens?"

Mama shrugged. "Pop was gone when I got up. Haven't seen him." She pushed back her chair. "I better get dressed. Will is picking me up in an hour."

I gripped the New Testament tightly. Although Grandma had told me that it was a sin to hate and you could wind up in hell for not opening your heart to people who didn't know God's love, she definitely hated Will Satterly. Grandma sucked in her breath, gathering air to spew out her disapproval, but before she could say a word, Mama wiggled her robe from her shoulders and naked as a newborn walked out of the room. Just before her bedroom door slammed, she yelled at Grandma. "Save your breath. I'll wait for him out front."

My mother had been dating Will for nearly a month, so I knew that he wouldn't be visiting our house much longer. None of Mama's beaus lasted for more than three or four weeks. Mama had gotten rid of Errol Newman after only one picture show, and Jake Lott held the record for keeping Mama interested for the longest time of six and a half weeks. Grandma didn't like any of the men Mama brought home, but she especially loathed Will because the weekend before this one he and my mother had come home at four in the morning to find Grandma sitting with the phone in her lap dialing the hospital emergency room number.

That night Mama and Grandma had argued until milking time when Papaw woke up and threatened to call the sheriff if they didn't shut up and get some biscuits in the oven. Papaw missed most of the fuss because he is a really sound sleeper, but even though I had squeezed my pillow over my ears, I heard every word they screamed at each other. Grandma called Mama a Jezebel, the devil's child, and a couple of other names I didn't know she knew. Mama retaliated by breaking two of the porcelain figurines on Grandma's whatnot shelf, and kicking the coffee table till one leg broke off, so that it looked as drunk as Mama. I was glad about the whatnots as they were a pain to move when I had to dust the shelves.

After we heard Mama's door slam, Grandma frowned at me even though I hadn't said a word. "Go change your clothes," she said. "I'm leaving in fifteen minutes."

Sunday afternoons Grandma and I visited the infirm. That's what she called anyone who belonged to Pisgah and skipped church. I was changing into a pair of shorts when Grandma came into my room and said that she had decided to go alone today because, as a newly saved Christian, I should spend the afternoon staying close to God by reading scripture and offering up prayers of thanks. I had expected just the opposite. If I wasn't a sinner anymore, it seemed to me I wouldn't need to read the Bible near as much. But I didn't argue because I welcomed the opportunity to have the house to myself. Papaw was most likely gone for the entire day, Mama wouldn't be back until late, and with Grandma out visiting, I could count on at least three hours or so of absolute freedom during which time I planned on experimenting with Mama's makeup.

Mama's business is makeup. She sells Elizabeth Arden at Salloum's department store in Zebulon. My mother got the job because she's beautiful. Her hair is the color of tobacco streaked with gold and it falls in soft waves that ripple across her shoulders when she walks across a room. Her smooth white skin, without a pimple or blemish of any kind, is as soft as a feather pillow, and she keeps it that way by applying moisturizers twice daily. Since I have entered puberty and am engaged in a war with pimples, Mama has brought home jars of a variety of pimple-fighting weapons that smell dreadful but seem to be winning. I have her nose, and I'm hoping that somewhere within me lies a gene that will develop into fabulous breasts exactly like hers. Mama says I got my long slender feet from Daddy's gene pool.

My father's name is Kenneth Woodrow Andrews, and because he died before I was two, I don't remember anything about him. I'm absolutely certain he was much nicer than any of the men who treat me like a kid when they stand in the living room waiting for Mama to make her appearance. I know what Daddy's voice sounds like because he talks to me sometimes when I get the hot fudge sundae blues. That's what Mama calls them. When you're feeling as rotten and low and hopeless as you can be and you think the world's biggest sponge couldn't mop up all the tears inside you, the remedy is this: You drive to the Tastee-Freez and order the large-size hot fudge sundae. And when it comes, the bright red cherry on top cheers you up a little, and then you spoon the first bite into your mouth and you taste the warm chocolate and the cool vanilla ice cream and the sweet sweet whipped cream, and you look at yourself in the rearview mirror of the car and you're wearing a white mustache, and you smile just a little, and after you've taken the last bite, satisfied and filled with that cup of joyful sweetness, suddenly you don't have the blues anymore.

But you can't always get to the Tastee-Freez, especially when you're only thirteen and you can't drive. So sometimes when I get the blues, my father comes and whispers words that sound like music and he tells me how much he misses me, how much he wishes he were here to hold me in his arms and kiss away my pain. I close my eyes and see him as he looks in the picture on Mama's nightstand. He is wearing a checkered shirt with the sleeves rolled up to his elbows. His hair, black as Jim's hooves, is swept back on the sides, and one piece falls across his forehead just above his laughing eyes. He is tall, with narrow hips and long slender feet encased in shiny brown alligator boots. I can feel his strong hands on my shoulders, his lips soft on my forehead. Sometimes he makes silly faces with his eyelids turned inside out and his fingers in his mouth stretching his lips out toward his wiggling ears. Other times his amber eyes are filled with pain, and I see his broken body lying beside the hunk of twisted metal that was his motorcycle. Mama often rode with him, but on the day of the accident, they had argued; Mama had thrown a potted plant against the wall where he stood, and she told me that he left the house brushing fine black dirt out of his hair. He hadn't stopped to pick up the helmet he usually wore. When Mama got the call from the hospital, she had finished repotting the asparagus fern and set it on the dining table between two candles that she planned to light when he came home.

After Grandma left, I did say a prayer, a plea for forgiveness for my latest sin. I knew that God couldn't be fooled like Grandma and Brother Thompson, so I asked Him to order the Holy Spirit to enter my heart and make things right. I also asked Him for breasts, Jehu Albright's love, and a daddy just like the one He had taken away from Mama and me.

Chapter 2

————

LIQUID EYELINER ISN'T EASY TO APPLY AND IT DRIES ON YOUR lids like cement. By the time Grandma got home, I had used up a third of a jar of cold cream trying to scrub off the wavy lines around my eyes. Right away she noticed the heightened color of my skin and felt my forehead for fever. All through supper she worried I was coming down with a summer cold or maybe the red measles or, Lord save us, scarlet fever. Papaw stuffed the last bite of pound cake in his mouth and, after a couple of swallows, said, "Bullshit! There's nothing wrong with Layla Jay. She looks fine to me."

Papaw hadn't been sick a day in his life and his theory was that churchgoers were more susceptible to disease because they spent so much time worrying about going to hell. And worry could kill you. He also believed a few swigs from the whiskey bottle he kept in the toolshed repelled germs and made you impervious to small aches and pains. Even Grandma had to admit that Papaw was a wondrous human specimen. We had seen him toss a two-hundred-pound hog out of the garden, swing a pickax like it was a piece of cardboard, and he was the longest hitter and fastest runner on the Elks baseball team. This was truly amazing because his lack of worry and his consumption of whiskey didn't extend to making him immune from accidents, which happened to him frequently and freakishly. He had lost three toes on his right foot when the jack broke and the car fell on him, half of his left ear had been torn off by a squirrel that for some unfathomable reason had leapt onto his head, he had a deep scar on his cheek from a flying fishhook, and two of his teeth were knocked out when he had a wreck in his Ford truck. We found them sitting straight up on the dashboard below the dent his head had made when his truck crashed into Mr. Moscary's delivery van. Although Grandma believed that these accidents were divine warning signs to her husband, none of these mishaps compelled him to go to church on Sunday. Papaw told her that God wanted him to use the time more wisely, and he continued on happily riding Jim across God's pastureland. After Grandma enlisted the preacher's help, Brother Thompson offered to pick him up for the men's supper after Wednesday prayer meeting, but Papaw refused, saying, "If God wants me sitting on a pew in Pisgah Methodist Church, He'll have to come down and give me a ride on His donkey."

When I asked Grandma why she hadn't chosen a husband more like herself, she took the longest time before answering. "Claude was such a cutup, handsome, of course, and very different from the other boys I knew. The first time I ever went out with him, I was smitten. Back then, I longed for adventure, and whenever I was with Claude, well, it was like my blood ran faster, like I was more alive. I could actually feel a sunset, smell the smoothness of glass, hear the taste of a ripe plum. He could make a simple walk to the pond seem like an expedition to some exotic place." She had smiled then, risking a quick glance at me before she turned her eyes to the quilt she was stitching. Lifting her shoulders in an uncharacteristic shrug as if she didn't care or maybe understand her allegiance to Papaw, she said, "Who knows, Layla Jay. Maybe it was as simple as that old adage that opposites attract. And to this day I don't know why your papaw fell in love with me. He knew I was a churchgoer, raised in a home where laughing too hard was frowned on. My mother believed that if you let go of your emotions and allowed them to take over you, then you were vulnerable to Satan entering your body. Papaw thought that was the craziest thing he'd ever heard and told her so. So Mother didn't come to our wedding. If you could call it that. Just a justice of the peace and me wearing a suit with a homemade camellia corsage." She gripped the scrap of material she held so tightly that her knuckles shown white. "I nearly didn't marry him because Claude told me straight out that he wasn't getting married in any church, and that he wasn't going to be preached to every week. I didn't think I could live with a man who was so opposed to my beliefs, but that next Sunday the sermon was about witnessing to others, how we ought to embrace the doubters and sinners, how it was our duty to be disciples for Jesus. I felt the Lord was speaking through our pastor directly to me, and that afternoon I told your papaw I would marry him."

If Grandma regretted her decision, she never let on that she did. I suspected that for all her nagging about attending church and fussing about Papaw's whiskey drinking and wild ideas, he could still make her blood run a lot faster than a revival preacher could.

After we did the supper dishes, Grandma and Papaw went to bed early like always. I slipped out of my room and tiptoed down the hall to Mama's room to wait for her to come home. When I was younger, I nearly always fell asleep before her return, but tonight I was wide awake when I heard the crunch of Will's tires on the gravel drive. Scooting across the bed, I knelt beside the window where I could see the entire circular drive lit by the porch lights.

When they got out of Will's Le Mans, I saw that Mama was wearing my favorite dress, the one Grandma had forbidden her to wear when the preacher came over for Sunday lunch. Mama said that God didn't give her great breasts intending for her to hide them, and the ruffle on the bodice of her bright blue dress was a perfect display shelf for them. Will took her hand as they walked toward the house, but the wide gap between their bodies was a sure sign that this was their last date. I propped the window up with the stick that we used to hold it in place, and with my nose pressed against the screen, the sweet scent of freshly cut hay wafted into the room as I watched Mama reenact the scene I had witnessed so many times before. Lifting her breasts, she breathed deeply, let out a little sigh, and shook her head. "It's been fun, Will, but Mama doesn't like you, and before we went out today, I promised her I wouldn't see you again." She offered him one of her half-smiles. "You know how much I like you, but I just can't go against my mother. I hope you understand."

I couldn't see his face, but Will said just about the same thing they all said when Mama used the sword of Grandma's disapproval to cut them off. "Aw, Frieda, you don't need your mother's permission to date anybody."

Mama fished for the house key in her purse. It was definitely over. When she held the key, she looked up at Will. "Hon, I am a widow whose circumstances are hard, and if it weren't for my parents, my little girl and I wouldn't have a pot to pee in or a window to throw it out."

Now came the moment that made me hold my breath. Would he walk away or would he snap up Mama's bait? He hesitated, most likely deliberating on how much he was willing to do to keep on dating her. Finally, he drew a long breath. "I guess I understand how it is with you and your mother, but, baby, I sure wish you'd change your mind."

Mama's voice sounded really really sad. "I'd love to, but I just can't. I've got Layla Jay to think about."

"Well, I guess this is good-bye then."

"Mmmm. Bye, Will." Mama leaned over and kissed him hard before he turned to jog across the wet grass to his car.

Looking up to the quarter moon, I smiled and whispered yet another prayer. "Thank you, Lord. Please send Mama a better man next time around."

Back in 1962, the year before this one, Darryl Thomas (who called me kiddo and tweaked my nose every time he saw me) had nearly been The One when he stepped right into the trap Mama set out to snare him. After her "pot to pee in" speech, he had offered to buy Mama and me a nice little house of our own, and Mama was dancing among the stars every day that week. But God is good. On the next date, Darryl reneged on his offer and admitted that he couldn't afford us on a policeman's pay.

Mama hadn't promised Grandma anything, of course, but she had promised me that someday she would find a nice rich man who would be a good daddy, who would get us a house of our own and take us to see the Eiffel Tower in Paris, France. Mama was crazy about all things French.

When I heard her key in the door, I slid down between the covers and closed my eyes. "You asleep?" she whispered.

I opened my eyes. "Nearly was. How was your date?"

She tossed her purse on the bed and kicked off her red high heels.

"Boring. Last week Will told me we would go dancing across the state line at Skinnys, but it was closed. We couldn't find one place that served liquor on Sunday in Zebulon and so we wound up going to see some stupid show he wanted to see about prisoners of war way the hell back in World War II. And the popcorn was as stale as the movie."

I sat cross-legged on my side of the bed next to the window. The wind had shifted and hot air drifted into the room. I lifted my hair from my neck and said, "Was it the one with Steve McQueen? *The Great Escape*?"

Mama came over to the bed and sat next to me. She sounded tired when she said, "Yeah, and when he rode that motorcycle . . . well, it just ruined the whole movie for me."

June and I had gone to the Palace and seen the show the week before, but when I had watched the scene of Steve McQueen driving that motorcycle like a daredevil, I hadn't thought about the connection between the bike and my being a half-orphan. I guessed that no matter how many men Mama dated, Daddy was the one she'd always love. I put my arm around her and kissed her cheek. "Will won't be back?"

She smiled then. "Nope. He got the boot tonight." Mama stood and went to her dresser and pulling her hair back with a silver clip, she smeared cold cream on her face. "Mother will be happy I'm sure."

Grandma tapped on the door and opened it simultaneously. "Happy about what?"

Mama lit a cigarette and blew a smoke stream toward Grandma. "I broke it off with Will, the devil's own disciple."

Grandma didn't say anything, but her face muscles relaxed with satisfaction. She looked over at me. "Get some sleep, Layla Jay. You might be coming down with something. Remember how red your face was earlier."

After she closed the door, Mama stubbed out her cigarette and pulled a tissue from the gold box on her dresser. "What's this about your face?"

"Just had to scrub it hard because I couldn't get that eyeliner off of me. I was trying to draw a line out toward my hairline like you do, the Cleopatra look, and you know how Grandma feels about me wearing makeup."

Mama laughed. "Practice practice. Next year you're going to get to wear all the makeup you want. We're going to get out of here soon. I promise."

Mama had made this vow every year since I was old enough to understand it. I knew it was important to her to think that someday we'd be free of Grandma's rule, but I didn't mind it nearly as much as she thought I did. There were a lot of good things about living with Grandma and Papaw. Grandma wasn't nearly as harsh with me as she was with Mama. Of course, I didn't disobey her openly like Mama did.

I jumped off the bed and kissed her. "I believe you," I said. "This year will be the one."

Mama smiled at herself in the mirror. "You bet. Now scoot! It's late, and tomorrow you register for school."

I skipped my nightly prayers as I felt I had prayed plenty enough for one day. I pulled back my spread and sheet and lay spread-eagle on the bed. The overhead fan was broken, and the heat lay as heavily as a winter coat on my body. I closed my eyes and saw Sandra Dee kissing Troy Donahue in the cave in the picture show I had seen before *The Great Escape* started playing at the Palace. Sandra and Troy had gone all the way, and she got pregnant. I figured this would probably happen to me if a boy ever fell in love with me, but I didn't need to worry because only one boy, Frankie Denham, had ever kissed me, and that was because he had to when we were playing post office at his birthday party back in sixth grade. After the kiss he told me that his mother had made him invite me because she and Grandma were friends.

Grandma had lots of friends. There were all the ladies at Pisgah Methodist who called her an angel when she showed up with covered dishes at their houses whenever they were sick or just had had a busy week. And she was the favorite pink lady at Zebulon Infirmary, the president of Beta Sigma Phi, and all of my teachers adored her because she volunteered for room mother every year.

Mama, on the other hand, had only one girlfriend, and Grandma didn't like her. Cybil Richards had been twice divorced and was Mama's best Elizabeth Arden customer. That's how they became friends. Mama had done a makeover on her that she said made her look the best she ever had. Of course, she wasn't nearly as pretty as Mama, but people were always telling her she looked like Ali MacGraw with shorter hair. She was tall, nearly six feet, dwarfing most of the other women who worked alongside her in the office building on Ninth Street. Cybil was Ned Pottle's personal secretary. Mr. Pottle was a certified public accountant, and since he filed tax forms for almost everybody in Zebulon, Cybil was, therefore, privy to the size of everyone's bank accounts. After tax season ended, Mama's friend had lots of free time to try on makeup at the Elizabeth Arden counter. Her nights were busier. She spent a lot of them with Ned when his wife played bridge or when an important meeting was devised as the means to spend the evening at the Slumbercrest Motel out on Highway 51. I knew this because Mama didn't believe in keeping secrets, especially when they were "so much fun to tell." I enjoyed being treated like a girlfriend instead of a daughter, and relished every detail Mama was willing to divulge, but the more she told, the more wary I became of confiding in her. And yet I usually couldn't help telling secrets I had planned to keep. Mama had a way of tricking me into revealing my most private thoughts. I could never figure out how she entrapped me because she was so damn good at it.

Thus far I had been able to keep my love for Jehu Albright a secret, although I knew it was just a matter of time until Mama got it out of me. In fact, I imagined she would unearth every pebble in my soul the next day when we registered for school. Because both Jehu's and my last names began with an *A,* we would be registering at Zebulon Junior High at the same time, and Mama would be sure to notice, even feel, my hunger for Jehu's love. I was ready for the spark to ignite, and my hopes were high. Hadn't a special look passed between us when he shook my hand after church? And reflecting back on the day, it now occurred to me that perhaps he had chosen to horse around with James Louis because he was *my* cousin. And I would be looking my best tomorrow in my blue denim wraparound, a madras blouse, and fake pearls Mama had bought for me at Woolworth's. With all of these positive thoughts swirling in my head, I was filled with confidence and bravado that night.

But when morning came, I awoke with a new pimple and a cowlick that defied lacquering, and when Mama and I walked into the school gymnasium, the first person I saw was Lyn Parks with her arms wrapped around Jehu's shoulders. She was wearing real pearls.

Chapter 3

I THOUGHT PERHAPS GOD WAS PUNISHING ME FOR FAKING SALvation. If crime doesn't pay, sin can make you go bankrupt. I had not only lost Jehu to Lyn, I had to pretend I was happy for June when she was chosen over me for cheerleader. Mama tried to convince me that the contest was rigged, but I knew better. June laid a sympathetic arm around my shoulder and told me I had gotten only five votes when I demanded a recount. I appreciated how hard she tried to disguise her happiness over her 137 yes votes, but she didn't look over at the table where I sat waiting for her in the lunchroom when she walked over to sit with the cheerleaders.

I think Grandma was secretly happy I didn't make the cheerleader squad. She didn't approve of girls spreading their legs showing the dark blue bloomer panties they wore beneath the blue-and-white-striped skirts that flared out when they jumped up and yelled "Go Cougars." She told me that the navy pants suit with the gold braid the band members wore was much more impressive to view from the stadium bleachers, but I knew that the beautiful silver flute I held to my lips as I marched across the football field couldn't compare with a megaphone held by a pretty cheerleader. Papaw said, "Bullshit, Layla Jay. What do you care about that lousy football team? I'd be ashamed to cheer for those losers."

Had I known what else God had in store for me, I would have marched across the field with pride and been more grateful for the five people who voted for me. (Well, four. I voted for myself.) But God doesn't give hints, or foreshadow the coming events in your life, and so you go on grousing over petty disappointments, wallowing in self-pity, never suspecting that your life is going to take a detour to hell.

Like so many events in my life, my descent into hell began with good news. I was about to begin my fifth week of school when Grandma announced that the revival preacher who was coming to Pisgah would be staying with us. At first I was excited that a semicelebrity would be sleeping in my bedroom as Wallace Ebert's name was well known and revered in our community. He was a missionary to Uganda who had sent the Pisgah congregation newsletters through the past year entitled "Epistles of Light from the Darkness," and I had tithed part of my allowance for support of his mission. That our family had been chosen to house him seemed like a special blessing from God himself, but what appeared to be good fortune reversed into disaster quicker than our band could execute an about-face.

When she heard the news, Mama was livid; she argued with Grandma during every meal, which was the only time she would sit in the same room with her. At breakfast she waved a biscuit in the air. "Do not expect me to stop smoking just because some Bible thumper thinks my body is a temple." At supper, she wadded her paper napkin and threw it across the table when Grandma dispensed new house rules that included no cussing, no inappropriate clothes, and no alcohol (she looked over at Papaw on this one), and she forbade Mama to bring her dates inside while Brother Ebert was in our home. I tried to ward off a full-blown war between them by speaking up just then. "When I meet the preacher, I'm going to say, *Mi casa es su casa.* That means my house is your house." I was taking Spanish I and my teacher, Miss Schultz, said I had a real flair for language.

"But it isn't your house, Layla Jay, or mine. Mother is making that perfectly clear. Why don't we just move out? Will that make you happy?" Mama's face was turning the color of her dark red lipstick, a new Liz shade called Poppy.

Papaw stood up and ran his fingers over his silver hair. "Enough enough. Frieda, it's only five days; you can handle that, make your mama happy." He turned to Grandma. "And Zadie, quit your fussing. He ain't the president or a motion picture star. He's just a man who's good at getting folks all worked up over the heathens." He leaned down and kissed my cheek. "I'm going to bed, honey. I suggest you do the same, save your ears further blistering by these two hot tongues."

I didn't heed his advice, surmising that Mama and Grandma might need a referee or a bandage if things took a turn for the worse. Mama wouldn't give in on the smoking, clothes, or cussing, but she said she wouldn't bring home any men. She offered to move us out two more times, and I wondered where she thought we would go as the reason the preacher was staying with us was that there wasn't a decent motel in Zebulon. Just the Slumbercrest, and everyone knew that the beds there weren't for sleeping.

Grandma started crying when Mama said she never dreamed that things would turn out like this on the night she moved her baby in after she couldn't pay the mortgage on her own home. When Grandma said that she couldn't understand the Lord's decision to take away a good man like Kenneth because none of this would be said if he hadn't been killed, Mama started bawling, too. Both of them agreed that they couldn't get along and probably never would. "I'll never understand you" was said in unison several times. I sat between them not knowing who to pat. Whose misery was the deepest? I thought that I should have taken Papaw's suggestion and gone to bed, but now my rear end was glued to my chair. "Mama," I began. "Grandma." I wanted to avoid crying at all costs, but I felt the lump rising in my throat. I clamped my top teeth down on my bottom lip and looked up at the ceiling where an orange stain circled over Mama's head like a little halo that God might drop down on her to change our lives. But I knew He wasn't going to concern Himself with this mess, and I would have to think of a solution without divine assistance. "Mama, I've got an idea. Why don't you ask Cybil if you could stay with her while the preacher is here?" Even though Grandma didn't like Cybil, I was banking that her desire to provide a holy place for the earthly messiah surpassed her disapproval of Mama's friend. When no one spoke, I scraped my plate onto Papaw's and reached for Mama's. "I could move into your room, the preacher can have mine, and Grandma, you won't have to worry about a thing." They stared down at their plates, neither wanting to haul out the white flag first. Before they could think up an argument, I stood up and said, "Okay, then let's do that. Call Cybil, Mama. See what she says."

Mama wouldn't look at Grandma, but she left the room, and as we listened to her dial the telephone, Grandma blew me a kiss.

I don't know what I had expected Wallace Ebert to look like exactly, but my mental picture of him included lots of white wavy hair on a big head, kind blue eyes, an imposing figure of at least six feet. When he got out of Grandma's car, I was at my post beside Mama's bedroom window and on first glimpse thought she had grabbed the wrong man at the train depot. The man who lugged a tan suitcase onto our porch was short, dark-haired, stocky, no more than thirty-five years old, and really handsome. While I had pictured him with fleshy jowls, looking somewhat like Katharine Hepburn's brother in *The African Queen,* he had a craggy face much more like Humphrey Bogart's after he cleaned up for his Rosie. When he held out his hand for me to shake after Grandma introduced me as her little angel granddaughter, the hard calluses on his hand bit into mine. He looked down, straight into my eyes, and I knew right away that this man would never tweak a thirteen-year-old girl's nose.

I was happy Cybil had agreed to allow Mama to stay with her, as I was now the only unmarried woman in the house and the recipient of all of Wallace's admiration. He loved everything about me. That first afternoon as we sat in the living room sipping iced tea from Grandma's good crystal glasses as though we routinely used them, he instructed me to call him Wallace, instead of Reverend Ebert as he wasn't an ordained minister and my calling him Mr. Ebert made him think his father had risen from the grave. He told us that his daddy had been a sinner, addicted to whiskey and something called cocaine, and that his poor mother had been the one to call the law after he had stabbed a neighbor and robbed him of twelve dollars. Wallace's father died in prison when the homemade knife of an inmate turned on him. Reaching for a tea cake, he said, "My mother, God rest her soul, died from grief and shame, and I became an angry young man who took out my rage on others. For several years, I followed my father down sin's highway, drinking, cursing, and blaspheming the Lord. I was headed for a wreck that would destroy my soul."

He took a bite of the tea cake. "Delicious," he said to Grandma and me, sitting side by side on the couch, our eyes wide, our mouths hanging open at this startling confession. He seemed unperturbed by our countenances. "So you might wonder what saved me from destroying myself, why I'm not in prison or worse." I nodded assent, wondering what Grandma was thinking about having an over-the-top sinner sitting on her best armchair in our spotless living room. I knew the punch line to the story although I didn't know just how God had turned up to save him.

"It was the year I turned thirty, my birthday in fact. There was no cake, no ice cream, no happy birthday song. I was wandering the streets of Memphis looking for an easy mark. And I found one. A young girl wearing diamond earrings with an expensive leather purse hanging on her arm. All I had to do was knock her down, grab the purse, and I would have money to buy whiskey." He sat up straighter as though swelled with pride that he had been a good criminal. "I followed her down Beale Street onto a deserted side street, and just when my arm stretched out to grab her, she turned around."

Grandma and I were both spellbound. This was better than *The Fugitive,* my favorite TV show. "What happened?" I said, clutching my glass. I had never known a real criminal.

He smiled, and that smile was truly holy; it was like the Lord Himself was sending out love into the room. I was sure Wallace could save every sinner in Zebulon if they felt the warmth of that smile. "The girl spoke to me. She said, 'Brother, I know you're in pain. Let me help you.' And she opened her purse and gave me three hundred and five dollars, all she had."

"Three hundred!" Grandma was probably wondering what a young girl was thinking carrying around that much money.

"Yes, but there's more. She took off those diamond earrings and dropped them in my hand, saying, 'I have no need of riches. You're welcome to them.' She was *happy.* Can you imagine that?"

"No," I said. I had thought that maybe the girl was giving him all of this because she was afraid he would hurt her or that maybe she was cracked in the head, loony as they come. I had seen a plot similar to this on *Dragnet* once.

"She *was* happy though. Her face was glowing with joy. Radiant! She said I looked like I needed a good meal and would I like to go to her house with her as she had a whole roast cooked with good nourishing vegetables in a nice brown gravy." He had finished his cookie and took another one as though all this talk about food was making him hungry. I looked over at Grandma. She had cooked chicken pie for an early supper before the revival meeting, and I knew she was worried that he was ruining his appetite.

He leaned forward in his chair, hands clasped between his legs and in a softer voice, he said. "Her name was Mary; appropriate, isn't it? Mary laid out her best china and crystal on a white damask tablecloth. She had prepared the best meal I had eaten in years, and as I ate, she told me the story of the Good Samaritan. I had no knowledge of the Bible or of Jesus' love. My mother was a good woman, but she was ignorant of the ways of the Lord, and I was raised in a godless home. Mary talked to me about God's love and told me the wonderful stories of Jesus' life, how He died for me. 'Not for someone like me,' I said to her. She took my hand and said, 'Yes, you. Life everlasting is for everyone who accepts Him as their Savior.' When the sun came up that morning, we were still sitting at that beautiful table, but I was not the man who had come there planning to steal the very silver from which I had been served. From that moment on, I was transformed by the Holy Spirit, and before I left that gentle home, I knew that God had called me to do His glorious work."

I looked down at the rose-patterned rug beneath the coffee table. What would Wallace think if he knew I had faked salvation that Sunday? A man with such a dramatic calling might see right through me, recognize me for the sinner I was. I squirmed on the couch and tried to calm myself.

Grandma frowned at me. "I don't think I've ever heard a stronger testimony in all my years."

Wallace folded his hands like he was about to pray, but he grinned and said, "Did you say you made chicken pie for dinner? It's my favorite."

After we ate and changed into church clothes, Papaw announced that he was going to drive up to Jackson and spend the night with his cousin Douglas. They were going to attend the big livestock auction and it opened the next morning at seven sharp. Papaw wanted to purchase a few more hogs and said that, although he could buy some in Zebulon, he might get a better deal at the auction. Grandma and I both knew he was lying, but I figured that Grandma was glad he had made up a good excuse for not attending the revival. If Wallace thought Papaw was cheap, that was preferable to him finding out that he was an atheist.

If an atheist was sitting in Pisgah Methodist that night, he would have turned into a Christian by eight o'clock. Wallace could not only preach as good as Billy Graham, he could sing, too. When he sang "In the Garden," I thought he sounded just like Frankie Avalon. Before the collection plate was passed around, he testified about his past and told the story of his conversion. He changed it up a little from what he had told Grandma and me. In this version, the girl gave him a diamond necklace instead of earrings and he ate seafood instead of roast. They were small details, but it bothered me some. My doubts fled though when he began reciting his adventures in Uganda. The hardships he had faced! Sleeping on the ground with wild animals nearby, eating roots and berries when he got lost in the jungle, and he had nearly been killed by natives wearing nothing but strips of cloth between their legs. The women were bare-breasted, didn't know to cover their nakedness, he said. But before he left the country, Wallace had those women in dresses sitting on a bench in the grass-roofed church he built with our donations. He saved fourteen sinners the first night, a record for Pisgah Methodist.

Papaw stayed up in Jackson the entire week, calling every night with another reason he couldn't come home. His truck blew a gasket, he had upset stomach, and his cousin needed his help on a roof leak.

Mama didn't stay away though. She came home on Wednesday because Ned Pottle's wife went to visit her sister in Tennessee and he showed up at Cybil's with a suitcase filled with gin and lacy underwear he had bought for mutual enjoyment that night. "I wasn't about to be a spoke in that wheel," Mama said, throwing her own suitcase filled with uninteresting underwear on the bed. "We'll have to bunk in together," she said.

Grandma was furious, but with Wallace in the house, she kept her voice low. "You best behave, Frieda. I won't have you ruining Brother Ebert's visit."

She needn't have worried. Wallace took one look at Mama and fell in love. He didn't care that she cussed, smoked, imbibed spirits, and showed a lot of cleavage. I think he secretly wished he was back in Uganda, where Mama would be running around bare-breasted with her cigarette and a glass of whiskey.

All of the attention Wallace had lavished on me, asking me to play the flute for him, listening to my Spanish recitations, complimenting my good grades, and so on, vanished the moment Mama told him she could play the piano and knew how to cha-cha. I didn't know she could do the cha-cha, but she put a record on the hi-fi and swiveled her hips like she was born in Latin America. By Thursday Wallace was doing the cha-cha nearly as good as Mama.

The biggest surprise occurred that night. When I went into Mama's room to change into Sunday clothes for the revival meeting, Mama was pulling a ruffled high-neck blouse from her closet. "Where are you going?" I asked as she snaked her hips into a dull black skirt.

"Revival," she said. "Can I borrow your circle pin?"

"You're going to church with us?"

"Wallace invited me personally. He said it would mean a lot to him if I would come hear him preach."

I handed over the pin with a glad heart. Now I understood. All this attention he had been showing Mama was just a ruse to save her sinful soul. I, on the other hand, was already saved (at least that's what he thought), and that was the reason Wallace had chosen to spend so much time with her rather than me.

Mama swept into Pisgah Methodist and strutted down the aisle like she was a model on a runway in New York City. After she took her seat beside me, she looked up at Wallace with a big grin on her face that she held the entire two hours Wallace sang and preached. He was inspired that night. As he talked, he became increasingly passionate, throwing off his suit coat, flailing his arms every which way with sweat streaming down his face. He bounced full circle around the pulpit, jumped down to the altar, and boogied back and forth down the aisle. When he neared our pew and Mama caught his eye, he stopped dead still and fell silent. Mama fingered her circle pin and crossed her legs. Then she blew him a kiss and fell back on the pew laughing loud enough to be heard three pews over. All eyes in Pisgah church were swiveled around to us and

Grandma's face turned as white as the altar cloth. I think my face was the color of blood.

"Mortified" was what Grandma said as we walked to the car. "Frieda is a shameless hussy. I thought she was sincere about coming tonight and had so hoped she would find salvation, but just look how she acted. I'm never going to be able to hold my head up in church again."

I looked back to where Mama stood laughing with Dean Tucker on the church steps. Wallace was nearby shaking hands and accepting the compliments that rained down on him like manna. "Well, at least she didn't wear that blue dress," I said. "She *looked* like a Christian." As we sat in the car waiting for Mama and Wallace, I wondered what Grandma would say if she knew I was a fake Christian, too. At least Mama hadn't run down the aisle and pretended to be saved like I had. I wasn't sure who the Lord would choose as the worst sinner, me or Mama.

Chapter 4

O N THE FIRST SATURDAY IN NOVEMBER, MAMA AND WALLACE got married at the courthouse in Zebulon and drove off in Mama's Volkswagen for their honeymoon on the Gulf Coast. I was the maid of honor and Brother Thompson stood in as best man for Wallace. Grandma didn't attend. I thought about how her mother hadn't shown up at her and Papaw's wedding and wondered if she were starting a tradition in our family that meant that Mama wouldn't be around to see me say my vows when the time came.

Grandma had good reason for being mad. After revival was over on the Sunday following Mama's debacle in church, she and Wallace didn't come home until the next day. When they came slipping in the back door at six a.m., Grandma was whipping up pancake batter and said she smelled whiskey on Wallace's breath.

Wallace left that afternoon as he was leading another revival in Tupelo, so I moved back into my room thinking Mama's little fling was now just another page in Mama's History of Lost Men book. Was I ever wrong! The next Sunday Wallace jumped off the 2:30 train back into Mama's arms, and whatever happened that night caused him to cancel his next revival in Greenwood, a town of far more sinners than we had in Zebulon.

Grandma blamed Mama. To hear her tell it, her daughter was a sorceress, capable of casting a spell over God Himself. If someone as holy as Wallace could be enchanted by Mama, no one was safe. Papaw got a big kick out of it all. "Bullshit!" he said. "Frieda didn't have to cajole that apple off the tree; he was dying to fall. The man's a fake; I recognized his colors first night I met him. Frieda ain't got no more magic in her than Sam." Sam was our mule that ate up all our butter bean vines when he wiggled underneath the garden fence. I didn't believe Mama held any magical powers either unless you counted the power her size 36D bra had over men.

Whatever the reason, Mama had finally gotten herself a man who was willing to move us out of Grandma's house. After the wedding and before they left for the coast, Mama and Wallace drove me home. Mama was still mad at Grandma and refused to get out of the car, but Wallace escorted me into the living room where Grandma was sitting on the couch with an open Bible on her lap. Wallace knelt down and took her hands. "Zadie, I love your daughter and I love Layla Jay. I longed to have a daughter, prayed for the good Lord to send me a wife and child, and now He has answered my prayers." Wallace may have guessed that Grandma is one of those people who can talk themselves into believing just about anything if they want it badly enough. When her sister forged Grandma's signature on a check and told her she had no memory of doing it, that it was automatic writing from the spirit world, Grandma believed her. And didn't she believe I was genuinely saved? Although she still had reservations about the whiskey-drinking episode and fornication that she figured had most likely occurred, she was going to convince herself that Wallace was speaking the truth. He smiled and said, "I've taken the position of choir director at Centenary Methodist and I'll supplement the small salary by selling shoes at Vest's Shoe Store." He said that he and Mama had rented a little blue house on Fourth Street in Zebulon. Mama and Wallace would drive to work together every morning. I was to catch the school bus on the corner of Fifth and Sycamore. "We'll make a good home for Layla Jay," he said. Grandma accepted Wallace's peck on her cheek, and after he and Mama drove away, she put her arm around me. "You'll have a good daddy who will take care of you and your mama," she said.

"Bullshit," I whispered as I walked away from her to my room.

Mama had a husband, but I knew that God hadn't sent me a father. I tried to be happy for Mama. I wanted to believe that I was a gift God had given to Wallace. I wasn't sure what a daddy was supposed to do with a thirteen-year-old daughter, but I tried to imagine the two of us watching television together, sitting at the table doing homework, him tucking me into bed at night. But I couldn't forget those discrepancies in Wallace's conversion story. Wouldn't a person remember the exact details of an experience that changed his life? I would have known what Mary cooked for me, which piece of jewelry she offered me. Ever since Mama had entered Wallace's life, he hadn't shown the slightest interest in anything I said or did. Would a piece of paper that said he and Mama were husband and wife make Wallace love me? I doubted it. I suspected that maybe Wallace had prayed for Mama's breasts, but he hadn't asked for the child who had suckled them.

As the autumn wind stripped the trees of their leaves, I tore away the pieces of my life and stood naked in spirit and heart in the room where I had slept since birth. As I laid my old dolls and stuffed bears into cardboard boxes, I mourned each of them as if I were viewing them in a collective coffin. The life I had known had ended, and my trash can held the miscellany of my former self: a paper plate mask on which I had drawn Papaw's face with a big smile above the Popsicle stick I had glued on for a handle, starred Sunday school papers, folded notes passed in school, a red leather leash for Ginger, my collie who had been hit by a car. As I folded the afghan Grandma had knitted for me, I held it to my face and breathed in the scent of her talcum that clung to the yarn. I packed the photograph of Daddy, the framed picture of me in a sunsuit sitting on Papaw's new tractor, a map of the state of Mississippi, and the prayer of St. Francis printed in red on parchment paper. The nail holes and white spaces on my bedroom walls would attest to my former presence, and before I packed my cologne in my train case, I sprayed it on the curtains, hoping my scent would linger for a long time after I was gone. I had nearly forgotten to pack the box of memorabilia on the top shelf of my closet, and when I opened it, I found all of my ribbons with crosses on them that I had been awarded for recitation of Bible verses, "For God so loved the world," "In my Father's house there are many mansions." Grandma and Papaw's old farmhouse wasn't a mansion, but on the day I sealed the last box that held my life, it seemed like one.

Grandma told me nothing could change our love for each other; I wouldn't be far away, only a few miles, and we'd see each other often. But I saw the sadness in her eyes before she looked away. Although she would never admit it, I think Grandma mourned Mama's leaving, too, because I caught her sitting on the bed in Mama's room, looking around at Mama's possessions as if she were trying to memorize her daughter's life.

If Mama had regrets about moving, she hid them well. On the day when she and Wallace returned from their honeymoon, she packed up her entire room in one afternoon, and we spent that night in our new two-bedroom home.

We ate a celebration dinner of boiled shrimp and potato salad, which Mama had brought back from Biloxi, on the old dining table Papaw had brought down from the attic where Mama had stored her furniture so long ago. I had expected Mama to shed a tear or two when she saw all of the things that she and Daddy had shared, but she laughed when Wallace carried in the mattress from her and Daddy's old bed and fell down on it with a leer on his face. I was standing in the doorway, and when he looked up and grinned at me, I turned and fled down the hall to my own room.

I liked my bedroom. It was at the back of the house, lighted by a bank of four windows that looked out onto the backyard, where I spotted a squirrel's nest in the branches of an oak tree. The owners had left a bird feeder on a metal pole, and I imagined watching the orioles, sparrows, cardinals, and blue jays flying gracefully across the yard to partake of the seed I would pour into the feeder. On the two side walls of my bedroom I hung my map, the prayer of St. Francis, and my framed pictures, adding a new photo of me in my band uniform that Grandma had given me the day before we moved. In this snapshot a tall white hat shades my forehead, but you can see my narrow nose and my dishwater blond hair hanging down my back. My lips are open, ready to blow on the silver flute that I am lifting with elbows tilted out from my side.

My bedroom set—bed, double dresser, desk and chair—belonged to Grandma, but she gave all of them to me, saying she thought it would help me adjust to my new home. I had still been sleeping in a crib when Daddy died, and after Papaw brought it down from the attic, Mama said to put it back as she didn't plan on having any more kids. Which was a relief to me. I hadn't thought of this being a possibility, but Papaw winked at me and said he'd keep it near the pull-down stairs just in case a little brother or sister turned up someday. I hoped he was wrong; I wanted that crib to stay in the attic. I didn't want any siblings, and something in my gut told me that Wallace and I were in agreement on this.

We didn't agree on much else. I had thought we would be reading the Bible nightly, saying grace every meal, spending hours on our knees praying for God's blessings, but Wallace rarely opened the big black Bible on our coffee table, and his hands reached for the platters of food on our kitchen table before I could bow my head. I couldn't figure it out. Across from me sat a man who had spent many years among the heathens, risking life and limb to save their souls. He had preached so hard to save sinners all over the South and yet he seemed unperturbed that Mama was still saying goddamnit every time she messed up her fingernail polish. And he drank more bourbon than she did. Three or four nights a week they would pour bourbon and Coke into the tall clear glasses Mama had gotten with S&H Green Stamps, and after a couple of hours, they didn't bother with the Coke anymore. Mama was a happy drunk, laughing and dancing to Bobby Rydell's record "The Cha-Cha-Cha," but when she'd had too much bourbon and couldn't do the steps correctly, she would set down her glass and go to bed. When I complained about the loud music that sometimes lasted far into the night, Mama yelled at me with the same defiant tone of voice she had used with Grandma, and I would miss her and Papaw so much my chest would hurt with the effort of taking a breath. I didn't see them often like Grandma had said I would. Grandma sat alone on our pew at Pisgah Methodist after we switched to Centenary Methodist, which I hated nearly as much as I detested every person in my new Sunday school class.

Lyn Parks was the president of the MYF, the Methodist Youth Fellowship, and she ran our meetings like a dictator in a room filled with ignorant peasants. She was pretty, had those real pearls she'd worn the first day of school, and a wardrobe Edith Head would have envied. Every boy sitting on a folding chair in our Sunday school classroom was in love with her, and they didn't give a flip whether we had a car wash for a fund-raiser or sold brownies at the bazaar. Lyn's best friend, Sarah Jane Patterson, was her slave. She laughed at every stupid little joke Lyn made, jumped out of her chair to get a pen or whatever Lyn needed at any moment, and actually worked up a tear when Lyn said she wasn't going to run for homecoming queen because she didn't think she was pretty enough. Of course, Sarah Jane talked her into running, and Lyn was crowned just before the game with Tylertown, which we lost.

I told myself I didn't care that I wasn't ever going to be a homecoming queen, or even a maid in the court. It didn't matter that Jehu was in love with Lyn and not me. And why should I care if those snotty kids didn't like me? I also tried to convince myself that Wallace would become a good father in time, and that Mama's happiness was worth the misery I was feeling every night as I sat in my room listening to her laughter. I tried, but in my sick heart there was a cancer of hatred growing faster than Mama's feet could cha-cha-cha.

Before Mama and Wallace got married, I had been an A student, but now I never studied for tests or did my homework or paid attention to my teachers, who no longer called on me for the correct answers. With one exception. Miss Schultz, my Spanish teacher, who had come to America from Panama when she was in her twenties, loved my sullen self, and kept on treating me like her prized pupil. When I failed the translation exercise taken from *Don Quixote,* she called me up to her desk after class and said she knew I could have made an A, so something must be wrong in my life and what could she do to help. I nearly gave in, wanting desperately to pour out gallons of unshed tears on her pristine desk, but the shame I felt over my unpopularity and my booze-soaked life contained them. I held my breath until I was dizzy, and clutching my Spanish I book against my chest, I said, "Nothing's wrong with me, and if there was, it's none of your business. Can I go now?"

Grandma tried to help me, too. Mama dropped me off for a visit one Saturday and when Grandma hugged me, she said she could feel my bones. How much weight had I lost? What was Frieda cooking for supper? Had I been sick? She put me on the bathroom scale. "Ninety-five!" she yelled. "A strong wind would blow you away, Layla Jay." I told her Twiggy probably didn't weigh as much as me, and the whole world thought she was perfect. Grandma didn't know who Twiggy was, but she said she didn't care if she was Jackie Kennedy, I was her granddaughter and I needed to get some meat on my bones.

I ate the entire day. Tea cakes, chocolate drops, mashed potatoes with brown gravy for lunch, a ham slice, whole milk, greens cooked in bacon grease, and lemon meringue pie. My stomach was stretched to its capacity and I shook my head "no" over and over as Grandma pressed me to drink the glass of buttermilk she held out to me. When she had run out of fattening foods to offer, she sat beside me on the couch and took my hand in hers. "Layla Jay, are you happy out in town? Is the marriage not working out? How are things between them?"

I looked over at the piano running my eyes over the yellowed ivories. Middle C, D, E, F. If I told Grandma the truth all the wrong notes would be played. Mama would be mad at me, and only the Lord knew what would happen when Wallace found out that I had ratted on him. I looked into Grandma's pale blue eyes filled with worry and knew I couldn't speak the truth. "Everything's fine, Grandma. We're all doing just great." I knew she didn't believe me, but she sighed, dropped my hand, and said she hoped Mama wasn't going to ruin this chance she had for a good life with a good man.

I knew Wallace wasn't a good man though. I knew that I couldn't trust him. My knowledge came from the way he stared at the pointy ends of the padded bra I wore beneath the new white sweater Grandma had given me for an early birthday present. And I came to fear him on the day when I caught him in my room opening the drawer to my dresser that held my panties and double-A-cup bras. When he looked up and saw me standing in the doorway, he said he was looking for some notebook paper and thought I kept a spare pack there. Wordlessly, I went to my desk and handed him the pack that lay beside my algebra book. When he took the paper, touching my hand with his, I looked above his head to the round white light globe overhead, and after he turned and left my room, I locked the door and sat on my bed staring out at the once beautiful trees that had lost their leaves.

Chapter 5

I WORRIED THAT GOD WAS STILL MAD AT ME ABOUT COUNTER-feiting salvation, that maybe He had sent Wallace over to Zebulon as my punishment. But I remembered Grandma saying that God's business was forgiving all the folks nobody would excuse. So with hope in my heart, I kept on praying. I asked for a motorcycle for Wallace, a tornado to whip down Fourth Street, a thousand pimples on Lyn's face. And breasts. I thought that if Mama had gotten a man with hers, then there was the possibility I could win Jehu's love with a set of C cups.

I knew that the chances of God granting any of my requests were slim, but I hoped that He would have a modicum of pity when He looked down and saw how things were going at our house. The day after I had caught Wallace in my room, I said with the sweetest smile I could muster, that the next time he wanted to borrow something of mine he should ask Mama for it first. "Mama keeps track of everything in this house," I said. "It's real hard to keep a secret from her." And Wallace had understood my threat because that night at supper he kept his eyes on Mama even though I was wearing my new sweater.

God chose Grandma to deliver the one blessing He bestowed on me. She had gotten chummy with the Albrights after they joined Pisgah Methodist, and so she had found out that Jehu's family lived on Third Street, one block over from my new house. After thanking God for helping me along with one of my prayer requests, I strolled around the corner every chance I got to spy on Jehu. He was hardly ever home because, besides football practice, he worked as a stock boy at the Piggly Wiggly on Saturdays, but occasionally I would see him sitting at his kitchen table eating a sandwich or I would spot him in the backyard tossing a football with Red Pittman, his best friend. I dreaded seeing Lyn through his living room window someday, and imagined them on the green velvet couch cuddled together watching a television show. But God was merciful enough to spare me that sight; Lyn never made it even to the front steps of the Albright house. And I have Mama to thank for that.

My birthday is November 19, and on November 9, Mama announced that she was throwing me a party. This was a bad idea. After the few votes I had gotten for cheerleader, I was afraid that no one would come. Even though I had moved to town, I would always be one of the country kids at school, and none of us were ever invited to the town kids' parties, so I couldn't imagine that they would show up at mine. But Mama wanted to show off her new den furniture: an aqua plastic couch and two matching chairs with black wrought-iron legs, and a coffee table that was carved in the shape of the state of Mississippi. She also wanted to use her punch bowl, a present from her first wedding that she had never filled with ginger ale. I begged Mama to return the thirty-five invitations she had bought at Zebulon Stationery. "Nonsense," she said. "Layla Jay, you've never had a party. How do you know you won't have a good time?"

"I just know," I said. "Besides, nobody is going to come."

"That's ridiculous. Of course they'll come. It's not just a birthday party; we're having a dance right here in the den. I've already put Wallace in charge of changing the records."

My heart sank from my stomach on down into my ovaries. "Is he going to be here?" I had assumed Wallace would want nothing to do with a bunch of teenagers crowding into his house, encroaching on his drinking time.

Mama smiled. "Of course he will. He loves you, Layla Jay. Wouldn't miss his stepdaughter's first party for the world."

I gave up and helped her write out the invitations. We invited my entire class and a couple of kids from Pisgah, whom I didn't like all that much, but I added their names to the list because I figured they might show up. Three days after we mailed the invitations with an R.S.V.P. on the bottom, only June had promised to come; after four days passed the two Pisgah kids accepted. Then the no's started popping up like freckles on a redhead.

On the night before the party I skulked into my room and sat on my bed, trying hard not to cry. The math was easy; besides Mama, Wallace, and me there would be three party guests, and one of them was a cousin. It would be too awful; I couldn't go through with it. I would tell Mama that I had come down with a stomachache, a migraine, signs of a deadly cancer. I headed down the hall toward the den to find Mama, but stopped short of the door when I heard her talking on the phone. "Well, I was worried something was amiss with Gloria when Layla Jay said she couldn't come to her party." I sank down onto the hardwood floor. She was talking to Gloria Reddick's mother! Gloria had said she was going out of town and couldn't come, which I had told Mama was a big lie. And now she was tattling. I placed my hand over my breast; my heart was on fire, melting down into my stomach. Then I heard Mama dialing again. "Judith, it's Frieda. I'm calling to tell you how sorry I am that Thad is ill and will have to miss Layla Jay's party." After a few seconds, she said, "He isn't?"

I sat with my back against the wall, feet spread out in front of me, listening as Mama called every one of the guests who had R.S.V.P.'d "no"! I stood up and crept over to the door to peep into the den where Mama sat hunched over the phone, a burning cigarette in one hand and the party list on her lap. I tiptoed back to my room and slid between the cool sheets where I lay in the dark trying to untangle the knot of confusion in my brain. I had never questioned Mama's love for me, assuming that all mothers love their children no matter what, but now I wondered whether she had to love me if I turned out to be a total flop in the world. She might resent having to beg other women to make their kids be nice to me. I worried that I was a terrible embarrassment to her.

When I heard Mama's footsteps coming down the hall, I turned onto my side and feigned sleep. I couldn't let her know I had overheard her telephone calls. But she didn't come into my room. She stood silently in the doorway, then switched off the hall light and walked away.

Mama's furtive telephone calling resulted in nineteen guests showing up for the party the next afternoon. I pasted on a big smile and tried to look surprised that so many sick people had received a miracle healing. Mama was the Academy Award–winning actress though. She greeted everyone at the door, smiling and waving to the mothers who dropped off their teens. No one would believe this sweet woman had sat at the telephone like a soldier in an army tank rolling over my enemies one by one. After everyone was crowded into our den, Mama and I met in the kitchen. She hugged me and said, "See, Layla Jay, you thought no one would come, and nearly everyone is here."

Even Wallace was nice, acting almost like I remembered him on that first afternoon when we sat listening to him in Grandma's living room. "The Lord works in mysterious ways," he told me with a wink.

I didn't want to ruin the party by telling him that I knew the Lord didn't give a shit about how many people would dance in my house that day. Mama might have suspected that I had eavesdropped on her calls though, because when I looked over at her, she bit her lip and turned her head away.

An hour after the party began, Jehu Albright knocked on the front door. When I opened it and saw him standing on our porch in pressed pants and a yellow shirt, holding a wrapped gift for me, my heart literally banged so hard I was afraid he could see it beating against the bodice of my dress. As I steered him toward the punch bowl, we passed by Lyn sitting on Mama's new couch, and I looked over and shot her a triumphant smile. Jehu might be her boyfriend, but he had come to my party, brought me a present, and was grinning at my mother instead of her.

I hadn't expected to enjoy the party. I had been prepared to deal with surly guests whose mothers had forced them to come against their will, and figured they would all pay me back someday. But if any of them resented coming, they changed their minds when Wallace put on the first forty-five and Cliff Richard and The Shadows started wailing "Do You Want to Dance?" Nearly everyone did. Including Jehu, who asked Mama if she'd care to try the watusi with him. I stood beside her, gripping the tiny handle of my punch cup, dreading the moment when Mama's hips would start swiveling into a spectacle that would be gossiped about for months to come. Mama flashed her brightest crimson smile. "Honey, Layla Jay is a much much better dancer than I am." She pushed me forward, and as I took Jehu's outstretched hand, Mama winked at me.

Watching Mama all those nights was paying off. I pretended I was her and all of my inhibitions fell away as I danced with uncharacteristic abandonment. On our tiled dance floor, rhythmically shaking my butt, I caught a glimpse of Lyn's fiery eyes and finally understood what winning feels like. It's like someone pulls a lever, switching on the thousand-watt bulbs inside you, and every organ, vessel, and strand of hair swells and pulses so that you can hardly keep from screaming your joy. Wallace was a good DJ, expertly switching the records before we had time to walk away, and I came into Jehu's arms with Elvis expressing my feelings exactly. "I can't help falling in love."

Jehu's breath filled my ear. His fingers were warm and fit mine perfectly. "Great party, Layla Jay," he whispered. "I'm glad you moved into town."

I looked up into his face with my best Sandra Dee smile. My eyes were probably sparkling just like hers. "Me too," I said. "I like living in town a whole lot better than the country."

June danced by, holding on to Matt Bradley, her latest conquest, and winked at me. Sharing my joy with June doubled my happiness, and I whispered a silent thank-you to God, who had more than answered my prayers . . . with a little help from Mama, of course.

Despite my euphoria, I couldn't entirely blot out Wallace's dark eyes, straying to the breasts of the most blessed girls. Some of them, Sarah Jane Patterson for one, didn't seem to mind his interest. I had forgotten that Wallace's good looks magnetized women, and now I remembered those first days we spent together during revival. Hadn't I played every song I knew on my flute, recited paragraphs of Spanish phrases, basked in the attention he had showered on me before Mama came home? And now the last thing on the earth I wanted was Wallace's eyes on me. Those eyes took on an unnatural glitter, and each time I passed by him sitting beside the record player, I looked away. I was relieved when Mama called us all into the kitchen for cake and ice cream, which meant Wallace's services were no longer needed, and he would be leaving the party to go to work at Vest's. They were having a sale and Mama told him to put back a few pairs of shoes in her size.

Just before he left, he asked me what size I wore. "I don't want anything from Vest's," I said. "Or you," I whispered.

When Jehu asked for my telephone number, the party was over right then as far as I was concerned. I obligingly cut the cake, blew out all the candles at once, but it didn't really matter since my wish had already come true. I opened the gifts of nail polish, cologne, stationery, and a few new 45's and thanked everyone. After the party I helped Mama clean up the wrapping paper and wash the dishes before going to my room to relive every moment I had spent with Jehu. I closed my eyes and saw his neat blond crew cut; his teeth, white as Gold Medal flour; the curling hairs on his forearm. "Can I call you sometime?" he had said. Call me, call me, call me. Jehu Albright had said that he would call me and now I hugged myself and rocked with excitement. I had a boyfriend at last!

I stayed in my room after I heard Wallace come home from work. When Mama called to me that *The Dick Van Dyke Show* was on TV, I said I had homework to do. And I did have some algebra equations to figure out, but I spent the rest of the night drawing hearts and smiley faces around my and Jehu's names.

Before she went to her own bed, Mama came to my room and sat beside me on mine. "Did you enjoy your party?" she asked, smiling with anticipation of my response.

"It was perfect. Thanks for all you did," I said.

Mama leaned over and brushed her lips across my forehead. "There's nothing I wouldn't do for my girl."

Reaching up, I hugged her tightly. I believed her.

After Mama said good night, I switched off the lamp beside my bed, and in the darkness, I made a vow to myself. From now on, I would share only my triumphs and good fortune with her. I would bear all of my failures alone. It was better this way, because if Mama shared my pain, the hurting would be doubled. I loved her that much.

Chapter 6

THREE DAYS AFTER MY BIRTHDAY, PRESIDENT KENNEDY WAS shot dead in Dallas, and the world turned upside down. Through her tears, Mama vowed she would never wear a pink suit again out of respect for Jackie. Wallace fell onto his knees in front of the TV set and prayed for our nation, and Grandma called up and said maybe Lyndon Johnson would be a better president. Mama slammed down the receiver, lit a cigarette, and swore she would never enter her mother's house ever again. Mama loved Jackie because of her stylish outfits and her connection to France, and she hated Lyndon Johnson, Lady Bird, and both of the Johnson daughters. Not that she knew anything about any of them, but they could never climb to the heights the Kennedys had risen to in Mama's esteem. Miss Schultz told our class that assassinations were common in her native land, but that she had never expected such a tragedy to occur again in America.

After the funeral, which everyone I knew except for Grandma watched on TV, school resumed, but a pall hung over us all. I guess I looked as sad as anyone because Jehu came up behind me as I was putting my science book in my locker and asked me if I was okay. I wanted to dance, shout, sing the school victory song, but somehow I managed to keep my eyes downcast, my shoulders hunched forward, washing myself in sorrow as best I knew how. "I guess," I said. "I just keep remembering that sad funeral parade. Even the horses looked like they were mourning the president. I can't imagine what Jackie feels. To lose the love of your life!"

The love of mine reached out and tilted my chin up to rest in his palm. "I know. Everybody feels pretty awful." He dropped his hand. "It's probably a bad time to ask, but I was wondering if you'd like to go to the school dance after the game next Friday."

Too quickly, I answered. "No, no, it's not. I'd love to go." Then remembering my grief-stricken role, I said, "What I mean is, I know we have to try to go on with our normal lives. President Kennedy would want us to."

Guilt weighs heavier than ever when joy spills into sorrow, and I was plagued with visions of burning in hell for my happiness. While poor Jackie was moving out of the White House enveloped in heartache, I was in tears because I didn't own a party dress. Mama flipped through the dresses in my closet and said we'd go to The Ideal Shop to find something wonderful. We never shopped there. The Ideal Shop catered to the rich teenagers in Zebulon like Lyn, who had gotten a date with Shawn Willoughby. I had overheard her telling a group of girls that she was wearing a black chiffon with a plunging neckline.

In the dressing room at The Ideal, Mama and I turned over the tag hanging from the armhole of the silver lamé sheath that fit me perfectly. "Fifty-four dollars," I screamed. "We can't afford it."

Mama slapped her hand over my mouth. She whispered, "Of course, we can't. We'll tuck the tag in and bring it back on Monday. We'll say you found something better in Jackson."

"But that's kind of like cheating, Mama." I hoped she wasn't listening to me. I looked nearly beautiful in the dress.

Mama giggled. "I know. It is a little naughty, but Layla Jay, it's fun, isn't it?"

Mama was right. Despite the tag scratching my underarm, I had a wonderful time dancing in the dress in Jehu's arms. The school gym was transformed into a fairyland with silver tinsel and blue-and-white crepe-paper streamers, and balloons that popped like firecrackers on the Fourth of July as we glided across the varnished floor. My dress was the envy of every girl at the dance.

In the girls' bathroom June made me slowly turn around twice. "Where'd you get it?" June wanted to know. "It looks like something Ava Gardner would wear."

"Ideal Shop."

"Must have cost a fortune," Sally McGruder said from two sinks over.

I knew she thought we were too poor to shop at The Ideal, and of course, she was right. Quickly I lifted my arm and checked that the tag was still in place. "My mother got a raise," I said. "And we're expecting a big inheritance any day now."

After she left June turned to me. "Really?"

"No, you know we don't have any rich relatives. That just popped out, and now she's going to wonder how come I keep showing up at school in fake pearls."

June opened the door and music and laughter wafted into the room. "She'll forget about it. She's so narcissistic, she can't think of anything but herself."

Ever since we'd begun studying mythology in Mrs. Peachon's English class, June had been using words like narcissistic and exchanging the deity Zeus for God as often as possible, like when she'd say "Only Zeus knows!" When I followed June out of the girls' room, I found Jehu waiting for me just outside the door.

The evening flew by, and it seemed like we'd just arrived when Jehu checked his watch and said we'd better go out to wait for his mother to pick us up. We were standing on the sidewalk beneath the overhanging branch of the one willow tree that had survived on school property when I saw Lyn and Shawn coming out of the gym. Jehu saw them, too, and as they walked toward us, he leaned over and kissed me so suddenly, I didn't have time to pucker my lips. Over his shoulder I caught a glimpse of Lyn's face illuminated beneath the streetlight, and it was a pitiful sight. It brought to mind the image I had seen on television of Jackie's face as she walked across the White House lawn holding on to the hands of John John and Caroline. After the kiss, Jehu turned around, and his eyes followed Lyn's black dress swirling around her calves as she disappeared into the darkness. Then looking down at me, he forced a phony grin. "You're a good kisser," he said. His left eye twitched, and I knew he was lying.

I stepped away from Jehu and looked down at the cracks on the sidewalk. "I'm sorry. I wasn't ready," I whispered.

When Jehu's mother parked their car in front of our house after the dance at eleven o'clock, Wallace's frowning face was visible through the living room picture window. He had been out at choir practice when I had come home to change out of my band uniform for the dance, and I didn't know if Mama had told him about my date. As we got out of the car and Jehu led me up the front walk, I could feel Wallace's eyes on us. Standing beside Jehu beneath the yellow porch light, I prayed. "Let me say the right thing, Lord. Don't be an Indian giver and take him away."

Jehu's lips brushed my cheek. "I had a good time, Layla Jay. I'll see you at school Monday. Got a lot of homework to do over the weekend." I was still waiting for help from God when Jehu wheeled around, flew down the walk, and hopped in beside his mother who had left the motor running.

After I locked the front door, Wallace called to me from the den. He was sprawled on the couch wearing only his Sunday pants, holding a half-filled glass of amber liquid I knew must be whiskey. "Come here," he yelled.

When I walked in, his eyes ran up and down my body like I was a list of unpleasant chores. "You look like a whore," he said in a menacingly quiet voice. "The whore of Babylon."

I looked around the dimly lit room. The lamp by the couch shed only a small circle of light across the coffee table. The television was silent, and I could hear Wallace breathing as he rose from the couch. "Where's Mama?" I asked.

"Gone to bed with a headache. Did she paint your face like that?"

I licked my pink lips. She had helped me with the liner and eyebrow pencil, but I didn't want Mama to fight my battle. "No, I did. I think I look pretty." I lifted my eyes to his. "Jehu said I did."

Wallace slammed his glass down on the coffee table sloshing droplets across the southern counties of Mississippi. "*Jehu. Jehu.* That pimple-faced twerp. He get your cherry tonight? You go behind the gym and smooch in the dark, let him touch you?"

I dropped my clutch bag and crossed my arms over my stomach. Bile rose in my throat, and I squeezed my eyes shut. "*No.* It was nothing like that." My nails dug into the flesh of my arms as I struggled to block the tears I felt welling in my eyes. I felt dirty, guilty, and I didn't know why. I'd barely felt that kiss.

Then he was there. Wallace grabbed my arms and held them out from my sides. My wrists burned from his grip, and when I smelled the sour whiskey on his breath, fear replaced my guilt. "I can tell if you're lying," he said. "I can tell by your stomach. Let me see."

I stared at the dark screen of the TV set and willed Dick Van Dyke and Mary Tyler Moore to appear there. Rose Marie was going to tell them some funny joke in just a minute. I would laugh along with them, and then Wallace would go away and Mama would come in and say "Did you have a good time, honey?" And I would go to my room and none of this would have happened.

"I asked you a question, Layla Jay. Did he touch you?" Wallace dropped my arms and ran his hands down the front of my dress over my breasts, my stomach, pausing above my thighs. I was trembling, unable to run, unable to speak. I was so hot I could have been standing in ten-foot flames, and I looked up at the pebbled ceiling expecting it to melt and descend down on me like white lava. "Please God, help me," I prayed.

Maybe I prayed a long time. Maybe I spoke aloud. Maybe God heard me and answered my prayer because, when I opened my eyes, Wallace was backing across the room away from me until the back of his legs hit the coffee table.

I told my legs to run away. Get me to my room behind a locked door. I could still feel his hands on my body though, holding me in place, nailing me to the floor. I watched his naked chest heaving out and in, out and in. He dropped his head. His voice was just above a whisper. "Okay, your stomach's still flat. You didn't let him fuck you. Not this time anyway." He reached behind him, lifted his glass from the table and drained it. He tossed the glass onto the couch. "You're not to go out with that boy again. You hear? Fourteen is too young to date."

I didn't want to cry in front of him, but I knew I couldn't keep the tears at bay much longer. I longed for Mama, for Grandma. I pictured Papaw with his shotgun pointed between Wallace's red-veined eyes. "Can I go now?"

"Yeah, go." I turned sideways, but his voice stopped me. "Wait! Layla Jay, you're not to tell your mother about this. She'll think you asked for it, that you like the touch of a man. I could see that about you the first day I laid eyes on you." A sort of half-laugh preceded the shake of his head. "You're no different from any of them. Even those little girls who came to your party couldn't take their eyes off me. Frieda knows how it is with me and women."

"What . . . I . . . I . . ." Before I could think what to say, his face tightened into a frightening mask, his lips drew into his mouth, his eyes glinted like two hard silver dimes; he clenched his fists. "I won't tell," I said.

He didn't speak again, but when he waved his arm in dismissal and lurched across the room to the hi-fi set, I ran for the safety of my room. I slammed the door, locked it, and then fell face forward on my bed. That night I slept in the dress, afraid to see my body, afraid that somehow the marks of his hands would be visible on my skin. Just before I drifted off to sleep, I heard Wallace singing the chorus of "Onward, Christian Soldiers."

Mama had to press the dress before she returned it on Monday morning. I hated it now, was happy I'd never have to see it again. I wanted no reminders of my first date. When I threw my corsage in the garbage, Mama fished it out. "Don't you want to save this, maybe pin it on your bulletin board?" She held the brown-edged flowers out to me, her brows knitted together like they did when she was trying to figure our budget for the month.

I shook my head. "I don't like Jehu anymore. He's a dope," I said.

Mama knew there was more than I was telling. When she dropped the corsage on the table and crossed her arms over her chest, I saw the long white scar shaped like a lightning bolt on her forearm and knew she would protect me if she could. The scar was proof of that. She had gotten it back when I was in first grade. Santa had left Carolyn underneath our Christmas tree that year. She had a vinyl head, legs, and arms; a light pink cloth body; and her painted face was fixed in a permanently sad expression. Papaw had laughed and said she looked like I did when I was about to cry, and although I knew he was right, I loved the way she seemed to need me and had taken to carrying her with me everywhere, even going so far as to sneak her into my book satchel when I returned to school that January. But on this day, the day I was remembering now, I had left Carolyn lying on the grass beside the front walk while I went inside to get a Popsicle I intended to pretend to share with her. Before I returned I heard a dog's furious barking and then a growl. I ran to the door and through the screen saw a black-and-brown German shepherd snatching Carolyn up into his wide mouth. As I watched her swinging from the dog's teeth, I imagined her screams of terror and pain and I began to scream, too. In an instant Mama was beside me, grabbing my shoulders. "What's wrong? What's the matter?" I pointed to the yard where the shepherd was continually dropping Carolyn and then attacking her again, ripping her soft stomach over and over as he ran back and forth across the grass.

I was crying now, and Mama looked into my face for only a second before she flew out the door. I followed her and stood watching on the porch as she chased the dog, yelling for it to let go of my baby doll. The dog paid her no mind and kept on shaking Carolyn until Mama lunged for her. Then I heard the growls that sent chills over me. I yelled for Mama to run, but she stood her ground even as the dog sank his teeth into her forearm after she pulled Carolyn from its mouth. Mama jerked sideways with a scream, but she held on to the doll as she kicked the dog until it yelped and finally ran away.

The German shepherd had bitten Mama more than once during that fight and she'd required nearly as many stitches as Grandma had sewn into Carolyn's torn body. Since we never found that hateful dog, Mama also had to endure a long series of painful rabies shots. I had overheard Papaw calling her a damn fool for wrestling a big dog like that over a doll. And I never forgot what Mama said then. "Pop, that isn't a doll. It's Layla Jay's baby. She loves it just like I love her, and there's nothing I wouldn't do for my baby. Every stitch on my arm is just a mark of my love."

Now, as I silently stared at the marks of her love on her arm, she shot me her "I'm going to find out what I want to know" look. She leaned closer to me. "What makes you call Jehu a dope all of a sudden? Did something happen that night that you need to talk about?"

"That night, that night," the words echoed inside my head. I could nearly feel Wallace's hands on me, hear his words, feel the violence that

I knew lay inside him, and I longed to tell her the truth. But Wallace wasn't a German shepherd, and I wasn't a little girl anymore. It was best to let her think my secret had to do with Jehu. "Nothing happened," I said. "I just changed my mind about him is all."

I SPENT THE CHRISTMAS HOLIDAYS with Grandma and Papaw because Wallace and Mama left for Rockville, Alabama, to attend the Christian Holiday Season Retreat. It was good to be back in my old room even though the single bed Papaw had moved in to replace my old one was narrow and the mattress was lumpy. I ate everything Grandma cooked. We made divinity and fudge and pecan pralines and fruitcake and red velvet cake and pinwheel cookies that melted in my mouth. By the end of the second week of my visit, I had gained eight pounds and budded out into an almost B cup.

Mama had pitched a hissy fit about spending the party season with what she called a bunch of holly berry nuts, but Wallace had talked her into going by promising her a side trip to the Florida panhandle, where it was rumored that Jan & Dean might do a New Year's Eve show. They didn't show up, but Mama came home with a little plastic trophy that she won for Best Costume at the Holiday Inn party in Pensacola. She told me not to tell Grandma that she had gone as Cleopatra. For her costume she had pasted two Skoal can lids on her breasts, put a black rinse in her hair, and fitted a chain around her hips to hold the nylon skirt she'd fashioned from a nightgown. When I asked her what Wallace had worn to the celebration, Mama frowned. "He stayed in the motel room praying for the Lord to save my ass after he chewed it out when he saw my costume."

Wallace had been born again at the retreat, repented of his sins, and before the first month of 1964 was over, was preaching at a little church over in Liberty called New Hope. Although I still hated him, the new Wallace didn't scare me, and as my fears subsided, I eventually stopped locking my door every night. I began to enjoy his daily Bible readings and prayers, figuring they might help me get true salvation and I wouldn't have to fake it anymore.

Wallace was back on his game, saving mostly female sinners who breathed in shallow pants when he jerked off his tie, spread his legs, and, with palms stretched to the ceiling and sweat dripping down his face, prayed for the devil to get out of New Hope. Grandma was euphoric over Wallace's return to the pulpit, but Papaw said, "Bullshit. A leopard don't change his spots." Mama didn't voice an opinion on Wallace's sincerity, but she only attended one service at New Hope before going back to her old habit of sleeping late on Sunday mornings. There was no out for me; every Sunday morning Wallace dragged me out of our warm house into the Volkswagen, sputtering with cold as we chugged the fifteen miles down Highway 51 to Liberty.

I hadn't protested about switching from Centenary to New Hope. I no longer had to witness Lyn's popularity in the Sunday school class and MYF meetings, and I assumed that as the stepdaughter of a preacher, I'd be treated with greater respect at New Hope. Was I ever wrong!

Besides me, there were only four kids in the teenage Sunday school class, three girls and one boy, all of them shabbily dressed and dumber than dirt. They hated me. Our teacher, Miss Mansfield, who looked like a crane with a steel-wool wig on its head, told the class that, now that the preacher's daughter had joined them, they'd have to work harder on learning scripture. "We wouldn't want Layla Jay telling Brother Ebert that we are lazy Christians." I didn't blame them for the cold, suspicious looks they tossed at me as we sat sweating in the overheated room on our hard folding chairs arranged in a tight circle. To them, I was untrustworthy, a tattletale. Sunday after Sunday I sat beside Miss Mansfield, smiling sweetly, all the while thinking that the tales I could tattle about their new preacher would scorch the pages of the dog-eared New Testament she held in her lap.

Wallace wasn't worrying about me blabbing his secrets. His previous sins had been washed away at that retreat, and he reminded me that God absolutely loves a repentant sinner. "To err is human, to forgive is divine," he said on the way home from church one Sunday. "Let him who is without sin cast the first stone." I looked away from his smug face and stared out the window at the leafless trees. Their branches twisting out toward the road reminded me of the fleshless bones of skeletons, and I shivered in my thin coat. I was a doomed sinner who wanted to cast boulders at Wallace, and God knew that my heart was hardened against my stepfather. I suspected that Papaw was right about him, and I knew I could never trust Wallace again unless God got busy and answered my prayers for help by sending the Holy Spirit down to soften my heart.

He didn't send the Spirit, but He gave me something much better. After church on the last Sunday in January, when Wallace parked the Volkswagen beneath the carport, Mama came out of the house and smiled. She pointed to a stack of boxes beside the door. "You're packed up, Wallace. Hit the road, Jack."

Chapter 7

WALLACE'S REMOVAL FROM OUR HOUSE TURNED OUT TO BE like eating a peach. After enjoying the sweet pulp of his leaving, Mama and I bit into the bitter center. I knew that Wallace had slept on the couch a couple of times, but I hadn't guessed that his getting kicked out of the bedroom would eventually land him on the street. I didn't ask Mama for an explanation for this gift of his departure. I wanted to bury the past and enjoy the present. The delicious beginning of our new life centered around dancing, and I was Mama's new partner. She taught me the cha-cha, the rhumba, and the Cajun jitterbug, and after practicing nearly every night, I could do the twist as good as she could. We ate chocolate ice cream for dinner, watched the late movie on TV, and walked around the house with red-painted lips, wearing only our underwear. After our three-day celebration, Grandma went to prayer meeting and heard the gossip about New Hope's preacher moving into the Slumbercrest after his wife had booted him out.

When I saw Grandma's car pulling into the driveway, I yelled a warning to Mama who was in her bedroom reading a paperback while her nails dried. We had planned to go out to dinner at Sal's Restaurant, and I was sitting at the kitchen table taking the rollers out of my hair. When Mama didn't answer Grandma's knock, I went to the door, expecting the usual hug and kiss she always bestowed on me no matter how long since she'd last seen me, but something was terribly wrong. There was a yellowish tint to her skin and her usually bright eyes had no light in them. She had lost a lot of weight, too, so that now her favorite gabardine dress looked two sizes too large. Before I could speak, Grandma tottered past me without a glance. "Frieda," she called out as she fell heavily onto the couch in the den. "Frieda, you'd better come out here and explain yourself."

In less than a minute Mama, in black lace bra and panties, sauntered in the room waving her wet nails. I glanced at Grandma's stormy face and groaned aloud. I knew what was coming and I sank down on the rug beside the door ready to dive into the fracas if needed.

Mama kept waving her nails up and down like she was batting balloons in the air. If she noticed how awful Grandma looked, she didn't let on. "Why, Mama, how nice of you to stop by. We're about to go out to dinner, but we can wait a while. How's Pop?"

Grandma glared at her like she was a roach running across her stove. "What happened between you and Wallace?" There wasn't any energy at all in her voice. It seemed every breath she took caused her effort.

Mama wiggled her shoulders; quivering white breasts straining against the black lace. "Oh, Wallace! Nothing happened. That was the reason I kicked him out." She lifted her foot and propped it on the coffee table. Her bright pink toenails tapped on the southeast corner of the state of Mississippi. "After he got saved, Wallace went limp. Soft as bread dough. I couldn't get him going no matter what I did. When the Lord took away his sins, He took away his tools, too."

Grandma had clapped her hands over her ears about halfway through Mama's explanation, and when Mama's lips stopped moving, she lowered her hands. She sounded like she was reciting the alphabet when she said, "Frieda-I-don't-want-to-hear-another-word."

Mama flopped back on the chair beside the couch. "You asked me. I told you."

Just then Grandma looked across the room and saw me sitting on the floor beside the hi-fi set. I had taken the remaining rollers from my hair and sat surrounded by a crescent of aqua, pink, and yellow plastic cylinders. "Layla Jay, honey, go to your room. This isn't fit conversation for a young girl's ears."

"But I already heard it, Grandma," I said, going over to sit beside her. I shook my loopy uncombed curls around my face. "And I'm glad Wallace is gone. I think Mama was right to throw him out. Not for the reason she gave, of course, but my own."

Grandma's eyes narrowed. "What reason did you have?"

I froze. Grandma knew me better than anybody. She would guess what had happened; I should have kept my mouth shut. I looked down at my knees to avoid her eyes that would detect the mess inside my brain. "Well," I said and stopped. My fear, disgust, guilt were all about to spew out like vomit, and I pressed my lips together so hard I winced in pain.

Grandma's voice was filled with dread. I think she suspected the truth. "Layla Jay! Tell me. Right now, this minute."

I could have ratted him out then. Should have done it, but something stopped me. Maybe it was the Lord, maybe it was that I couldn't bear to repeat those repulsive feelings, maybe I somehow felt that I shared in his guilt. Maybe, and this is the most likely reason, maybe I was worried Grandma couldn't stand the pain of knowing what Wallace had done to me. I lifted my chin and said, "He wouldn't let me wear makeup or go out on dates. He treated me like a baby."

When I saw the tears in Grandma's eyes, I felt worse than I had since I'd faked getting saved. I had chosen Mama over her and we both understood that I had broken something precious that might never be restored. My lips trembled; I wanted to fall into her arms, but she struggled to her feet and crossed them over her chest. Her face was as gray as a squirrel's back. "Well, I'll pray for you both. You have cast out a good Christian man. You've chosen to," her eyes swept Mama's sexy underwear, my rouged cheeks, "live as you please without regard to what's right. I wish I hadn't lived to come here this day." And then she was gone and Mama and I sat staring over each other's heads in the living room that had never seemed as silent as now.

We didn't go out to dinner after all; we split a can of tuna and topped it off with popcorn. After I went to bed, I smelled cigarette smoke in my room, and opening my eyes, I saw Mama standing beside my dresser. "What?" I said.

She took a drag, the tip of her Lucky Strike a small red glow in the dark. "Layla Jay, I want you to tell me the real reason you're happy Wallace is gone from here."

I was glad she couldn't see my face. I wanted to spill out all of it, the sneaking in my underwear drawer, the sleazy leers, his hands on my body after my date. I longed to run to her and allow myself the comfort I knew she would offer. But I also sensed that after Mama comforted me, she would go after him just as she had gone after that German shepherd. She might borrow Papaw's shotgun and shoot him. She'd go to prison and I would be left in this world with no parent at all. I turned on my side. "Just what I told Grandma. That's the true reason. He told me I couldn't go out with Jehu anymore. And he never loved me. Just you."

The red tip of Mama's cigarette circled her face. "Layla Jay, he didn't love me. He just wanted to throw himself into a pit of sin so he could feel righteous about getting out of it and start hollering his head off in the pulpit again. I provided the means to the end. That's all."

I sat up and turned on the lamp beside my bed. "But you loved him, didn't you? I mean, you married him. You had to have loved him to marry him."

Mama laughed like a loon. "Oh, Layla Jay, you're such a romantic. You gotta quit watching all those Sandra Dee movies. The only man I'll ever love is Kenneth, and Wallace could never be one tenth of the man he was." She looked like she might cry now. "You have no idea how much I miss your daddy. I'll never find another man like him. He was my everything. I remember how he . . ." She shook her head as if to clear away the memories, then lifted her chin and raised her voice. "Wallace had one purpose; he was my ticket out of Mama's house. I rode that golden chariot with him to get away from her, and for a while it was a fun ride. But that's all it was. Flight and fun. And now it's over and I feel like my old self again." She stubbed out her cigarette on the scarred wood of my dresser and walked to the door. "Night, honey. Don't worry about a thing. I'm calling the plays for the game now. You can date any boy you choose as often as you get asked."

ANOTHER CONSEQUENCE OF WALLACE'S ABSENCE was that I began missing my real daddy more than ever. I hadn't thought of him all that often when Wallace was living with us, but now, every night I would lift the photograph of Daddy from my night table and kiss his smiling lips. I thought of Mama saying he was the only man she'd loved. Maybe he was the only father I could ever love, too. "Daddy, I wish you weren't in heaven. I wish I could feel your arms around me. Hear you laugh. If you weren't dead, what would our lives together be like?" I imagined sitting on the back of his motorcycle, my cheek against his back, my arms encircling his waist, and I could smell his special scent like that of the sweet hay in Papaw's field.

When I asked her to tell me more about him, Mama refused to conjure up those memories. I knew she was lying when she said she could barely remember him herself. She confessed again that it made her sad to think of what might have been, but then she added that life was for the living, not remembering the dead. I understood that she didn't want to relive her pain, but it made me mad, too. Her memories were all I had, and she wasn't willing to share any of them.

Two days after Grandma's visit, Mama called up Cybil Richards and asked her to meet her at Skinnys. That night she wore the blue dress that showed nearly all of her breasts, and she pinned her hair up into a fancy French twist with tendrils of curls around her rouged cheeks. "Don't wait up," she called to where I stood on the porch as her high heels tapped across the drive.

After that night, she never had to ask Cybil to meet her again. Mama had plenty of escorts to take her wherever she wanted to go. Most nights I stayed in my room, not wanting to meet any of the new men. I knew the old ones who stood in our den waiting for Mama. Their names had been in Mama's History of Lost Men book. It seemed years had passed since I had waited by the window in Mama's bedroom back at Grandma's house eager to hear about her dates. Now I barely listened when Mama described her latest conquest. "He's got money, Layla Jay. He's been to France." And another one had a junior college degree, one drove a Mustang convertible, one Friday night date wore elephant hide cowboy boots. I hadn't known there were so many bachelors in Lexie County, and I couldn't figure out why I didn't give a damn about any of them.

I told myself I should be happy. Mama didn't care how late I stayed up on school nights. She never nagged me about what I ate or asked what I made on an algebra test. She let me borrow her makeup, laughed when I told her I had worn her new blouse to school, and said I'd never have to attend Centenary Methodist Church again. But I was miserable. Lonely. And I missed Grandma. I longed to call her, ask if I could visit her, but I was afraid she was mad at me now. I had thought she would call me, ask me to come over, but every time the phone rang, it was never her voice I heard on the other end of the line. I knew her heart was broken, and I was the cause, and there didn't seem to be anything I could do about it.

One cold Sunday morning while Grandma was at church, Papaw stopped by for a surprise visit. After shoving Mama's magazines off a dinette chair and sitting beside the table, his eyes swept around the kitchen where our dirty dishes were piled in the sink, Mama's bra hung on the refrigerator handle, and a pile of ironing covered the board set up by the window. "We weren't expecting company," I said. Papaw just laughed. He told me he didn't care if we were living like heathens. He said Wallace wasn't going to last out at New Hope, that he'd come crawling back, and he hoped to hell Mama would have better sense than to take him back.

Mama, still in her red nylon shortie nightgown, came in just then. She stretched out her arms and rolled her neck on her shoulders. "What time is it? You're out and about early, Pop," she said, brushing his cheek with her lips.

"You're looking fit, Frieda. Looks like the single life is agreeing with you."

Mama shoved my schoolbooks off a chair and sat down. "Layla Jay, we got any coffee? Pour your Papaw a cup."

Papaw held up his palm. "Already had my fill." Drawing a cigar from his shirt pocket, he stuck it between his lips, but didn't light it. "Your mama is pretty upset with you, Frieda."

"Oh, Mama, she's always mad at me."

Papaw's cigar rolled to the side of his mouth. "She's getting old, ain't been feeling up to snuff here lately. I'm worried about her. I think there's something bad wrong with her, but she won't go see a doctor. I wish you'd go out and see her."

Mama reached across the table for the nail file she'd left beside three bottles of polish and began filing her left thumbnail. "Well, she could call and invite me if she wants to see me. I'm not going out there without an invitation."

"You know how she is. Too prideful to let you know how much she's suffering. It's up to you to offer the olive branch." He took his cigar out of his mouth and pointed it at me. "She misses Layla Jay. You don't want to keep her only grandchild away."

Mama tossed the nail file across the table. "If you're trying to make me feel guilty, you're not succeeding. Mama is the one who came storming in here judging me. Judge not lest ye be judged. Isn't that what that Bible of hers says?"

Papaw stuck his cigar back in his mouth and pushed back his chair. His face was as stern and hard as I had ever seen it. I worried he was giving up and I didn't want him to leave. I wanted to go with him if he did. "Please God, do something," I prayed. "Make Mama change her mind."

Mama saw the look on his face. She tapped her nails on the table and looked over at him once more. Suddenly, she grabbed her hair and pulled it out from her head. "Oh, poot! I don't care. I don't care. I don't care. Layla Jay, if you want to go out for a little visit, you can. But I've got a date to go to the show this afternoon, so you'll have to get Pop to bring you home."

Papaw's lips curled into a smile around his cigar. "I can sure enough do that." He pinched my arm. "Let's get going. Grandma cooked a chicken pie for you."

She met us in the driveway and we both cried a little, but we pretended it was the brisk wind that whipped up our tears. The pie was delicious, and Grandma had made a chocolate cake, too. After I helped with the dishes, she said she was too tired to go visiting the infirm, and later when I went back into the kitchen for a second piece of cake, I found her lying on the tile floor with her arms stretched out like Jesus on the cross.

Chapter 8

WE BURIED GRANDMA ON VALENTINE'S DAY. I ORDERED A red-and-white-carnation heart that Mr. Davis, the funeral director, pinned onto the satin lining of the casket lid. Mama pitched in for the blanket of roses Papaw ordered, and Wallace showed up with a green plant that turned brown and died in less than two weeks. Mama and I didn't speak to Wallace even though he cried real tears when he went up to view the corpse. I believed he was truly sad, but Mama said I'd forgotten what a good actor he was.

I went through that day in a trancelike state. During the funeral and burial in the Whittington Cemetery, I couldn't get my mind to focus on the fact of Grandma's death. I kept thinking about desserts: red velvet cake, pecan pie, chocolate pudding, banana cream pie, sweet potato cake, Coca-Cola cake with thick creamy icing dotted with walnuts.

When we went back to the house for the post-funeral feast, there was Grandma's dining table laden with several of the very desserts I had imagined, but I couldn't eat a bite of anything. While our cousins and neighbors and fellow Methodists wandered around the living room whispering their condolences to Papaw and Mama, I went outside and knelt beneath the oak tree to pray, but I didn't know what to ask for now. God had taken Grandma before He'd sent the Holy Spirit to me and now she was up in heaven where all things are revealed to us. I wondered if she had met up with Daddy or if her spirit was still hovering over her grave. Wherever she was, she now knew me for the lying sinner that I was. She probably also knew that Mama had worn a low-cut red dress to her funeral, which the Pisgah members would be talking about for a long long time. I hoped Grandma knew though that Mama had said she believed in looking her best when she was feeling her worst. That made sense to me, but I couldn't summon the energy to care about my appearance and wore an unironed blouse and a black skirt to the funeral.

After all our guests had left, Papaw called Mama and me into the living room for a family conference. He wanted Mama and me to move back in with him. "Frieda, you can't afford the rent on that house in town, and I'll just rattle around in this big ole house without Zadie. It'd be good for both of us if you and Layla Jay moved back." He knotted his fingers together (two with Band-Aids on them) like he was plaiting rope. "What do you say?"

Mama kicked off her high-heeled pumps and flopped back on the couch. "Pop, I like living in town. I don't want to feed chickens and slop hogs. Why don't you sell this place and move in with us?"

I knew Papaw better than his daughter did. He wasn't about to give up riding Jim across the pasture. Papaw loved his land, the shaded pond he'd stocked with bream and catfish, the fields ripe with tall stalks of green and golden corn, the animals he fed and petted daily. He would never be happy in our little blue house on Fourth Street. I didn't want him to be lonely, but I didn't want him to give up the place where his heart belonged.

He dropped his hands into his lap. "No, I can't leave this place. I'm too old to start a new life in town. I wouldn't want to if I could."

Mama slid her right foot out, wriggling into her shoe. "Well, I'm not moving back here. If you want to stay, that's your choice." She forced her high heels onto her swollen feet and grimaced when she stood up. "You're right though. I can't afford the rent much longer; my savings are just about gone. I've got to find a better job or get another husband as soon as my divorce comes through."

Papaw must have seen the panic that fluttered as fast as humming-bird wings flitting inside me. I thought of all of the men Mama had recently been dating: the repeaters, Will Satterley, Errol Newman, Jake Lott; the new ones whose names I couldn't remember; I didn't want any of them for a stepfather. Papaw said, "No, you don't need to worry about money, Frieda. I don't need near all I have. I'll send you a check; your mama would want you to have a little inheritance from her."

Mama smiled and I blew out a stream of relief. "Thanks, Pop. Layla Jay and I could sure use a helping hand."

Mama and Papaw exchanged a look just then that told me they both knew what the outcome of this conversation was going to be way before it got started. I was the only one in the room who thought our futures were in doubt.

I believed that Mama regretted that her mother had died before they made up from their last fight, but she hid it well. While Papaw and I appreciated the notes and phone calls from people expressing their sympathy, Mama's face turned to stone. She had been through this before when Daddy died, and I don't know how she felt back then, but now she said it was none of anyone's damned business how she was feeling.

As soon as we got Papaw's check, she threw a party for her thirty-fifth birthday. Mama's birthday was March 15, the Ides of March, and Grandma used to say that a baby born on that day was sure to have pain in his or her life, but Mama wasn't feeling any of it that night, and neither was I.

Cybil Richards came with Ned Pottle, who was getting a divorce after his wife caught him at the Slumbercrest Motel with Cybil, and nearly all of Mama's beaus, old and new, came. A couple of women who worked with Mama at Salloum's department store came, too, but the men outnumbered the women five to one. Mama was gorgeous in a green velvet sheath trimmed in gold braid that snaked around her body as she danced the cha-cha, the twist, and a wild watusi. I sat eating salted peanuts from the glass bowl on the coffee table for the first hour or so of the party, wishing Jehu had come. I had invited him, but he said he was going to be out of town with his folks, and June, whom I had invited, too, said her mother wouldn't allow her to come because she knew for a fact that Frieda Andrews Ebert would serve liquor to minors. She was right about that. After Mama popped the champagne cork, she said a glass or two wouldn't hurt me. In fact, after my third glass I felt a whole lot better than I had in a very long time. All of my burdens and worries floated like feathers high above the heads of the couples who danced across our hardwood floors. I batted my eyes at Mervin Stevens when he passed by. He was one of the few men in the room Mama hadn't dated, although, from the way he looked at her as she flitted across the room, I was sure he was dying to ask her out. Mama had turned him down because he lived in the country and made little stone people, benches, fountains, and such out of concrete. "He's got white powder in his ears and talks about those figures like they're real people," she had told me when I said I thought he was nice.

When he walked by where I stood, I smiled at him. "Hey, Mervin," I said.

He wheeled around and grinned back at me. His thumb was stuck in the neck of a bottle of Papst Blue Ribbon that dangled from his hand, so I assumed he was on his way to the kitchen for another beer. "You want me to get you one?" I asked nodding down at his thumb.

"Sure, honey." He popped the empty off his hand, but then set it on the floor against the wall. "But you can get it after a dance. What about it? You like Chubby Checkers?"

I giggled. "I love him," I said, shimmying my shoulders just like Mama.

After we danced to two songs, Mervin and I had a couple of beers together in the kitchen, and that's when I got so numb I couldn't work my legs. But my stomach was moving plenty, and I wound up the evening curled up on the bath mat beside the toilet, which I vomited into about every fifteen minutes or so. Mama came in a couple of times to check on me, and the last thing I remember as she helped me to bed was her saying, "Beer on champagne, mighty risky. You should have known that, Layla Jay."

The next day, when I told June about the party, I enjoyed laughing with her over my first ever hangover. Later in the week I wished I hadn't confided in her. I told myself the reason she spread the news all over Zebulon Junior High that I got soused was that she was jealous. But I knew, too, that she had betrayed a confidence, and I'd never tell her another secret again. At Friday's basketball game against Brookhaven (we lost 30–86), all seven of the cheerleaders flashed me horrified looks when I walked down the bleachers to get a Coke. I didn't tell Mama about the kids at school whispering and gossiping about me, but she knew something was wrong. "Honey, would you like to spend the week-end with Pop? He's probably lonely with your grandma gone. Would that be fun?"

"Sure," I said, but I didn't think two days on the farm was going to eradicate my gloominess or Papaw's loneliness.

When Mama dropped me off, Papaw came out of the house wearing a bandage on his nose. "Crazy hen flew up in my face and bit the shit outta me," he said to Mama and me. "And I wasn't anywhere near the eggs she was sitting on."

Mama just laughed and advised him to wear protective clothing to gather the eggs, then drove off in a cloud of dust to get ready for a date. She was going out today with Thad Barnes, who had just moved to Zebulon from Meridian. Mama said he told her there weren't any women in Meridian as beautiful as she. We both believed him.

But I couldn't believe my ears when Papaw told me we were invited to dinner at Miss Louise Dunaway's house. I didn't know Papaw knew Miss Louise, and I had never met her, but I had heard a lot of stories about her. She was talked about around Zebulon nearly as much as Mama. She was a nurse, had moved to Zebulon when her husband was killed in a train accident that occurred the same year as my daddy's motorcycle accident, and although older than Mama, she was a lot younger than Papaw.

I didn't expect to like her. I sat silently beside Papaw on the drive over to her house in his battered truck that was beginning to look like a compact car with its missing bumpers and fenders. "You'll like Louise," Papaw said. "She's a good cook, too."

"Not as good as Grandma, I'll bet," I said, looking out the window as the sun bobbed its good-bye to me. I took off my sunglasses. "Nobody cooks as good as Grandma did."

I was wrong. Miss Louise made the best lasagna I'd ever tasted, and after eating junk food with Mama for so many nights, my stomach practically smiled when the lasagna hit it. As we ate, from across the table I watched Miss Louise laughing at Papaw's jokes. She was pretty, not beautiful like Mama, but she had sandy-colored hair that fell in curls around her shoulders, a spray of freckles across her nose, and when she smiled, a dimple appeared on her right cheek.

After the meal (she wouldn't dream of my doing the dishes), she got out a deck of cards and shuffled them like a professional gambler. That's when I noticed her hands. They didn't fit the rest of her; they were red and rough with unpolished short nails filed straight across her fingertips. I guessed that all nurses' hands looked like that considering what all they had to do with them. "Five-card stud," she announced nodding me into the dinette chair across the table from her.

I stole a glance at Papaw. Grandma had forbidden gambling in her house. The only cards we owned was a pack of Old Maid, which she grudgingly allowed me to play when I was younger. Papaw smiled. "What stakes are we playing for?" he asked, taking his seat at the head of the table.

"Two-penny ante."

"I don't know how to play," I muttered. "And I didn't bring my purse."

Papaw laughed. "She's a fast learner," he told Louise. "I'll stake you, Layla Jay."

As it turned out I had a real knack for poker. I won with ace high, a pair of threes, a straight, and a flush. As I raked in the pennies, Louise and Papaw wore twin looks of disgust on their faces. "Can't catch a thing," Papaw said, throwing his card down. "Time to get on home, Layla Jay."

It occurred to me that maybe Papaw and Miss Louise let me win on purpose, but I wasn't sure of that. When we counted our pennies, I had won one dollar and thirty-three cents. "You brought in a ringer," Miss Louise said to Papaw, showing nearly all of her big teeth. She flipped her curly hair around her face. "Poor me. I'm the big loser."

She was, but when I saw Papaw lean over and kiss her just before he got into the truck, I suspected that she had won much more than a poker pot.

On the drive home the next day I told Mama about our evening at Miss Louise's house, thinking she would be happy we had fun. But I was wrong; she was furious. Which surprised me. She and Papaw were so much alike, I had thought that she would be all for his having a "lady friend" as he called her. "You've had plenty of boyfriends since Daddy died," I said. "And Miss Louise is nice. She said she's going to start wearing Elizabeth Arden makeup just so she can visit with you at Salloum's. She thinks you're beautiful."

Mama swerved into the driveway and slammed on the brakes, nearly throwing me into the windshield. "All the makeup in the world couldn't improve her looks," she said. "And she's at least twenty years younger than Pop. He's an old fool. That's what."

Mama stayed in a bad mood the entire month. When she wasn't storming around the kitchen cussing the leaky faucet or the loud humming of the refrigerator, she was in her room, lying on her bed with the blinds closed. I could tell by her puffy eyes that she was crying a lot, but she told me she'd developed allergies and to stop looking at her like she was some goddamned bug under a microscope. She didn't even notice when one of her nails chipped, and when I pointed it out, she just shrugged her shoulders like she didn't care. Mama still went out to Skinnys, and she had plenty of dates, but her laughter sounded like false notes on my flute, and her pink rouge looked too bright on her pale face. I wanted to help her, talk to her like a best friend since she'd lost Cybil to Ned Pottle, but I didn't know what advice a daughter is supposed to give a mother. I gave up and asked God to counsel her. I didn't know that I was the one who was going to need His advice soon.

Chapter 9

GOD FINALLY ANSWERED ONE OF MY PRAYERS. SOMETIME BEtween New Year's and Easter, I grew real breasts, and just as I had thought, having big boobs changes your life. But not always for the better. I was still in love with Jehu, but he and Lyn had gotten back together and were going steady again. June double-dated with them several times, and she told me that Jehu and Lyn made out in the backseat of Red Pittman's car when the four of them went to the drive-in movies. Red had gotten his license before anyone else because he'd failed eighth grade twice. June said she was only dating Red until someone smarter got their license. She acted like she was Miss Goody Two-shoes on those dates, but I knew she let him French kiss her because she told me exactly how to do it. She even offered a demonstration, but I refused her when she wiggled her tongue too close to my face.

Ever since Mama's birthday party, I had been getting plenty of phone calls from boys I hardly knew, but none of them had asked me for a date as they didn't have driver's licenses. Then one Friday night when Mama was out on a date, Henry Quitman, a boy in my English class, borrowed his brother's motor scooter and drove over to my house. I invited him in for a Coke, but he said he would rather have a beer. "How 'bout it, Layla Jay? You got any beer in the house?" he asked as he plopped down on the couch and propped his feet on the northernmost corner of Mississippi.

"We're out," I lied. There was a six-pack of Buds in the refrigerator, but I didn't feel like giving him one, and I hadn't drunk one since Mama's party.

His chin dropped. "Well, I guess I'll take a Coke then."

When I brought the bottle to him, he took it with one hand and pulled me down beside him with his free hand. His eyes were on my chest. Mine were on his bangs. I assumed they were supposed to make him look like one of the Beatles, but they weren't even, dipping upward on his right temple. I longed to get the scissors and fix them for him. As I listened to him talk about his ride over, how fast he went, the route he took, the feel of the night wind on his skin, I counted the pimples on his face. Eight. His thin lips disappeared into his mouth when he fell silent. Where was Jehu tonight? Was he kissing Lyn, telling her that she was beautiful and that he couldn't believe he'd actually sunk so low as to go out with Layla Jay Andrews? Was Henry all I deserved in this life? I decided I would be an old maid. I wasn't going to spend my life straightening bangs and popping zits. I stood up. "You have to go," I said. "My mother will be home soon, and I'm not allowed to have boys in the house when she's not here."

Henry set his Coke down. "How 'bout a little kiss first?"

I shook my head sideways. "No way," I said. But he had risen and his arm went around my waist, pressing me against him. He slid his hand around to the side of my left boob. "You like this, don't you?" he whispered. "You let Don Perkins go all the way with you, didn't you?"

I punched him hard and he fell backward onto the couch. "I did not!" I yelled. "I never even went out with him. Who told you that?"

Henry rubbed his chest where I had punched him. "I don't remember. I've heard stories about you from lots of guys. Don, Jerry, Bruce, I don't know. The ones who come over here and get drunk with you. I heard you go all the way, let them do anything to you they want."

My legs turned to rubber, and I sank down on the couch beside him. How did all this get started? "It's all lies," I said. "Why would anyone make up these ugly lies?" I could barely get out the words, my throat constricted and I couldn't breathe. Suddenly my head was on his chest and my tears were making dark spots on his madras shirt.

Henry patted the back of my head. "I'm sorry. Real sorry, Layla Jay. I swear I thought what they were saying was the truth. Even June said some things, and she's your best friend, isn't she?"

I closed my eyes. June. June, my best friend. My only friend. Judas in a wraparound skirt. "What'd she say?" I whispered.

"She said that at that party your mother had, for her birthday I think it was. June said you told her you got drunk and went all the way with some old guy. She said you and your mother were just alike, wild women."

I guess something inside me broke then. Maybe it was my brain that came apart. I sat up. Wild women. Mama and me were wild women, and I imagined us running down the street, shrieking and beating our chests with our hair flying out in all directions. I laughed. Wasn't it all a joke? "Ha ha ha ha ha." I was screaming louder and louder. And then I was crying again.

Henry was so scared his bangs quivered across his forehead. "Uh, Layla Jay. Uh, I said I was sorry. I got to go. I need to get on home." He was easing away from me as if I might pounce on him like the wild animal I supposedly was. "I'll see you," he said, and then he was gone. I waited until the sound of the motor scooter died in the night before I cried until my eyes were swollen shut. I thought of the old saying "Sticks and stones may break your bones, but words can never hurt you." What a lie. Words were more lethal than bullets from a machine gun. There was no escaping them, no way to return fire that I could see.

Remembering the vow I had made the night of my birthday party, I wasn't going to tell Mama what Henry had said, but like always, she wormed it out of me. When she got home that night, I was still on the couch with swollen eyes, and it was a sure bet that Mama was going to know everything that had happened while she was gone.

Mama wanted revenge. After I told her about June's betrayal, she said, "That little bitch has always been jealous of you." She stood with her hands on her hips, her back against the kitchen sink, where the pile of stacked dirty dishes was listing precariously to her left. "We're going to make her life so miserable she'll wish she'd never spoken your name."

I was sitting at the table with a cold washcloth pressed against my eyes. It was three o'clock in the morning, and Mama had to be at work at eight-thirty. "But how? No one will believe me over her. She's a *cheerleader*."

"So what! All that means is that she's got a big mouth that needs shutting up."

As much as I, too, wanted revenge, I was more afraid of what Mama might do, and I wished I had at least left out June's name when I wailed out the entire story to her just an hour past. "I don't know, Mama. She's the president of Y-teens, reads the daily devotional over the intercom at school every Monday. The teachers like her."

Mama took a drag on her Lucky Strike. "Remember the golden rule. Do unto others what they've done to you."

Miserable as I was, I smiled. "Wallace would be surprised that you're quoting scripture."

Mama grinned. "Wallace would be surprised about a lot of things he'll never find out about." When she threw her arms out from her sides, her elbow struck the tower of dishes behind her. They teetered, but they didn't fall.

I dreaded going to school on Monday and begged Mama to let me stay home. "I'll clean the house," I promised. "I'll cook a nice dinner for you. I'll even iron some of your blouses."

"No sale. You're going to school with your head held high. We Andrews women don't allow people to dictate our behavior. You're not a coward; don't act like one. Think how Jackie would handle it. Would she let Lady Bird keep her from appearing in public? Of course not. *C'est la vie.* That's French for live it up, or something like that."

On Monday when the bell rang after homeroom, I spotted June sashaying down the hall with Cassie Greenberg, and when my Judas friend smiled at me, I burst into tears and ran to the girls' room where I locked myself in the first stall.

After the bell rang for first period, I left school and wandered around Zebulon for a while, trying to get up the courage to face Mama. She would find out that I had cut my classes when Mrs. Tremont, the school's secretary, called to report an absence, a new school policy that every kid I knew hated. I figured it was better that Mama hear the news from me than from the school's tattler, so I turned down State Street and headed for Salloum's. As I pushed open the glass door and turned left toward the cosmetics counter, I told myself that Mama would just have to accept the fact that I wasn't capable of *c'est la vie*.

I STOOD AT THE END of the counter watching Mama in profile as she held up a mirror in front of Mrs. Randolph's frowning face. Her voice was seductive and yet cheerful. "You see how that color brings out the blue in your eyes?"

Mrs. Randolph kept on frowning. "I don't know. It doesn't cover my liver spots all that well." Mrs. Randolph's husband owned the Palace Theater, State Street Drugs, and the new women's clothing store named Ruby's for his wife, so I knew Mama was hoping for a big sale. When Mama lowered the mirror, Mrs. Randolph opened her big tapestry purse and drew out a red wallet. "I guess I'll try it." She drew back the twenty-dollar bill just as Mama reached for it. "But if I don't like it, I'll expect my money back when I return it."

"Naturally," Mama said, as Mrs. Randolph finally let go of the twenty. "But you're going to get so many compliments you won't want to. Those spots are really beauty marks; everyone knows that."

I waited until Mrs. Randolph had walked across the aisle to the lingerie before I slid my hand down the glass counter to where Mama stood with a sad look on her face. "Hey," I said. "Even you can't make that ugly face pretty," I whispered.

Mama's eyes crinkled with laughter that was genuine, and I felt better already. "What are you doing here and why, Miss Layla Jay, aren't you in school where you belong?"

I spread my fingers wide on the smooth glass cool to my touch. "Don't be mad. I just couldn't stand seeing June smiling at me like she hadn't done a thing. It was too much to take."

Mama lifted my hands from the counter and kissed the knuckles on each hand. "Poor baby. You've got a lot to learn. Well, at least you tried. That's the important thing. To try." She glanced at the clock. "Tell you what. I get a break in about thirty minutes. Why don't you hang around and we'll go to the Tastee-Freez and order the large-size hot fudge sundae."

Mama was right! I had a case of the hot fudge sundae blues, and maybe, I thought, maybe Mama did, too. "I'll wait outside," I said and blew her a kiss before I turned and walked toward the sunlight streaming in through the open door.

I can't say the sundae cured the blues, but by the time Mama got home from work, I was feeling better than I had in days. Mama had just suggested that we go out for hamburgers when the phone rang. I sat on the couch listening to Mama talking in the tone she reserved for flirting, and disappointment wrapped around me tight as a straitjacket. She was saying, "Mervin Stevens, I can't possibly get there before seven." She laughed. "Well, you'll just have to tell your racing heart to slow down. You go ahead; I'll meet you there, and I promise I'll be worth the wait." I thought back to Mama's birthday party while I listened to more of Mama's bantering. I remembered how Mervin and I had sat at the kitchen table drinking beer and his face had gotten so fuzzy and then I'd seen two of him. Both of him were good-looking men with curly black hair, olive skin, the darkest eyes I'd ever seen. And he had been as drunk as I, laughing and spilling beer, staggering over to the washtub each time he got another bottle.

When Mama hung up the phone, she turned to me and said, "Imagine Mervin Stevens asking me to a party up at Dixie Springs Lake this late. I shouldn't go."

I brightened up right away. "Then don't. Let's get hamburgers."

She frowned. "The party is going to be at Dave Turner's cabin. I heard it's really something to see. Stone fireplace, bear rugs, rustic stuff. I've always wanted to go there. Bonita Garza goes up there all the time, always bragging to me about it. She'll be real surprised to see me there with Mervin, even if he does have white powder in his ears."

Before I could think of something persuasive to say, she left the room and headed for her closet. "I'll find something to eat," I yelled. "Maybe some arsenic is left in the fridge."

Mama didn't hear or she didn't think that merited a response. When I heard bath water running, I lay down on the couch and turned on the TV. *My Favorite Martian* was on. It wasn't my favorite, but I watched it anyway.

I woke up on the couch where I had fallen asleep. The TV screen was filled with snow and I switched it off. In the kitchen I glanced up at the white plastic wall clock and saw that it was 3:35 in the morning. Then I went to Mama's room and saw that she wasn't in her bed. I felt cold fingers gripping my arms, and I shivered with terror. My heart was beating so fast I could hardly breathe as I flew to Mama's unmade bed. Grabbing the sheet and spread, I huddled beneath them, pushing my nose into her pillow. As I breathed in the scent of Mama's Elizabeth Arden perfume, I suddenly knew something was terribly wrong. I sat up. Something had happened to Mama. I was sure of it. I looked around the dark room. No one was there, but I could feel Grandma's spirit all around me, telling me to get up, go, hurry. But go where?

I don't know how long I sat, frozen with fear and worry, in Mama's bed before I heard pounding on the door. After I ran down the hall and flung it open, Papaw reached for me and held me against his chest. "There's been an accident," he said. "Frieda. She's in the emergency room. Get your shoes. Let's go."

The nurse at the emergency room desk at the Zebulon Infirmary told us she didn't know anything about Mama's condition and directed us to the waiting room. As we came into the room, I saw two policemen and a fireman standing in front of three men seated on the gray plastic chairs lined against the wall. I recognized one of the policemen, Darryl Thomas, the man who had nearly been my stepfather but didn't have enough money to buy us a house. I also knew one of the men in the plastic chairs and I walked over closer so that I could hear what Mervin was saying. "I told her she shouldn't drive herself home, but she wouldn't let me have her keys. She said she didn't need a man to look after her, that she could take care of herself." He looked down at his folded hands hanging between his knees. "I was drunk myself. We all were. I don't know how in the hell we didn't get in that wreck. We were right behind her. I remember seeing her taillights and then she pulled out into the left lane and we saw the headlights coming, and Buddy slammed on the brakes hard and threw me into the dashboard."

Darryl had a pad in his hand, but he hadn't written anything on it. While Mervin talked, he kept nodding his head up and down like he was a teacher listening to a pupil give the right answers. He turned and saw me. "Layla Jay, you're here. Your mother's gone up to surgery."

Papaw was squeezing my hand so hard I cried out. I hadn't realized he was beside me until then. "How is she? Has anyone spoken to a doctor?" Papaw asked the group of men.

Mervin stood up. "Mr. Whittington, you know me. I'm the one who called you. I bought a Jersey from you last year." He stuck out his hand but Papaw ignored it. "All we know is Dr. Martin said she had a head injury, internal bleeding. She was on the pavement when I got there, so bloody it was hard to tell. That little Volkswagen crumpled up like a smashed beer can." He looked down at me. "I'm sorry. You don't want to hear all that. I just, I just, well, I just feel terrible about it."

I pulled my hand out of Papaw's grip and ran back down the hall. The scent of antiseptic and bleached tile floors wafted around me as I ran for the big glass double doors. Outside I skirted an ambulance and headed for the one pine tree beside the parking lot, where I knelt on the hard needles scattered beneath it. "Please God, let her live. Don't take her from me. You've got Daddy and Grandma; leave her for me. If you never answer another of my prayers and will answer just this one, that will be enough." Hot tears rained down my face and I could no longer speak aloud. Silently, I kept on praying. "Please please please please."

Chapter 10

GOD TOOK HIS TIME ANSWERING MY PRAYER. MAMA LAY IN A coma for eight days, and Dr. Martin said he didn't know if she'd come out of it or not. Papaw and I hardly left the hospital during those times. Night and day, we sat beside her bed where she lay with a bandaged head. Tubes and machines burbled and whined continuously, blocking out the sound of her shallow breath. I watched her chest; those magnificent breasts, rising and falling ever so slightly, didn't matter anymore. Nothing mattered at all, not eating, sleeping, changing clothes. Even praying became so routine and mechanical, I wondered if I should bother.

On the third day Wallace showed up. Papaw had gone home to feed the animals and I was sitting in the brown fake leather chair beside the window. I think I had dozed off as I remember jerking my head up when Wallace said her name. "Frieda. Frieda? Can you hear me? It's Wallace."

"She can't hear you," I said. "She's in a coma."

Wallace hadn't seen me; he jumped a little when I spoke. "Layla Jay. How are you?"

"I wasn't in the car. I'm fine," I said. Wallace looked like shit. The white shirt he preached in was wrinkled and there was a brown oval stain over his heart. His black pants hung on him, and his hair was matted down on his head and damp. As he walked over to my chair, I glanced out the window thinking it must have rained.

"I just found out," he said. "I was in Biloxi for a revival. What happened?"

I wasn't going to tell him that Mama was drunk, that I had heard the nurses gossiping that all sorts of outrageous behavior occurred in the cabin where she went that night. "She was in a terrible wreck," I said.

Wallace pulled over the only other chair in the room and sat beside me. "I heard that. And I heard about the party at the cabin. She must have been really drunk to hit an oncoming car. Was anyone else hurt?"

I shook my head. "No. She hit a big moving van, not a car, and the driver in the cab didn't have a scratch on him."

Wallace looked over at Mama lying still as ever. "Is she going to make it?"

"Don't know yet. Dr. Martin says she could come out of it at any time, or . . ." I shrugged.

Wallace's eyes filled with tears. "Let's pray together," he said.

My first thought was to tell him I could pray by myself just fine, thank you, but then I remembered Grandma saying that there is strength in numbers, and the more prayers lifted up, the better chance of God listening. I followed Wallace to Mama's bedside and folded my hands next to his.

WHILE MAMA WAS IN THE HOSPITAL, I stayed at Papaw's. Miss Louise moved into Mama's old room to keep me company during the hours Papaw was gone. I came to like Miss Louise even more than I had the night we played poker. She worked in pediatrics on the seven to three shift and tried to cheer me up with stories about the cute things some of the kids said. I didn't care about those kids, but I tried to smile at her stories so she wouldn't tell Papaw how miserable I was. He had enough to worry about. On his way to Mama's room on the third floor one night, he got in the elevator with an unlit cigar in his mouth, and when he leaned forward as the doors closed, somehow his cigar got stuck between them. Instead of letting it go, he clamped his teeth down on the cigar, fell into the metal door and broke off one of his false front teeth plus an incisor. No one could figure out exactly how all this happened, but Papaw swore that he was telling the truth. Miss Louise said it happened because he wasn't getting enough sleep and made him come home earlier each night. "You don't know how long Frieda will be there. Have to save your strength for the coming days," she told him.

I didn't go back to school. I told Papaw there was no point because I couldn't think of anything but Mama, and I'd just be a body with no brain sitting at a desk. I knew that the azalea bushes were all in bloom, a riot of purple, pink, and white lace-edged flowers. I knew a thunderstorm blew down the visitor sign in the hospital parking lot. I knew someone came into the emergency room with a gunshot wound. I knew these things, but I couldn't interpret any of it because nothing mattered except the rise and fall of Mama's chest. The nurses were kind to me; they brought me *Ingenue* magazines, a deck of cards, offered the leftover chocolate pudding patients didn't want. But I would sit in the chair too numb to read or play a game or even enjoy the sweet dessert. I stopped crying and felt worse. I dreaded seeing Grandma because I believed if she came to us, she would take Mama away, and every day I shook with fear when my eyes would grow heavy and the objects in the room would blur. That's when I thought she might appear, in that in-between time when my brain began to switch from reality to an unconscious state. But Grandma stayed away, and I kept my vigil, remembering the promise I had made to God, hoping he had heard my prayers.

I wasn't at the hospital when Mama came out of the coma. Papaw was there though, and he cried so hard trying to tell me that her first words were "Layla Jay okay?" that Miss Louise had to finish his sentence. We were standing in the hall just outside the room, and I rushed right in to see her. I guess I was expecting her to be just like she was when she left the house on the night of the accident, but this woman was nothing like my mother. She was weak and I could hardly hear her when she said, "Don't worrrr. I kay."

Mama had lost eight days of her life. She hadn't known we visited her every day, that Miss Louise and Cybil, Brother Thompson, and so many others from Pisgah Methodist and a few ladies from Salloum's had come, too. None of her boyfriends came, except Mervin, and he cried so loudly and carried on so much about it being his fault that we had to ask him not to come back. Luckily for Mama, Darryl Thomas had been the officer on the scene, and he was going to leave out a few details in his report, like the fact that Mama was drunk as a skunk. All of these things I told her that first day after she came back to us. But when I paused and looked up, I saw that her eyes had closed sometime during my long-winded chattering. I realized I had talked so long because I was trying to keep her awake, scared that she might slip back into the coma and that the next time she wouldn't come back.

But she came back to us after every nap, and each time she was a little more aware, a tiny bit stronger. Her legs weren't working right though, and her speech was slurred. Temporary brain damage, most likely, Dr. Martin said. She would need therapy and a lot of care for a long time. She had other injuries to deal with as well. They'd removed her gallbladder and patched up a perforation in her spleen, but she would live and that was what mattered.

I wasn't sure if it mattered to Mama. When she was finally well enough to understand her condition, she said she wished she had died. She couldn't face being an invalid, dependent on others to take care of her. It wasn't fair to ask her to live in a wheelchair; she was a dancer. And she was in a lot of pain.

Papaw tried to reassure her that she'd walk again. "You're going to have to summon up something you've never had, something called patience, Frieda. You'll heal, but it's going to take time." He smiled across the bed to where Miss Louise and I stood. "Louise has offered to help out. When you're well enough to go home, she'll be your nurse, help us take care of you."

Mama fingered the bandage on her head. "Who is 'us'?"

"Me and Layla Jay. Y'all will have to move in with me until you're well enough to take care of yourself."

Mama shook her head "no" for so long that Louise grabbed her cheeks and held her still. "I wan my bed," Mama said. "Go home? Pease?"

Papaw patted her hand and kissed her forehead. "We'll see. You rest now. Not good for healing to get yourself all upset."

"That's right," Louise said. "Happy patients get well a lot faster than unhappy ones."

I didn't think Mama would ever turn into a happy patient, but I smiled like I thought she could be one, too.

Since I had missed nearly two weeks of school counting the day I'd skipped, Papaw said he'd drive me to school the next day. I didn't mind going back to school now that Mama was out of danger. Anything was better than sitting in the hospital day after day. Of course, I'd probably see June, but now I didn't care if I did. Everything between us had been settled during the first days Mama was in the hospital.

Three days after Mama's accident, June and her mother had shown up in Mama's room with a potted plant. While Papaw visited with June's mother, June and I went down to the snack bar for a Coke and a pack of Nabs. That's where she cried and said that Henry Quitman had told her about ratting her out as the person who started all the rumors about me and Mervin. Now she wanted me to believe how sorry she was for making up all those lies. I wasn't going to forgive her that easily, so I pushed my chair back and stood up. "I'll never understand how you could say those things knowing how much it would hurt me. Everyone believed you, not me."

June grabbed my wrist. "Please give me a chance to explain," she said.

An intern or resident—I couldn't tell the difference—walked in and put his dime in the machine for a Coke. "Hi girls," he said. "Got a patient in here?"

"My mother," I said.

He lifted the Coke from the box, stuck the cap in the opener, and popped it off. "Well, hope she goes home soon. This place isn't much fun to be stuck in."

When he left, I sat back down. "Okay, I'll listen, June, but I want to get back up to Mama's room soon."

June bit her lip and her hesitation made me wonder if she was going to make up another lie, but then her eyes filled up, and she sobbed and shook her bubble hairdo until I thought the curl would fall out. "Go on," I finally said, and although I was enjoying her misery, I didn't think it could compare to mine.

When she finally got her breath, she said, "Dear Zeus, help me!" She rubbed her eyes and sat up straight in her chair. "Well, okay. Here's how this all got started. I was talking to Glory, Sue, Lyn, all of the cheerleaders after practice, and Lyn said something about you." Her breath hitched again.

"What'd she say?"

"She said she couldn't believe Jehu had taken you to that dance, that no other boys liked you, that you'd probably never get another date." June tightened her mouth the way she did every time she talked about Mr. Robinson our algebra teacher, who she thinks is a communist. "So I said, 'That's not true. I know for a fact that older men like Layla Jay.' They wanted to know how I knew and so I told them about how you danced and drank beer with Mervin." She looked over at me and lifted her palms. "You did say that, Layla Jay."

"I know what I said, but I didn't say we went all the way. I never even kissed him. He's *Mama's* boyfriend, not mine."

June looked over at the Coke machine. Her voice was fainter now. "I know. But after I told them that, they got real interested in me. I mean they were hanging on my every word for a change, and I'm not as popular as they are. I mean, I don't get invited to a lot of their spend-the-night parties, and I guess I was enjoying all the attention and so when they all screamed and asked what happened next, well, I had to think of something fast, and before I knew it, I heard myself saying you and he, well, you know."

I stared hard at June. It was like I had never known her, like we had never been best friends, swapping *Photoplay* magazines, rolling each other's hair, telling our dreams to each other and promising we'd never tell anyone else our secrets. We'd done all that, and yet June had told this awful lie. Our friendship had meant less to her than being popular with these snotty girls. I stood up. "So you did this terrible thing to me just so you'd be the center of attention with the cheerleaders? That's rich," I said. "And that's the best reason I'll ever have for ending a friendship. I'll see you around, June. Well, not if I see you first." Before she could reply, I jumped up and ran out into the hall. When I got back up to Mama's room, I told June's mother that June was waiting for her in the snack bar downstairs. I wanted her far away, out of the hospital and out of my life.

I dreaded seeing June at school, but she was absent. I overheard Lyn telling some girls that June had the flu, and I hoped she had the stomach flu and was in for a lot of vomiting before she got over it. All of my teachers asked about Mama, trying to be kind, and they tried to be subtle when they asked questions about what *exactly* had happened that night. Only Miss Schultz didn't quiz me. She put her arm around me and said she had prayed nightly to the Virgin Mary to lay her healing hands on Mama. I mumbled my thanks although Grandma had told me it was wrong to pray to the saints and not to God. I knew she meant well, and truth be told, I'd prayed to Grandma and Daddy and Papaw's neighbor, Mr. Thompson, who had died of TB when I was ten.

After Papaw picked me up from school, we drove over to the hospital. Mama was sitting up eating green Jell-O from the spoon Wallace held out. He smiled at us. "Look at our girl. Eating something at last."

Papaw and I stood with our backs to the door in shock. How had this happened? How could Mama allow Wallace to even be in the room, much less feed her? I had assumed Wallace hadn't returned after that one visit, and I hadn't dared tell Mama or even Papaw about his being in the room and our praying together. Now I wondered if he'd been slipping in to see her all along.

I walked over to kiss Mama's cheek and noticed a new bunch of flowers in a plastic vase beside the bed. "Hi, Mama, I see someone brought you some daisies."

"Wallace remembered they're my favorite," Mama said, except it sounded like she said, "Wallurce remember tday my fave right."

"That's right, Frieda," he said. Then looking over at Papaw, who was still at the door, he waved to him. "She's had a good day. I've been here since noon, and she's just getting better by the minute."

"Bullshit," Papaw said and walked out.

"Paaaaop," Mama said. "Go get im, Wallurce."

Wallace handed me the Jell-O and spoon. "Here, you get her to eat some more. I'll go see what's what with your grandfather."

After he left I put the spoon and Jell-O on the tray beside the bed. "Mama, what's up with Wallace? How come you're letting him stay?"

Mama smiled. I interpreted her slurred sentences as she spoke. "Layla Jay, he's the reason I'm alive, well, not him exactly, but his faith is the reason. God saved me for him. He told me."

It hadn't taken too much effort to figure out what the words she said were, but I didn't have a clue as to what they meant. "What? What are you saying? I don't understand."

"Roll the bed down, honey. I'm tired. Need to lie flat a while. Then I'll explain."

I turned the crank until she was lying flat and then sat down in the straight chair beside her. "Okay, so what'd Wallace say?"

Mama rolled her head on her pillow toward me and, in her new way of talking, began her story. "Take my hand, sweetheart. It was when I was in the coma. Late one night Wallace came in and my blood pressure was dropping. The nurse told him I might not make it through the night."

"No one said that to me and Papaw. At least not to me," I said.

"Well, no need to because when Wallace heard that, he said he knelt beside my bed and laid his hand on my heart and began praying to God to let me live. He promised Him that he would dedicate his life to Him, doing whatever He commanded. He begged God to give me to him as a helpmate, a kind of sidekick I guess, so that he wouldn't stray with other women, and then he just kept on praying and praying. He prayed so long, he lost his voice, and he couldn't feel his body at all. Wallace thinks God took him out of his body and held him in His arms. He said he could feel His love, and he knew then that I would live. When he opened his eyes, the nurse came in and said my pressure had risen, that I was out of danger, and Wallace wept with joy."

I was dumbfounded. Speechless. What was I to say to this?

Mama was worn out from talking so long, and now I saw that tears were streaming down her cheeks. I wiped them away with my thumb. "So you think Wallace's prayers are the reason you're alive?"

She smiled. "Of course, that's the reason, and that's why Wallace is going to take us home and we won't have to go to Pop's after all."

Chapter 11

———

PAPAW WOULD NEVER HAVE ACCEPTED WALLACE'S RETURN TO our lives except that Mama begged him to give her new/old husband a chance. Not wanting to upset her after all she'd been through, Papaw told me it was best to let her have her way for now. "When she's stronger, she'll come to her senses," he assured me. "You can stick it out with him until then."

We were in his truck with my suitcase in the back and my train case on my lap driving back to Fourth Street, where we'd be meeting Wallace, who was bringing Mama home from the hospital. I said I supposed I could stick it out, but I didn't for a minute believe God had chosen Mama for Wallace's sidekick, and I couldn't believe Mama's newfound faith was going to last very long. But then hadn't I faked salvation myself? What did I know? I knew I still didn't trust Wallace, and I knew that I was going to be miserable living with him again. "Okay, I'll keep my lip zipped," I said to Papaw, "but I wish I could have stayed with you."

Papaw swerved around a mongrel dog running across the road, and then patted my leg. "I wish you could, too, but we'll see each other a lot.

Louise is going to come by every day to check on Frieda and help her with her therapy."

We were on Broadway Street turning onto Fourth and my heart was pounding with anxiety. I dreaded seeing Mama in a wheelchair in her house. "I know, and I like Miss Louise. She's really nice."

"Made some lasagna this morning and it's in your icebox ready to heat up for your dinner tonight." He pulled into the drive behind Wallace's new Ford Galaxie. "Looks like they beat us here," Papaw said, shutting off the engine. I started to open my door, but Papaw held my arm. "Wait, I want to say one more thing before we go in."

"What?" I knew this was the important thing, the last "one more thing" always is.

"If this isn't working out, if he mistreats your mama or you, or well, just anything makes you upset, I want you to tell me. Promise me you'll ask for help if you need it."

His face was so white and his grip on my arm so firm, I wondered if somehow he knew what had really happened between me and Wallace in this house we were about to enter. I hadn't told a soul, but Papaw was a shrewd judge of not just cows and horses, but of men as well. I kissed his cheek. I tried to smile, but I could only spread my lips a little before I said, "I promise. Don't worry, Papaw. I'll be fine."

Mama wasn't fine. Her speech improved rapidly, and the ugly black stitches that had marred her body turned to bright pink scars, but she couldn't stand up without someone holding on to her. I brought her coffee, fluffed her pillows, and smoothed her sheets because she preferred staying in bed to being lifted into the wheelchair. Wallace, Miss Louise, and I suffered through her loud protests daily when we insisted she get out of bed. Occasionally, she'd forget she was God's gift to Wallace and yell out cuss words, but then she'd put her hand over her mouth and say, "Sorry, that just slipped out."

I have to admit Wallace was a good caretaker. Mama's wheelchair wouldn't fit through the bathroom door, nor could we wedge it beneath the kitchen table, so Wallace got cinder blocks to lift the table and carried Mama down the hall each day to her chair. He filled Mama's prescriptions at the drugstore, he did the grocery shopping, he even cleaned the house a couple of times before Mama told me to take over those chores. Wallace read to Mama until she felt well enough to read the Bible herself. She was fascinated by the biblical tales, and would read passages out loud to me. "I never knew the Bible was so *interesting,*" she said to me. "There's a lot more in it than just rules to follow. Have you read about David and Bathsheba? What a romance!"

"Yeah, I know the story," I said. We were sitting on the front porch and I looked across the yard and waved to Miss Graham, who was watering the gardenia bushes beneath her front-room windows. Wallace had gone to New Hope to write his sermon and counsel a couple who were thinking of getting a divorce, but before he left, he parked Mama beside me, telling her some fresh air was what she needed to feel better. We were expecting Papaw and Miss Louise, and they would help me get Mama back to bed when she got tired.

"Layla Jay, don't you feel grateful to the good Lord for giving Wallace back to us? I think of all those terrible awful days when I was out sinning, getting drunk, and fornicating, and taking His name in vain. Why, I was headed straight for hell, and Wallace has changed my direction to the path to heaven." Wallace had also changed our phone number because, when Mama came home from the hospital, quite a few of her old boyfriends didn't know that Wallace had moved back in with us.

I watched Miss Graham pulling the hose down the yard toward the bright yellow mums she'd planted around the water oak. Their lacy leaves drooped in the heat and I doubted they were going to last the season. "I don't think you were going to hell before he came back," I whispered.

"You don't? How could I not?"

I wiped the sweat from my forehead with the tail of my shirt. "I just don't. I can't explain it, and I wish you'd talk about something besides God and Wallace." I saw the hurt expression on Mama's face, and I felt terrible. I thought of Grandma, how we'd talk about God and the Bible and people getting saved, but I hadn't minded those conversations. Why was I feeling annoyed, maybe even a little bit angry, when Mama brought up the same topics? "I'm sorry," I said. "I guess I'm just bored now that school is over. I don't have any friends now that I don't see June anymore."

Mama reached over and squeezed my arm. "Oh, Layla Jay, I'm so selfish. I had forgotten about your fuss with June. Why don't you call her? God wants you to forgive her. You know that."

I jumped up so fast my chair tipped sideways and I caught it just before it crashed into Mama's wheelchair. "Forgive her! Never!" I yelled. "She's a liar and a bitch. I'd rather be friends with the devil himself."

Mama's eyes filled up. "Layla Jay, don't say such things. God is listening."

"Yeah, well, I hope He gets an earful because I've got a lot of other things to tell Him about."

"You're not making sense, and you don't mean that. You're only fourteen and you just don't understand what you're saying."

Just then Papaw's truck jumped the curb and veered toward the drive. "I understand more than you. And I know things you'll never know," I said, leaping down the steps to greet Papaw and Miss Louise.

It was Miss Louise who came up with a solution for ending my isolation on Fourth Street. "Why don't you take swim lessons? I saw a flyer at the grocery store that the lifeguards at the Zebulon City Pool are giving lessons for fifty cents for a half hour. Swimming is such good exercise, and maybe you'll meet some friends at the pool," she said.

Wallace was against the idea. He didn't think a young girl should parade around in public half-naked. I promised to get a one-piece suit and not the hot pink bikini I coveted in Salloum's department store window. Mama was on my side. "Wallace, she needs to have something for herself. She spends all her time taking care of me and the house, and now that I can walk a few steps, I can be left alone for an hour or so if you have to go somewhere during lesson time." She looked at me and smiled. "Layla Jay deserves to have some fun. At her age she should be thinking about makeup and boys and going to the movies, not what time Mama needs her pills."

I was so grateful to her I could hardly keep from jumping up and down, not just because she was fighting for me, but because the old mischievous light had flickered in her eyes for just a moment or so. Maybe Papaw was right; she might come to her senses when she was fully recovered.

Wallace gave in, and even though I was afraid of drowning, I decided I'd rather drown in a pool than die a slow death in my pious home.

My suit, though not a bikini, was cool. It was the color of a fire hydrant with white straps that matched the two white strips around the legs and across the low vee-cut bodice. Now that I had breasts, I filled out the top just fine, and even had a small line of cleavage to show off to the unlucky girls who didn't have any.

I fell in love with the swim instructor the first day. His name was Roland and he had sun-bleached hair and a dazzling white smile on his dark tanned face. The muscles on his upper body rippled when he leaned forward with his palm beneath my stomach, holding me up as I flutter-kicked my white legs in the aquamarine water. He was too old for me, twenty-one, a Mississippi State graduate, and he would be leaving to attend law school at Tulane University in New Orleans. But I didn't think about any of that. I thought about the light pressure of his palm on my stomach, the feel of him pressing against my back when he encircled my body with his arms and lifted mine to demonstrate a stroke.

Thirty minutes flew by, and after each lesson I would reluctantly knot my beach towel around my waist, slip into my thongs, and trudge the eight blocks back home where Mama would be waiting for me to get her a Coke or a cup of coffee or something to eat. She was gaining weight sitting in the chair all day, and Miss Louise told her she needed to try harder on her exercises. Mama got mad at Miss Louise two or three days of every week, but no matter what Mama said or how much she cried, Miss Louise was always serene and spoke to her in an even-toned voice, repeating her instructions to bend the knee and extend, bend and extend. I admired Miss Louise more than I can say. I wished I could be more like her and less like myself. Things with Mama weren't going as well though. When Mama cried, I cried. When she got mad, I got mad back. We just weren't getting along anymore, and while I wanted to blame our troubled relationship on her accident, I knew it was more about Wallace than anything.

Wallace was still preaching at New Hope and he worked part-time at Vest's, so he wasn't home all that much, but when he was, I looked for excuses to leave. He didn't make me go to church since Mama would be alone if we both attended, and I was glad I didn't have to see him parading around another pulpit. I could imagine his tearful testimony about the miracle God had performed when He healed Mama. Wallace was so sure she was alive because of him. I wanted to tell him that maybe it was my prayers that God had answered and not his. How could he be so sure *his* prayer was the one?

One day when Papaw came over and Mama was napping, I asked him what he thought of the story about the night in the hospital when Wallace had prayed over Mama. We were eating lunch at the kitchen table, and Papaw lifted his head from the paper plate in front of him and laughed. "Bullshit. All that concoction about God rocking Wallace like some big baby is just bullshit, Layla Jay. Your mama got well because she's got mine and Zadie's blood in her. We don't give up, and even in a coma, she was fighting to come back to us." He took a bite of the tuna fish sandwich I had made for our lunch, and with his mouth full said, "Forget about it."

"But don't you believe in prayer, Papaw?" I asked. "Grandma sure thought praying made the difference in the outcome of things."

Papaw's voice softened. "Yeah, Zadie was a real Christian, not a fake like Wallace." He leaned over and kissed my cheek. "You start thinking about having fun and learning to drive, and dating silly boys instead of dwelling on your mama's business."

It was good advice, and with Papaw's blessing, I asked Mama if I could stay at the pool for a few hours on Wednesdays. Mama didn't mind, and Miss Louise's shift was now from three to eleven, so she would come by and check on Mama while I was out.

I had learned to swim an awkward crawl, and I could float like a life raft, so Roland terminated our lessons, which was a big disappointment, but I could still watch him as he gave lessons to the other kids, all way younger than me. The Zebulon public pool was lined with fourteen white lounge chairs that tilted back so you could lie on your stomach and tan. There were at least thirty kids at the pool every time I went so I hardly ever got a chair, and usually wound up lying on my navy blue beach towel on the hot concrete. Every now and then all of us sunbathers would jump into the pool to cool off before returning to our chairs and towels, which we saved with personal belongings.

It was during one of my cool-off swims that I saw Jehu and Lyn walk though the turnstile into the pool area. Lyn, in a sheer lime green beach coat flapping out over a matching bikini, strolled down the side of the pool and swung a canvas drawstring bag with her initials monogrammed in big loopy letters. Jehu, in a T-shirt with the Cougars' logo on it and a red swimsuit the exact color of mine, carried a rolled-up brown towel under his arm. Both were wearing sunglasses to die for. By the four-foot marker, I ducked under and held my breath for as long as I could before I burst out of the water with a big spray that splashed droplets onto Lyn as she walked along the edge of the pool.

"Damnit!" She squealed. "My sandals!" I brushed my wet hair back from my face and saw that, unlike most of us who wore rubber thongs, she had on green leather sandals with gold seashells glued on top.

"Sorry," I said.

"You ought to watch out for people," she said. She lowered her sunglasses down on her nose. "Oh, Layla Jay, it's you. I'd think you'd be home helping out with your mother. She's still in a wheelchair after that accident she caused, isn't she?"

Before I could answer, Jehu squatted down by my bobbing head. "Hi. How is your mother?"

"Doing good," I said. "Our maid is with her." I directed this up to where Lyn stood taking off her wet sandals.

"Sure was sorry about her trouble," Jehu said. "I remember how much fun she was at your party. I liked her a lot."

Lyn had gotten her sandals off and tapped Jehu's back with them. "Come on. I see two vacant chairs."

I looked to where she pointed and saw that both chairs were saved with T-shirts thrown on them, but as I hoisted my body out of the pool, Lyn snatched them up and tossed them on the concrete a few feet away. I knew she'd try to tell their owners that they had blown off or been knocked off by a kid. They'd never get those chairs back.

My towel was laid out across the pool from where Lyn and Jehu were setting out their things, so I lay down and watched Lyn shrug off her cover-up. I smiled when I saw that the top of her bikini laid in folds around breasts the size of tennis balls. Mine were definitely better, and now it occurred to me that Jehu must have seen my cleavage when he squatted over me in the pool. As I breathed in the scents of suntan lotion and chlorine that rose up from the sunbathers and crowded pool, I turned onto my side where I had a better angle to observe him as he pulled his T-shirt over his head. Even though he was blond, a nest of curly brown hair curled on his chest between his nipples, and now I noticed the bulge in the front of his suit. I blew out a long stream of air and felt sick. He should be mine, I thought. He was mine, if only for a little while, and I hated Lyn almost as much as June.

Hoping to divert my attention from the agony of watching my love with another, I picked up my book and tried to read. I had stolen a copy of *Lolita* from the cabinet beneath Mama's bedside table where bottles of pills and a medical dictionary had replaced her nail polish, colognes, and the costume jewelry that she would toss there after a date. The foreword was hard to read and I almost gave up, but the first lines in part one got my attention. "Lolita, light of my life, fire of my loins. My sin, my soul. Lo-lee-ta." Fire of my loins. I remembered loins and loincloths in the Bible, and had always skipped right over the fact of them, but now I pictured loincloths and all that lay beneath them. Like Jehu's swimsuit, they probably didn't hide the fact of those biblical loins. As I read ". . . the tip of the tongue taking a trip of three steps down the palate to tap, at three, on the teeth, . . ." I licked my lips. I was hot, needing to take another dip to cool off. So what if Jehu was rubbing suntan lotion on Lyn's back now. Who cared? I was in love with Roland anyway . . . but he had barely said hi when I waved at him earlier.

I backed down the metal ladder into the deep end and hung there for a moment before I lay back and rowed with my arms to the side of the pool. Keeping my hand on the tile, I lodged myself there to keep from bumping into the other swimmers. Overhead, tiny wisps of clouds like pulled taffy stretched across the sky the same color blue as Mama's favorite dress. The heat of the afternoon sun made me feel languid and soft and I closed my eyes, imagining I was floating on one of the soft clouds where Daddy laid his palm beneath my back and gently we bobbed along across the heavens. Then suddenly I was spiraling down into the water, gulping, kicking and thrashing for air. I shot up, coughed, and snorted water out of my nose. "You okay?" I looked up into Roland's blue eyes.

"What happened?"

"Some kid," he pointed to a giggling freckle-faced boy around ten or eleven years old, "grabbed your ankle and pulled you under. I blew the whistle. Didn't you hear?"

"Uh uh. I guess I fell asleep." Looking around I saw that I had drifted down to the diving area and Jehu was on the board jumping up and down, springing the board so we could hear the thumping of wood hitting metal. He dove in, a perfect jackknife.

Roland was holding out his hand. "Here, I'll help you out."

Just as I came out of the pool to Roland and my breasts rubbed against his chest, Jehu swam by and gave me a look that maybe said he was jealous, or maybe he thought those rumors about me were true. Whatever he thought, I had his attention, and I threw my long wet hair back and breathed as deeply as I could so that my breasts were slightly lifting out of my suit.

But it wasn't Jehu who spoke; it was Roland. "When you're ready to go, how 'bout I take you home in my Mustang?" he said.

"That'd be cool," I said, flashing my Sandra Dee smile. But as I knotted my towel around my waist and glanced one last time at Jehu and Lyn holding hands across their chairs, I knew that I had outgrown Sandra Dee. It was Lolita I wanted to be now, fire of Roland's loins.

Chapter 12

ROLAND DID DRIVE ME HOME, ALONG WITH FIVE OTHER KIDS who lived in my neighborhood. I was stuffed in the backseat between the Banacheck twins, and the acrid smell of chlorine was so overpowering, I felt sick by the time he let me out on the street in front of our house.

Wallace's puke green Galaxie wasn't in the drive, so I was surprised when I walked into the kitchen and saw him standing at the sink. He told me he was getting the tires rotated and had walked home from the garage, intending to pick it up later. Too late, I realized that, with my towel still knotted around my waist and nothing over my suit above it, my breasts were on display. Wallace noticed them immediately. Ever since he moved back in, I had taken care to wear floppy shirts around the house, fearing this very moment. But now his eyes were on my boobs that had popped up like jack-in-the-boxes.

Wallace didn't bother to say hello. "You've been parading around the pool in that skimpy suit?"

"It's a one-piece. You should see the girls in bikinis. I look like a grandma compared to a lot of them."

Wallace turned away and lifted a handful of greens from the sink where he was washing them. He threw them in the aluminum pot sitting on the countertop. "You are not to go out in that swimsuit ever again."

"But Wallace, it's all I have. I need to get out of this house and the pool is the only place there is to go during the day." I hugged my towel closer and pulled my beach bag beneath my arm. All I needed was for *Lolita* to fall out onto the floor. I imagined the book burning a rectangle into the tile from the fire I saw in Wallace's eyes as I tried to reason with him.

He grabbed more greens and pushed them down on top of the others. "There are better places, decent places. I never liked that you were going to that pool in the beginning. I only said you could because I didn't want you arguing about it and upsetting Frieda."

Tears welled up behind my eyes, and this time they were tears of rage. How I hated Wallace and his damned piousness. "Well, I'm about to upset her now when I tell her how unfair you are. Where is she?"

Wallace grabbed my wrist before I could get out of the kitchen. "She's taking a nap. You leave her alone." He was too close; his eyes were on my breasts, and I could smell the bitter greens on his fingers before he let go of me. He lowered his voice. "Go change your clothes and help me finish dinner for your mother." When I backed a step away from him, he shook his head. "You've changed, Layla Jay. When we lived together before, I thought you were a good Christian girl. Now I'm not so sure about that."

"I was never sure of you," I said before I ran to my room and locked the door. Tossing my bag on my bed, I lay down beside it in my damp suit. If Wallace wanted to go to war with me, so be it. I could do battle with him, couldn't I? I turned over onto my stomach, reached over and pulled *Lolita* out of my bag. When I had first seen the paperback in Mama's nightstand cabinet, I remembered people talking about the movie, which a lot of kids' parents had forbidden them to see. A couple of boys had seen it in Memphis, and June told me they said it was just about the sexiest, weirdest movie they'd ever gone to. I had seen photos of Sue Lyons in nearly all of the movie magazines and I knew that she was supposed to be only fourteen in the role of Lolita, but I thought she looked a lot older than that.

I got up, dropped my towel on the floor, and walked over to my dresser, where I stood staring at my reflection. I looked older than four-teen myself. While my breasts had been growing larger, my face had been losing its roundness so that now my cheekbones stood out, and my neck appeared longer. I had straight white teeth behind my full lips, and as I turned in profile, I decided I liked the way my nose curved up just a tiny bit on the end. Backing up I could see that my now tan legs were long enough, but my waistline was too low, which made the upper and lower halves of my torso disproportionate. I wasn't going to be as beautiful as Mama, but I thought I might be pretty enough to turn a few heads.

My eyes fell on my flute case on the floor beneath the window. After football season ended, I had given up playing the flute; I was never going to be all that good. But I missed playing it, and now I took it out of its case and lifted it to my lips. I liked the feel of the cool silver against my lips, the slick cylinder that I wrapped my fingers around. I played a few notes. I had already forgotten most of the songs I had learned in band practice, but I tried to play "Greensleeves," and had just about got-ten the first bars right, when Wallace banged on my door.

"Layla Jay, stop that noise. You've woken your mother, and now she has a headache. Open this door."

"I can't. I'm not dressed," I said.

"Well, get dressed and come help me with dinner."

I pulled down my suit and fluffed the hairs I had recently grown on my mound of Venus and bounced my breasts before I strapped them in a bra. I was a woman in every sense of the word now, I told myself. And as a woman, I could handle Wallace, couldn't I?

I didn't stop going to the pool. I told Wallace I was spending the af-ternoons at the library, and began changing into my suit in the pool dressing room and drying my hair before I returned home. I stuffed books on top of my swimsuit in case Wallace peeked into my bag, but usually he wasn't around when I left or returned. I checked Charles Dickens's *David Copperfield* out of the library, and told Wallace I was really enjoying reading about poor David, who never knew his real fa-ther, just like me. "It's very educational, too," I said. "That Mr. Murdstone is so mean to David."

"Good for you. Maybe now you'll learn to appreciate having a step-father like me," Wallace said, looking pleased with me for a change.

At the pool my romance with Roland was going nowhere. Once in a while he'd come over and talk to me, but mostly he was busy giving lessons or blowing his whistle at boys running or horseplaying too rough. A lot of girls hung out by his chair, which was about four feet off the concrete and centered in the exact middle of the pool. Jehu and Lyn came to the pool almost as often as I did. Lyn never spoke to me again, but occasionally Jehu would pass by me on the way to the snack bar or the boys' bathroom and say hi or how's it going or hot, isn't it? Each time he passed, I planned to think of something interesting to say, but words always failed me, and I usually wound up saying hi back or yeah, it's a scorcher.

And then one Wednesday afternoon around two o'clock, June showed up. I didn't see her at first because she walked behind the chairs instead of in front of them like most people. I'd gotten lucky and had a chair of my own that day, and when she came up behind me and called my name, I nearly fell out of it.

"Hey, Layla Jay. Mind if I put my stuff down beside you?"

"It's a free country, public pool," I said in what I hoped was a bored-sounding voice.

I didn't watch as I listened to the squeaking sounds of her scuffing around her yellow beach towel in her thongs. She had brought a small transistor radio in her bag, which she held out over my stomach. "Mind if we listen to some music?"

What was this *we* like we were together? "Go ahead. I don't care." I turned over onto my stomach and laid my cheek on the cushion facing away from her. I thought about her hair. She'd finally gotten rid of the bubble hairdo and was letting her hair grow out into a flip, which was a better look for her. And she'd lost weight. When she was cheerleading, her calf muscles were plump-looking and her shoulders round with extra muscle. Now she looked frail. I had heard that she had been sick for a long time, but I couldn't remember with what.

"I'm Leaving It Up to You" was playing on WXIL when June switched on her radio. "You decide what you wanna do," she sang. She tapped my arm. "Kind of appropriate, huh? Deciding how to feel when someone leaves things up to you."

I turned my head to lie on my left cheek. "I don't know what you're talking about."

June uncapped her suntan lotion and smeared white cream on her arms and shoulders. "I'm talking about us," she said. "I'm asking if you would decide to give me a second chance."

I sat up and swung my legs off the chair so that I was facing her. "Why should I give you a second chance?" As soon as I said it, I heard Mama's voice inside my head, telling me I should forgive her.

"Because I'm sorry and I understand now how you must've felt when I treated you so bad." June capped the bottle of lotion and set it beside her. "You were right to be hurt and mad at me, and I was a stupid idiot. Those girls I wanted to be friends with aren't nearly as nice as you. They're backstabbers every one. I don't like any of them."

I sneered. "What'd they do to you?"

June's eyes teared up, but she didn't cry. She looked away and lowered her voice to a near whisper. "Uh, nothing. Nothing to me. Really. I just saw how they gossip about one another. They're mean and all they care about is money and boys and clothes. They don't ever talk about anything important like you and I did. And they think it's so cool to hate teachers and parents and really anybody over thirty. I loved your grandma. How could anyone dislike her? Or your grandfather? "

"I knew all that about them a long time ago. That's not news to me."

"Yeah, but Layla Jay, I didn't see it. You're the best friend I ever had, and . . ." She swallowed a few times before she went on. "And I'm just miserable without you. I miss you so much."

The cloud of her unhappiness ballooned out and enveloped me. I could feel her misery, and I admitted to myself that I was lonely, too. I had missed her as much as she missed me. Maybe Mama was right. It was better to forgive. I thought of how bad I felt when I got really mad. Thinking about the mean things June had said only made me feel worse. Two wrongs don't make a right, Grandma had said. Was I being just as awful as she was by not forgiving her? I looked across the pool to the chain-link fence that enclosed us. As I watched the T-shirts and towels draped on the fence, flapping in the light breeze like laundry on a line, it occurred to me that maybe my anger was a fence, too, imprisoning me, keeping me from the freedom to forgive.

"June," I said and stopped. Her head was bowed. "June?" When she lifted her face to me, I saw ribbons of tears winding down her cheeks. Her white lips, pressed together so tightly, matched the knuckles of her folded hands. "I missed you, too," I whispered.

"Oh, Layla Jay!" She scrambled across the concrete and fell on me. Her hug felt nearly as good as Grandma's, and I kissed her cheek for the first time ever.

When I told Mama that June and I had made up, that I had forgiven her, she hugged me, too. "Honey, I'm so glad, and I know just how June felt when you told her all was forgiven because that's how I felt when Wallace forgave me. And because of Wallace, God forgave me, too. I'm sure of it."

Wallace again. Her true savior. Savior of the world! God could re- tire and just let Wallace take care of His business. I was about to say "Maybe I should start praying to Wallace" when I saw Mama's shining eyes. I didn't want to take away her joy. "Yeah, I'm glad everything has turned out the way it has," I said looking down at my hands as I knew Mama would see that big lie written all over my face.

Lying to Wallace about the library wasn't bothering me one bit. Every chance I got, I met June at the pool and within another week, I was as brown as an acorn and my hair had blond streaks that contrasted with the darker browns of my hair. Even my boobs liked the sun; they were growing into showpieces like Mama's, and I thanked God every night for answering my prayer. I was also learning a lot from *Lolita*. I read slowly, often having to reread the long sentences this author Nabokov wrote, and there were quite a lot of words I didn't know, but it was very clear to me how this Humbert Humbert was feeling about his "nymphet." I hated Humbert, but I was fascinated by him, too. Lolita I couldn't figure out, but I thought I would eventually understand what made her tick if I could get through the novel. June thought I was nuts to have to work so hard to read a stupid book. She had amassed a large collection of magazines and read about fashion and makeup and stories about girls who didn't get invited to the prom. I thought reading should take you away from your regular life, but that's just me.

One Wednesday afternoon, June and I had just laid out our towels when a dark cloud rolled over the sun and in a short time, a clap of thun- der sounded overhead. "Everybody out of the pool," Roland called, tweeting his whistle in consecutive short blasts. With a lot of "aw's," "no fair's," and "There's no lightning," kids began clambering out of the water looking like the seals at the zoo waddling up on their rocks. Then they poured over the sunbathers, stepping on our towels, knocking over bottles of suntan oil.

"Let's go somewhere else," June said. "It's going to rain anyway."

"Where?" I said, getting up and sliding into my thongs.

"My house. Nobody's home. We can do our nails or something."

I glanced around the pool. Jehu hadn't come today, but Lyn was standing in a circle of girls, June's former friends and fellow cheerleaders. June was looking at them, too. "Let's get out of here before they do. I don't want to have to speak to them if they're leaving the same time as us," she said.

Glory and Sarah Jane were staring at June, and the disgust I saw written on their faces puzzled me. When they whispered to each other and laughed, I was sure it was June, and not me, they were gossiping about. "Okay. Let's hustle," I said.

Still in our suits, we walked over to June's cream-colored brick ranch house, where she lifted the potted mum beside the door and retrieved the key to the glass-paned door. "Mother thinks a burglar wouldn't find the key here. Can you believe she's that dumb?"

I didn't answer. I admired June's mother, had at times wished Mama was a little more conventional like her. June's mother was the president of the PTA at Zebulon Junior High, belonged to Beta Sigma Phi, and helped her husband in the office at his plumbing company. And her house was spotless. June loved our messy house and Mama's freewheeling life, and said she wished her mother was more like mine. I suppose Grandma was right about the grass is always greener.

June offered me a Coke from their refrigerator, which held oranges, neatly stacked Tupperware, several varieties of cheese, fresh asparagus and carrots along with the usual stuff. I thought of the limp carrots in our refrigerator. "Can I have one?" I said, pointing to the crisper.

"Yuck! If you want one, go ahead." June grabbed two Cokes and an opener from the drawer beside the sink, where their silverware gleamed in separated bins. I thought of how our utensils were all jumbled up so that we always had to fish around in the drawer to find a spoon or fork.

I followed June to her bedroom and dropped my bag on the floor. While June shrugged off her cover-up and hung it in her closet, I looked out the bank of windows that stretched across the back of her bedroom wall and saw the first drops of rain splattering on their brick patio. "Raining," I said. "We got here just in time."

June walked to the mirror and flicked the bottom of her bikini higher on her leg. "I'm blistered again," she said. "I wish I could tan as good as you." The fair skin of June's stomach had turned a bright red, and there were stripes of pink down her legs.

"Does it hurt?"

"A little," she said. "I'll put some cream on it. Maybe it won't peel."

After June left to get the cream out of the bathroom, I pulled my suit down and admired the line just above my nipples where the top of my suit came to. I smiled, thinking that Wallace was so dumb. Did he believe I was getting a tan beneath the fluorescent lights in the library?

"Wow! Look at your tan line," June said, holding up a jar of Noxzema. She set the jar on her dresser and walked over to me. I pulled the top of my suit back up and was reaching for my Coke and carrot when she said, "Can I see your line again?"

I hooked my thumbs in the straps and wiggled the suit down nearly to my nipples.

"Oh, you've got such beautiful boobs," June said, with envy in her voice. In her bikini top, hers looked to be about the size of Papaw's fists. "Are they hard like mine? Can I feel them?"

"I guess," I said, uncertain that I really wanted her to touch me.

June's hands, soft and cool, reached inside my suit, lifting my breasts into her palms. As she exhaled, puffs of air warmed my skin. Her thumbs brushed across my nipples, and when I felt them stiffening, I held my breath, heat rising up from below. I backed away. "No, June. Don't. I feel funny all over."

June's palms were flat on her yellow top. "I know. Me too. It's kind of nice though." She pulled her top off. "Feel mine."

I stared at the small pink-and-white mounds that she cupped in her hands. "No. I don't think we should . . ."

"Come on, Layla Jay, I'm not going to get you pregnant." June laughed, breaking the tension that was nearly tangible in the space between us.

I giggled. "I guess not," I said.

"Let's smush them together. See how that feels." She stepped over the fallen bikini top on the floor and pushed her boobs against mine.

"Maybe rubbing against yours will encourage mine to grow." She looked down at our chests, talking to her breasts. "See what you're supposed to look like?"

"You're goofy," I said, and just then, a loud clap of thunder made us both jump, and immediately lightning flickered in the room and sheets of rain pelted the windowpanes. June ran across the room to the four windows, raised the far left one, and knelt in front of it. The blowing rain hit her chest and face and water cascaded down her stomach. "Come on. Do this. It feels terrific," she called over the roar of the rain drumming on the tin roof.

She was right. The stinging pellets of cold water felt good on my breasts and I lifted my face with closed eyes to the refreshing spray. In minutes, we were getting soaked, and I slammed my window down at the same time as June. Before I could rise to my feet, June leaned over and licked the water that dripped from my nipples. I felt her tongue and the circle of her soft lips on my skin. "No," I said, but I didn't move away. This was wrong, maybe a sin, but my body ignored my thoughts, and my arms reached out and pulled her close.

Chapter 13

KNOWING THAT IGNORANCE IS OFTEN THE SOURCE OF OUR fears, I left June's house and walked straight over to the library, hoping to get smarter about what June and I had done. I had heard kids at school call Mr. Collier and Mr. Banks, who lived together in a big house on Delaware, a word that I couldn't remember, and I was afraid that June and I had become the female counterparts to whatever Mr. Collier and Mr. Banks were. I hoped to find that word in a book among the ones in the reference section.

Running up the steps to the redbrick building, I met Miss Schultz coming down them. She was holding three books against her chest and her fabric purse hung off her shoulder, bumping against her hip as she came toward me with a big smile. "Layla Jay! How nice to see you. Are you enjoying your summer vacation?"

I hated seeing teachers out of the classroom, but Miss Schultz would have been an exception, except that now I worried that what I had just done might somehow be visible to her. My cheeks burned and I drew my shoulders forward, pushing my breasts back as far as I could. "Yes ma'am," I said.

"How's your mother coming along?"

"She's better. Thank you. Getting around a little bit now with one of those walkers. Everyone has been surprised at what a quick recovery she's made so far."

"Well, I know she has a good nurse in you." She shifted her books to her left arm. "I'd better get home. Lots of reading to catch up on. I don't get a chance to read much during the school year. What are you reading this summer?"

I dropped my hand to my beach bag, covering the book outlined there as if it were transparent and the tall pink and yellow letters on the middle of the book cover that spelled *Lolita* were visible. "Uh, right now, *David Copperfield,*" I said.

"Oh, Dickens is just wonderful," Miss Schultz said, as she came on down the steps and stood on the sidewalk. "Well, I hope I'll see you again. Have a pleasant summer and best regards to your mother."

"Bye. Thanks," I said. As I watched her walking to her ancient Chevrolet, I thought that if she knew what pleasant activity I had just been engaged in, she wouldn't be hoping to see me again.

In the library I remembered the medical dictionary lying on Mama's bedside table, and went to the rows of encyclopedias and dictionaries. Running my fingers down the silver-lettered World Books, I came to a red-and-cream-colored book with the title *The Illustrated Medical Dictionary* and pulled it from the shelf. Sitting on the hardwood floor, I opened it, and then flipping through the pages, saw that it was in alphabetical order like a regular dictionary. I tried looking up "breast" first. I read about paired mammary glands, the growth depending on hormones, the size and shape depending on fatty tissue rather than glands. None of that was helpful. Next I found a color illustration of the female reproductive system that only named the organs, most of which I knew all about from health class in school.

Finally, just as I was about to give up, the word I was searching for popped into my brain: "Homosexuality." I turned to the *H*'s, and as my index finger passed Histoplasmosis, Hives, Hoarseness, and Hodgkin's disease and landed on the word "Homosexuality," Jehu popped out of the next aisle. I slammed the book shut and slapped my palm over as many letters of the title as it would cover. "Hi," I said.

Jehu had just come from work. I knew because he was wearing a red-and-white Piggly Wiggly shirt with the little pig's head logo on the pocket above his name. "Hey, Layla Jay. I thought you'd be at the pool."

"It rained earlier," I said.

He tucked the green-bound book he was holding beneath his arm. "Oh yeah, I was in the stockroom with no windows, but I heard the thunder. Big storm, huh?"

I wanted to know what the title of the book was he had hidden. Maybe, like me, he was seeking an answer to a question. "Yeah, it was. You checking that out?" I asked, pointing to the book.

"Uh huh. Baseball greats. I'm on the Pony League team this year. Second base."

"Oh, I didn't know you played."

"Yeah, you should come to a game sometime. I'm on the Firestone store team."

For a moment I forgot my misery. Would he ask me to come watch him if he didn't like me anymore? "I'd love to," I said. "I'll see if I can get a ride over to the field sometime."

"If you really want to go, you could ride with us," he said. "Red Pittman usually picks me up. He's on the team, too."

What about Lyn? I thought. What about her? He was asking me, not her, and I lifted my hand to my hair. Why hadn't I combed it before I left June's?

"That'd be cool. When's the next game?"

"This Saturday. I'll call you and tell you what time. Gotta get going. My dad's waiting for me outside. He's got to represent a client in court at three, so I've got to hurry it up."

"Okay, bye. And thanks," I said, smiling so big my cheeks ached.

After Jehu left, I turned back to the book. I had found what I was looking for, and now I would find out what was the matter with me. I read silently.

HOMOSEXUALITY, *sexual attraction toward persons of one's own sex rather than the opposite sex. In females it is called lesbianism. In psychoanalysis the term can also include sexual interest which does not receive genital expression. The causes of homosexuality are extremely complex and difficult to ascertain, and science or psychiatry have only partial answers to the treatment of the problem. This deviation from nor-*

mal heterosexuality may develop at puberty. A lack of hormones, or such
emotional factors as a father complex in the female adolescent, or a simi-
lar identification toward the mother in the male adolescent, may be the
basis of homosexuality.

June and I were lesbianism. I understood that we most likely had developed this problem (for which there didn't seem to be any treatment)
in puberty, but I didn't for a minute believe that I had a father complex.
I'd never had a real father to begin with. How could I have a complex
about one? Maybe June did though. We hadn't had genital expression,
but the term still applied, I assumed. Then I began to reread the paragraph, and the first sentence stopped me: "sexual attraction toward persons of one's own sex rather than the opposite sex." I wasn't attracted to
June; Jehu was the opposite sex and wasn't I drawn to him like a fisher-
man to a boat? I'd rather have Jehu's hands on my boobs than June's any
day. I didn't fit the definition of lesbianism. But maybe June did. And
now I remembered the girls at the pool staring at her, whispering behind
their hands. Did they know? Was that the real reason June had wanted to
resume our friendship?

I shelved the book back in its place, and beneath a cloud of still
unanswered questions, drifted out of the library and crossed Eighth
Street onto Delaware Avenue. Two blocks down I came to Centenary
Methodist Church and paused in front of the walk leading up to the
double wooden doors. Even if I wasn't lesbianism, I had sinned, or had
I? It wasn't fornication, and that was the only sin I could recall about sex,
except for adultery and that didn't apply to me. I walked on toward
home. I doubted God cared about girls enjoying each other's breasts.
And Mama had fornicated so many times, I'd lost count and, up until
now, she hadn't worried about going to hell. And I thought that, if there
were a lot of folks like Wallace up in heaven with Grandma and Daddy,
I wasn't so sure I wanted to spend eternity there anyway. By the time I
got home, I had begun thinking about the baseball game on Saturday
and decided to stop worrying about heaven and hell for a while and
enjoy watching Jehu swing a bat.

Saturday finally arrived, and I got up at seven in case Jehu called before he went to work. After Wallace left for work at nine, I went into
Mama's room, where she was sitting by the window sipping a cup of cof-

fee. She set her cup on the round cloth-covered table beside her and smiled at me. "Good morning, I heard you getting up earlier. Are you going to the pool when it opens?"

I smiled back. She hadn't mispronounced a single word, and now she sounded exactly like she always had. "No, I'm waiting for Jehu to call. He invited me to watch him play baseball tonight."

"Really? I thought you didn't like him anymore."

I sat down on the unmade bed. I could smell Wallace's aftershave lotion on the pillow beside me and moved farther down the mattress. "I just said that. He dumped me for Lyn, but now I guess they're broken up again."

"Well, he ought to make up his mind," Mama said. Although she was now overweight by about fifteen pounds or so, sitting framed against the windows with the morning sun streaming around her, Mama looked like a goddess in her long gown. Her hair had grown out in soft curls and turned into a rusty reddish color that made her pale skin look even lighter and the green of her eyes the color of celery. "Are you going to tell Wallace where you're going?"

The night of the school dance when Wallace had touched me and forbidden me to date returned, and a shadow of fear formed inside me. "I'd rather not," I said. "You know he'll say it's a date, even though Red Pittman is going, too, and I'll be sitting in the bleachers and Jehu will be on the field."

Mama had become my accomplice in deceiving Wallace about my near daily trips to the pool. She had caught me stuffing my suit into the bottom of my bag, and I'd confessed about lying to Wallace. Without hesitating, she had totally sided with me on the pool trips, so I was surprised when Mama frowned. "I don't like all this lying, Layla Jay. It's not right."

"I know, but Mama, Wallace is so unreasonable. I can't talk to him about anything without him lecturing me. He treats me like a two-year-old."

"Well, I have to admit you're right. He means well though. He loves you; just wants to protect you for your own good." As soon as she said those words, she couldn't stop the smile that began to spread. She shrugged her shoulders. "Oh, poot. Bullshit, as Pop would say. A girl

your age should have a little fun. I won't tell. You can say you'~
over to June's to play cards or something."

At the mention of June's name, I reached for the light blue she~ ~~
side me and crumpled the fabric in my fist. "I'm not going to June's
anymore," I said. Shut up, I told myself. She's going to ask why not.

Mama's eyes widened with anger. "I thought you said you'd forgiven her."

I released the sheet and pressed my palms against my cheeks. I
couldn't tell Mama about me and June. This was one secret she wasn't
going to get out of me no matter how hard she tried. "I did. We made
up, but now we've had another fight."

Mama looked genuinely concerned. "What happened?"

With Mama's eyes boring into me, I suddenly felt dirty. Even if I
wasn't a lesbianism, what I had done with June wasn't natural. Mama
would be disgusted, sickened to have a daughter who would do those
things.

"What happened, Layla Jay?"

"Uh, well . . ." I swallowed a few times afraid I was going to cry with
shame. "I can't tell you," I whispered. "I just can't." And then I was face
down on the bed, spotting Wallace's pillow with my tears. Somehow she
made it over to the bed without her walker, which stood beside her
chair. Mama hadn't taken one step without it before now. I cried harder
and then felt Mama's hand on my back. The scent of her perfume that
smelled like Grandma's tea roses enveloped me, and I sobbed louder.

"Honey, what's wrong? Let me help. We'll pray, ask God for His
guidance. No matter what it is, He can help you feel better."

I wiped my nose with the sheet. "No, He can't," I said, shaking my
head from side to side. "He doesn't care how I feel. Not anymore."

Mama wiped my hair from my face and cupped my chin, turning
me toward her. "What in the world would make you say something like
that? I feel like I don't even know my own child."

I jerked away and sat up, swinging my feet to the carpet. "How could
you? I don't know me myself." I also didn't know why I was crying, why
I felt so mad and sad and downright crazy. I knew I had traveled to some
unknown place in my life where there were paths in all directions, and
it seemed that any path I took would lead me into trouble. I had been

on the road to salvation, then taken a detour off when I lied about getting saved. I'd walked down liars lane with Wallace, run a ways down the lesbianism path with June, and there was always the road I longed to travel that led back to Grandma and the past that I could never retrace. But the highway I had to follow now curved toward Mama. I wiped my face and looked over at her high-necked pink nightgown and remembered the red see-through shortie gown that had been her favorite before the accident. Even her breasts looked smaller now, and it occurred to me that all that Mama had lost, the good and the bad, had been bestowed on me. I hugged her. "Don't worry. I'll be okay. I just can't talk about any of it right now. I need to figure out some things first. Please try to understand, Mama."

Mama wiped a tear from her face. I hadn't realized she was crying, too. "Okay, Layla Jay, if that's what you want. You don't have to tell me what's wrong, but I think you'd feel better if you'd ask God for help with whatever it is that's bothering you. He does care about you and He loves you."

In for a penny, in for a pound. I might as well say what she wanted me to. One more lie wasn't going to make any difference. "You're right. I know He does. I'll pray on it."

Mama didn't look convinced. "Promise?"

I stood up. "I promise," I mumbled, crossing my fingers behind my back.

Chapter 14

THE ONE PERSON I NEVER EXPECTED TO SEE AT THE GAME ON Saturday night was Roland. But there he was, sitting on the front row of the metal bleachers on the line from home plate to first base. Jehu and Red had hustled over to the dugout, where Mr. Matheny, the biology teacher at Zebulon High, who was also the coach, was talking to the team members with his left foot resting on the bench where they sat. I was about to hike up to the top of the bleachers when Roland spotted me. "Hey, Layla Jay. Haven't seen you at a game before."

I walked over to him and stood with my back to the field. "No, this will be my first one. I didn't know you were a baseball fan, thought swimming was your sport."

"It is. My brother Steve plays on the Gabriel Lumber and Supply Store team." He patted the space beside him. "Take a seat. You got a brother on the team?"

I was wearing my white shorts and the cool metal felt nice on the backs of my thighs. "No. I'm an only child." I grinned. "And I hope I always will be."

After the game started, Roland and I realized we were cheering for opposite teams. Each time I yelled and clapped for Jehu and his team members, Roland would put his hand over my mouth or grab my wrist so that I couldn't clap. Then when he called "Way to go" after the Gabriel team got a hit, I would punch his arm. Jehu looked over at me a couple of times, but for most of the game, he sat in the dugout with his eyes on the field.

After the fourth inning, Roland stood up. "Want a Coke? I'm going to the concession stand."

"I'll go with you," I said, pulling my sleeveless pale blue blouse down over my hips as I followed him on the muddy path, my sandals sidestepping puddles left over from the storm earlier in the week.

We didn't go back to our seats after we got our paper cups of lukewarm Coke, but stood watching the game to the left of third base. Red Pittman was at bat, and he had already hit one home run, so everyone was screaming "Miss it" or "Good eye" after he let a low ball go by. Dave Reddick was the Gabriel pitcher, and he had pitched two balls when he threw a fast ball that connected with Red's bat. I looked up at the fly ball that sailed into foul territory, right where we stood.

Roland yelled "Watch out," and flung his arm around me, throwing me onto my stomach on the muddy ground. Looking up, I saw the ball as it streaked on over our heads and landed at the base of the floodlights at the edge of the diamond.

We lay with our arms and legs entangled, and I could hear loud calls from the crowd in the stands and then a few people laughing and yelling, "You should've caught it, Roland."

I buried my face, burning with embarrassment, against Roland's chest. I knew how stupid we must have looked lying there in the mud. Roland was laughing as he pulled me to my feet. He waved and bowed to the stands and then caught my hand, and we jogged over to the concession stand. "Napkins, please. And water if you have any."

Mr. Webber shook his head, and before handing Roland a stack of napkins and a paper cup of water, said, "Y'all should have known better than to stand so close to the foul line."

I looked back at the field and saw our spilled Coke cups crumpled on the grass. He was right. "We're idiots," I said.

Behind the concession stand out of view of the crowd, Roland and I dipped our napkins in the water and wiped our arms and legs down.

With a dry napkin, I rubbed my blouse and the front of my shorts, but ended up smearing the red mud instead of removing it. Roland hadn't gotten nearly as much on him. Only one red streak down his chest and a quarter-size circle on his hip remained after he scrubbed his clothes. He took one of my napkins. "Here, let me see if I can get some of it off."

He began with the left side of my blouse and worked his way around and up until I felt his palm on my breast rubbing and then caressing. I didn't move away. The feeling I was having was just the same as when June had touched me. I wasn't a lesbianism. Roland was definitely the opposite sex. I lifted my eyes just as he lifted his. "I better stop," he said. "I shouldn't have. . . ."

I smiled. "It's okay. Really."

Roland dropped his hands to his sides. His eyes were on my breasts. "You sure don't look your age, Layla Jay. Lots of girls in college would like to look like you, I'll bet."

"I'm nearly sixteen," I lied. "Not that much younger than you."

He managed a half-smile. "Still too young for me." He leaned over and picked up the scattered napkins on the ground. "Let's go watch the rest of the game."

I looked down at my thin blouse clinging to my body now. "I can't. I look a mess."

Roland stepped back and surveyed me from head to toe. "You do look pretty bad." He tossed the napkins in the large metal can behind the stand. "Tell you what. You don't live very far away. I'll take you home and you can change quick, and I'll bring you back before the game is over."

"I don't want you to have to miss the game. Your brother . . ."

"Trust me. He didn't expect me to last more than a few innings. They're not the major league, you know."

Roland led me over to his red Mustang, and within minutes, I was sitting in the front seat beside him. I kept my eyes on his knuckles resting on the floor shift and the muscles in his forearm as he shifted gears. The black fabric seats held a faint scent of chlorine that mingled with the rich smell of the mud and spilled Coke on my clothes, but now I liked the tangy bouquet. Roland drove fast and too soon we were on my street. I spotted Wallace's car parked on the driveway, and said, "Go on down the block a little way."

He lifted his foot off the accelerator. "Why?"

"My step, Wallace, is home. I don't want him to see me. Just park down there." I pointed to the Masters' house three down from ours. "I'll go around back, and if you'll boost me, I can climb through my window."

"You're something else, Layla Jay," Roland said as he pulled over. "You sure he won't hear us?"

"Not a chance. He never comes in my room, and I keep the door closed when I'm out. And when I'm not."

Roland helped me pull out the screen on my bedroom window and lift the glass far enough for me to wiggle through. I changed into pink shorts with a matching ruffled top with lightning speed, stuffed my muddy clothes under the bed, and slipped on my pool thongs before jumping out into Roland's arms. "I'm going to start calling you Speedy Gonzales," Roland said, taking my hand as we ran across the grass to the car. "I never knew a girl who could get dressed that fast."

"Practice," I said as we reached the car. I ran my fingers through my hair, trying to untangle it. "I wish I'd brought my purse with a mirror and a brush," I said.

Roland leaned across the seat and opened the glove compartment. "You can use my comb."

"Thanks, but I still can't see what I look like."

When he said, "Got a solution for that," I thought he was going to turn the rearview mirror toward me, but he took the comb from me and began to work the tangles out of my hair, holding his left hand on the top of my head as he raked the comb down my hair to my shoulders.

Nothing had ever felt so good. My scalp tingled and goose bumps rose up on my arms. "Mmm," I said. "That feels so good." I laid my head back and my hair swept across my shoulders. The lights were on in the Masters' house and I could see the flicker of the TV screen through the sheer curtains on their living room windows. It was dark and cozy in the car, and as Roland turned my head toward him, combing the tendrils of hair around my face, I closed my eyes with contentment.

He kissed me, and just as it had been with Jehu, I wasn't ready. When I opened my mouth to say sorry, his tongue touched mine and slid along the roof of my mouth. "Let's go somewhere," he said, moving away and turning the ignition key. He cocked his head toward me. "Okay?"

"Okay," I said, unsure of what I was agreeing to.

We drove to the gravel pit just outside of town. As soon as we rolled to a stop and he turned off the engine, Roland got out of the Mustang and opened my door. A flicker of fear rose up in me. I knew lots of kids parked here but I had never been here at night. And I really didn't know Roland all that well, did I? I thought of Jehu. He would be wondering what happened to me. Looking up at Roland who stood smiling down at me, I eased out of the car, shut the door, and leaned back against it. "Maybe we should get back to the game," I said. "It's probably nearly over."

"I'll take you if that's what you really want," Roland said, moving forward, pressing his body against me. The hard metal of the car against my back contrasted with the softness of his lips on mine, his chest pressing against mine, his hands running down the sides of my hips. Suddenly, I didn't want this to happen. I thought of June saying she wasn't going to get me pregnant. Roland could though, and I wasn't dumb enough to not know where he was headed.

When I felt him sliding down the zipper of my shorts, I pushed him away. "I've never. I'm not." I didn't know how to say what I wanted him to know.

"Your first time?" he asked. "I thought from the way you kissed and all . . ."

I don't know what made me ask, "Have you done it before?"

He smiled, his white teeth flashing bright against his dark tanned skin. "Yeah, I've known a few girls before now." He held my face between his hands. "If you say no, we'll go."

I bit my lip. I wanted to say no, go back to the lighted ball field and be a fourteen-year-old fan again, but I also didn't want the feelings I was having to go away. And I wanted to know for sure that I wasn't a lesbian-ism. "Kiss me again," I said. "I don't know what I want just yet."

We never made it back to the game. I heard that the Gabriel team beat the Firestone team 6–5, and in the last inning when Jehu Albright came up to bat with the bases loaded, he struck out.

Chapter 15

JUNE HAD BEEN CALLING ME DAILY BEFORE SHE LEFT FOR CAMP up in Tennessee, but I always made up an excuse to get off the phone, and when she came over one Saturday, I didn't answer the door. The week after the baseball game, Roland, who didn't call at all, left for summer school at Tulane in New Orleans. So I went back to the pool where I made friends with Jeanie Rawls and Faye Porter after I sat beside them and offered to save their chairs.

Lyn and Jehu were going steady again. Jehu's initial ring glistened in the sun on its chain around Lyn's neck, and when I bumped into them at the snack bar, they looked right through me like I was one of the elementary school kids all of us teenagers ignored.

On the morning after the game, I had wanted to call Jehu and apologize for leaving with Roland. I had practiced the lie that I was going to tell him: "When I went home to change, Wallace wouldn't let me go back out." But each time I reached for the phone, my hand shook and I knew he would hear the lie in my voice. I hadn't had to lie to Wallace or Mama. They'd been asleep when Roland brought me home for the second time that night, and I'd tiptoed to my room without waking them.

They were sleeping soundly, Wallace thinking I was playing games at June's house, and Mama believing I was with Jehu and Red Pittman.

I had still been asleep when Wallace left for New Hope the next morning, and for the first time, Mama had gone with him. She was getting around without her walker now, and felt stronger with each step she took. Wallace left me a note on the kitchen table beneath the salt shaker. "Layla Jay, Frieda is feeling well enough to attend services this morning. She wouldn't let me wake you, so while we're gone do the laundry and start on lunch. Pork chops are thawing in the sink. Dad."

I stared at the signature. What had caused Wallace to suddenly declare himself "Dad"? He'd never be that to me.

I would have done the laundry anyway to hide my muddy clothes and my panties with rusty red stains on them, visible proof that I was no longer a virgin. I threw them in the washing machine without looking. I wanted no reminders of what had happened in the backseat of Roland's Mustang.

After I turned on the washing machine, I went out into our shady backyard and sat in the green metal lawn chair with my knees against my chest, my bare feet curled over the edge of the seat. I thumbed through *Lolita* to the middle section where the word "lesbian," not "lesbianism," leapt out at me. I read "she had been coached at an early age by a little Lesbian." I read on to the part where Humbert asked Lolita, his Lo, to tell him about her first time, to what Humbert referred to as her being debauched. Lolita and I had begun similarly: she with this Elizabeth Talbot, and me with June. But there we parted, at least in thought. Lolita "held Charlie's mind and manners in the greatest contempt." I, on the other hand, knew that my opinion of Roland went beyond the word "contempt." I hated him.

I closed my eyes, remembering lying on the backseat of Roland's Mustang with my head resting on his bunched jeans. His hands traveled over me, crisscrossing the country of my body from North to South from East to West. Through the open windows I listened to the incessant croaking of a bullfrog as the peculiar scent of the gravel pit wafted into the car. When Roland eased my shorts and panties down my legs, the night air cooled my skin and I thought of the cold rain hitting my breasts as I knelt in front of June's window. I didn't want to think of her, of what I had done with her. "Roland, I love you," I said, and I knew that I did not. Shouldn't I love the person I was about to give myself to? What was I doing here? How had this happened?

This was wrong wrong wrong. "No," I finally managed to say. "I don't think . . . I want to go home."

Roland raised his head from my breast. "No, you don't," he said. "It's too late to stop now. You know you want this," he said. "I promise you'll like it. I won't hurt you. Doesn't it feel good?" he asked.

He was right about the sensations shooting through me, but he didn't know my heart was breaking, thinking now of Grandma and Mama and Papaw and how they trusted me. With my hands on his chest, I tried to push him away, but suddenly his body was weighing me down, and I tasted the salt of his sweat as he hovered above me. Before I knew what was happening, a sharp pain shot through me and he clamped his mouth on mine. The top of my head hit the window again and again as his hips slapped against mine. I think I said "Stop" aloud, but I may have only been screaming it inside. Crying silently, I stared out the rear window at the moon shaped like the slice of the cantaloupe I had served Mama for breakfast that morning. When it was over, I couldn't stop shuddering with hatred and fear and shame. "I want to go home," I whispered. "Take me home."

After we were dressed and Roland was safely behind the wheel again, I sat in the bucket seat with my head resting on the window and my arms crossed over my chest. I wanted to be as far away from him as I could be in the small car. On the drive home, Roland told me I was making a big deal out of nothing. "You didn't do anything lots of girls haven't done. I don't get what all this crying is about. You wanted to do it, too. You know you did."

I didn't bother to answer him. I closed my eyes and prayed all the way to Fourth Street. "Please, God, I'm sorry, I'm sorry. Help me, help me."

I kept on praying until June 12, when I got my period and knew that my secret was safe. Mama suspected something was wrong with me because I avoided our usual morning chats and I abandoned my former lazy habits in favor of industry. I defrosted the refrigerator, took down the blinds and scrubbed them with a brush and bleach in the backyard; I scoured the grout in the bathroom with a toothbrush, and each night I fell into bed too exhausted to care about what had happened to me in

Roland's car. Mama tried her best to worm my secret out of me, but now, after her accident, she was easier to fool. Maybe tragedy, instead of making you stronger as I'd always heard, can also make you vulnerable. I was determined to protect Mama from the pain of knowing that her daughter had become what the boys at school called "used goods."

A voice inside my head repeated the chant, "It wasn't your fault. You said no." But I had voluntarily climbed into the backseat of Roland's car, hadn't I? And I couldn't deny that Roland had been right about my wanting to do it. Then I told myself I had the right to change my mind, didn't I? But it really didn't matter. It was too late. I was used goods and nothing was going to make me a new product again.

Wallace and I had formed a silent truce. Now that I had done what he accused me of, I felt I deserved his criticism. Once in a while when we were alone in a room, which I tried to avoid as often as possible, I would see him looking at me with the same look I had seen on Roland's face when he pressed the napkin on my breast at the baseball game. It was the eyes that were alike, focused on my body. I could nearly feel them piercing my skin, cutting through my blouse and bra to expose my bare breasts.

But Wallace and I weren't often alone, and when we were, Mama was always nearby as she still couldn't drive. She could walk fairly well, dragging one foot just a little behind the other, and only occasionally losing her balance, which Miss Louise said wouldn't happen at all in another month or so. Mama was a miracle really. She gave God all the credit for her recovery, but Papaw said it was determination that got her on her feet.

I hadn't finished *Lolita,* but I put it back in Mama's nightstand. I didn't want to read about Humbert's and Lolita's travels, and I thought that June was right. You shouldn't have to work so hard to read a story. You never had to look up the meaning of a word in *Seventeen* magazine, and I tried to get interested in the easy reading of the stories and articles in it, but most of them bored me. I didn't care if blush on my forehead would give me a sun-kissed look. With no help from cosmetics, the sun had kissed every inch of my exposed skin at the city pool, and Papaw had begun calling me "chocolate drop" when he stopped by for a visit. Jeanie and Faye weren't nearly as dark as me, even though they were using the iodine and baby oil mix I suggested would tan them better.

Miss Louise told me I ought to stay out of the sun. "You'll get more wrinkles when you're older," she said. I didn't care. I didn't plan on getting all that old. I was sure that I would die young tragically, and Jehu would regret that our star-crossed romance hadn't worked out.

INDEPENDENCE DAY MARKED yet another life change for Mama, Wallace, and me. Papaw and Miss Louise invited us to join them at Dixie Springs Lake for a Fourth of July picnic some of Miss Louise's friends were throwing at their house on the lake. I didn't want to go, thinking it would be boring, until Papaw told me that there would be fireworks and waterskiing behind their speedboat.

I was afraid Wallace wasn't going to allow me to wear my swimsuit and I wouldn't get to try skiing, but on the morning of the Fourth of July he came into the kitchen where I was making potato salad to bring to the picnic and said, "Frieda said the Mizells have a ski boat and there'll be swimming in the lake."

I dropped a spoonful of mayonnaise onto the cooling potatoes. "Papaw told me. He said they might teach me to ski."

I nearly dropped the mayonnaise jar when Wallace said, "Well, you'd better bring your swimsuit then."

The Mizells weren't anything like the people I imagined Mama and Wallace hung around with at New Hope. Mrs. Mizell, who told me to call her Dottie, was about Mama's age, but her husband was much older. He was a lawyer like Mr. Albright, Jehu's dad, but I guessed he was a better one. Their stone house was four times the size of the Albrights'. They had three bathrooms, five bedrooms, and a dining room with a glass wall looking out on the lake where at least twelve people could sit and eat dinner off of their gold-rimmed china plates. I was enchanted with everything I saw, including Dottie's daughter Frances and her boyfriend Joey. Frances was sixteen and Joey was a senior at Zebulon High. He was going to drive the boat and said he'd be glad to help me learn to ski later in the day. A few more high school kids showed up, and two other nurses Miss Louise knew came with their husbands and two little toddlers each.

There were snacks everywhere. Dips and chips, peanuts, little wieners in barbecue sauce, boiled shrimp with a hot red cocktail sauce, olives, pickles, and a ham spread shaped like a porcupine with pretzel sticks for the quills. The drinks were iced down in metal washtubs and there was a bar set up for the adults on the patio. I was reaching for a Coke when I heard Jehu's voice. When I turned around, I saw Jehu, Lyn, and his parents walking across the yard toward me. I snatched a Coke and ran down to where Joey and Frances were standing in the beautiful blue-and-white speedboat tied up to their pier. "Get your suit on if you want to ski," Frances said. She had changed into a red bikini top above navy shorts that I assumed covered a matching bikini bottom.

I looked back at the crowd and saw that Jehu and Lyn were sitting on the patio beside the French doors leading into the den, where I had left my beach bag. "Maybe later. I'll just watch for a while," I said as Joey backed the boat out onto the lake. "Have fun," I called as they roared off with the boat riding low in the back and the bow lifted as it skimmed across the calm water.

It was a beautiful day, and I sat down on the rough wood of the pier admiring the tiny crystals of sunlight dancing on the water, the line of pines on the far shore that shaded the water to a darker navy color. Cattails waved beside me on the bank and an occasional egret painted a streak of white in the blue sky overhead. I leaned back onto my elbows and stretched out my tanned legs, wishing I had worn my suit. When the boat circled back, I watched Frances and her friends taking turns skiing behind the boat. Only one girl, I think her name was Kathy, couldn't get up on the skis. Over and over she fell into the lake, sideways, headfirst, backwards, and her skis came off each time she fell so that Joey had to drive in circles to retrieve them. I was afraid I'd look as foolish as Kathy and decided I didn't want to try it after all. As they roared past the pier, Joey waved at me, and each time he passed by, I shook my head no.

By two o'clock the temperature had risen to the high nineties and the humid air off the lake was sapping my energy. I lifted my heavy damp hair from my neck, wishing I'd brought a ponytail holder. I longed to take a cooling dip in the lake, and when I saw that Jehu and Lyn were nowhere in sight, I ran back toward the house to change into my suit. I passed by Papaw sitting in a white wooden lawn chair next to Miss Louise. His usual unlit cigar jutted out of his mouth. Everyone was laughing at something he had just said. "Oh, Claude, you don't need a nurse, you need a team of them," Miss Louise said, smiling at him from beneath her wide-brimmed red straw hat. I smiled, too, thinking that Papaw must have told them about his latest mishap. He had gotten the fingers on his right hand caught in the door of a phone booth, then, with his left, he grabbed the receiver, jerked it loose from the box, and got hit in the nose with the metal cord. He held up his bandaged fingers and pointed to the Band-Aid on his nose. "Bullshit! I doctored myself without any help from you pill pushers," he said.

I didn't see Mama or Wallace until I walked into the den where they were sitting on the white sectional couch with Falstaff cans in their hands.

Chapter 16

NEITHER MAMA NOR WALLACE NOTICED ME STANDING WITH my back against the French doors. With their heads together, holding up their Falstaffs, they sang, "Big girls don't cry-yi-yiiii." There hadn't been any liquor in our house since Wallace moved back in and poured it all down our kitchen sink, and now they were drunk as skunks. I looked down at the crushed cans lined up on the white stone coffee table. Drunk on three beers each.

I sidled over to the huge fireplace to stand beneath a colorful tapestry hanging over it when Mama looked up and spotted me. She stopped singing, and after a moment Wallace's voice died away, too. "Having a good time, Layla Jay?" Mama asked.

"Looks like you are." I pointed to the empties on the table.

"It's the Fourth of July. Independence Day. We're entitled to a few beers to celebrate. No harm in it." She kissed Wallace's nose. "Is there, babe?"

"Not a bit." Lifting his beer, he saluted with it to his forehead. "Want one? There's plenty in the washtub out there." When he cocked his beer to point to the door, it spilled on the crotch of his light blue pants.

Mama howled. "Oh, Wally, looks like you peed on yourself. Doesn't it look like that, Layla Jay?"

I don't know why I felt disgusted with Mama. I never had before when she had too much, but this time I thought about how neat Dottie Mizell was in her crisp camp shirt and khaki Bermudas and saw that Mama looked like a floozy in her white ruffled low-cut blouse and tangerine shorts that showed the bottom of her cheeks when she crossed her legs. Wallace was patting his crotch with a big grin on his face. A strand of hair, black as crow's feathers, fell forward over his dark eyes, and when he grinned at me, I think he half-expected me to adore him like most women did.

I frowned instead. "You said after the accident that you'd never drink alcohol again," I said. "Who's going to drive us home?"

"Oh, little worry wart, stop your fussing. Wally can drive and, if he doesn't feel up to it, Pop's got his truck." Mama stood up. "Speaking of pee, I gotta go. Where's the john in this hotel?"

"There's one down the hall," I said. "I'll show you."

Mama had been walking normally for the first time since her accident, but now she staggered worse than she had in months as she limped along behind me.

When I opened the door to the bathroom, the big round lightbulbs around the huge mirror over the countertop made me think of an actress's dressing room. The potty was behind a white louvered door that Mama didn't bother to close as she rushed into the tiny room. When she was done, she sat on the white wicker chair in front of the mirror and propped her elbows on the pink-veined marble counter. In the bright light, Mama's beautiful white skin had turned sallow, her mascara was smeared beneath her glassy eyes. "I don't feel so good," she said, dropping her head into her hands, and then before I could hold on to her, she leaned over and vomited onto the white carpet.

"*Oh no,*" I yelled, staring down at the mess on the carpet. As I grabbed a handful of the decorative gold-rimmed hand towels, Mama staggered to the potty where she dropped to her knees and heaved over and over. The stench was awful, and I squirted the little rubber ball of the atomizer on a perfume bottle that I snatched from the counter all around the room. I tried to scrub away the big brown stain in the shape of a star on the carpet, but it was no use, and finally I gave up. Just as I was about to go in search of Miss Louise and Papaw to take Mama home, she flung back the louvered door and smiled. "Feel better now. That label on my pill bottles that says don't drink booze is there for a good reason." She leaned over the sink and rinsed her mouth. I handed her the last of the towels to wipe her face, "Go get my purse, Layla Jay, honey. I need fresh makeup," Mama said, fluffing her hair with her splayed fingers.

"You need to go home," I said, longing to be far away from the shame I felt when I looked down at the ruined carpet.

"No, I'm having fun. I haven't had any fun for a long time. Don't you think I deserve to enjoy myself just a little bit?" She ran her tongue over her teeth. "Never mind, I'll get my purse myself. I can't remember where I left it."

I didn't think Mama needed any more fun on this day, but there was no use arguing with her. I followed her to the door, where I turned out the light to hide Mama's mess. I never knew if Dottie Mizell suspected that it was Mama who had ruined her carpet. If she did, she was too polite to mention it, just as she pretended she didn't see the big wet stain on Wallace's pants when he and Mama went back outside.

In the guest bedroom, where earlier Dottie had directed me to change if I wanted to swim, I wiggled into my suit and dashed past the adults down to the lake. I jumped off the pier into the cool water, and then, turning onto my back with my eyes closed, I tried to shut out the voices that drifted out across the lake. I didn't care that Jehu was with Lyn. I didn't care that Mama and Wallace were making fools of themselves. I didn't care that I was used goods. I didn't care that Grandma was dead, that God had taken my daddy from me. I didn't deserve them. Nothing mattered to me. Nothing, nothing, nothing. I am nothing, I thought, and maybe I'll float away and no one will even notice that I'm missing. Not even Papaw, whose laughter rang out above everyone's chatter. He had Miss Louise now. He didn't care about me, and if he knew what I had done with Roland, he would be ashamed that I was his granddaughter. I rolled over and paddled farther out into the lake. My arms and legs were cold and heavy, and I turned onto my back again with my arms stretched out from my shoulders and squinted up at the sky. A blue heron soared above me. She flapped her broad wings several times and dove toward the water before lifting again out of view. I closed my eyes and then scissored my legs and regained my balance as the calm water beneath me began to roll slightly. I heard the motor of the boat before I saw it coming toward me.

I dropped my legs and treaded water, circling around to face the boat. Joey stood at the wheel, looking back at the skier. I knew it was Frances skiing because I saw the two strips of her red bikini jumping across the wake behind the boat. With one hand hanging on to the rope, she waved the other over her head.

No one in the boat had seen me. I hollered as loudly as I could. *"Hey, I'm here. Hey, hey hey!"* But I couldn't be heard over the roar of the boat's engine and the laughter of the five kids on board. I kicked and thrashed my arms, swimming as fast as I could, but the fear hammering my chest weighed me down, and when I gasped with effort, my mouth filled with water. I stopped and coughed and waved one arm, cried "Hey," one last time before Joey turned his head and saw me. His smile turned into horror as he frantically turned the wheel so hard, the boat tilted up on its side, nearly overturning. Screams rang out from all directions. I saw Frances's body jerking sideways, and then her skis were in the air. At nearly the same instant, the rope whipped across my neck before I sank down into the water.

I remember very little of what happened next. Blurry worried faces, vomiting, smooth cold fiberglass, Frances's leg touching mine. I hadn't died, and I hadn't even thought to ask God to save me.

They carried me to the guest room where Miss Louise and the other two nurses hovered over me as I lay on the soft bed with the sweet-smelling sheets. They discussed what to put on my neck, whether I needed an X-ray, and whether there was still any water in my lungs. Joey, who knew CPR, had saved my life, but I didn't remember his mouth on mine before I vomited what seemed like half of the lake into the boat.

The irony of Mama's and my dual spewing wasn't lost on me. Now our entire happy little family had disgraced themselves. Nearly everyone had asked me why I'd done such a dumb thing as to swim out to where people were skiing. I didn't care what they thought. I was just glad I hadn't died a sinner, especially one who had faked salvation, and then gone right ahead and committed even more sins. Had I died I would have been burning in hell instead of lying in this beautiful bedroom.

As soon as I recovered we left the party. Miss Louise drove Mama and Wallace home in Wallace's Galaxie and Papaw and I followed them in his truck. I laid my head back on the seat and closed my eyes, hoping to avoid Papaw's questions. If he had any, he kept them to himself. The only words he uttered on the long drive home were "Louise drives too damned slow."

Jeanie, my so-called new friend, telephoned me from the pool the next afternoon. She pretended that she wanted to know how I was feeling, but after a lot of hemming and hawing with this and that about how she and Faye missed me, she let slip that Lyn had told everyone at the pool that I had tried to commit suicide by drowning myself in Dixie Springs Lake. "She said if it weren't for Joey saving you, you'd be lying in Hartman's Funeral Home right now."

"Did she also tell you why I was supposed to have been drowning myself?"

Jeanie hesitated, then blurted it out. "Yeah, she said it was because of Jehu dumping you for her."

I thought of June. She would be glad to know that she wasn't the only person who told lies about me. "Oh, right," I said. "I would end my life over a twerp like Jehu. I could care less who he dates," I said. "I gotta go. My mother needs me." When I hung up, Jeanie was still talking. Now she could be the center of attention at the pool because she'd been the one to talk to poor old brokenhearted, crazy Layla Jay. Suddenly, more than anything, I wanted to move out of Zebulon, go someplace where no one knew me or Mama or Wallace.

Afraid that someone else might call, I told Mama I was going to the library. She had a hangover and was lying down on the couch in the living room. "You're not going to the pool today?"

The pool was the last place I wanted to be, not just because of the gossip, but also because I didn't plan on ever submerging myself in water anywhere except the bathtub for the rest of my life. "No, the library," I said, going out the door before she could ask me any more questions.

I didn't go to the library. I wandered aimlessly around the neighborhood without caring where my feet took me. I walked past the neat lawns, edged walks, trimmed hedges, and stately trees surrounding me, thinking that it was all fake. Inside the tidy exteriors lived people like Wallace and June and me and Mama with disheveled lives. Who knew what went on behind the lacy curtain in Mrs. Paterno's kitchen window? Or what evil lurked within the walls of the Esterbrooks' white ranch-style home. Maybe Mr. Esterbrook beat the little boy who sat on the steps with molding clay, a cup of grape Kool-Aid beside him. Perhaps there were fornicators and drunks and lesbians and people trying to kill themselves in houses all over Zebulon. And God saw that the world He created hadn't turned out like He expected at all. But maybe He didn't care one whit. Maybe He felt like I had when I made a beautiful peach cobbler for dinner. I had been so pleased with my handiwork: the smooth, lightly browned crust over perfectly cut peaches and round dumplings resting in a thick rich creamy nest. Then Wallace had stabbed a tablespoon in the middle and slopped the cobbler onto our plates, mashing up the dumplings, chopping the peaches and crust into a messy glob that was so unappetizing, all of my former pleasure was stolen away.

In front of June's cream-colored house I stopped walking and stood on the sidewalk. All of a sudden a peculiar feeling came on me, prickling my skin so that I felt a chill creeping up my neck. It was as if a voice was urging me forward up the walk, and slowly I obeyed and stepped onto the porch. I peered into the dark house and saw that no one was home. I rang the bell anyway to make sure, and when no one came to the door, I lifted the potted mum and picked up the key. I let myself in and tiptoed into the living room. The house was eerily quiet and I looked up at the silent clock on their mantel, wondering if it was broken. Everything was as I expected. No dust anywhere, no tossed newspapers, or clothing heaped on the floor. In the kitchen there were no dishes to be washed, no ironing flung over the six chairs pushed into the table in perfect alignment. I went into June's parents' bedroom and lifted the book on the mahogany night table that Mrs. McCormick was reading: *The Spy Who Came in from the Cold* by some author named John le Carré. A spy was what I felt like, standing in the dark room as though I were looking for a clue. But what I expected to find, I didn't know. Whatever it was, it was most likely in June's room, and I wheeled around and headed down the hall.

The only hint that June was away was that the stuffed white dog that usually lay on her bed was missing. Nail polish bottles lined her dresser beneath the mirror, and the clear glass jar that held her barrettes and ponytail holders was in its usual place. Staring into the mirror, I traced the faint red line on my neck with my forefinger. It didn't burn any longer. Turning away from my image, I went to her chest of drawers and pulled out the top one, where only a few pairs of panties lined the bottom of the drawer. I yanked out the second and third ones, both empty except for a lone pair of frayed shorts, but when I tugged on the bottom drawer, it resisted. I jacked it up and down and stuck my hand in the small opening and removed a notebook that had jammed there. Sitting on the floor, I sorted through the mess of papers and miscellany of school mementos I found there. June had saved scraps of her entire life. Drawings, macramé jewelry we had made in Brownies, ribbons from the fair, programs from school plays, dead corsages, her cheerleading booklet "Go Cougars," and graded papers from nearly every class she had taken. Beneath her Spanish I final exam paper (on which she'd gotten a C), I pulled out a brown photo album.

I carried the book to the window where I had knelt in the rain. Sitting cross-legged with the book on my lap, I opened it. The first picture I saw was of me when I was around ten. I remembered June taking it in the yard at Grandma's house. I was acting silly, posing with one hand on my cocked hip, the other behind my head like a pinup girl. I shifted my eyes to the next photo. Me again. This time outside of Pisgah Methodist Church in my Easter dress, holding a basket of candy. Quickly, I scanned the rest of the pictures on the first page; I was in all of them, and I turned the page to see who else June had fitted between the black triangular tabs. More of me. I caught my breath and flipped another page, me, June and me, me and Mama, Grandma with her arm around me, me on Jim . . . I flipped page after page until I came to the end where the last photograph she had taken of me was centered alone on the page. I could hardly bear to look at it, and yet I couldn't take my eyes away. I was lying on my side with my head resting on my right palm on the floor near this very spot where I sat. I was smiling softly with a dreamy expression in my eyes that I hadn't known I possessed. The word for it that came to my mind was rapture. I looked enraptured. I forced my eyes down to what I dreaded to see, and there above my pushed-down suit, shining with moisture, were my bare and glorious breasts. Beneath the picture, June had written "My Beloved Layla Jay."

Chapter 17

I CLOSED THE BOOK, PUT IT BACK WHERE I HAD FOUND IT, AND then walked over to June's dresser and opened her jewelry box. "Lara's Theme" drifted out from the rose-colored velvet-lined box and I listened for a moment, staring at the assortment of rings, bracelets, and pendants. June hardly ever wore jewelry, and it occurred to me that probably these trinkets were gifts from her mother, who was always as bejeweled as Elizabeth Taylor in the movie *Cleopatra*.

I retraced my steps down the hall and opened a closet door adjacent to the bathroom. In the cupboard towels were folded and stacked in neat rows exactly like they were on the shelves of Salloum's department store. There were three rows of robin's egg blue, one canary yellow, and four towels with matching hand and washcloths the color of Grandma's lavender hydrangeas. I took two of the blue cloths and opened the cabinet beneath the sink where the extra toilet paper was kept beside bathroom cleansers. I lifted the green Comet can, wrapped it in the towels, and left the house, checking to make sure the door was locked.

The next day I went back at the same time, confident no one would be home since I had remembered June telling me that her mother volunteered during those hours at the Zebulon Infirmary as a Pink Lady. I watched *The Match Game* on their TV set, lying on the slate blue couch. After the show was over, I ate an orange from the fruit bowl on their kitchen table, and before I left I took the wire whisk I found in the drawer beside the refrigerator.

By Sunday I had gone back to June's house three more times and added a china figurine of a boy reading a book, an unopened box of Tussy's dusting powder, and two of Mr. McCormick's belts, one black, one brown. I kept these treasures in a box beneath some old stuffed animals in my closet, and when the house was quiet and I was sure Mama and Wallace were asleep, I would take them out, run my hands over them as though I were blind, and then I would lift them to my face and breathe in any scent that lingered on them.

Every night before I fell asleep I would see the photograph June had taken of me lying on her floor. I dreaded turning out the light when shadows danced on the wall and I would hear "Lara's Theme" playing and replaying in my mind. I often awoke frightened and confused in the early morning before daylight. In one dream that recurred frequently I walked into Dixie Springs Lake, wearing June's yellow bikini, and lying on my back, I floated on calm water. Above me white egrets and blue herons flew in tiered circular patterns. I floated, arms akimbo, peaceful and silent, until the sky darkened with hundreds of dissonant cawing crows. They attacked the egrets and herons and white and blue feathers fell like arrows from bows all around me. They pricked my neck and peppered my breasts, and I rolled over, swimming as fast as I could with my arms and legs thrashing, spraying great jets of water that washed over my head and pounded me down, shooting me toward the lake's sandy bottom. In other nightmares Wallace appeared with hands the size of roasting pans that plucked my breasts from my body like flowers from their stems. I dreamed of June and Roland and I saw Mama swathed like a mummy from head to toe chasing me down the hall in June's dark house. I couldn't stop crying after these dreams, and sometimes I couldn't muffle the sounds of my screams. Mama would rush into my room to shake me and holler, "Wake up, Layla Jay. For God's sake, wake up!" I never told her about my dreams. Always I said, "I can't remember."

By August, Mama was well enough to go back to work. She slept late on Sundays again, but Wallace didn't seem to care whether either of us attended New Hope with him. They were getting drunk three or four nights of every week, and although Mama couldn't dance as good as she had prior to her accident, she played all the old records she had boogied to on the hi-fi set. I wasn't happy about the drinking, but I liked the fun-loving Mama much better than the pious one, except that it was mostly "Wally" who she told her stories to, not me. I had feared the sober Wallace, but the drunk Wally terrified me. I could feel his eyes following me everywhere around the house, and I stayed in my room more and more. Twice on nights when Mama went to bed drunk, I had heard Wallace turning the knob on the bathroom door when I was taking a bath. I never forgot to lock it.

I stayed away from the house as often as possible, and I couldn't help comparing Mama to Mrs. McCormick. I preferred the tailored suits in conservative colors in Mrs. McCormick's closet to the brightly colored tight skirts and low-cut blouses Mama wore. Mrs. Mac's closet was more interesting than June's. Far back on the shelf there was a box of old love letters tied with a pink ribbon and some of them were from a boy named Shawn. He lived in Ireland, where Mrs. Mac had traveled in search of her ancestors. Evidently, "Delia, my daffodil" and this Shawn had fallen in love, but obviously nothing had come of it. He wrote that he wished she'd return, and she must have written that she wanted him to come to the United States instead because in the last letter in the box, Shawn wrote, "Ah, my daffodil, what might have been."

Mrs. McCormick also owned six evening dresses, which I tried on, but they were all too big, except in the bodice. They smelled heavenly, even the ones wrapped in heavy plastic bags held a soft scent of lavender, and when I discovered the tiny sachets lining the bottom of the bags, I saw why this was so. I especially liked the full-skirted silver gown that felt like soft hands caressing my body when I stepped into it and wiggled it up my legs. I wore her pearls with it and then tried the ruby choker she kept in a velvet box. I decided the plumbing business must be a good one to go into to afford such things and then remembered Mrs. Mac's family lived in a big antebellum-style home on Delaware. Delia had probably been wearing real jewelry since she was a baby.

She kept her fur stole in the hall closet. The fur was so silky and luminous, it rippled like waves when I brushed my palms against it. I figured it must be mink, and I pretended to drink a glass of wine from one of the crystal glasses in their china cabinet as I strolled around the house with the soft fur against my face. I took the stole's padded coat hanger but left the mink with her initials embroidered in the lining on a wooden hanger. We didn't have any nice coat hangers in our house, and I decided I would give the padded one to Mama. She didn't have a mink or even a fake fur coat, but she did own a black-and-white cape that would benefit from the hanger.

When I gave it to Mama, she looked puzzled. "Why in the world would you give me this, Layla Jay?"

"It's for your cape," I said. "It won't get those lumps on the shoulders if you hang it on this."

Mama sat on her bed and kicked off her shoes. She'd just come home from work and her poor feet were swollen with red stripes beneath her toes. "But where did you get it?"

"Found it. I was walking to the library and saw it hanging out of a trash can on the street. It doesn't smell or anything."

Mama pulled her striped knit top over her head, stood, and unzipped her olive green skirt. "Well, thank you for thinking of my cape," she said, as she tossed her skirt on top of the hanger. "You're not going back to the pool then?"

I shook my head from side to side. "No way. I've had enough swimming to last me a lifetime."

Mama wiggled out of her half slip. "Well, at least we don't have to lie to Wallace anymore. And that's good, huh?"

She walked to her dresser in her panties and bra and I noticed that the scars on her stomach had faded to light pink. Mama had gotten her waistline back and her legs were shapely and long. "Yeah. I guess, but I don't really care about lying to Wallace."

Mama was silent as she zipped her shorts and buttoned her blouse, then pinning my arms to my sides, she looked straight at me. "Layla Jay, why do you hate Wallace so much?"

I stared back. "I don't hate him." *Of course you do*, a voice inside my head said. *He's Humbert Humbert and Roland and every man who wants what he wants from a girl whether she wants it or not.*

I tried to back away, but Mama held me firmly and said, "Don't lie to me, too. I've seen the way you look at him from across the table. I know you try to avoid being around him as much as possible. Are you still mad because he didn't want you to date or wear makeup? Is that the only reason?"

I didn't answer her. She wasn't going to believe me if I said yes, that was the reason, and I was terrified of what she'd do if I told her the real one.

She shook me. "Is it? What's wrong with you? Ever since that night you went to the ball game with Jehu you've been different, and . . ." She was shouting. "I don't like who you are."

I wouldn't cry. I hated her now. "I don't like you either," I said. "I hate you."

She slapped me. "I hate you and Wallace both," I yelled.

Mama slapped me again and then burst into tears. "Oh, Layla Jay, I'm sorry. I'm just so frustrated with you. I don't know what to do, what to say, how to help you. Something's terribly wrong. I don't know where you are most of the time. I don't know why you're mad at June, why you never went out with Jehu again. Why why why?"

I stood silently staring at her as she sank down onto the bed and shook her head back and forth. My heart was empty; I felt nothing for her at that moment. If she wanted to help me, she shouldn't be Miss Pious one day, Miss Party Girl the next. *C'est la vie,* Layla Jay, on Monday, and pray for your soul, Layla Jay, on Sunday. Mama was the one who needed help, not me. She didn't know who in the hell she was. Compared to her, I was just fine.

I wheeled around and fled to my room, slammed the door and locked it. I didn't cry, but I threw myself on my bed and kicked the mattress until my legs ached. I felt so tired, so empty. I couldn't think properly, and I was scared. Was this Tuesday? Had I gone to the McCormicks' already? Yes, the coat hanger. It was Wednesday though because it was trash pickup day. I said I had gotten the coat hanger out of a trash can. I didn't hate Wallace. I wasn't a lesbian. I wasn't used goods. I wasn't anything but the girl with the stiffened body and clenched fists that lay on this bed staring up at a white ceiling that needed a coat of paint.

Hours later when Mama pounded on my door, I heard Wallace's voice. "Leave her alone, Frieda. She'll come out when she gets hungry. Let her blow off some steam in there alone."

"But she's so upset." Mama's voice was wavy sounding as though she might still be crying a little.

Wallace's voice was cajoling. "C'mon, I'll fix you a gin and tonic. You'll feel better after a while."

I wasn't hungry. I had eaten a slice of German chocolate cake at the McCormicks' and now I thought of Grandma's red velvet, her tea cakes, and I traveled back to Grandma's sweet-smelling kitchen where we stood at the wooden table cutting dough into circles with jar lids. I remembered that Grandma was humming the chorus of "In the Garden."

"Annnd, He walks with me and He talks with me," I sang along.

When we came to the last line, Grandma hugged me against her side. "I'm so happy you got saved, Layla Jay. Now you're in God's arms forever."

"Yeah," I said. "The spirit finally landed on me, and now I'm going to heaven when I die."

But I wasn't going to join Grandma in heaven because I had faked salvation, and of all the sins I had committed, that was by far the worst of them. I had fornicated, been a lesbian, broken the commandment "Honor thy father and mother." I saw myself unlocking the door to the McCormicks' house. I was a burglar and a thief, too. But the worst sin, the one that had started it all, was that I had lied to Grandma and the entire congregation of Pisgah Methodist Church. That lie was definitely going to mean I would burn in hell for all eternity.

I lifted the photograph of Daddy and held it against my heart. Surely, he was in heaven with Grandma, and now I would never get to meet him. I bowed my head. "Please God, don't throw me into hell. Save me!"

Mama came to the door again and this time she only tapped on it. "Layla Jay, honey, don't you want something to eat? It's getting late." She'd had a few drinks now. I could tell by the slowed rhythm of her speech. "Wallace wants to go out for a while. We're going to the store for a few things in a minute."

I knew a few things meant they were out of gin or whiskey or both. I lifted my head and shouted, "Not hungry. Go!"

Mama was angry again. "All right! If that's the way you're going to talk to me, we're leaving, and you can starve yourself to death in there."

I guess I fell asleep for a while because Grandma came into my room and sat beside me on the bed. She leaned over and kissed my forehead. "I love you, Layla Jay. God sent me. He wants you to know that He forgives you for what you've done. He knows you're sorry, and when you die, you'll go to heaven. Your daddy and I are waiting for you. Come to us," she said.

I sat up and snuggled against her. Her arms were soft and comforting and she rocked me like she had when I was small. My tears fell on her light blue gown and then disappeared instantly. Suddenly, she, too, vanished and I fell forward onto the foot of the bed. "Grandma," I called, waking up on my damp sheet. My tears had been real; maybe I hadn't been dreaming. Maybe God had sent Grandma to save me. Maybe God was answering my prayer. Grandma and Daddy really were waiting for me, and if I were up there with them, I wouldn't have to live with Wallace anymore. I wouldn't have to face June when she returned. I wouldn't have to face all the kids at school who thought I'd tried to commit suicide. They thought killing yourself meant you were crazy, but now I thought that maybe they were the crazy ones, believing that life on earth was better than life in heaven. Who wanted to walk on streets of asphalt when you could be walking on streets of gold?

I got up and went to my closet and dug out all the items I had taken from the McCormicks' house. I laid them in neat rows on my bed and then tore a sheet of paper from my notebook. I wrote, "All of these things belong to the McCormicks. Please return." Then I sat at my desk and wrote a letter to Mama. "Dear Mama, I have gone to be with Daddy and Grandma in heaven. God has called me, and someday I hope He will call you, too." But not Wallace, I thought, but I left that off the note and signed it, "I'm sorry about yelling at you. I do love you, Layla Jay."

I put on my band uniform that Grandma had loved and got out my flute. I would probably get a harp in heaven, but just in case I'd have my flute nearby. Now I sat on my desk chair to consider the best way to get to heaven. We didn't have a gun. Papaw had several, but I had no way of getting one of his. I couldn't stand the sight of blood, so knives and razor blades were out. I looked around the room; I didn't have any rope or a really good place for hanging anyway. So what was left? Charlotte, Lolita's mother, had been hit by a car, but that was just a lucky event for Humbert. Nobody in Zebulon would run over me. The police gave out speeding tickets like Mama gave out sample perfumes to her customers.

I took off my band uniform and put my flute back in its case. I needed more time to figure out how to get to heaven. I would pray for

Grandma to come back and give me a few good tips on suicide. After tucking the notes in the box with the McCormicks' possessions, I stowed it back in my closet and went in search of something to eat. I stood over the sink eating cold leftover tuna casserole and washed out the dish before I went to my room to pray.

Chapter 18

I AWOKE EARLY THE NEXT MORNING WITH THE SUN STREAMING across my bed. I had forgotten to close the blinds, and looking out onto the backyard, I saw a cardinal enjoying breakfast at the bird feeder. Across the lawn a gray squirrel chased an identical one up the oak tree and they leapt from branch to branch higher and higher until they were hidden from my view. It was a beautiful day, a catfish jumping day, and I thought of Papaw with the fancy new rod and reel he'd gotten for his birthday the week before. Mama told me that he'd gone down to his pond with it and caught a big catfish. But when he'd tried to get the wriggler out of the fish's mouth, he'd somehow gotten tangled in the line, tripped and fell into the water, snapping his line as the new rod and reel sailed over his head out into the pond. This time he hadn't sustained much injury though, just a twisted ankle that swelled up so that he limped around on one shoe for a few days.

As I pulled a pair of shorts out of my dresser, I realized that I hadn't dreamed of Grandma all night. In fact, I couldn't remember a thing I'd dreamed. Apparently, God was going to take His time answering my request, and I would have to postpone my suicide until He was ready to help me.

After I finished dressing, I found Mama in the den about to leave for work. She didn't welcome me with a smile, so I figured she was still mad at me, but she thanked me for washing the casserole bowl. Before she left for the Elizabeth Arden counter, she topped all the bad news I'd gotten all summer. "Wally is still in bed. He has a cold and isn't going to work. You're to take care of him. See that he drinks plenty of water or 7-Up. And give him an aspirin if his fever goes up. I left the thermometer on the table beside the bed." She swiped her purse off the arm of the couch and then gave me a mean look. "Be nice, Layla Jay. Wallace is really sick."

After she left, I crept down the hall and saw that the door to their bedroom was open, so I sidled down the wall and craned my neck around the door facing. The blinds and curtains were closed, and in the dark room I could barely make out the mound of Wallace on the far side of the bed. He was lying on his right side with his back to me, so I couldn't tell if he was awake or not, but I crossed my fingers that he'd sleep all day.

Back in my room, I got out my Spanish dictionary and looked up the word for hate. We hadn't used it in any of our translations. The verb was *odiar* or *destestar*. "*Te odiao tu'?*" I said out loud. "*Te destesto tu'*, Wallace." Suicide was *suicidio*. *Mi suicidio* was definitely postponed now.

"Layla Jay?" Wallace hadn't been sleeping.

"What?" I yelled.

"I want something to drink. So thirsty." His voice was weak, and I grinned. Maybe he was really suffering and this cold would turn into pneumonia and his lungs would fill with pus and he'd die.

"Coming," I called.

When I brought him a glass of water, my heart sank. He didn't look all that sick after all. With the sheet drawn down to his waist, I saw that he was wearing an undershirt exposing a slight sheen of perspiration on his shoulders and arms. His face was a bit flushed, but he sat up and held the glass firmly as he gulped all of it down. "Thanks," he said, handing the glass back. "Turn out the light, would you? It hurts my eyes and my head aches." He lay back on the pillows and I flipped the switch. "Layla Jay?"

I waited by the door. "Huh?"

"Nothing. You can go," he said.

This was the longest day of my life it seemed. My life that was nearly over. I thought that I should be out admiring the beauty of the world before I left it and here I was stuck in the house watching stupid game shows and a soap opera about a dying woman who had a secret to tell before she croaked, but no one could understand her. Then just when she was about to take her last gasp, a good-looking doctor rushed in the room holding up a big hypodermic needle saying he'd found the serum that would save her life. I didn't want to be saved at the last minute though. God would make sure there wasn't a remedy for whatever He decided I was going to die of.

Wallace had taken a three-hour nap, but when I heard the toilet flush, I knew he was awake and would be calling me any minute. "Layla Jay, is there any soup left? I'm hungry."

I glanced over at the sink where I'd left the pot of chicken noodle soup. There was enough for half a bowl. "No."

"Oh, well, then bring me a Seven-Up and some crackers."

I wrapped a few crackers in a napkin and grabbed a 7-Up bottle from the fridge and headed for the sick room. Wallace was lying on his back. "Don't turn on the light," he said, pushing himself up to a sitting position.

Standing by the bed, I waited for him to finish the crackers, then balled the napkin up in my fist. "Anything else," I said, using the tone I'd heard the nurse use on the soap opera.

Wallace set the 7-Up bottle on the bedside table and lay back down. He looked up at me. "No," then, "Yes, could you fluff my pillow up like you did for Frieda when she was sick?"

Wallace wasn't Mama, and I sure as hell didn't care if his big head was comfortable on his pillow or not, but I figured the quicker I did what he wanted, the sooner I could get away from him. "Okay," I said, leaning forward, trying to fluff from only one side. But I wound up having to put my arms on either side of his head to do it right. My chest was nearly brushing his face and suddenly, my arms were jerked out and I was lying on top of him with my feet dangling off the bed. Wallace's arms were tight around my back and he pushed his head between my breasts. "Let me go," I yelled, stupidly thinking he would obey me.

His mouth moved to my ear. "I saw the look in your eyes; you leaned so close to move the pillow because you wanted me to feel your breasts against me. You want this as much as I do."

I pushed against him as hard as I could, breaking out of his grip, but before I could get up, he grabbed my arm and flung me down on the bed beside him. He fell on top of me, pinning me down on the soft blue sheets. I bucked and kicked like a wild horse at the rodeo, but I couldn't throw him. One hand moved to my hair and he yanked my head so hard tears came to my eyes. His other hand was pulling up my T-shirt, working his fingers beneath my bra. I slapped at his head, his back, pounded him with my fists, and tried over and over to get my knee up to his loins, but Wallace didn't seem to feel my nails scraping his back. I could feel his legs against mine as he squirmed on top of me trying to release his penis from the flap of his boxer shorts that was my only protection. This will not happen, I told myself. I remembered Roland and I knew how quickly and easily he could get what he wanted. This will not happen, I screamed inside. But it was happening. Wallace held my wrists with one hand, jerking my shorts and panties off with his other. With the weight of his body pressing down on me, horror washed over me as I felt his skin against my thighs.

I must have been screaming because I didn't hear Mama come home, but there she was standing beside the bed with the 7-Up bottle in her hand. I think she yelled "You son of a bitch" or something like that before she slung the bottle across his head with so much force, it broke, and glass and sticky 7-Up rained down on us both. I squeezed my eyes shut as I felt Wallace rolling off me onto the floor. Mama was yelling. "You bastard, you piece of shit." Wallace cried out something I couldn't understand that maybe was the word "Don't."

When I opened my eyes and raised up on my elbow, across the room I saw Mama's purse lying on the floor where she had thrown it. I heard Wallace thrashing on the floor. When Mama lifted her head, she looked up at me and whispered, "I think I killed him."

I sat up and looked down to where Mama knelt in a pond of blood and saw Wallace's red-spattered face beside her knees. Beneath his jaw a jagged shard of 7-Up bottle stuck out of his neck like a triangular bow tie. "I think you did," I said.

Mama rocked back on her heels and pressed her lips together. Neither of us moved or spoke as we stared into each other's faces acknowledging a truth that we'd never expected in our lifetime to share. Finally, Mama said, "Are you okay? Did he rape you?"

"Noooo," I said. "You saved me," and then we were crying and holding each other as we huddled on the far side of the bed. I don't know how long we sat shivering as though we were locked in a freezer afraid to look past each other's faces to where Wallace lay making no sounds now. I remember thinking we could call an ambulance, that maybe he wasn't dead, but I knew he was. I'd seen his eyes staring at the ceiling emptied of his black soul.

When it was dark, Mama eased off the bed. "I'll call Pop," she said. "He'll know what . . . what to do about . . . about . . . about what we have to have to."

I nodded like she was making perfect sense. "Okay."

After I pulled on my panties and shorts, we waited for Papaw in the den sitting side by side on the couch in front of the coffee table, Mama overlooking northern Mississippi and me the southern counties. Mama had a lot more blood on her than I did, but now I noticed small drops dotting my right arm. I shivered. It was Wallace's blood, and jumping up, I ran to the bathroom to scrub him off my skin. I tore off my clothes and climbed into the bathtub, twisting the taps as far as they would go. Crying, without making a sound, I washed away every speck of the Reverend Wallace Ebert from my life.

I hurried into clean clothes, and by the time I got back to where Mama was still sitting like a block of ice, I heard Papaw's truck in the driveway.

After Papaw went into Mama's bedroom and saw Wallace, he came back through the den and went to the wall phone just inside the kitchen door. "No need to call an ambulance," he said, "but we'd better call the law."

The sheriff and a deputy we didn't know arrived in record time, but it seemed like hours before the coroner's stretcher took Wallace away. The sheriff questioned me first. He sent Mama into the kitchen and sat across from me in the arm chair facing the couch. I couldn't stop shaking and I crossed my arms tightly over my chest, feeling that if I let go, my body would fly apart. During the entire time the sheriff asked about what had happened, I could feel Wallace's presence in the house, feel him lying there on the floor. Dead he seemed more present than he had all day. I was so distracted by him I couldn't pay attention to those questions. They were about sequence of events, rape, my clothes, evidence, 7-Ups, a napkin filled with cracker crumbs. I could hear Mama and Papaw murmuring in the kitchen with the deputy as the sheriff scribbled my answers down in his notebook.

Then it was Mama's turn, and we played fruit basket turn over, switching rooms and people. In the kitchen Papaw let me sit on his lap with my head resting on his shoulder like I was a little girl again, and for a little while, I pretended Wallace wasn't lying on the bedroom floor deader than last year's gardenias. The deputy was nice. His name was Rob Yellin, and he said he had a little girl named Marcie who was three years old. I liked him much better than the sheriff, whose name I hadn't bothered to remember.

It must have been after midnight before the coroner carried Wallace out of our house for the last time. The sheriff stood beside Mama, still huddled on the couch, and closed his notebook. "We'll have to take you in for booking, Mrs. Ebert," he said. "You have the right . . ."

"Bullshit!" Papaw stood eye to eye with him. "She'll come down in the morning. My daughter's in shock; she needs rest, just now recovering from a car wreck."

But the sheriff didn't care about any of that. Mama left with the sheriff and I didn't see her again until the next afternoon when Papaw brought her home. I had just woken up and was coming down the hall when I saw Miss Louise throwing open the door. For a moment I wondered what she was doing in our den, and then remembered that Papaw had called her to come stay with me after Mama was taken away. I didn't know if he had stayed with me, too, because, after I swallowed the sleeping pill Miss Louise gave me with a muffin and a glass of milk, I barely made it to bed before I fell asleep.

"Made bail," Papaw said. "Charged her with voluntary manslaughter at the arraignment this afternoon. We'll get this nonsense cleared up, but there's a helluva lot to do first. We need to get a good lawyer, the one they appointed doesn't know shit, and after the autopsy, somebody's got to do something about burying that skunk."

Mama collapsed then. I hadn't gotten all the way into the den where Papaw, Miss Louise, and Mama stood, but as I took a step toward them,

Mama crumpled down onto the floor like someone had wadded her up like a paper cup.

As I watched Papaw carrying Mama down the hall to my bed, I trailed behind praying out loud. "Please God, take care of Mama. She saved me. It's Your turn now." Then it came to me that God hadn't answered my prayers for suicide. He knew that I didn't really want to die. I wanted to live.

Chapter 19

PAPAW DIDN'T KNOW ANY LAWYERS, BUT I KNEW ONE. "WHAT about Mr. Albright?" I said. "You met him. The Albrights were at the Fourth of July party at Dixie Springs Lake."

As Miss Louise laid a bowl of chicken gumbo in front of him, she said, "I remember the Albrights. Isn't their son the one you dated for a while?"

I held my bowl out to her. It had been a long afternoon and my appetite had returned when I smelled the gumbo bubbling on the stove. How Miss Louise had managed to make it was a mystery to me considering she'd been so busy. She had helped Mama bathe before giving her the same small blue miracle pill she'd given to me. Then after Mama was tucked into my bed, Miss Louise had taken up the rug in Mama's room, washed the sheets, vacuumed up every sliver of glass and even cut some maroon mums for a vase that now sat on the center of the table where we sat waiting for Mama to wake up.

"Yeah, I went out with him once. He's going steady with somebody else now though. The girl he brought to the picnic."

"Well, if the son takes after the father, he's got bad taste in women. I don't know that we'd want him defending Frieda," Papaw said, as he blew on his spoon before lifting it to his mouth. "Good gumbo, Lou. You've got good taste in food and men."

She smiled and sat down with us. "Maybe we should say grace," she said.

I looked over at Papaw. I remembered the one time Grandma had made him say the blessing and he'd said, "In the kitchen, down the hall, hope to God I get it all." But he bowed his head and kept silent.

After a moment Miss Louise said, "Pass the butter please, Layla Jay."

MAMA DIDN'T EAT ANY GUMBO; she slept on in my room until the next morning. After Papaw and Miss Louise left around ten o'clock, I got back into bed with her and lay with my arm wrapped across her body so that I would know if she got up during the night. Although she mumbled a few times, frowning and crying as she twisted the sheet into funnels, she never opened her eyes until the phone rang around eight o'clock the next morning.

It was Papaw. He was on his way over with Mama's lawyer, Mr. Gordon Albright.

I threw on the clothes I'd tossed on the floor the night before, and while I made coffee, Mama got dressed. When she came into the kitchen, I was relieved to see that she'd put on some makeup, pinned her hair up in a twist, and put on our favorite blue dress with the low-cut ruffled bodice. I grinned, thinking that no matter what had changed in our lives, old habits resurfaced easily. A man was coming to our house, and Mama was going to look her best.

Papaw looked like hell. He hadn't shaved and white stubble covered his cheeks and chin. His eyes were red-shot, I couldn't think blood anymore, but the ever present unlit cigar was clenched between his teeth. Mr. Albright was immaculate in a suit, clean shaven, and as I shook his hand, I noticed that his long slender fingers were exact replicas of Jehu's.

Mr. Albright talked a lot about damage control after showing us the Friday edition of *The Lexie Journal*. A reporter named Jason Dowell had written the front-page story about the "alleged murder." He'd done a lot of homework for his report in a very short time. He quoted statements from several New Hope members. My old Sunday school teacher, Miss Mansfield, said, "Brother Ebert was a wonderful pastor. Everyone loved him. This is truly a great loss to our community and New Hope Church." Jason Dowell's characterization of Mama was accurate, if not flattering. He said she was employed at Salloum's department store as a "beauty consultant" who had been involved in a serious accident on Highway 98 after attending a party at Dixie Springs Lake. In the last paragraph, he noted that "Mrs. Ebert dropped her membership at New Hope recently." The only person who said something nice about Mama was, unfortunately, Tilly Bryant, who worked at the package store. She said, "Oh, Frieda Ebert comes in nearly every week to buy her gin. She's a darling lady, has a smile for everyone, and she always pays cash. I can't believe she would hurt a fly, much less murder her husband."

"Isn't this self-defense?" Papaw asked Mr. Albright after we all got settled at the kitchen table to review Mama's situation, as she called it.

"Technically, I'm afraid not," Mr. Albright said. "He didn't have a weapon, was sick in fact, and Layla Jay here," he nodded his head across the table toward where I sat with my feet crossed in the chair, "says he didn't rape her."

"But he was going to," Mama said. "I got there just in time."

"That's right, and it wasn't the first time he'd tried stuff with me."

"What!" Papaw and Mama spoke in unison, both of them grabbing a wrist.

I didn't want to tell them more with Mr. Albright sitting there looking like he wished he hadn't agreed to take on this case. "Well, it's just he, uh, a long time ago, put his hands on me, on parts, you know, private." I was whispering by the end of the sentence.

Papaw slammed his fist on the table, and all three of us jumped along with the salt and pepper shakers. "I knew it. I told Lou I didn't trust that son of a bitch."

"When?" Mama wanted to know. Then before I could answer, "Exactly what happened, Layla Jay?"

I tried not to cry, but I shook my head back and forth and the sobs came out before I could answer.

Mr. Albright laid his hand on Mama's arm, pinning it down onto the table. "Let's give Layla Jay some time. She can tell us more later. Right now we need to put out the fires we've got burning us. File a motion to dismiss and get a date for a hearing on that. We'll get the police reports, autopsy, and so on." He stood up. "Mrs. Ebert, I . . ."

"Call me Frieda," Mama said. "I don't want to hear that name anymore than I have to."

"Should've never had it in the first place," Papaw said.

Mr. Albright closed his leather briefcase and pressed the gold latches shut. "All right, Frieda. I want you to write down every detail you can remember about that afternoon from the time you got home until you called your father." He walked around the table to where I sat, blowing my nose on a napkin. "And Layla Jay, you, too. I want you to write down everything you remember, not just about that day, but any other times you felt threatened by your stepfather, things he did or said that frightened you."

"Okay," I said. And while Mama and Papaw walked him to the door, I sat wondering whether he would tell Jehu about all the awful things I was going to write. Why had I suggested him for a lawyer? I hadn't thought of the consequences, hadn't thought about my secrets all coming out now that Wallace was dead. "Damn you," I said to Wallace looking down at the floor over hell. "You may be dead, but you're still screwing up my life."

Mama and Papaw were taking a long time saying good-bye, and I went to the kitchen window and looked out at the three of them standing by Mr. Albright's white Chrysler. Mama was shaking her head "no," and Papaw's cigar was going up and down in his mouth as he chewed on it. Mr. Albright held up his palms and shrugged his shoulders. When I saw Mama look back toward the kitchen window with tears in her eyes, a sinking feeling came over me. They were talking about me, not Wallace.

I waited until Mr. Albright got in his car and then I headed back to my room and sat on the bed. A few minutes later, Mama tapped on the door as she opened it. "Layla Jay?"

I wasn't going to answer any questions until I got good and ready. "Huh?"

"You need to get your shoes on. Pop's going to drive you to the hospital now." Still holding on to the doorknob, she wasn't looking at me.

"Why? I'm not hurt or sick."

"Mr. Albright wants you to be examined. Thinks that's the best thing to do. Just to be, uh, you know sure about Wallace."

I threw myself across the bed. *"No! I told you he didn't rape me."*

"Well, I know you did, and I believe you, but Mr. Albright, he says it's what we need to do. Sometimes people block these things out. Like if you don't want it to be true, then you believe it so much, it isn't to you, but it is true." She waited until I lifted my head and finally came into the room. She sat on the bed. "I argued with him, baby, but it's for the best, I guess. You don't have a choice and neither do I. Even Pop said we have to cooperate with our lawyer, not hide things from him." She kissed the top of my head. "Do this for me, will you? If it's not true, this is the only way you have to prove it."

I sat up, bit my lip, trying not to cry. "Can I take a bath first?"

"No, he said it would have been better if you hadn't taken one right after . . . after. Why don't we just go and get it over with?"

I knew what I knew, but now I understood that in a way it would have been better for Mama if Wallace had raped me. As I tied the laces on my tennis shoes, I thought about Roland. When he examined me, the doctor would find out I wasn't a virgin. He'd know that, but he wouldn't know who I had had sex with. Unless I confessed, and I wasn't about to tell him or Mama the truth. It could have been Wallace, nearly was . . . and then the first glimmer of a plan formed in my mind. I kissed Mama and told her not to worry, that everything was going to turn out just fine.

Of course, there was no semen, nothing to swab except my own secretions, but Dr. Harrington twirled his swabbing stick inside me anyway. After I got dressed, he called Mama into the exam room and delivered the surprise news that my hymen was not intact.

"He did rape you!" Mama said, covering her face with her hands. "Oh, Layla Jay! You said he didn't!"

I jumped off the exam table where I had been sitting. My legs were rubber. I was a wreck. I wasn't sure I could go through with the lies I had concocted in the car on the way over. Now I couldn't remember exactly what I had planned to say at this moment. I kept my back to Mama and pressed my stomach against the exam table. I had to do this, and I had to do it just right, or Mama was going to go to prison for ridding the world of a man who should never have been in it in the first place. The time had come for me to tell my lie, but the antiseptic smell of the exam room was making me sick, and I swallowed bile. I wanted to get out of this room, away from the odors of sickness and disinfectants, away from the constant distant ringing of the phone in the reception room. And I wanted to say that Wallace had raped me before Mama got home, just before she killed him, but there was no way I could explain what the doctor didn't find inside me. "He didn't rape me that day. But . . ." I stalled for time. Looking down at my hands, I saw that I had shredded the white paper on the exam table into ribbons. "Wallace did rape me, just not that day. He was trying to do it for the second time." There, that was it. I had said the lines I'd rehearsed inside my brain over and over while the doctor examined me. Wallace had done it once; he'd do it again. They would believe me, wouldn't they?

Mama was so pale I was afraid she was going to faint again, but she squeezed her eyes shut and took a deep breath. Gradually the color returned to her face. "When? What happened? Where was I?"

I didn't have any details worked out yet. There hadn't been time to flesh out my story, and now heat was rising inside my chest. Right now, there wasn't a lie left in me. My brain couldn't handle any more on this day. "Can we talk about it later?" I begged. "I want to go home now."

Dr. Harrington saw that I was near tears and he rescued me. "Maybe you should take her home, Frieda. We'll let you know the results of the test. But my guess is she's telling the truth now. There were no tears or bruises around the cervix. I'd guess she wasn't raped recently."

Mama stood up. She clutched her red patent purse against her chest and bobbed her head up and down like a Kewpie doll on the dashboard of a car. "Okay, okay, okay, we'll go home." She stared into my eyes for a long time then said, "But you've got to talk to me, Layla Jay. You've got to tell me everything."

"I will," I promised. Given more time to figure things out, I was confident I could make up a story she would believe. It wouldn't be nearly as hard to counterfeit a rape as it had been to fake salvation.

Chapter 20

THE CHAPTER IN MY STORY I HADN'T FIGURED ON WAS MAMA'S. She blamed herself. "I knew you hated him. I knew something and I just wouldn't look at it, ignored all of the clues. I'm so selfish, thinking about me me me all the time, leaving you to deal with all this by yourself. How could I have ignored the facts, not known about this? I'm an awful mother. Horrible. Terrible." She ranted on and on like this sitting beside me in Papaw's truck all the way home from the hospital.

Papaw never said a word. Driving like we were three criminals being chased by a fleet of cop cars, he chomped down on his cigar so hard, it broke off and fell onto his lap. After he ran up onto our lawn, he didn't bother to back up, but got out and slammed the truck door before I could open mine.

I tried to reassure Mama. "You're a good mother," I told her. "I should have told you. It's my fault, not yours."

"No, no, it's mine. Girls never want to tell. I've read that. They feel so terrible they can't talk about it." She clenched her fists and pounded her thighs. "But a good mother would recognize the signs, would know to protect her child."

"You couldn't have protected me," I said. "Wallace threatened to kill me if I told. And he would have. You saved my life. That's protecting your child."

Mama wanted to believe me so badly, she hesitated before she said, "Well, but still I should have done something, suspected." Her eyes widened when she said, "And you know I did in the beginning. I remember asking you about why you were so glad I threw Wallace out that time."

"Yeah, you did, and so did Grandma, and I just lied to you both. He wasn't having sex with you because he was raping me," I said.

"More than once?"

"Well, no, just that once on the way home from church at New Hope." I had chosen the backseat of Mama's Volkswagen for the crime scene, trying to stay as near the truth as I could. I *had* lost my virginity in a car.

THE NEXT TIME we saw Mr. Albright we went to his office where I was to repeat the story I'd rehearsed over and over as I paced around my room.

Mr. Albright's office was the most beautiful I'd ever been in. It was in the old McCroy's building, which he owned, and he'd converted the front store space into a reception area with plants and oriental rugs and brass floor lamps. Down the hall were three offices, a coffee room, and a huge library. One office was filled with a copy machine and file cabinets, the second door led to the office of Mr. Blankenship, Mr. Albright's partner, and at the end of the hall we entered Mr. Albright's haven. As soon as Mama and I walked into the room, I smelled the rich aroma of leather and lemon oil polish. There was a chocolate brown leather love seat, two wingback chairs, a cherry coffee table, and a desk nearly the size of Mama's wrecked Volkswagen. Shelves of books bound in kelly green and wine and tan lined two walls, and a tapestry covering the windows that looked out onto an alleyway hung behind the love seat. I wanted to live in that one room for the rest of my life. Mama preferred bright colors and she said, "Kind of dark in here, isn't it?" as she flung her purse down on the coffee table and plopped onto the love seat.

Mr. Albright laughed. "Well, Frieda, I can turn on more lamps for you," he said, switching on the brass floor lamp, a twin to the ones in the reception area. Mama's beautiful face glowed in the soft light, and I marveled that she could look so radiant when her life had turned so dark.

Mr. Albright seemed disappointed that the test results proved I hadn't been raped on the day Wallace died, but he said that Wallace's raping me earlier certainly improved Mama's chances with the judge. He asked a lot of questions about the day I had been raped, and I tried to reinvent my night with Roland as closely as possible. I had to fabricate much of the story though since I'd willingly climbed into the backseat of Roland's Mustang, and there were a lot of other differences. With Roland it was summer, Wallace, winter, so what was I wearing? Only kids parked at the gravel pit, so where did this occur? How did I disguise my bruises? What did I do with my bloodstained panties? What did Wallace say exactly? What were the precise words of the threats he made to me if I told?

On and on the questions came firing at me like a hundred kids playing dodgeball against just me. Then Mr. Albright leaned forward and said, "Have you told anyone before now about Wallace raping you? Maybe a girlfriend? It would help if someone could corroborate the time of your rape. The DA might try to say you made this up just to get your mother off, that maybe you and a boyfriend . . ."

"I don't have a boyfriend," I said, thinking not of Roland, but of Jehu.

"Okay, but if we go to trial and someone could testify that you told her or him about this and were afraid for your life . . . before the day Wallace was killed . . . well, that would help us a great deal."

I thought of June. If I needed someone to back up my story, June would be perfect. After all, I knew plenty about her to use as blackmail, and I nearly smiled thinking about the time in church when she'd taken money out of the offering plate. I had gotten a lot of mileage out of that little sin, and now I knew something she wouldn't want known that was a much bigger sin. I hesitated. I looked over at Mama, who was drumming a cigarette on the armrest of the couch, her eyes searching around the room for an ashtray. I wanted to save her more than anything in the world. June owed me, too. She'd told lies about me, so I knew for sure that she was capable of backing me up. And further, there was the last resort: If June didn't care about her debt to me or didn't care about my telling on her, she might trade another afternoon with me for telling another little lie. But was I willing to do that? Mama put her cigarette back in the pack and bit her lip. She looked so young today and sad. Two dead husbands now and all those lovers who didn't give a damn about her.

"Well, there is one person who could . . ."

Mr. Albright uncrossed his legs and practically rose up from his chair. "You did tell someone about Wallace?"

"Yes, but she's away at camp for the summer. I don't know when she'll be back."

"June, of course," Mama said with a big smile. "We can call her mother, find out when she's expected to return."

WHEN I CALLED MRS. MCCORMICK later that afternoon, she said they would be driving up to Tennessee over the weekend to bring June home. She'd be sure to tell her that Layla Jay needed to talk to her as soon as she returned. She was so sorry to hear about my stepfather and my mother. It was just unbelievable!

You don't know unbelievable, I wanted to say. Look to your own house, but I thanked her and immediately after I hung up the phone, it rang.

It was the coroner's office calling to tell Mama that the autopsy had been completed and they could release the body for burial. "You can throw him in the trash. That's where he belongs," Mama said. Evidently the members at New Hope expected Mama to say as much because they had already asked for her consent to sign over the body to them. "They're welcome to him," Mama said when she got off the phone. "They can pray all they want to for Wallace's soul, but it won't do a damned bit of good. He might have fooled them, but God knows him for the piece of shit that he is."

I was as nervous as a dog in heat about seeing June again, but when she called, I calmed my voice and asked her to come over as soon as she could. She sounded so happy and excited over the invite, I felt a twinge of remorse for what I was about to do. But then I imagined Mama living out the rest of her life sitting in a cell wearing a drab prisoner's outfit, and I knew I would do anything necessary to save her from that fate.

When I opened the door, June threw her arms around me and hugged me so tightly, I could barely breathe. "Let's go out in the backyard," I said, not wanting Mama to hear what I was going to say.

June was predisposed to come to our aid. As we sat down side by side on the metal lawn chairs, with tears in her eyes, she said, "Layla Jay, when Mother told me what all happened, I felt like I might throw up. I feel so bad for you and your mama. I wish there was something I could do to help."

I smiled inside, but kept the sorrowful look on my face. "Well, maybe you can, June," I said.

My smile turned upside down when I saw the horrified look on June's face. "Me? I don't know how I could help. I mean, I didn't know your stepdad. I barely saw him the few times I was over here."

"But you know me, June," I said. "You know me better than anyone." I stared at her breasts, reminding her of just how well she and I knew each other.

June brushed a mosquito off her leg. She had finally turned a light tan color and gained some weight back. Camp had obviously agreed with her. "I knew you hated him if that's what you mean, but you never said why exactly."

I turned my chair around to face hers. "If you'd asked, I would have told you. You're my best friend."

June busied herself tightening the rubber band around her ponytail. She was suspicious now of where this conversation was headed, and I knew she was having second thoughts about her offer to help. No one would want to get publicly involved in the mess Mama and I were in. I kept my eyes on June's face and finally she said, "I'm sorry I never asked. I guess I just figured if you wanted me to know, you'd tell me."

"I want you to know now." I worked up a few tears. "It means the world to me that you understand, June, that you know what he did to me. You're my best friend," I said again. "We're *more* than friends. I've thought about that day in your house when it was raining and you took the picture of me over and over, and June," I swallowed, barely able to get the words out, "I missed you so much."

June's body went limp in the chair. "Oh, Layla Jay. Me, too. I missed you awfully. I didn't like any of the girls in my cabin."

I reached out and took her hand while I told her the story of my rape, which had become so real after all the telling that I almost believed it myself. When I finished, I squeezed her hand and said, "So June, all you have to do is repeat what I just told you. The only difference"— I was careful not to use the word "lie"—"is you have to say I told you back in January instead of today. If you'd just do that one little thing, you could help save Mama, and I'd be grateful to you for the rest of my life."

June drew her hands back and crossed her arms, hugging herself as she slid farther back into her chair. "I don't know, Layla Jay. Wouldn't that be a crime, lying to a judge or a lawyer even? It's called something, per-junery or something like that."

"Perjury," I said. "Yeah, but people do it all the time. I've heard that just plenty of people lie on the witness stand and it's okay if it's for good, if it's to make sure they don't convict the wrong person for a crime."

June looked doubtful. She wasn't as dumb as I had thought she was for all these years. "What if someone found out though? Can't you go to jail for lying in court?"

I tried for a smile like Grandma gave me when I was little and used a word wrong in a sentence. She'd given me the perfect opening to use all of my ammunition and buy insurance. "Who's going to find out? No one will ever know except you and me. I haven't ever told any of *your* secrets, and I know how bad you feel about making up those lies about me. But this is different. Besides, if the case gets dismissed like we hope, we won't ever go to trial."

She blinked twice. She had caught on to the fact that she didn't really have any choice if she wanted to continue our friendship and keep her secrets safe. She half-smiled. "Yeah, I guess there's no way anyone would ever know."

"Not unless the squirrels learn how to talk," I said, pointing to a gray squirrel darting across the lawn. "How about a Coke? I'm hot; let's go in. You can tell me all about camp," I said, pulling her up from her chair and pushing her toward the door. As we walked across the yard, I looked down at the grass and imagined Wallace far below standing in a circle of flames. I hoped he knew that I had just added a keg of powder to the fire.

Mr. Albright was pleased that June was willing to come in and tell him what she knew. He said it didn't matter if she remembered my exact words, only the date of my saying them. He wouldn't allow me to be present while he questioned her, so I waited in the front reception room sitting on one of the soft leather chairs across from Mrs. McCormick. She was wearing a pink shirtwaist dress from her closet that I hadn't tried on and the short eight-inch pearls that I had tried on with the blue two-piece suit. They looked better with the suit. She hadn't spoken to me during the first fifteen minutes we sat listening to the receptionist answering the phone intermittently as she typed on the humming IBM Selectric. I picked up a *Time* magazine and flipped through the pages without reading any of the articles about what Lyndon Johnson was up to. Mrs. McCormick sat as still as one of the lamps, staring at the picture of a flying duck on the wall.

"They're taking a long time," I said.

Mrs. McCormick looked at her white-gold watch. "Mmmm. Lawyers are all long-winded. And June talks too much to everyone." Her eyes went back to the flying ducks. "Now I know that you're pretty garrulous, too."

I knew that she didn't want June involved in our sordid story, and I couldn't blame her. I understood that June's testifying to save Mama's disorderly life would be terribly upsetting to a woman who would never mix the colors of her towels, leave dirty clothes on the living room floor, or let milk sour in her refrigerator. But she was also a woman who believed in doing the right thing. She was a Pink Lady volunteer and the clubs she belonged to raised money for the needy and collected toys for tots at Christmas. Now Mama and I had become another of her projects.

When she came out of the office with Mr. Albright, June circled her thumb and forefinger in the okay sign. She'd done it. Lied for me. For Mama. For the good of all mankind it now seemed to me. I hugged her and she squeezed my hand as we walked out of the cool air-conditioned office into the stultifying heat on Main Street.

As we walked to June's mother's white Lincoln, June said, "Let's go swimming. The pool should be open now."

I had forgotten that June hadn't heard the rumors about my suicide drowning. "I can't swim anymore," I said, and as soon as I said those words, another inspiration came shooting into my head like a rocket. What if those kids were right? What if I had tried to kill myself because

I couldn't live with the fact of Wallace's raping me? Wouldn't my being tortured by the memories of the rape and the fear of Wallace doing it again put an exclamation point at the end of my testimony! I saw the headlines: "Daughter tried to kill herself; mother kills the monster instead."

"Why not?" June wanted to know.

My face instantly rearranged itself into the mask of sadness and reluctance to confess that I assumed so effortlessly now. "Oh, I don't want to talk about it."

Mrs. McCormick unlocked the driver's side door and rolled down the window. "Fine. I need you to help me weed the garden anyway, June. We'll take Layla Jay home."

June and I slid in beside her mother, sweat popping out on both of our foreheads. "It must be a hundred degrees, Mother. Let's wait till it cools off. I want Layla Jay to spend the day with me." She turned to me. "You loved to go to the pool. What's happened?"

Mrs. McCormick interrupted. "We have things to do. Layla Jay has to go home and that's final." She turned the key in the ignition and glanced in the rearview mirror. "Where'd all this traffic come from?" she said as a line of cars moved down Main behind us.

I was determined to get the news of my suicide out while I had another witness sitting in the car with us. We were backing out of the parking place and it wasn't far to Fourth Street from here. I lowered my voice, injected with as much pain as I could muster in my tone. "I tried to drown myself in Dixie Springs Lake," I said.

Mrs. McCormick slammed on the brakes. "You what!"

"It was the Fourth of July. My family went on a picnic to Dixie Springs Lake, and some kids were skiing. I swam out to where their speedboat was headed, hoping that it would hit me."

June grabbed my arm. "But why, why would you want to die?"

"Wallace," I whispered. "I was afraid he'd rape me again. He told me he would. And after he moved back in with us, I thought that I'd rather die than have it happen again."

Mrs. McCormick had pulled back into the parking place, and now she cocked her head across June and stared at me. "Well, obviously you weren't successful. Does your mother know you did this crazy thing?"

The cool-pack air conditioner in the car was blowing hot air into our faces and I was sweating like I'd been running for hours in the heat. I lifted my damp hair off my neck. "No, a boy named Joey saved me. Everyone at the lake thought it was an accident, except Lyn and Jehu. They were there," I said to June. "I couldn't tell Mama, didn't want her upset. She was just getting better after her accident. Lyn thought I had tried to kill myself over Jehu, but it was Wallace who drove me to it."

Mrs. McCormick slid the gear shift into reverse again. "You should go see a psychiatrist, Layla Jay. You need to talk about all of these feelings. It's not good to keep things bottled up inside. You probably need therapy to deal with all of this anyway."

I could fool a lawyer, a judge, Mama, and a lot of other people, but I knew I most likely wasn't good enough to fool a head doctor. I had heard that they had ways of getting inside your brain and sucking out all of your secrets. I tried for a half-smile. "Oh, I don't need help. I'm fine now. I mean, Wallace is dead. He can't hurt me anymore. Mama saw to that."

Chapter 21

I WAS WRONG ABOUT FOOLING MAMA. SHE DIDN'T BELIEVE ME, and neither did Papaw. "Bullshit," he said. "I was there that day and you looked and acted perfectly normal. The two nuts were your mama and Wallace."

"I might have had a few beers, but I agree with Pop. You acted just like yourself the whole day, and when they carried you inside, you were glad to be alive. I could tell. I may not have known Wallace, but I know you."

Miss Louise took my side. The three of us were sitting at Grandma's dining table in front of a beautiful ham decorated with pineapple slices and cherries that Miss Louise had baked in Grandma's ancient oven. "Some suicidal people are very good at hiding their true emotions," she said. "Those who don't really want to go through with it usually call for help before they try. Layla Jay wasn't one of those."

Papaw reached for the big earthenware bowl of fluffy mashed potatoes. "Layla Jay isn't either one. She's a normal girl, who made up this story to help out her mama." He slapped a huge spoonful of potatoes onto his plate. "Isn't that right, Layla Jay?"

I ducked my head, trying to decide how to respond. I'd forgotten that Papaw could pick out liars better than most of us. I was pushing my luck with him now.

Miss Louise was disappointed in me. Her face crumpled up over the ham platter she passed to Mama. "Honey, if what your grandfather is saying is true, you're not helping your mother's case. If you lie, the DA could find out and then your mother will be worse off than she was. Lying is not how to handle this. There's always someone who will catch you in a lie."

A cold knot of fear rose inside me. There was someone who could catch me in my lies. Roland. Roland could expose me, ruin my plan. If he came home from law school in New Orleans, he'd hear about my "rape" and know it was a lie. He wanted to be a lawyer, so wouldn't he feel that it was his duty to come forward and set the record straight? I imagined him on the stand. He'd be dressed in a dark suit with a Tulane tie, his blond hair grown longer, but neatly clipped around his ears. His tan would have faded some, but his face would still be the color of ginger. The DA would ask him if he had knowledge of the case, and he'd say, "Yes, I know for a fact that Layla Jay Andrews was a virgin when we had sex in the month of May, long after she said her stepfather raped her." And I'd go to jail for perjury along with Mama for manslaughter.

Mama saw the fear on my face and assumed I was in agony over my suicide lie. "Honey, I appreciate your wanting to help me, but lying is going to hurt my case more than help."

I remembered her tucking the tag into the armhole of the silver lamé dress in the dressing room at The Ideal Shop. She'd said yes, it was naughty, but wasn't it fun? Lying had turned out not to be fun at all. I debated what to do. Should I spill my guts, confess to everything? Admit the one lie, pray that they'd never find out about the other? I thought of the box in my closet filled with the things I'd taken from the McCormicks' house. If I wanted a clean slate, I'd have to go all the way back to my faking salvation. I closed my eyes, praying silently. "Tell me what to do, Lord. Help me know what's the best course to take." He wasn't going to answer. I knew that, but I waited a minute or so more before I spoke. "I wasn't lying," I said. "Mama, you were taken in by Wallace with his story about his prayers saving your life after your accident. What makes you think I couldn't fool you, too? I was only pretending I was glad to be alive. I wanted to die, and as a matter of fact, I was going to try it again, was planning it on the day you caught him trying to rape me again." This part was perhaps true, I thought. I *had* written a suicide note the day before. But I avoided Papaw's eyes. Wallace hadn't fooled him.

Everyone sat silently for a long time. Finally, Papaw's voice boomed out. "Let's eat. Food's getting cold, damnit."

My appetite was gone, but I lifted my fork and speared a crispy green bean.

MR. ALBRIGHT FILED A MOTION TO DISMISS and the date for a hearing was set. We had two weeks left to find out if she'd be bound over for trial, and Mama was getting tired of playing the role Mr. Albright had assigned to her . . . that of a devoted wife and mother who had been forced to defend her daughter against a man who had taken advantage of her innocent love for him. "I want to go dancing," she said. "I want a tall glass of Old Charter. I want to have some fun, can't stand being cooped up in this shitty house any longer."

When she went to the telephone, I knew there was no arguing with her. She called Mervin and played him like she was first chair flute. "You have no idea how difficult this all is for me," I heard her say. "I was just wild with fear, in shock for days." She twisted the cord around her finger and smiled. "Uh huh. It does get lonely without a man in the house."

I walked into the kitchen, which now that Wallace wasn't barking orders, had returned to its former chaos. I surveyed the mess. There were dirty dishes of smelly leftovers on the table and countertop, Mama's nylons hanging over the back of a chair, and the trash can overflowing beside the back door. More trash bags were lined up along the wall. These held Wallace's belongings that we were waiting to burn in celebration after Mama was acquitted.

Against Mr. Albright's orders and my pleas, Mama went out to Skinnys that night with Mervin. I knew she was making a terrible mistake, but trying to keep Mama from men, music, or booze was like trying to keep a starving hog from a trough filled with slop. She was grinning when she left and smiling even more when she returned around two a.m.

I had fallen asleep on the couch in the den, but I heard her laughing as she said good night to Mervin.

I sat up and watched her weave her way across the room. She was drunk. "Did you have fun?" I asked, hoping she'd gone drinking some-where far away where no one knew she was an accused husband killer.

"Yesssss," she said. "You wouldn't believe how many people are cheering for me to get off. Everyone at Skinnys wanted me to tell them my story. It was like I was a celebrity, Layla Jay. All the attention was on me. The women were jealous; Bonita Garza shot me the bird and said she would think I'd be mortified over what had happened." Mama threw her purse on the coffee table. "Her date, I don't know who he was, kinda cute with a Kirk Douglas dimple, said I was a heroine. Did you ever imagine your mama was going to turn out to be a heroine someday?"

All of the air inside me rushed out, deflating my hopes of Mama get-ting any sympathy in the courtroom now. If she was going to parade around in public acting like she was some movie star, she was going to play out the last scene in a prison cell. She sat down on the couch and patted the cushion beside her. "Sit down. Let me tell you the best part of the evening. Mervin. He was so wonderful to me. I never noticed how like Kenneth he is. Mervin used to ride motorcycles, but he sold his, said it was too dangerous. Did you know he went two years to Southwest College where your daddy went?"

"No, and I don't care. I'm going to bed," I said. "I'll leave the light on for you."

Mama had been sleeping with me ever since the day she'd stuck the green glass in Wallace's throat. Even though Miss Louise had scrubbed the room, she couldn't wipe away the memory of that day, and each time Mama went in there, she'd snatch her clothes or jewelry or whatever she needed and run out as quickly as she could. I understood; I never went in there at all. But tonight Mama was drunk, and she must have forgot-ten her horror of sleeping in the bed she'd once shared with Wallace. Or maybe now that she saw herself as a hero, she wanted to lie on the set where she'd gained stardom.

I put on my nightgown and got into bed, but after my nap on the couch, I wasn't sleepy, and I tossed back and forth on my pillows for a while before I gave up. I tiptoed down the hall and saw that Mama had fallen asleep on top of the spread in her panties and bra. I hesitated before going in, but forced my feet to her side of the bed and covered her with the edge of the spread before running back to my room. We needed to move away. After the trial, I would suggest another town, another state. We could go to Mama's Promised Land: France. I was good at Spanish; I could probably learn to speak French in no time, and I'd meet some dark-haired, black-eyed handsome Frenchman who would be mad for me and take me for drives in his fast sports car convertible. I saw myself with a scarf wrapped around my head, the tail of it flying behind me. I'd be wearing big sunglasses like Audrey Hepburn, and I'd smoke cigarettes in a long gold holder. I got back into bed and pulled the sheet over my face.

Lying there in the dark I turned onto my side and drew my knees up to my chest. I knew better. We weren't going to France or anywhere else. Mama was going to get convicted and no telling what would happen to me. I bit the back of my hand until tears came. I was the reason Mama was going to jail. The complex threads of my lies were going to weave a maze that would trap me like a bug in a black widow's web. And now Mama seemed determined to destroy her chances as well. I closed my eyes and prayed. "Daddy, Grandma, Jesus, can't y'all help us? Please help us. We need you. Save Mama. Save me."

IT CAME TO ME THAT MAYBE GOD might be more inclined to help me if I went back to church, so I called up June and invited myself to attend Pisgah Methodist with her family on Sunday. When they picked me up fifteen minutes before the service was to begin, Mrs. McCormick welcomed me into the car with a warm smile. I guess she was glad I was seeking God's help and not depending totally on June anymore, but she seemed disappointed when she asked where Mama was and I had to admit that she was sleeping late again.

When we hurried down the aisle nearly late for the service, my first thought was of Grandma, dusting pews, sweeping, and straightening songbooks. I supposed some other woman had replaced her now and was getting God's reward for the job every Saturday. After we slid into a pew midway down, I stood for the Affirmation of Faith. "I believe in God, the Father Almighty," I said with true conviction. I did believe, and

I knew He would help me out eventually. The first song we sang was "Let Go and Let God," and I belted out "Your burden will vanish your night turn to day" with renewed hope in my heart. "Give your burdens to God; let him carry your load," Brother Thompson had said. I had a ton to lay on God's shoulders, and I prayed that He was willing to bear the weight. I was feeling nearly happy when Brother Thompson stood up to deliver the sermon. Then something shattered inside. I don't know what happened, but all of a sudden, Brother Thompson's face melted and distorted into Wallace's. I saw him strutting down the aisle, shouting and swiveling his hips as he came toward me. I looked down at the floor, but I could feel his presence all around me. I squeezed my eyes shut, praying, "Make him go away. Go away." I lifted my head to where Brother Thompson stood behind the pulpit. He was talking about how Jesus drove the devils out of the demented man into the swine, and how that miracle frightened the disciples. "They were terrified of His power," he said. And then Wallace was back with a long piece of glass sticking out of his throat above his tie. Blood was spurting out from his neck, covering his body, running down the altar steps, flowing on down the aisle toward where I sat.

I clapped my hand over my mouth to stifle the scream inside me and shivered. June leaned over and whispered, "What's wrong? Are you okay, Layla Jay?"

Her voice brought me back and I reached for her hand. "Yeah, okay," I said, as I squeezed her fingers against mine.

I didn't want to stay for coffee and cake in the reception hall, but the McCormicks were into socializing and shepherded June and me across the parking lot to the new building. The Methodist's Women Circle had bought a window air-conditioning unit for the cinder-block rectangular hall, and the cool air felt good on my skin after walking across the parking lot in the oppressive heat. There was pound cake, coffee, and red Kool-Aid, but I passed by the food and drink table. My stomach felt queasy and I was still haunted by Wallace's appearance in church. I wandered over to the chairs lined against the wall and had just sat down to wait for the McCormicks when Jehu and his parents walked in. I hadn't noticed them in church, but I should have known they would be attending the service.

The last person I wanted to see was Mr. Albright, and second to last was Jehu, but there was nowhere to escape to as I watched them pause in front of the open door. Mr. Albright, sharp as the best knife in our cutlery drawer, spotted me right away. When he waved, I lifted my hand in response, but couldn't work up a smile to match his pleasant expression. Jehu hesitated, took a step, stopped, and then took another as he looked around the room before coming over to sit on the vacant chair beside me. "Hey, Layla Jay. How you doing?" he asked without really looking at me.

Of course he knew all the gossip about Mama and me. "Just taking it one day at a time," I said.

Jehu shrugged. "Guess that's all you can do. I came over 'cause I wanted to say that I'm real sorry about what all happened with you and your mother. I really like her a lot. It's too bad she's, uh, she's, you know, got to, uh, have to need my dad." He looked right into my face then, and his eyes were filled with the same softness Papaw's held when he said he loved me. Now I remembered why I had fallen in love with Jehu all those months ago. He wasn't like all the other boys in ninth grade; he was special, and it wasn't just his Steve McQueen good looks, it was his Claude Whittington heart.

"Thanks," I said. "Mama really likes you, too." And so do I, I wanted to say, but I was going to be cautious this time. He was Lyn's boyfriend, not mine, and I couldn't risk being humiliated again. I remembered Mama's advice on how to handle men. "Always ask them about themselves, honey. That's their favorite subject." I thought first of baseball, but that wasn't a safe subject. Then I smiled. "So how's Piggly Wiggly?"

"You know. Lift that box, tote that carton of canned peas."

"Not much fun, huh?"

"No," he looked down at his brown Sunday loafers. "It's been a pretty rotten summer all around. Not much fun for me."

When Jehu said that, it got me to thinking that when awful things keep happening for a long time and you've spiraled into a depression that even a hot fudge sundae won't cure, sometimes the only answer is to *c'est la vie*. I needed to find joy in the world and maybe Jehu did, too. "Yeah, it'd be good to have some fun for a change. I wish I could turn the clock back and"—I was going to take the big risk—"and we'd be back at the school gym dancing with balloons floating around us."

He *smiled*. "I did have a lot of fun that night."

I knew the Bradley kid had spilled his Kool-Aid on Mrs. Dunn's white patent shoes. I knew June was eating cake, trying to get away from old Mr. Griffin, who was always telling dumb jokes to kids. I knew other people were having all sorts of conversations on many different topics, but no one had just heard a sentence that made them feel like I was feeling now. "Me too. I had a ball."

Jehu leaned closer. "Lyn was really mad about me taking you."

"I know. She doesn't like me very much." Understatement of the year, I added silently.

Jehu grinned. "She's jealous. I told her that I kinda liked you, and that set her off. You know, I don't really like all those girls she hangs around with. Lyn's a pretty nice girl, but when she hangs out with them, she changes, acts all snooty and starts telling me how I ought to cut my hair, what clothes she wants me to buy, like I have to be whatever they think is cool."

I leaned forward and put more weight on my feet that had begun to tap nervously on the tiled floor. Every muscle in my body wanted to wiggle and jiggle with all the excitement pumping through me, and I fought to gain control of it. "I've never cared much for any of them either. I guess they think I'm a square."

He grinned. "No, just the opposite. Lyn would give anything to look like you."

My boobs, of course. They were the one thing I owned that any girl, popular or not, would envy. I looked across the room to June, whose back was turned to us. My face burned. Was I always going to think of June every time I thought of breasts?

Jehu didn't notice my discomfort. "I told her that you liked somebody else, that she didn't need to be jealous, but she didn't believe me."

I liked somebody else? Who? Then I remembered. He meant Roland, of course. The baseball game. Finally, I now had a chance to set things straight. I looked down at my white flats. "I've been wanting to explain what happened that night at the baseball diamond, but I was scared to call you."

When I glanced up at him, I saw that Jehu's smile turn upside down. "Red Pittman and I waited a half hour for you, and when you didn't show up, the man who was closing down the concession stand said he saw you leave with some boy."

I nodded my head up and down. "I did. It was Roland, from the pool? He and I were all muddy after we fell ducking that ball, and he took me home to change was all."

"But he didn't bring you back."

"No, he was going to, but . . ." I could hardly bear to say his name to Jehu. "Wallace wouldn't let me go back out. He was against me going just about anywhere. I even had to lie about going to the pool, told him I was at the library on those afternoons."

Jehu stood up. "Well, you could have called me and told me what happened. I thought you just liked him better and were giving me the brush-off."

I jumped up beside him. I couldn't let it end like this. "I know, but I was scared you wouldn't understand, wouldn't believe me, and I've never called a boy before. Not ever."

He rubbed the side of his face with his palm. I held my breath. "Lyn calls me all the time. My mother doesn't like it though. I guess you and she think alike."

His mother! I didn't want to be like his mother although I had no idea what she was like, having only just met her that one night when she drove us to and from the dance. "But do you believe me? I wanted to come back to the game. I really did." And I remembered that I *had* told Roland we should go back. I pressed my lips together. But I hadn't in-sisted, had changed my mind when Roland leaned against me rubbing his hands down my thighs. I held my breath. Just then some kid began playing "Chopsticks" on the old upright piano against the back wall. "Bom bom bom." I wanted to yell "Stop it!"

Jehu twisted his initial ring and I sucked in air. Lyn wasn't wearing that ring around her neck anymore. I couldn't believe I hadn't noticed it before now. Jehu's voice rose over the irritating plunking sounds flying out from the piano. "Sure, I believe you, Layla Jay. It's just that back then, I didn't know what all you were going through with your stepdad, how it was so awful for you." I turned my head to the side to hear him better as his tone softened. "I'm sorry now that I didn't know. Dad doesn't talk about his cases, but it's not hard to figure out some of it."

Well, he figured out that you're not a virgin, Layla Jay, I said to my-self. Or at least he's guessing you aren't. I crossed my arms over my breasts. "Thanks for saying that. You're right. I just couldn't talk about it. It's still, you know, hard to talk about."

When he moved closer and looked at me like I imagined he would look at the winner of the Miss America pageant, I understood what Mama had felt like on the night she went to Skinnys. We were celebrities!

"Time to go, Jehu." I looked over his shoulder and saw Mrs. Albright bearing down on us. Her high heels clicked on the floor as she made short hurried steps across the room in her slim navy skirt.

Jehu turned around. "Okay, in a minute," he said.

The kid had finally stopped playing and Mrs. Albright's voice was way too loud. "Now," she said, without looking at me. She stood so close to Jehu he must have felt her breath on his reddening neck.

"I'll call you," he said before he turned and followed her across the floor.

As I watched them go over to where Mr. Albright stood talking to Mr. Greer, I realized she hadn't bothered to say so much as hello to me.

Chapter 22

WHEN I GOT HOME FROM CHURCH, I FOUND MAMA IN HER nightgown, with red-rimmed eyes, sitting at the kitchen table drinking coffee. "Hangover?" I said.

"The worst. Where've you been?"

I tossed my bulletin on the table. "Church. Pisgah with June and her folks. Mr. Albright was there." I smiled. "And Jehu. He's going to call me. Broke up with Lyn again."

"Jesus! He can't make up his mind who he wants. You ought to get a guy that will stick." Mama tapped a fresh pack of Lucky Strikes on the table, pulled off the cellophane strip, and fished one out.

I waited until she lit up. "He's going to stick this time." Waving smoke out of my face, I said, "At least I think so. Gotta get changed." Before I made it out of the kitchen, I heard a car outside. "Company."

Mama stood up and looked out the window. "Shit! It's Mervin. It can't be twelve-thirty already." She pushed me toward the door. "Tell him I'll be ready in a minute."

"Where you going?" I hollered after her as she headed down the hall.

"Dixie Springs. Dave Turner's having a barbecue at his cabin." Mervin was banging on the door. "Answer it, will you?"

Mervin was wearing baggy plaid Bermuda shorts and a big grin. "Hey, Layla Jay. Frieda ready?"

I moved aside and let him in. "Nope. She'll be awhile, most likely. You want some coffee?"

"No thanks." He followed me into the dark den and sat on the couch while I opened the blinds. "You been to church, I take it," he said eyeing my pink skirt and white blouse as I walked back to the chair beside the couch.

"Yeah."

"Your mama tells me you're real smart. Did good in school."

"Not really. I did okay." I couldn't help feeling mad that Mama was taking up with the man who had been the reason she had gone to that party at Dixie Springs Lake. He shouldn't have let her drive, no matter what she said, and now he was taking her back to the same place. People would hear about it and say she shouldn't be enjoying herself when she was about to face judgment for taking a life.

We could hear Mama banging drawers, running the water in the bathroom sink. I crossed my legs, swung my foot back and forth. I wished she'd hurry so I could go to my room, and then I wondered why I felt I had to be polite when I didn't give a shit what Mervin thought. I stood up. "I have to change. I'll see you," I said.

Mervin reached up and curled his long fingers around my wrist. "Wait a second, will you? I want to ask you something."

I jerked away, but remained standing, looked up at the ceiling. "What?"

"How do you feel about . . ."

"Fine. Bye." I turned to head for my room.

Mervin's hand stretched out, but he didn't touch me. "Please? Give me a minute. Please?"

I hated being rude, couldn't keep it up, so I sat down on the chair beside the couch and tried not to look surly. "Go ahead then. What do you want to know?" I wasn't going to tell him jack about what had happened with Wallace if that was what he was after. It was none of his business.

"I want to know how you feel about me and your mama dating

again. I hold myself responsible for her accident, figure you blame me, too, and I understand if you do. But I'd like a chance to make it up. I'd like to keep seeing Frieda. I've been sweet on her for a long time, and when all this mess is over with the hearing, I'd like us all to take a little trip somewhere, kind of like a family vacation. I can take some time off, got a good inventory right now." Mervin owned Written in Stone, which was a wonderland of cement figures, tables, benches, and fountains that he sold for grave monuments and yard ornaments. Mama had changed her mind and decided to overlook the white powder in his ears. Now she was calling him an artist. She acted like his praying angels stuck in the ground measured up to Michelangelo's *David*. "So Layla Jay, what do you say to that? Think you could accept me as a friend of yours?"

A vacation? Like a family? It was such a remote possibility he might as well have said we were invited to the White House to eat Sunday dinner with Lady Bird. "I knew you liked Mama" was all I could think to say.

His eyes were honest to God shining like a kid's lit up by candles on a birthday cake. "And I'm pretty sure now that your mama likes me, Layla Jay, but the question is can you like me?"

I smoothed my skirt. I had liked him the night of Mama's party when he was drunk and told funny stories and jokes, but that seemed like twenty years ago instead of a few months. I opened my mouth to say something smart, then closed it. I was tired of lying, worn out with plotting and figuring out people and trying to make things the way I wanted. Here lately, nothing ever turned out the way I wanted, so what did it matter whether I wanted to be his little pretend daughter for a few days or not? "I don't know, Mervin. I just don't know. Right now I'm doing good to know what day it is."

Mervin shot me a look with such tenderness that for a moment I understood why Mama liked him. Had my daddy looked at Mama as Mervin was looking now? I was beginning to understand why she might fall for him. He smiled. "Layla Jay, I understand. That's fine. Fine if you don't know, but I hope you'll think about it sometime. I want to make it up to Frieda and you. If you'll just consider giving me a second chance, that's good. That's all I'm asking for."

"Almost ready," Mama called, sounding younger than me, and now I remembered that they were headed right back to the scene that had caused Mama to get drunk.

I lowered my voice, hoping Mama couldn't hear us. "If that's all true, then why are you taking Mama back up to Dixie Springs? You know she'll get drunk again."

He frowned. "I know it. But she's not driving. I am." He put his hand over his heart. "And Layla Jay, I don't drink anymore. After the accident, I gave it up, drank a Coke at Skinnys last night. I'll take good care of her."

"Okay, but I still wish she weren't going up there. I don't think going to places like that, anywhere where there's lots of drinking, is a good idea right now with all that's going on."

Mervin leaned over and squeezed my arm, put his mouth close to my ear. "I don't either, but you know your mama. If she's set on doing something, no one can put the brakes on her. Dave invited her last night at Skinnys, and she's hell-bent to go. Better that I take her."

I liked him for saying that. He was right about Mama. She could be stubborn as Papaw's mule, and time and again, he'd said to Grandma, "You can't fight Frieda; might as well join her." Of course, Grandma hadn't joined her in anything even once. I smiled. "I'm glad you're driving. Mama hates to drive Wallace's car anyway. It took her a long time to get back behind a steering wheel, and she said she sure wished her maiden voyage didn't have to be in the piece of shit Galaxie Wallace bought when she threw him out back in January."

Mervin grinned. "I bought a Caddy. It's real old, but she doesn't mind riding in it one bit."

When Mama finally came out of her room dressed in a low-cut green blouse tucked into white short shorts I saw that she'd lost all of her weight, and as she twirled around the den, she looked like a woman made to ride around in a Cadillac.

When the phone rang around two that afternoon, I raced to it, waited a moment to calm down, and lifted the receiver, certain it would be Jehu on the line. "Hellllo," I said.

"Hey, Layla Jay." It was June. "I'm going to the matinee at the Palace. *From Russia with Love* is showing. It's gonna be fab. You want us to pick you up?"

I wanted to see the movie, but I didn't want to spend the afternoon with June. "I can't," I said. I wasn't going to tell her about Jehu, so I said,

"Mama asked me to stay home. She's expecting an important call. About the case."

"Oh, well, if the movie is as good as they say, maybe I could go see it again with you." June's disappointment ran through the wires and spiraled into my body. I squeezed my eyes shut. Telling another lie so quickly after going to church and hurting June's feelings again made me feel like a piece of lint.

"Okay, we'll do that and thanks anyway," I said before I hung up.

An hour later when the phone on the hall table rang again, I ran for it shouting, "Let it be him."

And it was! "Layla Jay? It's Jehu." His voice was so low I could barely hear him.

"Hi" was all I could think to say.

"Uh, I need to tell you something." He was practically whispering.

"I can't hear you," I said.

"I don't want my mother to know I'm calling. She's in the kitchen," he said.

Uh oh, uh oh, uh oh, I thought. She hadn't spoken to me at church. I'd suspected this. "Why not?" But I knew.

"She thinks with Dad taking your mother's case and all, it's not a good idea for people to think we're anything but casual friends. Casual was the word she used."

"Oh."

"And Dad said she's right. He said, if the charges don't get dismissed, you might have to testify, that I shouldn't be dating you until this is all cleared up."

"I see." I was trying hard not to cry, but I knew my voice was wavering. I pressed my lips together as hard as I could and took a deep breath.

"It's them. Not me. But I can't, you know. They're my parents."

"Yeah, I guess." Why couldn't I say something smart, something to make him change his mind? Why did I have to be punished for Wallace's sins and Mama's mess? I hated them both. It wasn't fair.

"But I wanted to tell you, didn't want you to think that I didn't mean it when I said I'd call. So you know now. It's not because I don't like you."

I counted the stripes of white, green, yellow, and blue on the wallpaper. Fourteen stripes from the phone to the doorway. The yellow was halved where it was cut to fit. There wasn't anything to say and I wasn't going to think anything about anything. Empty. I'm empty.

"Layla Jay? You still there?" His voice was louder now. Jehu's mother must have walked out of earshot.

"Yeah. I'm here. It's not because you don't like me," I repeated.

"Right. Well, now you know. So, I guess . . ."

"Yeah, you can hang up," I said, picturing him rubbing suntan lotion on Lyn's back at the pool. He'd never stroke any part of me now. "Good-bye." I never knew if he said good-bye back. I hung up and then swiped the phone off the table. It clattered with a ring onto the floor, a dial tone humming as I stepped over it and ran outside.

I wanted to go to June's house, lie on their couch, eat something fresh out of their fridge, smell June's mother's perfumes lined up on her dresser. But today was Sunday. I couldn't risk it. Mr. McCormick would probably be home, maybe mowing the yard, or watching baseball on TV. Mrs. McCormick would be in the kitchen in her white apron with the cherry appliqués, stirring a pot of spaghetti maybe, slicing French bread without a speck of mold on it. Or maybe she was sitting in the blue velvet chair wearing her reading glasses with the gold chain around her neck. She would be reading the Sunday paper, smiling at the huge sandwich Blondie had fixed for Dagwood in the comic strip. She wouldn't want a daughter with big boobs that men ogled, a fourteen-year-old who had had sex, who had witnessed a murder, and who was going to be gossiped about for the rest of her life.

I lay on the grass, wishing now that I had gone through with the suicide. Closing my eyes, I imagined sinking down into the warm earth. I crossed my hands over my chest. I heard the mourners as they looked down into my grave. "Poor Layla Jay. She was so beautiful and smart. Such a shame. She'd barely lived any of her life." But Mama would be there, looking sad and beautiful in a red dress surrounded by men who wanted to comfort her. She'd get all the attention even if I was the one in the casket. I sat up. She was the reason for all of my suffering. If not for Mama, I'd be dating Jehu. I'd be popular. I'd be a virgin. I'd be everything Grandma believed I was. Everything was Mama's fault. Her marrying Wallace was the worst fault of them all. And she hadn't even loved him. I remembered her saying that all he was was a ticket out of Grandma's house. Maybe I could forgive her if she'd loved him. But she hadn't. She'd loved my daddy; he was the only one. And if she hadn't had the fight with him, he wouldn't have forgotten his helmet that day and maybe he'd still be alive. I didn't care if she went to prison. I hated her. I didn't see how I could live with her for another minute. But where would I go? I looked up into the canopy of leaves overhead. I wasn't ready to go to heaven, but I could go back to the last place that was closest to it. I'd call Papaw and ask him if I could live with him again.

Before I got to the kitchen door, it opened and Papaw stuck his head in. "Phone was off the hook. Been trying to call you," he said.

His coming just when I needed him was a sign. This was going to work out perfectly. Grandma had sent him to me. He was surely a gift from her or God. I ran to him. "Where've you been all weekend? Mama tried to call you from Friday night through today."

Miss Louise had followed him into the kitchen. "Well, that's what we came over to tell you," Papaw said, winking at Miss Louise. She blushed, and an alarm bell went off in my head.

Papaw threw his arm around my shoulder and hugged me close to his side. "We've been to Biloxi, left on Friday morning, just got back."

He went to the beach! He'd never liked the beach. I'd begged him to take me plenty of times and he'd always said, "Sand's for Arabs and crabs. Nothing grows in it. We got good dirt right here, we don't need to go sit on grit."

Papaw let go of me and went over to Miss Louise. He lifted her left hand where a gold band ringed her fourth finger. "Say hello to your brand-new stepgrandma, Layla Jay. We got hitched on the beach."

Chapter 23

———

PAPAW AND MISS LOUISE (I WASN'T GOING TO CALL HER "grandma") had another surprise. Papaw's wedding gift to Miss Louise was a 1963 canary yellow Corvette, which they were planning on driving across the country to the Grand Canyon, Las Vegas, and Disneyland. "Of course, we won't leave until after your mother's case is decided," Miss Louise said.

"Yeah, we're delaying the honeymoon until we know what's what with her. And you." I was an afterthought.

I must have looked how I was feeling because Miss Louise pulled away from Papaw's grip and walked over to me. Putting her hands on my shoulders, she looked into my heart. "Honey, I know how much you loved your grandmother, and I want you to understand that I'm not trying to take her place. No one can do that." She looked over at Papaw for help, but he was fishing in his shirt pocket for a cigar. "You and I have been friends for a while now, and I'm hoping that we can build on that. Maybe in time you could come to love me a little?"

I wasn't mad at her. I sort of loved her already. But I was mad at Papaw. We'd buried Grandma only six months back, and it looked to me like he had already forgotten her, wiped her out like chalk letters on a blackboard. He was moving Miss Louise into their big bedroom where Grandma's clothes were still hanging in the closet. Dating Miss Louise was one thing; moving her into Grandma's house was another. I didn't smile, but I said, "Sure, Miss Louise, we're friends. I don't know what we'd have done without you after Mama came home from the hospital." Above her head, I could see Papaw peeling the cellophane off his King Edward, ignoring me, like I was some bellowing calf he'd have to feed eventually. "And Mama's grateful, too. I guess she'll be surprised when she hears she's got a stepmother now."

That got Papaw's attention. He licked his cigar to soften it before he said, "Well, Frieda's gonna have to accept the fact, surprised or not."

I wasn't so sure she did have to, but I kept my mouth shut for once. I dreaded finding out who was right about her reaction. Either way I wasn't going to be happy.

Miss Louise wanted to go home and I'm sure Papaw did, too, so he could get on with the honeymooning, but they knew I'd tell Mama their news, and they were determined to deliver the glad tidings themselves.

We ate hamburgers from the Tastee-Freez that Papaw picked up since Miss Louise couldn't find anything worth cooking in our house, and after we ate, she suggested we play poker, but we didn't own any cards. Mama hated games and I had no one to play with, so we'd never bought a deck. I wished we had as the hours we waited seemed like days, and Ed Sullivan didn't have anybody I was interested in on his big sheeow.

Around nine o'clock when we heard Mervin's Cadillac, all three of us jumped up like we were fifty-yard-dash sprinters who'd been waiting for the starting signal. We stood crowded together at the door, waiting for Mama to come in. In the large square of porch light cast across the front lawn, we watched her and Mervin get out of the Caddy Mervin had parked behind Miss Louise's Corvette. As they approached it, suddenly, Papaw sprang out the door, ran down the drive, and met them as they leaned down to look in the Corvette's passenger window. Miss Louise shrank back against me, and then I knew. She was scared of what Mama was going to say about her new stepmother.

After showing Mama and Mervin every little thing on the car (he cranked it up and even tooted the horn for them as though a Corvette's sound was special), Papaw pointed toward our heads framed in the panels of the kitchen window where Miss Louise and I had gone for a better view. I watched Papaw's cigar waving faster in his mouth as he told them the news. I knew this because Mervin stuck out his hand and clapped him on the back as they shook hands like Papaw had won the Indy 500. Mama stood still as the birdbath in the backyard. She didn't wave when Mervin drove off, tooting his ordinary horn.

Papaw said something to her, and then Mama rushed in and hugged Miss Louise. "It's just wonderful," she said without a slur in her voice. Although I could smell whiskey and smoke around her, she was only a little high, not dead drunk as I had feared. "Love is in the air, love is everywhere," Mama was practically singing the words. She hugged Papaw next. "I'm so happy for you, Pop." She obviously didn't care one bit that Papaw had jilted Grandma, and the three of them stood in a little circle with beaming smiles all round. When Miss Louise showed Mama her simple gold band, Mama acted like she was admiring a marquise diamond Richard Burton would buy for Liz.

Everyone was talking at once and my mind drifted away from them. I wouldn't be going to live with Papaw after all; I was stuck with Mama unless she went to jail, and then Papaw would probably sign me over to live in foster care or maybe the home for orphans in Jackson. I was about to go to my room, unable to stomach watching the happy little three-some any longer, when Mama looked over at me. "Layla Jay. Come here. I've got news to tell, too."

I froze. "What?"

Mama ignored the scowl that must have appeared on my face as I stood waiting for her answer. "Love *is* in the air, just like the song says. Tonight Mervin told me that he loves me, and he wants to take me on a trip." Mama's hair swung on her shoulders as she turned back to Papaw and Miss Louise. "Of course, we can't go until we get all this manslaughter mess cleared up, but after it's all over, and he's sure I'll get off, then he wants to drive all the way down Florida to Key West. He says a lot of artists like him live there and we can watch the sun go down in the water, snorkel and see colored fish, dance beneath the stars. It'll be so romantic."

Maybe I hadn't been paying attention, but I was pretty sure she said "take me," not *us*. Papaw and Miss Louise were going west, Mama and

Mervin south and east, and I was the center of the compass that was stuck in place, going nowhere. Mervin had invited me, hadn't he? So it was Mama who didn't want her baby bird chirping in her love nest.

"How exciting!" Miss Louise said. "We're going to take our honeymoon at the same time, going all the way to California and stopping at the Grand Canyon and Las Vegas on the way." No one had given a thought as to what would happen to me, where I'd be, while everyone was on their dream trips.

I backed down the hall toward my room as they all babbled on about their plans. Mama hadn't said she loved Mervin, only that he loved her, but I thought that maybe she did. She hadn't gotten drunk and stayed out late like she usually did. That might be a sign. And if Mama did love him, she'd marry him, and then I'd be getting a new stepfather besides a new stepgrandmother. I was just too too lucky. I kicked my bedroom door shut.

I stood with my back against the door wondering if they'd even notice I had vanished. I took the photo of Daddy to my desk and sat staring at him, willing him to speak to me. If only I could have heard his real voice just once, to know the tone and timbre he would have used when he said "I love you, Layla Jay."

After a while, the excited voices died away and soon I heard Papaw and Miss Louise at the door. "We're leaving," Papaw said. "Come give us a kiss good night."

"I'm not dressed," I said. "Bye."

"Bye, sweetie. You come out to visit soon," Miss Louise said.

"Okay," I responded, and then, "Don't hold your breath," too softly for her to hear.

Mama changed into a long mint green nightgown before she opened my door without knocking. I was still sitting at the desk, and silently she walked over and lifted the picture of Daddy, staring at it for a long moment before she said, "I wish you could have known him." She traced his grainy face with her forefinger. "Every time I'm with Mervin, he reminds me more and more of your daddy. Something in their way of gesturing when they speak. And their hands are alike, long tapered fingers. Artist's or pianist's hands." She handed me the photograph, twirled around and fell onto her back across my bed. "Oh, Layla Jay, I think Mervin is the one I've been waiting all this time to give my heart to."

I couldn't help it; I was so mad and hurt the words just popped out. "Well, you've given just about everything else to half the men in Zebulon," I spat at her.

She sat up. Her jaw dropped down. I could see bewilderment in her eyes. "*Layla Jay!* What a thing to say to your mother."

"It's the truth."

She stared hard into my eyes, and then lowered her voice. "What's the matter? You're starting to sound like Mama. Judging me like that. Next thing you know you'll be quoting scripture, too."

"Thou shalt not commit adultery." I scooted my chair closer to the bed and leaned forward with my palms on my bare knees. "Or how about thou shalt not kill."

Mama's head snapped back like I'd slapped her. The color drained from her face. "Oh, my God," she said. "What's happened to you? You know I didn't mean to kill Wallace. And the only reason it happened was that I was trying to protect you. I saved you."

"You were just mad. Jealous maybe that Wallace wanted me."

Mama opened her mouth a couple of times but no words came out. I lowered my eyes to her arm where the scar rose red and ugly against her white skin. And then all my anger left. It had felt so good to hurt her, but now I felt only pain. The vision of her calling all those mothers on the night before my birthday came to me, and then I saw us eating hot fudge sundaes together, remembered us in The Ideal Shop dressing room, her hugging me and saying how beautiful I was. And there were the marks of love she'd wear until the day she left the earth. She wasn't anything like June's mother, but she had been a good mother at least some of the time. "I'm sorry, Mama," I said, looking down at the scarred oak floor. "I didn't mean it."

When I dragged my eyes up, Mama patted the bed beside her. "Come here. We need to talk."

A whiff of whiskey and tobacco lingered on her body, but there was also a hint of sweetness from her Elizabeth Arden perfume. "I shouldn't have said those things," I mumbled. "I didn't mean them," I said again.

"No, no, it's all right for you to tell me how you feel. I want you to. I know I've made a lot of mistakes and I haven't been such a great mother to you this past year. I feel terrible about what's happened, what happened between you and Wallace. I brought him into this house, and it's my fault, all mine, that you've suffered so much. You can't know how guilty I feel, not for killing Wallace, but for hurting you, making your life hell these past years."

"I guess I just don't understand you," I whispered. "Sometimes I think you don't even love me, and then you do something wonderful that proves you do. It's hard to know how to feel about you from one day to the next." I knotted my hands together, twisting my fingers back and forth until they ached. "You just confuse me all the time and it makes me crazy."

Mama gave me a half-smile. "You know what? Your grandma used to say almost those exact words to me back when I was a teenager. You're a lot like your grandma in so many ways, and I guess I haven't changed much since I was your age."

"Why didn't you try harder to get along with Grandma? It seemed like you went out of your way to aggravate her sometimes."

"I know. I guess I did. I wish I had been different. Wish I'd told her how much I loved her. I miss her so much. When she died, before I got a chance to make up our last fight, I wanted to die, too. First Kenneth and then Mama. I can barely stand the guilt of knowing that the last words I said to both of them were said in anger." She wiped her face with the back of her hand and sat up straighter. "But I can't take back the things I said or did. It's too late now. Mama's gone and Louise will be moving in now, and I'm trying to be happy for Pop. He's lonely, can't cook, doesn't know how to turn on the washing machine, I'll bet. He needs a woman to take care of him, and Louise is willing to do those things, and she loves him."

"You were mad about them dating at first."

Mama smiled. "Yes, I was, but that was before I got to know her. She's a nice person, has a good heart. I don't want to make the same mistakes with her that I made with Mama. I'm going to try hard to be a better stepdaughter than I was a daughter." Then she reached for my hand and squeezed it way too hard. "And you need to try, too. You've got to accept the marriage. I could tell you weren't happy for them, or for me and Mervin. Sometimes I feel like you resent me having any fun, that you want me to be like Delia McCormick, who's boring as a stick."

I pulled my hand away and looked toward my closet where I had stowed Delia McCormick's possessions. For a second I thought Mama had discovered my secret, and as I thought of all of the shameful things I was holding inside, my face burned like fire. I tried to smile, but I gave up and bit my lip, trying hard not to cry. "I do want you to have fun, Mama. It's just that I'm not having any, and it's hard to be happy for others when you're so unhappy."

Mama pulled me to her side and squeezed me against her. "I wish I could change things for you. Maybe when this is all over and we go on our trip to Key West, things will turn around. Who knows? Maybe you'll meet some cute boy at the beach down there, and the four of us can go dancing together."

"I'm invited?"

Mama pulled away and, drawing her brows together, she cocked her head. "What? You thought I was going to run off and leave you alone? Of course, you're coming with us. Mervin said he'd already hinted to you about going. I thought you were only acting like you didn't know so I could be the one to tell Pop and Louise about it."

This was news to me! And welcome news for sure. "I didn't know I'm going, too. I guess I just assumed you didn't, he didn't, I wasn't . . ." I covered my face with my hands. "I guess I've got to stop expecting the worst all the time," I muttered.

Mama laughed. "Well, it's pretty understandable that you would. But things are going to change. After the hearing is over and the case gets dismissed, you'll see. Everything is going to turn out just fine." She kissed me and then at the door, she turned around. "I'm going to sleep in my own room from now on. Wallace isn't going to run me out of my comfy bed. Yours is hard as a rock."

TIME CAN'T BE MEASURED with any exactitude. Sometimes it goes too fast; other times too slowly. But always when you're anticipating something, good or bad, time damn near stands still. Each day that passed during the remaining days we waited for Mama's hearing date seemed like a month. Mama had work to keep her mind busy and she and Mervin went out most nights, but I had only June for a diversion, so in desperation, I went over to her house. I timed my visits when I knew Mrs. McCormick would be home, so June and I wouldn't be alone. But after I walked over on Wednesday, Mrs. McCormick said she had a meeting to attend that she'd forgotten about. "I always write down appointments in my little red book I keep beside the phone. I don't know how I could have forgotten," she said, after Mrs. Winrock had called her for a ride. "And I've been misplacing things around the house for quite a while. I don't know what's wrong with me."

I wanted to confess that all those "misplaced" things had been placed in a box in my closet so she wouldn't think something was wrong with her, but, of course, I couldn't. I'd just gotten there and couldn't think of a reason to leave, so I followed June into her bedroom after her mother left. "Want to show you something," she said. When she opened the bottom drawer of her chest of drawers, I knew she was going to take out the photo album. I felt like I was in a movie, in the scene where some girl is standing by the window and an arm reaches in and grabs her. She knew it was out there, but she had to stand there and just wait for it to happen. June sat on the floor and motioned me down beside her. Flipping through the pages, she quickly came to the last one she had taken of me. "Look! This is what I wanted to show you. Aren't you beautiful?" she said. "I got it developed before I went to camp at one of those one-hour photo booths while Mother was playing bridge all day."

I didn't want to see that picture again, but as I stared down at it and saw that dreamy expression on my face, I thought that June was right. I was beautiful. "I shouldn't have let you take it," I said. "What if your mother finds it?"

"Oh, don't worry about it. She'd never go through my things. We respect each other's privacy. I barely go in her room and wouldn't ever open any of her drawers without permission."

I thought of all the days I had sifted through Mrs. McCormick's lingerie, her jewelry, her makeup, her letters. June probably didn't know that her mother had had a lover before she married her dad. "Still, I wish you hadn't taken it," I said. "It makes me feel weird to look at myself."

"You mean your boobs, don't you? Well, they're absolutely gorgeous. If I had them, I'd want to show them to the world." June closed the book. "Hey, I've got some film. Maybe I could take one of you with your shorts unzipped and your blouse open, like the models in those magazines they keep behind the counter at Gillis's Drugstore."

"No. I don't want to."

"But Layla Jay, you could be a model someday. You're tall and you've got the figure. They make lots of money and live a glamorous lifestyle. I'll bet most of them have swimming pools in their backyards."

"I don't want to be a model."

"Then what do you want to be?"

"I don't know. Maybe a Spanish teacher."

June ran to her dresser and snatched her camera. "Well, why don't you just try one or two shots? I'll be the photographer and you move around while I shoot, like on a set."

She looked so funny crouched down like she was a professional photographer for a fashion magazine, I couldn't help laughing at her. A flash followed a click, and I automatically lifted my hair and posed, jutting my hips left and right. "Like this?" I said, putting my hands on my knees and drawing my mouth into a cupid's bow.

"Yeah. Now unbutton your blouse and zip your shorts halfway down."

Uh oh, I thought. I didn't want to replay the scene from the photo that was still taunting me from where June had left it on the bed. I was going to have to say something, make her understand. I dropped my hands and straightened up. "Wait, June. I don't want to. I mean I'm not . . . Can we just stop and talk? I have to tell you something."

June lowered the camera, her face already a mask of pain as if she knew what I was going to say next. "What?"

I couldn't tell her here where that shameful girl in the photo stared out at me. I walked over to June and reached for the camera. Laying it on the dresser, I said in a near whisper, "Let's go somewhere else, the living room. Please?"

She followed me to the couch and I moved over to the armchair where I could see her face. "June, you're my best friend, you know that. You've done some things I didn't like, but I know you're sorry and have a good heart. I forgave you for all that lying about me at Mama's party. That proves I care about you."

June's eyes were misty. "I know you do," she whispered. "And I care about you. I'd do anything for you, Layla Jay."

I knew that what I had to tell her would maybe end our friendship, or worse, maybe hurt her terribly, and I didn't want either of those things to happen, but I had to take the chance. I couldn't go on pretending I was a lesbian like her.

Chapter 24

JUNE SAT WITH HER HANDS HIDDEN BENEATH HER THIGHS, AND when I saw the frightened expression in her widened eyes, I nearly lost my nerve. But something in my life had to be resolved, and this situation with June was the only one I had any control over. I pushed my butt back in the chair and took a deep breath.

"That day you took the photograph. After I left, I went to the library, and I found a book a doctor wrote about girls . . . and boys, too . . . who like each other. I mean girls liking girls, boys liking boys."

June looked down at her orange-polished toes sticking out of her sandals. "Don't, Layla Jay, don't say any more."

"I have to. I need you to understand. You have a condition, June. It's probably not curable, but you're not alone. There might be lots of lesbians in Zebulon who feel like you do. That's what I read you are. A lesbian."

"I know that," June snapped. "You think you're the only one who can look things up in the library? I've known for months. Way back when I first started going out with boys, I knew something was wrong with me. I didn't feel the same as all the other girls. I tried to pretend I liked boys to kiss me, I wanted to like it, but what I felt was . . ." She shivered. "Those guys were just gross to me. I couldn't stand them touching me." Her voice softened and pulling her hands out from beneath her, she pressed her palms together. "I know for sure that I could never feel the same about a guy as I do you. I guess I've always loved you. You're soft and beautiful and exciting. I can't help the way I feel, Layla Jay." Her eyes filled with tears. "I can't help that I love you. That day you let me take the picture, I thought maybe, maybe you loved me, too. I thought you liked what we did." She was trying hard not to cry.

I felt as awful as I had on the night I said those terrible things to Mama. Mama couldn't help being the way she was, and neither could June. "I do love you, June," I said. "But not in that way. I want to have boyfriends, get married, have babies someday. Don't you ever want those things?"

"Of course I do. But I probably won't ever have them. I wish I could. I wish I were like you and most girls, but Layla Jay, I can't be something I'm not."

"June, are you sure? Couldn't you try harder to like a boy? Maybe you just went out with the wrong ones." I thought of Roland. "I know for certain that all some boys care about is getting what they want. They scare me, too. That's why I like Jehu. He's not like them." I hadn't meant to tell her about Jehu, but now the cat was out of the gunny sack. I had twisted the knife I'd stuck in her heart, but I went on, hoping she would understand that I only wanted to help her. "Jehu is sweet and gentle and he wouldn't ever try to make me do something I didn't want to. Maybe if you met someone like him."

June sniffed. Her voice was filled with dull disappointment. "I knew you were still stuck on him, no matter what you said."

"Yeah, but now I need to get unstuck on him." Then I spilled out everything that had happened between us. I ended saying, "So now his parents won't let him date me." I tried to smile. "I guess we're both longing for something we can't have."

"Could I have a hug?" June said. "Just a hug."

I stood up and when she reached around me and pulled me close, I could feel her heart beating against me. The hug felt good, and just for a moment, I wished I did love June in the way she loved me. Quickly, I pulled away from her and looked toward the kitchen. "How about something to eat? I'm starved. Mama hasn't been to the grocery store in a week."

In the kitchen over sandwiches of leftover pot roast, June watched as I ate. She'd only nibbled the crust of her bread, and I was worried sick about how she felt about us now. June took a sip of Coke and then looked over at me. "Layla Jay?"

"Yeah?"

"You know, in a way, I feel better now that we've talked about this. I guess I knew all along that you didn't feel the same about me as I do about you. I just wanted it so bad that I had to keep trying." She pushed her saucer away. "You won't tell anyone, will you?"

I laid my sandwich down. "No, I'd never." I held up my pinkie to cross fingers like in the old days. June smiled as our fingers touched. Then remembering the looks from the girls at the pool, I said, "I think Lyn and some of her friends already suspect though."

"Yeah, they saw me staring at them when we changed into our nightgowns at a sleepover. None of them are very modest, not like you."

"They're all bitches. I wouldn't worry about what they think."

"I don't, but I care what you think. You're my only friend, and I need you so much."

I smiled. "And you're all I've got, June. I guess we're stuck with each other no matter what comes." I picked up my sandwich again. "You never know. Maybe this is just a phase you're going through. You may have the complex about your father or something mental like that and you'll work it out someday. Or maybe you'll meet the right man and you'll feel the same about him as you do me."

June shook her head from side to side. "I doubt it. But if it happens, you'll be the first to know," she said. "You can be the maid of honor at my wedding if I ever have one."

"And you'll be mine."

THE NEXT DAY JUNE'S MOTHER cooked up a trip to Tupelo for June and her to visit her aunt Martha. I suspected that she wanted to keep June away from Zebulon in case Mama was bound over for trial, but she did leave her sister's phone number with us. Mr. Albright said not to worry, that he could subpoena her if necessary. Mama was sure he wouldn't need to, and her confidence was beginning to scare me more each day. The bounce in her walk and the smile on her face, caused I supposed by her falling in love with Mervin, wasn't the proper demeanor I thought a woman who'd killed her husband should have, and Mr. Albright agreed, warning her to stay out of Skinnys and the liquor store.

Mervin was of the same mind as Mr. Albright and he persuaded Mama to stay home a lot of nights when she would have ignored Mr. Albright's admonitions. I hadn't wanted to like Mervin. After Wallace, I didn't feel I could trust any man Mama brought home. Although Mervin was sweet and kind, I reminded myself that, when I'd first met Wallace, I had liked him, too, and that miscalculation had been an error I couldn't afford to make again. I didn't understand why Mama didn't feel the same as me, but I suppose that you don't have a choice about falling in love. And Mama was definitely in love. She sang in the bathtub, she hurried home from work, never complaining about tired feet anymore or cranky customers or the heat that was beating down mercilessly on sticky asphalt streets. The world was just one big old playground to her and she was the kid swinging the highest, believing she'd never fall.

Mama must have been right about Mervin's being more like my daddy. He certainly was the exact opposite of Wallace. He was quiet, shy, soft-spoken, and although he went to church occasionally, he never judged Mama, who still slept late every Sunday. Papaw and Miss Louise liked him, too, and I did trust Papaw's judgment. He hadn't been taken in by Wallace like everyone else, so when he called Mervin a regular guy with a good head on his shoulders, I took notice. "The first man Frieda ever went out with that's not full of bullshit," Papaw said. The proverbial fly in the ointment for Mama was that Mervin lived on a farm out in Amite County, and there are always lots of big green horseflies swarming around cow shit. Mervin had invited her out to his place several times, but Mama wouldn't go. "Let's stay here," she'd say. "I don't feel like a long drive." Or she'd invent some excuse to stay home, like she was expecting a call from Mr. Albright. Finally, one morning after Mama left for work, Mervin called me and asked if I'd like to come out and see his workshop where he molded the statues and yard ornaments he sold out of his shed. I figured he didn't really care about my opinion of his property, that he was hoping I'd have a good time and beg Mama to take me out there again. It was just a ploy, but I was bored with June gone. I agreed to go.

Mervin had warned me to wear old clothes, so I put on a pair of cut-offs with strings hanging down my thighs, pulled on a yellowed gym blouse, and slipped on my tennis shoes, tying my hair up in a ponytail. I needn't have bothered with my hair. I'd expected Mervin to pick me up in his work truck, but when I ran out to the drive, he was sitting in the ancient Cadillac with the top down. I had never ridden in a convertible, and wasn't expecting the force of wind that blasted across the car as we picked up speed on Carterdale Road. I closed my eyes and my earlier vision of myself in Audrey Hepburn sunglasses with a scarf flowing behind me returned, and I laid my head back against the soft leather seat and pretended we were driving through the Pyrenees instead of rural Mississippi.

On the fifteen-mile drive out to Amite County where Mervin lived, he told me that he'd inherited the place from his parents, who had died less than a year apart five years earlier. His older brother, Jake, lived in Knoxville, Tennessee, and his younger brother, Mike, had joined the army, so he lived alone in the redbrick two-story house surrounded by several outbuildings. A two-car garage was attached by a breezeway to the left of the house, and beyond it there was a metal-roofed workshop with a sign hanging over the closed double doors that bore the block letters spelling out the name of his business, WRITTEN IN STONE. As we pulled into the crushed-oyster-shell drive that wound to the left toward a display of cement figures beside the shed, I saw a red-roofed barn, a small cow lot similar to Papaw's, and behind that an open field of verdant green pastureland. Farther back tall pines, oaks, chestnuts, and maples rimmed the perimeters of the field. When I breathed in the countrified air—a mix of cow manure, chicken feathers, chemicals, and wild buttercups and bluebells that dotted the lawn—I felt right at home again and realized how much I missed roaming across Papaw's land. I guessed I was a country girl at heart and always would be. Living in town might be more exciting, but walking down steaming sidewalks inhaling the acrid odors that spewed out of exhaust pipes couldn't compare to the natural scents of land and beast that God had given us. If Mervin's plan was for me to extol the virtues of country living to Mama, he had succeeded. "It's glorious. If I lived here, I'd never want to leave," I said to him.

Mervin pulled onto the grass beside a cement angel. "Maybe some-day you will," he said. Then shutting off the engine, he shrugged, "Of course, your mama would disagree with you. I can't even talk her into driving past this place."

"I know," I said. "She hated living on Papaw and Grandma's place, couldn't wait to get into town. That's the main reason she married Wallace," I said as we got out of the Cadillac and walked over the brittle grass to the row of statues. I wished I hadn't mentioned Wallace; it seemed like farting in church.

Mervin didn't react to my talking about Mama's dead husband though. He swept his arms across the array of figures. "So what do you think?"

"Wow" was all I could think to say. Covering nearly a half acre of land were cement tables, benches, fountains, and numerous statues arranged by type and subject. Most of them were unpainted gray ce-ment, but there were colorful ones, too. In the first row I walked past were the religious figures: angels, the Virgin Mary, St. Francis in a monk's robe, and Jesus Himself with a lamb beside Him. There was a grouping of animals: a rooster, deer with and without antlers, a standing pig with a piglet curled beside her, a turtle on a rock, swans, ducks, and even an alligator. I liked the people best: cherubs playing musical instruments, a girl dressed in a peasant costume with a basket on her arm, a shapely woman with a water pitcher on her shoulder, a jockey, a colored boy with a fishing pole, and enough dwarfs for two Snow Whites to live among. I was enchanted.

"Did you make them all?" I asked.

"No, only some of them. Others I order and have shipped to me. I do make a few figures though and all of the fountains, tables, chairs, and benches. I get more calls for fountains than you would imagine." He steered me toward one with a cross on its top. "This one is going in the church on Eighth Street tomorrow."

"And you deliver it in your truck?" I asked, running my hand around the scalloped tiered bowls.

"Yeah, it comes apart. To me, that's the hardest part of my job, delivery and setup." Mervin grinned. "Want to see my workshop?"

"Sure," I said, following him past a mound of gravel toward the shed. The smell of gasoline rose up inside the shed to greet us, and he turned on the big fan just inside the door. As the cooling breeze blew across the workshop, Mervin explained the process he used to create his work. He kicked a bag of cement that he said weighed nearly a hundred pounds. "I mix half a bag of this in a five-gallon container filled with pea gravel. Start with the gravel and cover it in a couple of inches of water, then I pour in the cement and mix that. Lastly I pour in the same amount of sand as the gravel, and add more water until I get the proper mix, not too thick, but not too watery." Mervin showed me the big mixer that towered over the bags of cement before we moved on over to the molds into which he poured the cement mixture. The molds, made of rubber, fiberglass, and metal, were of varying shapes and sizes, and nudging one with his foot, Mervin said, "I pack this with a trowel, then shake the mold to get out all the air bubbles. If you don't get all the bubbles out, you'll ruin your work and have to start all over. Then I just walk away, leave it to dry overnight."

"Why doesn't it stick to the rubber?" I asked, thinking of how hard it was to get a cake out of a tube pan without leaving chunks in the bottom. "Do you flour and butter it like a cake pan?"

Mervin laughed. "No, but it's the same principle. I coat the mold, using gas and oil as a release agent, to prevent sticking. When I take out the product, I shake it in the mold. I used to bump it on the ground but that cracks whatever is inside it. Learned that the hard way. Eventually, the mold will rot when the rubber gets hard and deteriorates, but I take care of my molds, recoating them after each use to keep them in good shape as long as I can. Some of these are like old friends, I've had them for so long."

"Could I try one sometime?" I asked. "Maybe a squirrel or something else small?"

Mervin was thrilled I had asked. His face lit up in the dark interior of the shed. "Be my apprentice, you mean? Sure, I've always wanted a helper. You could do all of the painting just as well as I can I'll bet."

"What do you paint them with?"

"Silicone acrylic paint. First black and then your color over that." He grinned. "When do you want to start?"

"How about now?" I asked, thinking how wonderful it would be to take my mind off Mama and apply it to something that might turn out to be beautiful. "How many can you make each day?"

"Sometimes as many as ten or fifteen." Mervin grabbed the handles of the wheelbarrow. "Let's get started," he said, as he bumped the wheels across the grass to the pile of gravel.

We made a dwarf and a bench, and as we worked, Mervin told me how he'd been an apprentice himself to an old man who lived on the other side of Zebulon. "I didn't know this was what I'd want to do for the rest of my life, but when a customer bought my first cement table, and I saw how happy the lady was with it after I set it beneath a chestnut tree in her yard, I was hooked. I meet a lot of really nice people, and giving them something beautiful that will last for years is what I love about the job."

Mervin dragged the two molds out into the yard where they'd receive the benefit of the sun. "Makes 'em dry faster," he said, "and it's not supposed to rain, so tomorrow you could come back and see the finished product."

"I wish I could," I said. "But with all the goings-on, who knows what tomorrow will bring?" I scratched my arms. "This powder itches like crazy."

Mervin led me to the faucet, but the powder didn't wash completely off. He then produced a bottle of Jergens Lotion and rubbed it up and down my arms to remove the last of the powder. His touch was light and gentle; it wasn't a bit like when Wallace would put his hands on me. And this surprised me. Mervin was the first man to touch me, except for Papaw, after that last day with Wallace, and yet I wasn't afraid for even a second. Somehow I knew I could trust him. It seemed like I had known Mervin for a long time, like he had always been a part of our family. It even crossed my mind that maybe this is the way my daddy's hands would feel. Hadn't Mama said their long fingers were alike? For sure he wasn't like all of the other men Mama had brought home.

I think Mervin sensed the good feeling inside me because, when he looked up at me from where he squatted beside my feet, his eyes were gleaming with what may have been love for his new apprentice.

Chapter 25

THE NEXT MORNING I WAS BACK AT LOOSE ENDS, WANDERING through the empty house with nothing to do. I thought about calling Mervin to ask if I could return to his farm and see how my dwarf had turned out, but I replaced the receiver before I dialed. I didn't want to ruin the memory of the wonderful day by going back too soon. Memories are like stews and gumbos and chicken pie. After they sit awhile without partaking of them, the next time you have them, they're even better than the first time. I figured my next visit to Mervin's would be just like that if I could make myself wait for a few days.

I decided to practice my flute, but I got frustrated and put it back in its case after I kept playing sour notes. My fingers just weren't nimble anymore, and it had been so long since I'd practiced my breathing exercises, I couldn't hold a C for more than a second. Fishing my sandals from beneath the couch, I decided I had to get out of the house, and within minutes, I strolled around the block to pass by Jehu's house.

After being in the country for an entire day, the sounds of the light traffic on Fourth Street seemed deafening, and now I wished I had called

Mervin anyway. Although it was only nine o'clock and Third Street was lined with sycamore trees to shade the sidewalk, by the time I rounded the corner, beads of perspiration popped out on my forehead. My camp shirt fell limply over my shorts, and as I walked, my sweat-soaked hair clung to the nape of my neck. Brown sycamore balls that had fallen from the trees crunched beneath my feet, and every few steps, I irritably kicked one or two into the street. Just as I passed the walk leading up to Jehu's house, the front door opened and he came out onto the porch. My heart skipped a beat. He'd know I had no reason to be standing on the sidewalk in front of his house, wouldn't he? I quickened my pace, hoping to get past before he saw me, but I'd only taken a couple of steps when he called to me. "Hey, Layla Jay. Where're you going?"

I stopped walking and turned my head to him, lifting my arm in a half wave. "Hi. I'm on my way to, uh, a friend's house," I said, trying to remember if anyone I knew lived on his street.

"Do you have a minute? I saw you out the kitchen window. Could we talk? Just for a second or two?"

"I thought your folks didn't want you to talk to me," I said, but my sandals were already moving up the walk.

"They're not home." He came farther out onto the porch and met me on the concrete steps. "Can you stay a little while?"

"I guess. I didn't say what time I'd be there." Wherever "there" is, I said to myself.

We sat a couple of feet apart on the top step, Jehu with his back against the white post. "I've been thinking about you," he said.

I waited. Thinking what? That I'm a pariah? That I'm the daughter of the accused? That I'm not a virgin?

We watched a Flowerland delivery van slow in front of the house and then turn into the drive across the street. Jehu looked back at me. "And what I was thinking is that my parents aren't being fair about you. They don't have the right to tell me I can't see you if that's what we both want." He pulled a brown camellia bloom from the bush beside the step and tossed it out into the yard. "Do you still feel the same way about me? You said you wanted to have some fun and I thought we kinda agreed to do something together."

No one was home across the street, and I watched the woman, who had gotten out of the van with a vase of roses, walk back to the van after leaving the flowers on the porch. I wiped the sweat from my face and then swiped my palms across my shorts, and breathing in the scent of the few remaining camellias, I felt light-headed. I hadn't eaten anything, and I wasn't sure if I felt so weak because of my empty stomach or because I was filled with dizzying hope. "Sure," I finally said, "but when you called last Sunday and told me you had to do what your parents said, I assumed you wouldn't want to risk seeing me again."

"I'm willing to risk it now. If we didn't go anywhere in public where they might find out, we could still do something or other together."

The delivery van backed out of the drive and went back down the street from the direction it had come. I hoped the lady who was getting the roses would be home soon before they wilted in the heat. "Do something or other," Jehu had said, but what and how? "You mean sneak around?"

Jehu frowned. "Well, I don't see it as sneaking, just not telling them. I wouldn't lie about it if they asked, but what they don't know . . ."

"But where would we go?"

Jehu stood up. "Not here. Mother is usually home most days. What about your house? Your mother works all day, doesn't she?"

Praise God, she does, I thought. And now that Papaw had gotten married, he didn't come by very often, and even if he did, he wouldn't tell. "Yes, she works from eighty-thirty till five-thirty Monday through Friday. Sometimes half a day on Saturday."

"My hours at Piggly Wiggly are from two to six, so we could do something before that."

I looked across the lawn, and then shifting my eyes to the sycamore, I lifted my gaze on up to the sky. The greens, blues, browns, and white clouds were suddenly brighter, the perfume of the camellias sweeter. Piggly Wiggly two to six was a poem. "Do you want to come over right now?" I whispered.

"I thought you had to be somewhere."

I'd forgotten the lie of my excuse for parading in front of his house. "Oh, I can go later. I didn't say what time I was coming exactly. It's not a big deal."

Jehu stood up and held out his hand, pulling me up to stand beside him. "Then let's go," he said.

We bumped hips twice on the short walk, and as we neared my house, I began to worry about what Jehu was going to think when he saw that we lived like pigs. I took a mental inventory of all that he would see: last night's dishes on the kitchen countertop, Mama's nightgown on the hall floor, my tennis shoes in front of the couch, several glasses strewn around on the coffee and end tables, some of them half-full of orange juice, Coke, and red Kool-Aid. And a coat of dust lay on every piece of furniture, including Mama's new exercise bike sitting in the middle of the den. As I felt for the house key in my pocket, I said, "I haven't cleaned the house yet. I was going to get to it this afternoon. Things are kind of a mess."

"You don't have to apologize. My mother's the Clorox queen, drives me and Dad crazy worrying about germs. It's nice to know somebody who cares about more important things."

I stuck the key in the door. "Exactly," I said with a huge grin.

He stayed two hours and they were the fastest 120 minutes of my life so far. During all of the other times we'd been together, at my party, the dance, riding to the game, brief snatches of talking together, we hadn't ever really gotten to know each other all that well. Everything I did know about him made me think he was just about perfect, and I didn't change my mind about that as he sat on the floor of our den sorting through Mama's records. "Man, your mother's so cool. She's got all of the latest and a lot of the Top Forty that I like."

I eased down beside him and hugged my knees against my chest. "We listen to music every day, and Mama and I dance around the house like we're trying to win best couple on *American Bandstand*. You're a good dancer," I said, remembering being in his arms in the school gym.

"I'm not that good," he said. "Lyn was always wanting to practice with me in her living room."

Suddenly music and dancing didn't appeal to me anymore. "You want something to drink? I think we've got some Coke." I thought of all the 7-Ups in our refrigerator. I hoped he wouldn't follow me into the kitchen. If I opened the door, he might see them and want one. Neither Mama nor I could touch the bottles, even though we both badly wanted to throw them out.

Jehu did come into the kitchen, but I managed to block his view as

I snatched two Cokes from the top shelf. "What's all this?" he asked. He was pointing to Wallace's belongings stuffed into the trash bags lined up beside the back door.

I opened the Cokes and handed him one. "Uh, just old stuff. Trash."

Holding his Coke in his right hand, he reached down with his left and lifted the nearest bag. "I'll take it out to the street for you if you want."

"*No.* No, we're saving them for the celebration."

He dropped the bag. "Celebration? What do you mean?"

I took a long swallow of Coke. "I'll tell you, but let's sit down first." He followed me to the couch and set his Coke exactly on the spot I had identified as Lexie County on our state of Mississippi coffee table. "Those bags are Wallace's stuff. Mama got the idea to burn it all for a celebration when all this manslaughter stuff is over."

Jehu looked miserable. He hadn't come over to talk about our scandal. "Oh. Well, I hope my dad can get her off."

"Me too, but, Jehu, can we not talk about it? I don't want to think about Mama right now."

The tightness of the muscles in his face loosened and he reached for his Coke. "Right. We're here to have fun. That's what we said at Pisgah that Sunday." He drank from the bottle and then held out his hands. When I laid mine in his, he pulled me over and began tickling me. As his fingers played along my ribs, I kicked my feet against the couch, shrieking with surprise and laughter. "Is this fun? You having fun?" he said with a big smile on his face. "You must be having fun. You're laughing. You like being tickled?" And he grabbed my left foot and pulled off my sandal, raking the bottom of my foot with dancing fingers.

"Stop. I'm very ticklish. Stop it, Jehu." He was grinning so widely I could see his back molars. "I'll get you back," I screamed, as I wrested my foot away and ran with one shoe on across the room. He came after me and we raced around the exercise bike, and down the hall. I darted into my bedroom, slamming the door just before he reached for me.

"Let me in," he said in a deep voice. "I'm the big bad tickle wolf who will blow your door down."

I giggled and leaned back against the door crossing my hands over my racing heart. "I'm not scared of you," I gasped.

Jehu scratched on the door and howled, nearly sounding like a real wolf. "Let me in," he said.

I opened the door before running to my bed and jumping up onto it to stand in the middle with my feet wide apart. "Go away, wolf," I said. "You . . ." and before I could say any more, he was in the room, grabbing my ankle. I fell onto my back, and Jehu leapt onto the bed, nearly on top of me with his legs weighing down on mine. I rolled my shoulders sideways and fell to the floor.

"Gotcha now," he cried, as he tumbled off the bed beside me and threw his arm across my stomach, pinning me down.

I looked up into his face and smiled. "I give," I said. "You've got me."

He bent his face close to mine. "Do I? Do I have you?"

"Yes," I said, closing my eyes. I would be ready for the kiss this time. And when his lips touched mine, I opened my mouth slightly and knew I'd done it just right.

He kissed me once more and buried his nose in my hair, nuzzling against me as my arms encircled his back. When I pulled his chest against mine, he raised up on his arms. "We'd better go back into the den," he said. "I don't want to, but I think we better."

Disappointment welled up inside me as I watched him stand and adjust his shorts with his back turned to me. I sat up and laid my palms against my warm cheeks. He was right, of course. I shouldn't have led him into my room, let him kiss me so easily, and now I worried that he might think the rumors about me were true. I wanted to cry. "You're right. I was just going to say we shouldn't be in here. You're the first boy who's ever been in my room. Honestly, you are."

Jehu turned back around and pulled me up. He kissed my nose. "I know that, Layla Jay. I don't listen to gossip." And then I felt like we were floating side by side as we left my room and went back down the hall.

For the rest of the time we spent together, Jehu talked about himself. I wanted to know everything. I asked him how he felt about going to a country church like Pisgah, and he said that it was much more personal than Centenary. "I feel closer to God there," he said. "I don't know what it is, but it just feels more holy than a big fancy church."

He told me that he'd had a little sister who had died with a defective heart when she was only a few weeks old. He was only two, and didn't remember her, but he felt sad anyway whenever he thought of Melissa Kay, who was buried in the Zebulon Cemetery nearby. He said his father told him that his mother's sadness over the death of her baby was the reason sometimes she was too protective of him. Jehu liked western movies, and he used to pretend to be Johnny Weissmuller as Tarzan. His favorite color was purple, but he'd never buy a lavender shirt. Lyn was the only girl he'd ever dated besides me, and he wished now that he'd never called her to begin with.

I knew he had questions he wanted to ask me, but I didn't give him a chance to satisfy his curiosity because I was afraid that some of them might lead back to the bags that lined our kitchen wall, and before we knew it, it was time for him to go home to get ready for work.

After we agreed to meet the next morning, I said, "What will you tell your mother?"

"I'll let her think I'm going over to Red's. Don't worry. I'll figure something out."

At the door, he turned to me and placed his palms on my cheeks. "I had fun. Just like we said we would."

I didn't have to think about being ready for his kiss. I knew exactly how to do it now.

Chapter 26

By the time Mama came home, I'd cleaned the house from top to bottom. Although Jehu had said he didn't mind the mess, I worried he was being polite and was secretly appalled by the way we lived. I had just rolled up the vacuum cleaner cord and stowed it in the hall closet and was thinking about baking some brownies for Jehu when I heard Mama slam the front door. "Hey," she called. "Good Lord, Layla Jay, you've been busy. Is Steve McQueen coming over?"

"No, I just felt like cleaning up a little."

Mama kicked off her shoes and slung her purse down on the couch. "Good. Mervin's bringing Chinese food over in a little while. He had a delivery to make somewhere over in Tylertown and is going to stop here on his way back."

She had her dress off by the time she walked past me to her bedroom. I followed her to the door and leaned against the doorjamb. It still bothered me to come into the room, so I hadn't cleaned it, but it sure needed maid service. Clothes were tossed helter-skelter everywhere, there was spilled powder on the dresser, three coffee cups sat on the bedside table, and the sheets on the bed were hanging on the floor. "Can we go to the store? I want to make some brownies, and we don't have any cocoa or milk."

Mama jerked a pair of pedal pushers off a hangar. "What's up with you? How come you're wanting to be Suzy Homemaker all of a sudden?"

I tried to look nonchalant. "No reason. Just bored."

"Well, we don't have enough time to go before Mervin gets here. Maybe he'll take you later. After your birthday, we'll get your license and then you can drive yourself." She brushed past me and darted into the bathroom. "You sure nothing's up with you?" she yelled across the hall. "Come in here while I'm freshening my makeup." Mama gave me the long appraising look that meant she was determined to reach into my brain and suck out the one thing I didn't want her to know. The power of her suction skill when she was really dogged about finding out something was equal to our Electrolux vacuum cleaner's. "Now what's the big secret?"

I leaned against the bathroom door watching her pencil her brows with deft whisks. "Don't have one."

Mama laid her lipstick on the glass shelf above the sink. "No sale. The truth."

I might as well get it over with. She was going to find out eventually. "Jehu's coming over. He came over today."

Mama smiled. "Why didn't you want to tell me?"

"Because his parents don't want him to date me, because . . ." I hated to tell her why.

"Wallace?"

"Yes, but Jehu doesn't think it's fair. And neither do I."

"Well, you're right. It's not fair. You shouldn't be punished for what I've done."

"Don't tell Mr. Albright."

Mama smiled. "I won't tell. After the judge dismisses the charges at the hearing, they won't care if he dates you anymore."

She squirted Elizabeth Arden's newest scent into the air between us, and I leaned my head into the heavenly mist. "I hope you're right. About the hearing and about Jehu," I said.

An hour after Mama left for work the next morning, Jehu knocked on our front door. I had dressed in my best pair of navy shorts and sprayed that new Elizabeth Arden fragrance all over myself and most of the house. Jehu breathed it in. "Smells like gardenias in here," he said looking around our immaculate den. I could tell he was going to be a man who appreciated the little things a woman did for him.

I hadn't gotten to the store so there were no brownies, but I'd made cinnamon toast, which he said he liked. He only nibbled at his though as we sat across from each other at the kitchen table. When Jehu asked about the hearing, I shook my head from side to side. "Mama thinks the charges will be dismissed, but I'm real scared she'll go to trial."

"My dad will get her off. He's gotten a lot of people out of some big trouble."

"He hasn't had my mama for a client." I debated how much I was willing to tell him. I didn't know how much he already knew, but I suspected that the lawyer-client privilege Mr. Albright had talked about didn't extend to his family. "Did your dad tell you what happened that afternoon?"

He dusted sugar off his fingers onto the plate. "No, he doesn't talk about his cases, at least not with me."

Then maybe, I reasoned, he didn't know about my not being a virgin after all. And if he found out, would he still like me? My face must have shown my worry, because Jehu reached across the table and took my hand. "Layla Jay, you don't have to tell me anything you don't want to."

"I know," I whispered. "But if Mama goes to trial, you'll hear all about everything there is to know." I felt the pressure of his fingers against mine and squeezed his hand so hard he winced. "You may not like me when you learn the truth about what really happened."

Jehu let go and came around the table; he pulled me up to his chest and wrapped his arms around me. "I've already guessed a lot of it, and it doesn't matter. None of it was your fault. Or your mother's either."

"I wish everybody felt the way you do." And then I knew I had to tell him everything. I couldn't bear to spend these sweet mornings with him with the hope of his love and then have it taken away when the truth came out. I couldn't afford to hope for something I might not get. I led him to the couch. "I want you to know everything," I said.

I began with the night Mama told me she and Wallace were getting married. As I warmed up to my story, I realized that this was good practice for my testifying if it came to that. And it felt good to pour out my fears and my feelings about Mama and Wallace and even Papaw and Miss Louise. As I talked, I watched his face for a reaction, but Jehu sat silently, the muscles in his face as immobile as Mervin's cement figures. When I came to June's role in our drama, I left out the part about blackmailing her into testifying, and I never mentioned Roland. I longed to unburden myself of those worries, too, but I wasn't going to test Jehu's forgiveness that far. "So now you know why I'm so scared. I'm not what you thought I was," I said with my heart rising into my throat.

I had been talking for a long time, and Jehu hadn't said one word. Still silent, he stood up and paced around the exercise bike and then stood looking out the window into our side yard. When he turned back to me, I saw a look on his face I'd never imagined he was capable of. His eyes were narrowed, his jaw so tight, it seemed he would never be able to unlock his mouth to speak. His fists were clenched, and in his eyes, I saw what I'd seen in Mama's when she swung the 7-Up bottle at Wallace's head. Panic rose up so fast inside me, I could barely breathe. I'd said too much, and now he saw that our little blue house was filled with ugliness and he was disgusted and enraged that I'd tried to trick him into thinking we were nice people like him and his family. I felt physically sick. Why hadn't I killed myself and never lived to this day? "I'm sorry," I tried to say, but I choked, and it came out "I'm sor."

"Son of a bitch, bastard," he yelled across the room. "I wish I'd had a chance to beat the crap out of him before your mother killed him."

I tried to stifle the hope that was reemerging inside. Wait, Layla Jay, I cautioned. Make sure of what he means. I kept my eyes on him, as wary as a cornered animal.

"For God's sake, why didn't you tell somebody before all this happened?"

"I . . . I . . . couldn't."

He talked over my reply. "I mean if you'd told your mother, or your grandfather. Well, anybody. You should've . . ."

I bowed my head unable to look at his accusing eyes. I wanted him to go home now. I needed to cry and I wasn't going to release one tear until I could be alone with my misery. I heard his steps across the floor and then felt the weight of him on the plastic-covered couch. His palm was on my chin and he lifted my face. "I wish I could have helped you somehow. If you'd told me, I would have done something. I'm sorry for you, and I'm sorry for your mother."

"I don't want your sympathy," I said. "You don't have to pretend with me. You can go home. I'm fine."

"You can't get rid of me that easily," he said. "I care about you, Layla Jay. Really care. I mean maybe I love you."

Maybe he loved me! Maybe. "You don't know?"

He kissed me, a long kiss that seemed to draw out all of my love and hope and maybe even part of my soul. He slid his mouth across my cheek to my ear. "I know I think about you every morning when I wake up. I want to be with you all the time, and I want to kiss you again." And he kissed me again and again until we were both breathing hard and my face felt as warm as it did with a fever.

I pulled away first, scared of where all of my feelings were headed. Never had I felt such emotion bubbling like furiously boiling water inside me. Something had to spill out or I'd explode. "Oh, Jehu. I wish I could tell you how I feel. I've loved you for a long time," I said. "You can't imagine how much I hoped for you to love me." I touched my fingertips to his lips. "But I thought you were in love with Lyn."

Jehu's face was as flushed as mine felt. He kissed my fingers and held them against his cheek. "No, I was never in love with her. I guess I thought maybe I was, but I didn't really know what being in love is supposed to be like. Lyn just wanted me to say it all the time. I love you, over and over, and every time I said it, I wondered if I really did." He leaned closer and kissed the tip of my nose. "I'm not wondering with you. You're different."

I was different all right. "But, Jehu, now you know it all, about me, I mean. I'm not, not . . . pure." I hated that word, but I couldn't think of another one to use to describe my nonvirginal self.

"It doesn't matter," Jehu said. "It wasn't your fault. You didn't allow it. He forced you." He held both of my hands in his. "When we do it, it'll be because we're in love, because *you* want to. You'll be the first and only one I'll ever make love to."

When we do it, he had said. Not if, but when. He still wanted me. Used goods were good enough for him. I'd be his first, but he wouldn't be mine. I tried to push thoughts of Roland away. Could I have an honest relationship with Jehu if the night with Roland was always going to be between us? I looked at the sweet smile on his lips, saw his love for me in his eyes. He didn't deserve the pain my confession about Roland would cause him. I'd have to live with my deceit, and then when he kissed me again, I thought that keeping one secret wouldn't be that hard to do.

Chapter 27

W̱HEN MERVIN CAME OVER THAT NIGHT, HE BROUGHT A handful of travel brochures with him. "After Key West, we might get bitten by the travel bug and want to go some other places," he said, spreading the colorful brochures across our kitchen table. The first pamphlet he opened was about Gatlinburg, Tennessee, where you could ride in a chairlift up to the top of a mountain. There was another depicting the colors of Ruby Falls, and the third one he unfolded showed a glossy photograph of a family playing in the sand on Panama City, Florida. I wanted to see all of those places. The most interesting trip I'd ever been on was to the state capitol in Jackson when our sixth-grade class went there on a school bus tour. I knew he was trying to keep Mama's mind away from the upcoming hearing and on something pleasant, but Mama barely glanced at the brightly colored pictures. In the last day or so her former confidence had begun to wane for no reason we could discern. Tonight she flip-flopped into total pessimism. Now she was sure the charges against her weren't going to be dismissed. "I'm not going anywhere," she said. "All I'm going to see are three cement walls and some bars with a big lock on them."

"Frieda, you've got to think positive," Mervin said. "If you expect defeat, that's what you'll get. When I talk to a customer, I don't think they won't buy anything. I think they'll want everything I've made and have trouble choosing between an angel, a squirrel, or a gnome. And usually that's just what happens. Good thoughts bring big rewards."

I thought about this philosophy. Maybe it worked for some people, but Mervin's life hadn't been anything like ours, and I suspected that people like Mama and me could burn up our brains with good thoughts and the reward would just be more bad news.

Praying was our only hope, and Mama wasn't even doing any of that. I prayed everywhere. When I took walks around the neighborhood, I prayed beneath Miss Westheimer's maple tree, over a bed of red salvia, beside the corner mailbox. "Please God, please God, please." I prayed on my knees in my bedroom, while I sat watching Ed Sullivan, while I stood in the kitchen in front of the open refrigerator door as if God was the lightbulb that illuminated our leftovers. If I'd had a megaphone like the ones the cheerleaders put to their mouths to scream "Go Cougars go," I would have lifted it toward heaven and shouted into it, asking God to save Mama and me.

On the morning of the hearing, I began praying at nine when it was scheduled to begin, and I kept on praying until I saw Mama drive up in Wallace's Galaxie at eleven o'clock. She didn't have to tell me. As soon as I ran out and saw her sitting behind the steering wheel with her hands wrapped around it and her eyes staring straight ahead at the back of the carport wall, I knew. God hadn't answered my prayers. Grady Abadella, the Lexie County district attorney, had won the day. We were going to trial.

Mama got fired from her job the next day. I couldn't blame Mrs. Salloum for sending her home. She was a zombie, walking around so stiffly with glazed eyes, no one would want to be around her, much less trust her to sell anybody face powder. After Mama was sent home, she spent the days reading paperback novels with covers of wild-haired women and men entwined in front of castles. Mervin tried to get her to go out to dinner; Papaw begged her to visit him and Miss Louise; even her old friend Cybil, who hadn't called in a couple of months, asked her if she'd like to go to the movies with her some night. Mama just kept reading, turning page after page, lost in the world of fictional romance where maidens got rescued by handsome men with muscular thighs.

I was nearly as depressed as she was, and I was scared, scared of not only the outcome but of the road that was going to lead to it all. Night after night I lay in bed seeing myself sitting on the chair in the witness stand. Grady Abadella pointed his finger at me and shouted "Liar liar" over and over until I would leap out of bed pressing my palms against my ears to shut out the accusing tones. And worst of all, I had learned that there would be many nights of dread because the trial wouldn't begin until months from now. I would be back in school by then, and from Monday through Friday each week, I would suffer the curious looks, the whispers, the thrill of horror the kids would feel sitting in a desk next to the daughter of a murderer on trial. I had thought that having Jehu's adoration would change everything in my life. God had granted my request for his love, but now I wished I hadn't prayed for him. I considered that maybe God only answered a limited number of prayer requests, and I had used up too many of mine asking for trivial things like breasts and madras skirts, and a great tan that wouldn't peel. I thought again of suicide, of running away, but I couldn't abandon Mama. She needed me more than ever.

Late on Wednesday afternoon I was setting the table for dinner for three as usual now that Mervin ate with us every night. "Layla Jay, come here a minute," Mama called from her room. "I want to talk to you before Mervin gets here." She wanted to tell me that Mr. Albright had phoned and wanted her to come to his office the next morning. "I want you to go with me," she said. Mama held out her hand without looking at me. When I reached forward and took it, her fingers were as cold as an ice cube. "I'm scared, honey. I need you with me."

Fear struck like a lance in my chest. "Why?"

"The reason Mr. Albright wants to see me is the district attorney sent him the reports for the discovery."

"What's that?"

"It's any evidence that he's got to use against me."

"What's he got?"

"That's what we'll find out tomorrow. All Mr. Albright said was that I had an enemy I didn't know about." She pressed her cheeks with her palms. "Somebody wants me to get convicted, and I don't know who or why."

That night I left Mama and Mervin cuddled up on the couch and went to my room, saying I was exhausted. I was, but I couldn't sleep, worrying and wondering what the DA had up his sleeve. Who would want Mama to go to jail? Every man in Zebulon adored her. A lot of women were jealous of her, but none of them would know anything about what had happened that afternoon. On our first visit to his office, Mr. Albright had explained that, according to the legal definition for voluntary manslaughter, Mama had killed Wallace in a heat of passion caused by adequate provocation. When I had asked what that meant, he said, "Heat of passion may be provoked by fear, rage, anger, or terror. Your mother lost self-control and acted on impulse, without reflection, to protect you. When a person witnesses a crime against a close relative, that's justifiable cause for adequate provocation."

But now someone was saying that Mama didn't have justifiable cause. How could anyone know if she did or not? I was never going to figure it out, and I was never going to get to sleep. I remembered Papaw saying that worrying about something never kept him awake. "You can't do anything about your problem when you're in bed, so why worry about it until you get up the next morning?" Good advice, but hard to follow, I thought. I turned to God. "Dear Lord, smite Mama's enemy like you did the Philistines. Forgive Mama her past sins and me mine. Be on our side."

WHEN WE ARRIVED at Mr. Albright's office the next morning, the receptionist, Miss Kathleen, who reminded me of Miss Kitty on *Gunsmoke,* ushered us down the hall to the library, where a large conference table took up most of the room. Mama and I sat side by side in two of the eight burgundy leather chairs placed around the dark polished table. In minutes Mr. Albright came in. He walked over to me first and offered his hand. "Good morning, Layla Jay. How are you doing?"

I watched his eyes for any sign that he knew I'd kissed his son the day before. Nothing there that I could discern. "Fine," I said.

He pressed Mama's hand in both of his and then pulled out a chair directly across from her. Mama didn't look like herself. Despite wearing a bright red-and-white polka-dot dress with fake pearls, she looked awful. Fear had aged her, and I imagined that this was a preview of how she would look when she turned into an old lady with loose papery skin and liver spots. Even her voice sounded years older. "So what's up?" she asked, crossing her arms over her breasts. "What's in that discovery report that I should be worried about?"

Mr. Albright looked down at the typed pages and yellow legal pad he had laid on the table in front of him. "I'll get to that, but first let's summarize the process and the facts from the beginning."

I looked up at the twin brass chandeliers that hung over the table. There were no windows in the room and the lights that illuminated the table and chairs didn't extend to the dark corners. In the shadows an artificial ficus sat in a terra-cotta pot, and across from it a pedestal table held a bronze bust of some ancient Greek or Roman man. Mr. Albright shuffled the papers, and with his pen pointing to the top line, he began his summary. "Now, after your arrest, at the arraignment, you were formally charged with voluntary manslaughter." He looked over at me. "You remember the definition?" When I nodded, he went on. "You pled not guilty to the charge, so now the burden of proof is on the prosecution. Grady Abadella, the DA who's got the case, has to present evidence that the state is going to use against you. They must prove that, although you lost self-control, you committed an unlawful act without proper caution or requisite skill, and this constitutes a reckless disregard for human life, amounting to criminal negligence."

"Can you just say all this in plain English? Sounds like legal gobbledygook to me," Mama said.

"I thought I was," Mr. Albright said with a smile. "Okay, let's go at this from another angle. If asked . . . which he was by me . . . the DA is required to disclose the evidence that he intends to use at the trial. This discovery material includes the police report, medical records for the autopsy and for Layla Jay, and all witness statements."

"I gave a statement about what happened," I said. "He wrote it all down."

"Right. And your mother gave hers, which she didn't have to do without counsel, but volunteered." He frowned a little at Mama then. "So the DA looks at all of these things and decides how he's going to prove his case. Now, there are several ways to prove your culpability. For example, Frieda, if you had come into your bedroom, seen what was happening, and done nothing at the time, but later broken a bottle over Wallace's head and stuck the glass in his throat, then you'd have had time to control your actions, to calm down, and we'd have a difficult time proving you acted in the heat of passion after a time elapse."

"But it didn't happen that way," Mama said. "It couldn't have been more than a couple of minutes before I slammed the bottle across that bastard's head."

"Right, and Layla Jay corroborates your time line, which, unfortunately, included a lot of hours before you reported what happened. And it's mother's and daughter's word only. There were no other witnesses."

"We wouldn't commit perjury. Put me on the stand," I said, thinking that I most definitely would be committing perjury if I told my rape story in court.

"Okay, there aren't any other witnesses," Mama said, "except Wallace, but he's busy pleading with the big judge in heaven to save his soul."

Mr. Albright ignored Mama's attempt at humor. I knew she was trying to overcome her nerves with a little levity, but Mr. Albright was more concerned with the facts than our emotions. "Another avenue the DA can take is to prove you acted with excessive force. This is the road we don't want him taking, the one we've got to worry about. We can't claim diminished capacity as you're intelligent, weren't drunk or taking drugs, so we want to prove you didn't realize that you were using excessive force."

"And the DA will say that I did? That I meant to kill Wallace and knew what I was doing?"

Mr. Albright hesitated, as though he was about to lower the boom on Mama, and I squeezed my fingers together so tightly my knuckles turned as white as the paper on the table. "Here's what he's going to say to the judge and jury." He smiled across the table at Mama. "The little judge on earth. He's going to go through the physical evidence first."

Mr. Albright went on delivering the bad news in a quiet tone without a flicker of emotion on his face, and I marveled at his composure and wondered if one of the courses they taught in law school was on how to mask your feelings in front of clients who were scared shitless. All of the physical evidence was damning. Mama had no self-defense wounds, and neither did I, there was no semen inside me, Wallace had multiple bruises on his legs from where I'd kicked him, and the blow to his head had caused a deep gash two and a quarter inches long, which meant that he couldn't have fought back when Mama grabbed the piece of glass (with her thumbprint on it) and stuck him in the external jugular vein. At some point Mama said she didn't see how she was supposed to know that he wasn't able to fight back. "I'm not a doctor; did he expect me to check his pulse and take his temperature?"

Mr. Albright reminded her of the term "excessive use of force." "He had no weapon," he said.

"Yes, he did," Mama said. "And he was trying to get it inside Layla Jay." Mama was mad now. Her face flamed and I imagined her testifying in court, losing her temper when she was questioned, and I prayed silently that it wouldn't come to that. She'd get herself convicted for sure. She calmed down some, but then reached in her purse and snatched her cigarettes and lighter. After lighting up, she blew smoke across the table and said, "So let's skip the rest and get to the part about my so-called enemy. What's the dread news? Go ahead with it. I'm ready."

Mr. Albright rose and went to the door. "I'll be right back," he said.

Mama and I looked at each other. "I don't think you're allowed to smoke in here," I whispered. "There's no ashtray."

"I don't give a shit," Mama said, cupping her palm, tapping her ashes onto it. "For what this is costing us, he ought to have an ashtray the size of a plate made out of solid gold on the table."

He brought back a small glass one, handed it to Mama, and then sat back down in his place. "Do you know Bonita Garza?"

Mama laid her cigarette on the ashtray and brushed her palm off into it. "Yeah, I know her. She's a bitch. She bought some face cream from me, stuck her dirty finger in it, and tried to bring it back for a full refund. She'd used up a third of the jar, too. I can't stand her."

"You've got a lot stronger reason for not liking her now. According to her statement, she told the DA that you threatened to kill Wallace some months ago."

"What?" Mama and I said the word together.

"Threatened to kill him."

"Bullshit," I said in Papaw's absence.

"Well, if she gave a false statement, we can press charges. But let me tell you what she said; then you can tell me how to refute it. She says that at the party at Dixie Springs Lake on the night of your accident, you and Wallace were separated and you got drunk and said," he looked down at the report, "said—and this is a quote—'Wallace is lucky he got out with his limp dick still in his Sunday pants. I ought to have cut off that useless piece of flapping skin between his legs.' Do you recall saying that?"

Mama sucked in her breath. "Sort of. I was drunk. But I didn't say I wanted to kill him, just castrate him."

Mr. Albright looked down again. "Miss Garza goes on to say, 'Frieda was bragging about how she could shoot her daddy's shotgun as good as any man, and she said that if Wallace or any man ever made a fool of her, she wasn't afraid to use it on him.' "

Mama stubbed out her cigarette, grinding it into the glass so hard, bits of tobacco flew out onto the table. She stood up. "Well, I'm going to go find that little black-eyed bitch and shake the crap out of her. I ought to get Pop's gun and shoot her right in her big mouth."

I looked across at Mr. Albright; he was pressing his temples with the heels of his palms. "Frieda, please. Sit down. It's saying things like that that got you in this situation. Let's try and remain calm. Now, did you say that about your father's gun?"

Mama slid down in her chair. She shook her head back and forth. "I don't know. Seems like I may have said something like that. But I was drunk; I'm not sure." She sat up straighter. "What I do remember is that she grabbed my arm when I was dancing with Scooter Peachon and told me to keep away from her man. She's always been jealous of me. There were a couple of other times she got pissed at me because she couldn't stand her dates flirting with me, and I can't help it if men find me more attractive than her. I ought to charge her with assault. I think I had a bruise on my arm." Her voice drifted down an octave. "But I had the wreck and . . ."

Mr. Albright lost his lawyer composure and sighed. "That's the other damaging part of her statement." He didn't bother to read from the paper in front of him this time. "She says that she works for State Farm Insurance Company and that you filed a claim for your car and injuries and that it was out-and-out fraud because you were drunk and they were, therefore, not obligated to pay your claim."

"They did too pay, and they paid the Worldwide Movers for the damage on the van. I wasn't charged with drunk driving, so she has no proof that I was drunk."

"Miss Garza says that you and Darryl Thomas conspired to commit fraud, that he admitted to her he filed a false report when he didn't reveal that you were drunk, and Miss Garza says, if they had known you were drunk, they'd never have paid you a dime."

"Why would Darryl tell her what he wrote?"

Mr. Albright rolled his pencil up and down the legal pad as he talked. "They were engaged for a short time, and I guess he told her when they were together."

"But they're not now?"

"No, he broke it off, and now she's out for his blood as well as yours. As Byron wrote in *Don Juan,* 'Sweet is revenge—especially to women.'"

"Yeah, and hell hath no fury like that of Frieda Andrews, right now," Mama said. "That bitch better watch her step. Still, I don't get how all of this affects the outcome of the manslaughter hearing."

I didn't listen to Mr. Albright's explanation. I didn't need to because I already understood. If Mama was the kind of woman who would cheat an insurance company, conspire with a cop, and threaten to cut off Wallace's dick and shoot him, then she might have meant to kill her husband, lie about it, and then force her daughter to back up her story. I laid my head down on the table. Suddenly, I was so tired I felt I could fall asleep with my cheek against the warm wood. I hadn't slept more than a couple of hours, and now I longed to crawl back into my bed, pull the cover over my head, and sleep until Christmas when all of this would be behind us.

Chapter 28

ANGER IS A GREAT ENERGIZER, AND MAMA'S RAGE OVER Bonita Garza's statement propelled her into a frenzy. After our meeting was over and we were back at home, Mama jerked off her clothes, and in celery green bra and panties, she hopped on her exercise bike. Hunched over the handlebars, she pumped the pedals, rotating them as fast as an airplane propeller. When Mervin came over hours later, he tried to talk her off the bike. Standing in front of the handlebars, he crooned, "Frieda, sweetheart, you've got to calm down. Whatever has happened, this isn't helping."

Mama ignored him. Her breath was ragged, sweat coursed down between her breasts and trickled across her stomach, dampening her panties. When she spoke, Mervin leaned closer. "Bitchbitchbitchbitch," she gasped, pedaling harder.

Mervin looked across the room to where I sat on the couch as if to seek my help. "Been on the bike on and off all day," I said. "Her feet will slip off the pedals pretty soon, and then she'll get off for a while." I pointed to the bruises on her calves where the pedals had caught her each time one of her feet slipped. "She can still feel pain, I guess."

"What happened?" He left Mama to her pedaling and sat in the chair beside the couch.

I explained about Bonita's statement and told him the facts as Mr. Albright had laid them out for us. "It doesn't look good for Mama," I said. "I could tell Mr. Albright is worried."

Mervin dropped his head in his hands. "Oh shit," he mumbled to the floor.

"Yeah. Mama's scared . . . and reeeeal mad at Bonita Garza."

Mama screamed a short little yelp and fell sideways onto the floor. Mervin rushed over and helped her to the couch. She was crying, making the most pitiful sounds I'd ever heard come out of her. "I'm going to jail," she wailed. "I'll spend all of the good years I've got left with a bunch of *women*."

Mervin pulled her head against his chest and patted her every place his hands would reach. "No, no, no," he said. "You're going to stay right here with me and Layla Jay. We'll get this worked out. I was there that night, too. Did you forget it was me who invited you?"

Mama rubbed her wet face against his shirt and looked up. "No, yes, well, I didn't remember who was standing around when I was talking to Bonita. Did you hear me saying something about killing Wallace?"

Mervin's eyes shifted across the room over Mama's head, and I knew he was considering whether or not to tell a lie. A lifetime of thirty plus years of honesty was a high hurdle to jump over into Mama's messy life. "Let him lie," I prayed. "Just this once, bend Your rules, Lord. It's for a good reason. Mama needs his help so bad."

God won out. My prayer wasn't answered. Mervin eased Mama up into a sitting position and wiped tears from her face with his long fingers. "Well, no, I was outside most of the night sitting on top of the picnic table with Rafe and Howie. You kind of dumped me at the party." He chewed his lip. "But I could say I know you wouldn't hurt a fly. And I've known Bonita since high school. It wouldn't be the first time she's exaggerated something. I could testify to that. Might help some."

"Oh poot, nobody will care if you say that." Mama stood up and shot him a mean look with her eyes narrowed. "I understand now. You were only pretending you were going to help me. I need a shower. I'll see you, Mervin. Why don't you get on home to your stupid cows and little stone people? They don't ask you to do much for them."

Mervin watched her sauntering across the room toward the hall. "You want me to lie? Say I was there?"

Mama stopped and turned back around. She adopted a Scarlett O'Hara drawl when she said, "I wouldn't dream of it, Mervin. Why, everyone in Zebulon knows you're too perfect to do such an awful thing."

Mervin looked miserable, like he might even cry. "Frieda, honey, it wouldn't matter if I did. Bonita knows I wasn't there when you said those things. Besides, lots of people know we're dating, and they'd say I was just trying to get you off because . . . because I love you."

Mama turned her back to us and unhooked her bra and stepped out of her panties. She held them up and then sailed them over her right shoulder to land on the coffee table. "A souvenir," she said. "We're *not* dating. I don't want to see you anymore."

We watched her naked butt shimmying down the hall, then looked at each other with open mouths. "Wellll," I said, not having any other words to say.

Mervin stood up, then sat down again. He grabbed the back of his neck, pulling his elbows together in front of him. "Damnit to hell and back," he said.

"She's desperate," I whispered. Tears were on their way and I'd never cried in front of him. I thought of the day he'd taken me to his farm. I thought of the little angel holding the bird in her outstretched hand. I understood that a man who spent his days creating angels to watch over the deceased would have a hard time lying to a black-robed judge in a courtroom. Maybe if Mama had gone out there and seen what I had, she'd understand, too. But she hadn't gone.

"I know she's desperate," he said.

As we sat listening to the sound of the rush of water in the shower, I considered the character flaws that I seemed to have inherited from her. I hadn't thought we were all that much alike. Hadn't Mama said I took after Grandma when I'd judged her? But Mama judged, too. We were both slobs, both stubborn and proud. We cared about breasts and makeup and men. And *c'est la vie*. And, worst of all, we were both expert liars. As I tallied our behaviors, I worried our multiplying faults equaled bad character and only the Lord knew what we might be capable of next. "I'm sorry," I said to Mervin. I didn't know what I was sorry for, but maybe I wanted forgiveness for Mama. "Mama didn't mean what she said. She's just real real upset."

Mervin almost smiled. "Well, if she thinks I'm leaving she's got another thought coming. I don't give up easily. When an arm breaks off one of my figures, I don't throw it away. I fix it."

I doubted Mervin was going to fix things with Mama as easily as he could repair a statue, but I nodded my head in encouragement. I remembered Mama's triumphant smile when Wallace and I drove up that day and saw his things boxed up. "Hit the road, Jack" were the words she had said. And Wallace had known that there was no use in arguing. But Mervin wasn't Wallace. Not by a long shot.

When Mama came back into the den, she was wearing a white turbaned towel and her green satin robe. Her face, scrubbed clean of makeup now, was etched with worry lines between her thin eyebrows. She brushed past Mervin's chair as though he were a cloud of smoke from the lit cigarette she held and went into the kitchen. We heard her slamming a pot on the stove, and I shrugged my shoulders. I had no idea what she was going to do now that she knew Mervin hadn't obeyed her and gone home.

She boiled a wiener. Only one, and from that I deduced that she had placed me in Mervin's camp and wasn't about to feed a traitor. I remembered the day I had sided with her against Grandma not long before Grandma died, and I broke out in a sweat, worrying this was another precursor to tragedy. With the boiled wiener in her hand, she flipped on the television set, backed up, and sat on the floor watching the screen light up with Walter Cronkite and the evening news.

"Frieda, we need to talk," Mervin said.

She ignored him.

"Mama, don't be mad. You know Mervin would help you if he could."

"Shhhh, listen," she said, waving her wiener toward me. Walter was talking about our state. The bodies of three civil rights workers had been found in Philadelphia, Mississippi. "Now that's a real crime. Three bodies, not just one, and whoever killed them will probably get off and I'll be hearing about it from prison."

"You're not going to prison, Frieda," Mervin said, as he walked over and squatted beside her. Mama dropped her head toward the floor. "Look at me. Please, honey."

Mama jumped up, wheeled around, and crouched down like she was going to fly at him. He leapt up and took a step back as she moved toward him. "You're not here. I told you to leave." She pointed her half-eaten wiener at the door. "Now go!"

I couldn't stand it any longer. I wasn't going to let her ruin the one good thing she'd invited into her life. "Mama! Don't do this. Mervin loves you. Finally, somebody loves you, don't throw him out."

Mama looked around Mervin's big frame and her eyes locked with mine. I knew I'd overstepped the boundaries of a daughter, but I held my ground and didn't look away. "You love him," I said. Then in a much softer voice, "Don't you, Mama?"

She dropped her eyes to the floor, then lifted them to Mervin's face. Slowly, she nodded her head up and down. "I guess I do," she said. His arms encircled her and I let out a big whoosh of air.

I was flat worn out. I felt like I'd been on that exercise bike pedaling to the moon and back. "I'm going out," I said, figuring they needed some time alone. Locked in a clench without a sliver of light between them, the wiener on the floor beside their feet, they didn't hear a word I said. I opened the door and crept out to the carport, where Mervin's work truck was parked behind Wallace's Galaxie. I peeked in the bed of the truck and saw a stack of cement bags, a wheelbarrow, and a big tin drum. Climbing over the tailgate, I stepped over the cement bags and sat down on the drum. The setting sun cast a golden radiance over the houses across the street, and I imagined all of the happy families sitting down to a nice dinner of fried chicken and creamed corn. They would all be laughing, telling one another stories about what had occurred during the day. The mothers would smile at their children and remind them to brush their teeth before they came in to read them a story and tuck them in bed. I tried to remember if Mama had ever read to me, but all I could conjure up was the image of Mama weaving up the walk at Grandma's with a man wrapped around her like honeysuckle vines twisted around a fence pole. I told myself I didn't care. Who wanted to live in one of those boring houses where nothing exciting ever happened? Not me. I was destined to have a life filled with adventure. I'd travel someday, get out of Mississippi, go to Paris, France, and scores of other exotic places.

Ten-year-old Gaylord Daniels brought me back to Fourth Street as he came running toward me yelling, "Here, Daisy, Daisy, come. Stop." His brown-and-white cocker spaniel was making a getaway. I cupped my hands around my mouth. "Run, Daisy, run," I yelled. "Don't let him catch you." Gaylord snapped his head around as he passed in front of our drive, but kept on running on his fat stubby legs down the middle of the street. He'd never catch that dog. "Stupid boy," I said. But I was jealous of him. I missed the animals on Papaw's farm. I'd wanted to bring one of the yard dogs or barn cats when we moved into town, but Mama said they weren't house-trained and she wasn't going to spend her days cleaning up after them.

I wondered how long I should stay outside. How long did it take to have sex if you were in love? It wouldn't be as quick as what had happened with Roland, and in the movies, they always cut away to an ocean or a grove of swaying treetops, so you didn't know how much time had passed until you saw the couple readying themselves to go home, and sometimes they even skipped that part.

Gaylord came back down the street carrying the dog beneath his arm. "Too bad," I said. "You didn't escape, did you, Daisy?"

"Shut up, Layla Jay. You wish you had a dog to chase. All you've got is a mama who's a murderer," he said, picking up his pace.

I stood up, thinking I could catch him since he was fat and now weighed down with the dog, but then I sat back down. I didn't have the energy to smack him, and he was only saying what everyone in Zebulon was saying. After the trial everyone would know I wasn't a virgin, they would know all of our ugly secrets, and they would twist the truth of us into hideous lies just for the fun of telling it. If Mama was found guilty and hauled off to jail, a lot of the women would be smug and happy that Mama, the most beautiful woman in Zebulon, the woman every man wished was his, was locked away from their men's eyes. They'd probably pity me. "Poor Layla Jay," they'd say. "Her life is just ruined. What's to become of her?" I wouldn't be sitting in a truck bed on Fourth Street, that was for sure. And I wasn't going to live with Papaw, who'd be sleeping with his bride in Grandma's bed. Where would I go? Who would take me? I thought of June, but her mother wouldn't want me. I kicked the cement stacks. Maybe I could live with Mervin and his statues. I could be his apprentice like he'd said, learn how to use the molds and pick up the craft of carving my own statues. We'd go fishing in his pond and I'd help with the cows and chickens. It would be a good life, except it wouldn't be the life I really wanted.

I laid my head on my knees and prayed, "Please God, keep us safe from harm. Why won't you send the Holy Spirit down to save me?" I lifted my head and swayed back and forth on the tin drum, and raising my eyes, I waited for God to form an answer in the stars that were beginning to appear in the darkening sky. But the only sound I heard was the whooshing of the wind as it passed through the chinaberry trees next door.

MAMA TURNED TO BOOZE to numb her fears during the day and Valium to obliterate them at night. She began with a few beers and an occasional Valium, but before the week was out, Mama was drinking whiskey all day with a Valium chaser. I thought it would hardly matter now if she were convicted because she'd already abandoned her life. And consequently, I was forced to give up mine. Each time Jehu called, I'd hang on to the phone like it was a life raft, but always I'd look over at Mama passed out on the couch or slumped over the kitchen table, and I'd tell him I didn't want to see him.

Mervin showed up every night, begging Mama to stop her crazy binge drinking. They fought over a bottle of Evan Williams like two lions over a kill, and I was terrified Mervin was going to lose patience with Mama and give up on helping her. He took me to the Piggly Wiggly, helped me with the dishes, and carried Mama to bed plenty of nights, but I couldn't quite trust that he wasn't going to turn out to be another name in Mama's Book of Lost Men. After Mervin and Mama had another big fight, this one worse than all the others, he didn't show up for three nights in a row. I told myself I hadn't really liked him all that much anyway. Who wanted to spend their lives with a man who talked to cement people every day.

Since God didn't seem to be listening to me, I looked to Papaw and Miss Louise as our saviors. Every time they came over, Mama fought with Miss Louise just as fiercely as she had with Grandma. Miss Louise was worried that Mama would become addicted to Valium, although Dr. Bonner, who gave her the prescription, said it was perfectly safe to take and Mama needed it to calm her nerves. Miss Louise told Mama that her alcohol intake was going to damage her liver irreparably. Maybe she should see a psychiatrist. "I'm not crazy and my liver is working as good as yours," Mama screamed at her.

When Mama called Miss Louise a meddling bitch, Papaw slapped her. It was me who cried when the red streak appeared on Mama's cheek. Mama slapped him back and ran to her room, locking the door. Papaw suggested that I stay with them for a while, but I couldn't leave Mama. I had been a witness to every triumph and tragedy in her life since I was born, and no matter how much I wanted to pack my train case and squeeze into Miss Louise's Corvette to ride away with them, I couldn't leave her alone. If it weren't for me, she would never have killed Wallace. I was her witness, her only hope, and although I hated her some days, I knew I'd hate myself more if I followed Papaw and Miss Louise out the door.

Chapter 29

PAPAW AND MISS LOUISE DIDN'T GIVE UP AS EASILY AS Mervin. After the night of exchanging slaps, the next morning they were back, Papaw looking as angry as his bull before feeding time. He had a plan for Mama. "We're not quitters, Layla Jay. Get Frieda out of bed. Lou, you make us some coffee." He hadn't shaved and the white stubble on his jaw made him look like a tough guy Mama wouldn't be able to stand up to. And as I hurried down the hall to Mama's room, it occurred to me that I hadn't seen a single bandage or bruise anywhere on him lately. Marrying Miss Louise had somehow made him less prone to accidents.

As I shook Mama out of her drugged sleep, tiny drops of hope dripped down through my body. Papaw was in charge now, and when he made up his mind to get something he wanted, there was no stopping him. He'd just needed some time to figure out how to get it. "Papaw's here," I yelled into her ear. "He's mad. You'd better go talk to him or he'll be in here dragging you out by your hair."

Mama's startled eyes flew open revealing a network of red crisscrossing veins. She'd slept in a pair of turquoise shorts and a white bra. I handed her the rumpled yellow blouse that lay beside the bed. "Hurry up," I said, pushing her arm through the short sleeve. "The longer he waits, the madder he'll be."

We walked side by side into the kitchen, where Papaw stood at the sink, pouring Evan Williams down the drain. Mama didn't say a word, but pulled out a chair and eased down onto it like it was made of briars that were going to stick in her butt.

Miss Louise was ladling Folger's coffee into the percolator when Mervin knocked once and opened the door. When he walked into the kitchen, Mama looked up at him. "What are you doing here?"

"Your father invited me," he said, kissing the top of her head where a nest of tangled hair stood up like a woodpecker's tuft.

Mama couldn't seem to focus on him or anything else, and I guessed last night's Valium was still calming her nerves. "Oh" was all she said as Mervin sat down beside her.

After Miss Louise served the coffee, a bit of color resurfaced in Mama's face, but her eyes remained dull and lifeless. Papaw pulled her chair around to face him. "Now listen to me, Frieda. All those times your mama told you to straighten up and fly right, you ignored her good advice. I've watched you make mistake after mistake, and I never interfered. I thought it was best to let you figure things out on your own, but this behavior of yours has got to stop. You're not going to ruin your life and Layla Jay's, too. Not if I can help it."

Mama looked down at a spilled circle of yesterday's bourbon on her shorts. "My life's already ruined, Pop. I'm going to be found guilty and go to prison. I wish it'd be tomorrow. I can't take the waiting."

"Bullshit! You get off your ass and fight back."

I broke in, unable to keep quiet like I knew I should. "But how, Papaw? All the evidence makes it look like Mama meant to kill Wallace, and she can't even act like she's the tiniest bit sorry about it."

Miss Louise smiled, and I knew I'd hit on something that had already been discussed.

Papaw looked over at me. "She can act. She can act better than any of them movie stars up on the screen at the Palace Theater. You've seen her in some of her best roles. Think about it."

I did, and I remembered the "I don't have a pot to pee in" speech she used on all of her boyfriends way back before Wallace ever came into our lives to ruin them. "Yeah, she could do a number on her dates if she felt like it," I said. I glanced over at Mervin, wishing I had kept this thought to myself, but all of his attention was on Mama. "But I don't understand how that's going to help her."

Papaw explained it. "You and Frieda are going to practice a little play for the trial. After your testimonies, the jury will give you a standing ovation. Louise has already begun to write the script for it."

It was a good plan, but I wasn't sure it would work. Neither was Papaw, but he said it was worth a try. What did we have to lose? The major role would be played by Mama, of course, but first she had to stay sober, get her wits back together. "You can't pull this off unless you get yourself healthy. No more drinking, no more pills." Papaw said it like one of the commandments God had given to Moses.

Mervin was to be Mama's guardian angel. He would keep her safe from herself. I thought he was really her jailer because, in the following days, he never once let Mama out of his sight. He moved in with us, and although I knew there was now more fodder for the neighbors to gossip about (Frieda Andrews Ebert living with a man and her husband not even cold in his grave) their judgment of us seemed insignificant compared to the benefits of having a man to take care of us.

I don't know if Mama's hope was proportional to mine, but she quit drinking and flushed the Valium down the toilet, and she began writing down everything good she'd ever done in her life. "Mr. Albright said that I need character witnesses, people who can attest to my being a solid citizen."

My hopes were sinking. No one had ever judged Mama to be a solid citizen. She had a list of minor violations that was longer than my Christmas wish list when I was six and believed Santa Claus would bring everything I asked for. Mama had a drawer filled with speeding tickets, parking violations, fines that she'd never paid. If it hadn't been for her dating a cop, her driver's license would have been revoked a year ago. She didn't belong to a church, or a club, not even the square dance group that dosey-doed every Saturday night at the Community Center.

Mervin sat in on our brainstorming sessions, as Mama called them. They were more like light showers though. "What about a book club? Didn't you join Tina Haskins's book club one time?" he asked.

"Yeah, but I only went to one meeting. They were reading the most boring books. I couldn't get through the first one. It was a play called *Our Town,* I think. It was just as dull a place as Zebulon."

My list wasn't much better. I had joined Pisgah Methodist, but then church-hopped to Centenary Methodist to New Hope back to Pisgah, which showed I wasn't loyal to any preacher who would vouch for my being a good Christian. And, of course, one of them was dead. When I thought of my membership in the Spanish Club, I considered asking Miss Schultz to testify on Mama's behalf, but Mama had never attended a PTA meeting, much less gone to any of the Meet the Teacher nights. I scratched Miss Schultz off the list that now numbered two character witnesses . . . Mervin and June, an artist and a lesbian.

"Not to worry," Mama said. "It's our testimony that's going to do the trick for me. When you get on the stand and tell about Wallace raping you, and how scared you were of him, every mother on the jury will look at me and think, if he had raped their daughter, they'd have killed him, too. Next to me, you'll be the star witness," Mama said. I looked at the pencil she held over the piece of lavender-bordered stationery that had as many cross-outs as my list. Her pencil bore so many teeth marks it looked like a tiny comb instead of a writing implement.

I didn't want to be the star. I was having the testifying nightmares nearly every night, and no matter how much I polished and practiced my lies, I was certain I wouldn't be able to convince a jury I wasn't another Lolita, who had seduced Wallace and cost Mama her freedom. And even if I was successful, if Roland didn't show up, if June said all the right words I'd told her to say, everyone would know all the filthy details. I imagined sitting on the witness chair beside the judge with hundreds of pairs of eyes fixed on me. Those eyes would reflect their revulsion or pity, and I'd never have a chance to finish growing up like a normal girl.

Jehu assured me that this wouldn't happen. He actually believed there were hordes of nice people in Zebulon who would be praying for Mama to get off. After Mervin moved in, I had called Jehu and told him he could come back over if he still wanted to. I was sorry for how I had acted, and he understood. "With what all you're going through right now, I don't expect you to feel like seeing me some days," he said. "But I want to be there for you whenever you want me." His saying that only made me feel worse. I didn't deserve him, and I knew it. But I clung to the hope that at least some of his faith in me was justified.

June came back from Tupelo and called me before she'd unpacked her suitcase. "I thought about you the whole time we were sitting up there listening to Aunt Martha go on and on about her operation. It was torture. Mother, of course, was in heaven, taking care of her and all of the old ladies who came to visit us."

"I'm glad you're back. I missed you, too," I said, realizing that this was true. I needed a friend more than ever.

When she invited me over, I was out the door before she'd hung up the phone, yelling to Mama that I'd be back before dinnertime. June's mother didn't look happy to see me. "My goodness, Layla Jay, I swear you're so thin, you wouldn't make a shadow next to a lamppost. Is June expecting you? I don't think she's had a chance to unpack."

I had lost a lot of weight during Mama's drinking spree, but I was gaining it back now with Mervin's help in the kitchen. Mama had even rallied and made tuna casserole the night before. "June called and asked me over," I said, easing past her and hurrying down the hall toward June's room.

June was bending over her open white leather suitcase, and when she turned and saw me, she dropped the blouse she held onto the floor and ran to me. When she threw her arms around me, her hug felt nearly as good as Jehu's.

I filled her in on the days she'd been gone. She was upset for Mama and I think more than that, upset at the prospect of having to testify for us when the time came. "Let's talk about something else," I said. "Tell me about your trip." Looking relieved to stop worrying about the trial, June smiled and held up her arm to show me the charm bracelet her mother had bought for her. A tiny gold cheerleader's megaphone and a charm that was shaped like the year "64" dangled from the clasps. "I'll add to it, of course," she said, "and if you plan on getting me a present for my birthday, I'd love to have one from you."

"Sure," I said. I'd forgotten her birthday was in August. I hoped she wasn't going to have a party. I wasn't ready to face any of the kids from school just yet. I lay on her bed, beside her suitcase, and watched June as she carried stacks of clothes from the suitcase to her chest of drawers and back. "Jehu and I are going steady now," I said.

June stopped with a cosmetic bag in her hands midway to her dresser. "You are?"

"Yeah, he comes over nearly every day now."

"Oh, well, I guess I won't be seeing much of you then." She tossed the bag on the dresser and looked into the mirror where she could see my reflection.

I smiled. "Yes, you will. Nothing can change how I feel about you. You're my best friend. A boy can't be a best friend."

June's frown disappeared. "Yeah, they don't care about the same things as girls. Hey, you want to come with Mother and me tomorrow? We're going shopping for school clothes. We'll be registering soon, and all the fall fashions are in the stores now. Everyone is going to be wearing culottes this year."

I didn't know what culottes were, and since Mama had lost her job, I knew I wouldn't need to know. "We can't afford much of anything. Mama got fired."

June plopped down on the bed beside me. "Oh, that's terrible. Why?"

"Right after the hearing, she was too upset to work, and even though she's better now, I doubt they'll hire her back."

"Maybe they will. Everybody knows your mother is the best makeup artist in Zebulon. Maybe in the whole state." She stroked my hair, running strands through her fingers as she talked. "She ought to go down there and ask them to give her another shot."

I closed my eyes. Her fingernails against my scalp felt wonderful. "Well, right now she's just trying to figure out what to say on the witness stand."

June leaned over and kissed my cheek. "Is that all right? Just a kiss on the cheek? I know how you feel about, about the other," she said.

I sat up and kissed her forehead. "It's all right. Sometimes I wish I felt the same way about you as you do about me. Girls are much easier to love than boys in a lot of ways. Jehu will never understand me the way you do."

June's happiness spread over her face. She wrinkled her nose and laughed. "And you want me to like boys and get married."

"I want you to be happy," I said, and I meant it. If it turned out that June was going to be a lesbian forever, I hoped she'd be a happy one, and that someday a girl or some woman would love her the way she wanted to be loved.

Chapter 30

$\mathcal{A}$s the stifling hot August days passed and the begin-ning of another school year loomed closer, I began to have panic attacks. The first one occurred in front of Mechanics State Bank. Mama had gone into the new gray stone building to transfer her savings into our checking account, and I was waiting for her in the Galaxie outside. She didn't want to go out, but Mervin and Papaw both insisted that she needed to put on a look of innocence and not hide out in the house like a guilty person. So Mama had donned her least sexy dress, applied pink lipstick, and brushed her hair into a soft page-boy style for this outing. "I feel like Donna Reed or Harriet Nelson," she said when we left the house. "The two most pathetic women on TV. Next thing you know, I'll be baking cookies in a housedress every day, begging Mervin to let me pack him a lunch."

"You look nice, Mama," I told her. And she did. I didn't care about the cookies, but I figured Mervin would die of happiness if she offered to make him his favorite meatball sandwich.

She had just come out of the bank and was standing by the door talking to some man I didn't recognize when I looked up and saw

Roland, swinging a Vest's Shoe Store bag, walking across Main Street. As he came closer, I slid down in the seat, hoping he wouldn't see me, but I hadn't reacted quickly enough. He jogged up to my open window. "Hey, Layla Jay," he said. "How you been?"

His tan had faded to a light caramel color and his blond hair had darkened to the shade of wheat bread. "Fine," I mumbled, looking across the sidewalk willing Mama to stop talking so we could leave.

"I'm on break between summer school and fall semester," he said. He reached through the window and touched my arm. "I heard about what happened with your stepdad. I remembered how you crawled in the window so he wouldn't see you that night."

I couldn't breathe much less speak. Something heavy had landed on my chest and was cutting off all the air that was supposed to be flowing through my body. The pain was excruciating and I pushed back against the seat, trying to relieve the pressure. I tried to suck in the hot air but my vision was blurring and my stomach rose up in my throat. I could hear Roland's voice, but it was a roar of unintelligible sounds. Then Mama was there pushing my head down between my knees, fanning my face with her deposit slip. I fell sideways onto the seat, and although the pain subsided, my arm ached so badly I didn't feel I could lift it. Roland had brought water from the cooler inside the bank, and as I sipped a little from the paper cup, my vision began to clear.

"My Lord, Layla Jay, you scared me to death," Mama said. "Can you sit up? I need to get you home."

"I'm all right now," I said. And except for the exhaustion and aching, I was. "I don't know what happened to me."

"You turned pale as a ghost," Roland said. I hadn't noticed him standing outside the open car door. He shifted his eyes to Mama. "I was saying how sorry I am for your troubles, and all of a sudden, she started looking funny."

"Well, thanks for your help. I'm going to take her home and put her to bed." Mama leaned over me and closed the door, and we drove away, leaving him standing there in the parking lot beside his Vest's bag.

By the time we got home, I was feeling nearly normal, but Mama insisted I lie down for a while. The aching was subsiding, but I had never felt so exhausted and I quickly fell asleep.

When Miss Louise came over with Papaw later in the day, she said it sounded like I'd had a panic attack. "What's that?" I asked. She sat down beside me on the bed and waved everyone away. "Let me visit with Layla Jay alone for a while," she said. After Mama, Papaw, and Mervin left my room, Miss Louise explained that a panic attack wasn't an illness. "You're not sick."

"But why did it happen?"

"Well, usually a panic attack is brought on when someone is feeling very very anxious or fearful. Did something happen that really upset you?"

I thought of Roland and my heart began to beat fast again. "No, I was just talking to a boy I know. Nothing big happened." I worried there was no conviction in my voice.

But there must not have been, because Miss Louise lifted my hand in hers. "Honey, did he ask you about the trial? Was that it?"

Tears formed so fast I didn't have time to hide them from her. She held me in just the way Grandma had in the dream. Crying had never felt so good, and I wished I could stay cuddled against Miss Louise until the trial was over. After I blew my nose on the tissue she handed me, she lifted her legs onto the bed and sat with her back against the headboard of my bed. I scooted up beside her. "Now, let's talk," Miss Louise said. "I want you to tell me what you've been keeping deep inside you that's causing you to be so upset. Of course, you're worried as we all are about your mama, but is there something more?"

I wanted to tell her everything, but I said, "Not really. You're right. I'm just worried about the trial like everybody is."

"And you're scared about testifying, having to tell about Wallace raping you?"

I bowed my head. Miss Louise was a nurse and I wasn't sure if nurses had a sixth-sense skill that could diagnose lies. "Yes. I don't want to have to say it all in front of a bunch of people. You know what they'll all think of me after."

Miss Louise patted my thigh. "The judge will clear the courtroom when you testify if Mr. Albright asks him to."

"I know, but there'll still be all the jurors and the DA and the court people who don't leave."

Miss Louise looked as serene as she had when she was directing Mama's exercises after her accident. "Well, that's true, but your mother has a better chance with a jury than with a judge. She needs some women to be on the jury who will understand why she did what she did, and the more people there are to decide her guilt, the better it will go for her."

"I know, but it's still too many people, and even if it were only the judge, I'm worried I might mess up, say the wrong thing, and then Mama will be found guilty and it will be *all my fault*." I was about to cry again, and I pressed my lips together and clenched my fists.

Miss Louise looked upset now. "Oh, Layla Jay, bless your heart. It's not your fault. You must believe me. You'll do fine. Mr. Albright will see to that. By the time you take the stand, you'll be so prepared, it'll seem like you're reciting the alphabet."

I didn't believe her for a minute, but I tried to smile. "Yeah, I guess I'm just a worrywart. Mountains out of molehills is what Grandma used to call it."

"Your Grandma was a smart lady, and you take after her." Miss Louise leaned over and kissed my cheek. "I'm so proud to have you as my stepgranddaughter. I love you as much as if you were my own blood."

"I love you, too," I said. I was feeling something so warm inside sitting there beside her, I felt that maybe I could call it love.

I had asked Miss Louise not to tell Mama what I'd said that afternoon, and she didn't tell until days later . . . after I had another attack. It happened the next Sunday when I went with June's family for the service at Pisgah Methodist Church. Wallace showed up again, and this time he didn't vanish, but pointed his finger at me and called me a liar in the same voice as the DA in my nightmares. After I fell over on June's shoulder clutching my chest with my sweat dripping onto her lap, several ladies helped me back to the fellowship hall and brought tissues and water. This time I knew what to expect, and although I was still scared that something might be wrong with my heart, I recovered in less time and was able to eat a cookie before we left.

June's mother told Mama she thought I ought to see a doctor, and Mama agreed even though I told her Miss Louise said a panic attack wasn't an illness. Mama wanted to be sure she was right and made an appointment with Dr. Tunnekin, who was new in town and didn't know our history. "He won't know anything about us and can be objective,"

Mama said. "And Louise said he was a resident at Johns Hopkins. That's in New York or some big city like that. He'll know a helluva lot more than these Zebulon hacks."

I liked Dr. Tunnekin. He was from Istanbul and had a lilting accent that enchanted Mama. And although he was pretty old, in his forties, he was a handsome man with coppery skin and dark almond-shaped eyes. After hooking me up to a cardiogram machine with a ticker tape, he said my heart was perfect. I was the healthiest patient he'd seen since he'd arrived in Zebulon three months ago. And Mama could have saved a lot of money because his diagnosis was the same as Miss Louise's. I was having panic attacks, nothing life threatening. "Athletes often experience these same sensations after intense activity, such as running a long race. Their heartbeats accelerate exactly like yours did. You wouldn't worry about yourself if you reacted this way after participating in a strenuous sport, would you?" When I shook my head "no," he smiled. He did have one concern though. "If you were an automobile driver, I would prohibit that activity until these attacks subside," he said in his lovely cadence. "And if the attacks continue or become more prolonged, I would suggest seeing a specialist."

"What kind of specialist?" I asked, bumping my feet against the exam table.

"A therapist. Someone who could ascertain the source of your anxiety."

A head doctor. The last person I wanted to see was someone who would find out everything about me, discover all my secrets. "Can't you just give me a pill or something?"

Dr. Tunnekin shook his head. "I'd prefer not to right now. All of these new drugs like Valium, I feel they only mask our patients' problems. They don't effect a cure for the source."

Mama shook her head up and down in agreement. She had loads of experience in masking. When Dr. Tunnekin asked me to step outside while he talked to Mama in private, an alarm bell bonged in my head. I didn't know what he was going to say, but I figured I wasn't going to like it.

Mervin was waiting in the outer office and I sat with him while Mama and Dr. Tunnekin talked. "You okay, kiddo?" Mervin asked.

"Fit as a fiddle. He thinks I might be crazy though. He's talking to Mama about it now."

Mervin laughed. "Well, she'll set him straight." He pinched my arm. "You're the sanest one in the bunch, and nobody knows that better than Frieda."

But when Mama came out of the office, she looked so upset I thought she might be the next panic attack victim. "We need to talk, Layla Jay," she said.

With my heart pounding, I followed them out to the Caddy and asked Mervin to put the top down even though I'd just curled my hair. The wind cooled my hot face and I laid my head back and stretched my arms out across the leather seat. We were headed for Gatlinburg, where I would sit on the chairlift that would take me to the very top of the mountain.

I waited all afternoon for Mama to call me for the big powwow, but she never did. When I asked to go over to June's, I expected her to say no, but she said, "Take off, but be back by six. We're going out to dinner tonight."

When I told June about the doctor visit, she said she was glad there was nothing seriously wrong with me. "If anything terrible happened to you, I don't know what I'd do," she said. "Did he say why you're having these attacks?"

"He doesn't know why, but I do," I said.

"And you don't want to tell me the reason?"

"I can't," I whispered. "I can't tell anyone, not even you." I knew June was hurt that I wouldn't confide in her, but I figured she was better off not knowing that her best friend was a liar who had stolen an entire box of her family's stuff.

Mama, Mervin, and I went to The Little Caboose for dinner. The owner, Mr. Headley, had been a conductor on the Illinois Central, and when he retired, he bought a caboose that was being retired at the same time and fixed it up as a small restaurant. As I sat in the booth staring at our reflection in the window, I thought that we looked like a normal happy family, laughing and clinking glasses to toast our new life that would commence as soon as Mama's trial was over. But every now and then, when Mama thought I wasn't looking, I would catch a flash of sorrow crossing her face; then just as quickly, as if she were a magician, the vanished smile would reappear. I thought of Papaw bragging on her acting skills and knew that I was the audience for tonight's performance. "Isn't this the best fried chicken you ever ate?" She was nearly squealing with delight as she waved a drumstick over her plate. Mervin didn't notice that for all her enthusiastic food waving, very little of it was headed to her mouth. But I did. Something was terribly wrong, and Mama had devised this little outing to keep me from finding out what it was.

Chapter 31

MAMA WAS GONE ALL MORNING THE NEXT DAY. SHE'D LEFT the house before I woke up, and since Mervin was back at home with his cement people now that Mama was safely off the booze and pills, I had the house to myself. I called Jehu who arrived within fifteen minutes with a bouquet of red carnations. "For me?" I said, as I took them from his outstretched hand.

He kissed me. "For you. I bought them yesterday while you were at your doctor's appointment."

I found a glass vase in the kitchen with only one chip on its rim and filled it with water. As I cut the stems on an angle with a knife like Grandma had taught me, Jehu stood behind me rubbing my back. "So what's the occasion?" I asked.

"I thought you might be sick, and you'd be in bed and need flowers to cheer you up."

"You cheer me up." The vase was too large and some of the stems were bent, bowing the flowers over the side, but it was still a lovely arrangement. We hadn't had any flowers in the house for a long time, and now I realized how much I had missed their beauty. "There," I said. "Aren't they gorgeous?"

"Not any prettier than you," he said, kissing my neck.

I brought the vase into the den and set it on the coffee table north-west of Meridian. "Thanks. I can't remember the last time anyone gave me flowers. It was probably the corsage you gave me before the dance."

"Think of all the time we wasted," Jehu said. "I could have been bringing you flowers for all those months."

We sat on the couch and I snuggled against his chest. "A lot has changed this past year."

Jehu slid his hand up and down my arm, tickling my skin. "So what did the doctor say was wrong with you?"

"Panic attacks. Over the trial and all I guess. It's like a runner feels after a race. Nothing to worry about." I wasn't going to mention the shrink. Jehu might not want to go steady with somebody who turned out to be a nutcase.

"My dad said Judge Middleton is trying your mother's case."

"Is that good or bad?"

Jehu shrugged. "I don't know. I think he's an old fart though. I wish there was something I could do to help. We didn't make it to church on Sunday, but I prayed for you and your mother."

"Maybe God will listen to you more than He does to me," I said. "Here lately, I don't feel like He's taking my calls, and something's up with Mama. I don't know what it is, but she's hiding something from me. When she was on the phone last night and I passed by her, she stopped talking until I went down the hall to my room."

"I think she was talking to my dad. I heard him say 'Frieda' a couple of times while he was on the phone."

"Wonder what it's about." I sat up. "Do you think something has happened I don't know about?"

"I doubt it. She'd tell you if it was important, wouldn't she?"

"Maybe," I said.

"What I have to say is very very important," Jehu said. Cupping my chin in his palm, he lifted my face to his. "And it's this. I'm sure now. I love you, Layla Jay."

The next hour was pure bliss. Lying in his arms, feeling the length of his body against mine, every kiss and every touch was packed with the love we both felt. After he left, I lay on the couch feeling as languid as a cat taking a nap in the sun. I couldn't imagine having a panic attack ever again.

I BELIEVE THAT IF BAD MEMORIES weaken us, good ones strengthen us for the terrible moments that are sure to come. I held on to that belief when I saw Mama's ravaged face as she came into my bedroom late in the afternoon. I was sitting on the floor writing in the diary Miss Louise had given me. She told me that writing down my feelings would be a good way to release some of my fears. "Sometimes we can put on paper what we can't say aloud," she said with a wink. I had just written "Today Jehu told me he loved me. He brought me flowers, too. They are . . ."

When I looked up at Mama and saw the misery written on her face, I dropped my pen. "What's the matter?"

"We've got to talk" was all she said as she turned toward the door.

"Okay, let me finish this sentence," I said. After scribbling the date on the bottom of the page, I told myself that no matter what she was going to say, Jehu's love would get me through it. I felt strong, able to overcome any bad news Mama was going to tell me.

MAMA WAS WAITING FOR ME slumped in the armchair in the den. She noticed the flowers and I told her that Jehu had brought them, but I didn't tell her he'd said he loved me. Our love was to be a secret between just him and me. I wasn't even going to tell June right away.

I sat on the couch on the exact place where Jehu had sat. A hint of the English Leather cologne he wore lingered on the cushion and I took a deep breath. I tried for a cheerful tone. "So what's up?" I asked Mama. "You don't look so good." Her French twist had come undone on one side and curly strands of hair fell over her left ear. She was pale and hadn't reapplied lipstick so that only a red rim circled her bare lips. Her yellow linen dress, wrinkled and limp hanging off her chair, wore a look of defeat.

"I don't care how I look," she said, kicking off her shoes. After rubbing her feet, Mama straightened up in her chair and put her hands on her knees as she leaned toward me. "Layla Jay, honey, I'm very worried about you."

"I'm . . ."

Mama held up her palm. "I know. You're fine. Today, right now, you are. But you haven't been okay for a long time. I've heard you crying in your sleep, you're having these panic attacks, and you've lost weight, too. I've been so wrapped up in preparing for the trial, getting myself straight with the drinking and the Valium and all, well, I knew I needed to talk to you about your feelings, but I just couldn't handle it." She crossed her legs and drew herself into a little tight ball. "Now I have to tell you about where I've been, who I've been talking to."

I guess my mind was trying to protect me from what I knew was coming because all I heard for a few minutes was a little girl singing, "Catch a falling star and put it in your pocket. Save it for a rainy day." Rainy day rainy day rainy day chanted inside my head.

"Layla Jay! Are you all right?"

"Uh huh. Go on."

"I called Louise yesterday while you were over at June's house and she told me what you said that day when you had your panic attack at the bank." I opened my mouth, but before I could say that Miss Louise wasn't supposed to tell, Mama said, "I needed to know, Layla Jay. She did the right thing telling me. And I talked to Dr. Tunnekin about this; he thinks, considering that you're already having these panic attacks, the trial could cause you to get a lot worse. So last night I called Mr. Albright and we met at his office this morning."

I didn't tell her that Jehu had already told me about the call. I stared at my flowers. It had been a good day, a good day, and it was getting worse, a lot worse, like me after the trial.

Mama's voice was calm, way too calm to suit me. "Now, let me just tell you what all has happened, what I'm thinking, and what I'm going to do." She lifted her purse from the floor. She'd made notes on her lavender paper. "I'll just go through the facts one by one." Her unpolished fingernail followed the list down the page as she talked. "First. Judge Middleton drew my case for the trial. This isn't good. He's not sympathetic to women, he belongs to New Hope Church, and he and his wife have never been able to have children. So all of that means I would definitely need to go with a jury trial."

"I thought we'd already decided that anyway," I said.

"Yes, but I wanted to see if there was a chance of just having the judge hear the case, so we wouldn't have to select a jury. But Mr. Albright said he wouldn't feel as confident with Middleton as he would another judge. So back to where we started, I asked Mr. Albright if I had any chance of getting off with a jury if you didn't testify." She tried to smile and failed. "I thought maybe I could give a stellar performance like Pop suggested, but Mr. Albright said even if I were Elizabeth Taylor it wouldn't make any difference unless you testified, too."

My hopes had risen and then fallen, but I was an actress, too. I shrugged as if she'd said we were out of milk again and I'd have to eat dry cereal. "So I'll testify like we expected. So what?"

Mama didn't answer for what seemed like minutes. I heard Gaylord calling, "Daisy, come. Daisy, stop." I noticed one of the carnation stems was tangled with another and not getting any water, and I reached over, pulled it out, and reinserted it in the vase. Mama's lips were moving silently like she was practicing what she was going to say, and a dread came over me like I'd never felt before. My charade couldn't last. "Mama, please. What is it?"

She closed her eyes. "Layla Jay, I just can't let you testify. I'd never forgive myself if you did. There's enough gossip going around all over Zebulon already, and after you take the stand, there won't be a person within fifty miles who won't have heard about Wallace raping you."

"The judge can order the courtroom cleared when I testify. Miss Louise told me that."

"Yeah, but do you think the jury and the other people who'll be there won't tell afterward? You know all the juicy details will leak out."

"But if I don't testify, Mr. Albright said you'd get convicted."

"Right. So there's only one door left to open for my freedom."

I took deep breaths, tried to slow my galloping heart. I couldn't have another attack. I had to find out what she meant. "What door?"

"It's called a plea bargain. Mr. Albright is going to ask Mr. Abadella, the prosecutor, to meet with us to discuss a plea bargain."

I thought of the banner over the Black and White Store on Main Street. "Bargains galore!" A bargain meant getting something cheap. What did the DA have to sell? And then suddenly I knew. He owned the store, and Mama was going to ask him to give her a bargain. Less time in jail. I prayed I was wrong. "What's a plea bargain?"

"It's a negotiated deal between the prosecution and me. In other words, I'll say I'm guilty, that I meant to kill Wallace, and then Mr. Albright will ask Mr. Abadella for a reduced sentence."

"Mama, no!"

"Honey, my mind is made up. The meeting is all set for day after tomorrow. No more waiting and worrying. We'll just get it over with." She wadded up her list and tossed it on the table beside the vase of carnations.

"But you can't say you're guilty. You didn't mean to kill Wallace."

Mama sighed. "Maybe I did. I don't know what I meant to do anymore. I know I never hated anybody as much as I hated Wallace when I saw him on top of you."

I was shaking so violently my voice wavered like an old old lady's. "But you'll go to prison. Please don't do it. I'll testify. I don't care what anybody thinks. I don't care. Please, Mama, please."

Mama moved over to the couch and pulled me against her, wrapping her arms around me in a viselike grip. She kissed the top of my head, and I thought of the night after my birthday party when she had said, "There's nothing I wouldn't do for my girl." She had meant it. She was willing to go to prison for me. "There's still a chance I could get probation or maybe even get off."

"No, you won't," I said. My fingers dug into her back and I couldn't tell whether the tears that fell between us were hers or mine.

When we finally let go of each other, we both sniffed up mucus and wiped our faces, but tears eked out as we talked. Mama said she would still need my help. And as she unfolded the plan she and Mr. Albright had discussed, a minuscule hope resurfaced inside me.

Mama asked Mervin, Papaw, and Miss Louise to stay away because we needed some mother/daughter time alone. She didn't tell them what we were going to do. "We'll wait until it's over. I don't need their advice. This is just between Mr. Albright and me and you. Our secret."

We stayed up most of the night outlining and redefining our plan. We would still follow our original ideas of what to say and how to act, even how to dress. I was to wear a Sunday dress, no makeup, socks with flats. In other words, I was supposed to look like a ten-year-old instead of a sexy fourteen-year-old. "We can't do anything about your height," Mama said, "but an Ace bandage will hide those breasts." As we schemed on through the night, I pretended we were rehearsing for a stage performance. We were the stars of a Broadway play. But every now and then as I modeled dresses for Mama's appraisal, we would look into each other's faces and see terror mixed with sorrow mirrored in our eyes.

The sun was casting a pale pink light into my bedroom when exhaustion finally overtook us and Mama and I dropped onto my bed with our arms around each other. Just before she fell asleep, Mama whispered, "Mr. Abadella has four daughters. That's lucky for us."

I didn't think we were lucky, and even if we were, we needed more than luck. When I closed my eyes, Grandma's radiant face appeared. She was smiling, nodding her head in approval. Mama's sacrificing her freedom for me was exactly what Grandma wanted. She was proud of Mama. I opened my eyes. But what did she think about me? She knew I was going to lie to the DA, break the commandment "Thou shall not bear false witness," but I hoped she understood that this time I was lying for the right reason. I wondered if God granted plea bargains. Was obedience to His commandments absolute, or was there, in Papaw's words, any wiggle room? I thought of all the prayers I had offered up. Most of them requests. And I thought of the ones God had answered and the ones He hadn't. He hadn't shown me the way to kill myself, but He had given me breasts and Jehu. Now I wished I didn't have those breasts, but I couldn't regret asking for Jehu's love. I'd prayed over and over for God to send the Holy Spirit down to me, and He still hadn't done that. How did He decide which prayers to answer and which ones to ignore? Was there even any point to my asking Him to save Mama from prison? His mind was probably already made up.

I prayed anyway. "I don't know if you will answer this one or not," I said, "but I'm asking anyhow. Mama needs your help, and I need your forgiveness for what I've done and what I've got to do. Please send the Holy Spirit down before day after tomorrow. You know we can't get through this alone. Amen."

Chapter 32

THE MEETING WITH THE DA WAS ON FRIDAY, CRUCIFIXION DAY, and Thursday held lots of surprises before we bore crosses of our own. Mama and I woke up at ten and had to hurry to get to the office by our appointment time at eleven o'clock. Mr. Albright wanted to talk to me about what I was to say to Mr. Abadella, but I felt I was already well rehearsed.

He was waiting for us by the receptionist's desk. Miss Kathleen was taking notes with her head bobbing up and down like one of Papaw's chickens pecking worms out of the ground. Mr. Albright shook my hand and waved us back to his office. "No calls," he said without looking back. I figured Miss Kathleen knew better anyway, but as we walked down the hall, I heard her faint "Yes sir."

We sat in our usual places, Mama on the couch, Mr. Albright and I in matching leather chairs. There was an ashtray on the coffee table, and as soon as Mama sat down, she opened her white purse and got out her Luckies. When she took out a cigarette, Mr. Albright leaned forward and whipped a silver lighter out of his jacket pocket and lit her up. He was prepared for us, and somehow this underpinning made me even more scared than I already was. What he said next really worried me. "Layla Jay, how's my son?"

I had no idea what to say. "Sir?"

"Jehu. I believe you see him more than his mother and I." He was smiling.

I wasn't going to start this meeting with a lie when there'd be so many coming out of my mouth later. "He's fine," I said. "I know he wasn't supposed to see me; Jehu told me, but . . ."

Mr. Albright held his pleasant expression. "Kind of a meant to be thing, huh?"

"I guess," I said, looking over at Mama for help. She was staring at the bookcase like she was in the library searching for a good read.

He crossed his legs and reached for his yellow legal pad on the coffee table and said, "It's all right. His mother and I had a talk with him last night. He's allowed to see you, just not too often. Okay?"

"Okay." Why are we talking about Jehu, I wanted to ask. We had much more important things to discuss than teenagers in love.

"Now, let's get down to it," he said, and now I saw that he was trying to help me relax, feel safe when we "got down to it."

Mr. Albright suggested questions Mr. Abadella might ask and seemed happy enough with all of my answers. Occasionally, he would suggest another word like stepdaddy instead of stepdad. "Sounds less grown-up," he said. I caught on quickly. I was a fast learner, and I had been Mama's understudy for handling men for years.

After Mr. Albright deemed us prepped for our meeting, I asked him what time we were supposed to come back the next day. "Not here. We go to him," he said. "Eight-thirty. He has to be in court by ten-thirty. Your mother knows where to go."

My heart skipped a beat. I had thought we'd be right in this room in familiar surroundings, in the room I loved so much. Going to the DA's office was going to add to my fear. I looked at Mama, and she shrugged. "That's the way they do this, Layla Jay. We'll have to follow his rules."

Just like God, I wanted to say. And how could I follow all the rules when I didn't even know what they were?

MAMA AND I WENT FOR HOT FUDGE SUNDAES, but mine melted in my hand before I'd taken a few bites. "Let's take a drive. Sitting around the house all afternoon is going to drive us crazy," Mama said.

I agreed and we took off in Wallace's Galaxie, speeding past the County Co-op, Mississippi Power and Light, and Mac's Hardware, and then we left civilization behind as Mama turned off the highway onto an unpaved road. "Where we going?" I asked.

"You'll see. Let's pretend we're pioneer women traveling across Indian Territory. We're on our way to the prairie where our men are waiting and worrying about us."

I patted the seat between us. "Is this our covered wagon?"

Mama laughed. "Yeah, it is." Driving with one hand, she fished a brush out of her purse and handed it to me. "Here's your shotgun. Use it if you have to." Mama had never been this silly, and while I smiled along with her, enjoying the playacting, I could feel my organs knotting up with anxiety. This was a little too weird, even for Mama.

We passed a row of shacks with colored people sitting and standing on their porches, fields of yellow withered cornstalks, red plowed earth that awaited the fall crops of peanuts and mustard, turnips, and collards. The rutted road jostled me against the door over and over, and I rolled up my window against the dust billowing into the car. Mama was driving too fast, and when we came upon a cow standing in the middle of the road, she slammed on the brakes and skidded us sideways. I squealed, but Mama didn't say a word. She shifted into reverse, turned the wheel, and rocketed us back forward, accelerating quickly to the same speed we'd been going. "Should have shot him," she said to me. "Next time, take aim."

Somehow Mama seemed to know the road. She would let up on the gas just before a curve like she knew it was coming up even when I couldn't see it and there were no warning signs. We crossed a one-lane wooden bridge over a little creek and she pointed to it. "Mills Creek," she said. "Used to be much bigger."

"You know where we are?"

"Yep, used to come out here all the time with Pop when I was a little girl."

When she didn't say more, I asked, "Why? What did you do out here?" I was sure they weren't visiting the residents, who were all colored people.

"You'll see in just a minute," she said.

We drove maybe two more miles before she turned into a graveled drive with a posted sign PRIVATE PROPERTY on it. "Whose is it?" I asked looking down the long stretch of three-stranded barbed wire.

Mama didn't answer me. She pulled the set of keys out of the ignition. "Get out," she said. "I want to show you something." I followed her to the locked gate, where she used one of the keys on her ring to open the padlock.

"Is this all yours?"

Mama grinned. "Come on." And she set off walking across the field, a mosaic of white-top sedge, Queen Anne's lace, yellow goldenrod, pink bull thistle, and purple milkweed. It was a glorious spectacle worthy of a movie scene.

I hurried to catch up. Wiping sweat from my brow and lifting my hair from my neck, I followed her through the waves of suffocating heat. After we trudged up a small hill, I looked down and saw a beautiful sparkling pond surrounded by pines as tall as any I'd ever seen. "Oh, it's beautiful," I said.

Mama scampered down the hill, and when she reached the pond, she kicked off her shoes and sat on the bank dangling her legs into the water. I joined her and splashed the cool water up my burning legs. "Did you buy this land?"

"No, Pop did. When I was a little girl, he bought it for me. Eighty acres of timber, the pond, and that creek I pointed out to you. It meanders over this way and runs all the way across the back of the property line."

I swatted a mosquito. "But why didn't we ever come here? Why didn't you ever tell me about it?"

Mama lay back on the grass. "Because I was hardheaded and stupid and thought I knew everything. When I was a teenager, I told Pop to sell it, that I'd rather have the money than some old land with nothing on it but red dirt and trees. We had a terrible fight, one of the only times I think Pop and Mama agreed on anything. They told me they weren't selling it, that it would always be here for me, and that someday I'd come to appreciate it." Mama sat up and swept her arms around her. "The deed is still in Pop's name, but he's told me many times that he'd sign it over to me if I would promise not to sell it." Mama grinned. "I knew better than to make him a promise I wasn't going to keep. I figured someday, after he was gone, I'd sell it and use the money to go to France, maybe buy a villa and live there." She looked down at her damp dress. "But I'm going to prison instead. I never imagined that I'd be sitting here with you wishing we lived in a house on this land."

"You don't want to go to France anymore?"

"No, not anymore. All those years I hated living in the country, scheming to get into town and away from my roots, and look what's happened to us. Sometimes we have to get what we want to know that it's not what we thought it was." She shrugged. "There's no place far enough away to escape who you are. I was raised in the country and it will always be a part of me no matter if I go to France or Timbuktu." She stood up and offered me her hand. After she pulled me to my feet, she placed her hands on my shoulders. "I wanted to bring you here today to show you your legacy. I don't know how long my sentence will be, but on every day of it, I'm going to close my eyes and see all of this, just as it is now with you and me standing beside the pond. And that's going to be my strength and my goal. I'll have a dream to hang on to, something to give me courage when I need it." Mama twisted me back and forth and smiled. "Now don't you feel like a pioneer woman out here in the wilderness? When I get out, maybe we'll build a log house with a stone fireplace. We'll ask Mervin to move in, and he can bring all of his little stone animals and people out here to live with us."

"I'd like that," I said. I was crying, but I was smiling, too.

THAT NIGHT I WOKE UP AGAIN and again to look at the clock as it ticked away the hours until our meeting the next morning. When I heard Mama stirring in her room, I knew she hadn't slept much either. Throwing back the covers, I went to my closet and pulled out my little girl dress. It was finally time to begin preparations for my performance. Staring at myself in the mirror, I leaned forward and whispered to my reflection. "You're ten, you're a little girl." I took a step back and thought that

I could never pull it off. I was just too tall and my breasts were still visible. Mr. Abadella would see right through our ruse, wouldn't he?

When Mama came out of her room, I felt better. She had transformed into June's mother. She wore pink lipstick and a light dusting of blush, just enough to give her a healthy glow, and she'd pulled her hair back with little silver barrettes shaped like musical staff notes. Her dress was perfect. It was mint green, full-skirted with a cloth belt around her small waist, and trimmed with a white lace collar and dainty white buttons. She wore low white patent heels and held a matching clutch purse. She spun around. "What do you think?"

"Perfect!"

"So are you," she said. She checked the clock in the kitchen. We had an hour to kill before we were due at the DA's office. "We've got time for breakfast. You want some cereal?"

I knew if I ate anything, it was sure to come back up. "No, do you?"

"Maybe some coffee," she said. But when she walked over to the counter where the empty pot sat beside a roll of paper towels, she turned back around. "Maybe not. What I'd really like is a shot of bourbon right now."

"There isn't any in the house. Papaw poured it down the drain," I said. But I knew there was a bottle in the house—the one I'd found beneath the sink and hidden in the cabinet over the refrigerator. I didn't know then why I'd kept it, why I hadn't poured it out, but I knew why now. "Wait! I think I know where there might be some left." I scooted a kitchen chair over and climbed on it to open the seldom-used door. There was the half-empty pint of Old Forester, and when I reached for it, the Ace bandage around my breasts slipped down. "Whoops," I said, jumping off the chair. "I'll have to remember to keep my arms down or my boobs are going to pop out like jack-in-the-boxes."

Mama didn't laugh, but she smiled and took the bottle from me. "Holding out on me, huh? Don't worry. I'll just have a tiny bit to steady the nerves," she said.

My nerves needed steadying, too, didn't they? I remembered how good I'd felt after the first couple of glasses of champagne at Mama's party. "Can I have some? My insides are rattling like castanets."

Mama took two glasses out of the cabinet. "Why not? We'll just have one," she said. "One won't hurt you." She made it a ceremony, setting the bottle between us, lining our glasses in front of it; then she carefully measured three swallows into each glass. Passing mine to me, she lifted hers and held it up for a toast. "Here's to freedom," she said.

We clinked our glasses and threw back our heads, filling our mouths with hope.

"Remember to brush your teeth," Mama said. "If old Abadella thought I was feeding you whiskey for breakfast, he'd lock me up just for being a bad mother."

"He'll never know," I said, throwing back the last drops.

We brushed our teeth together, something we'd never done before, and then we picked imaginary lint from each other's dresses, fussed over an errant curl behind Mama's barrette, and finally, when we could think of nothing else to distract us from our dread, Mama put her arms around me and said, "It's time to go. You ready?"

I hugged her tightly. "Almost," I said, "but there's just one more thing I need to do."

"What?"

"I'm scared. I need to say a prayer. Would you say one with me?"

Mama didn't answer, but she followed me to my room and knelt beside me. I don't know what she said to God, or even if she prayed at all, but with her shoulder brushing against me, I opened my eyes and saw her folded hands on the bed beside mine. On this morning we'd drunk whiskey and brushed our teeth together for the first time, and now I was sure Grandma was watching us share something else we'd never done before.

When we lifted our heads in unison, I laid my hands on top of Mama's folded ones. "I'm ready to go," I said. "I'm not scared anymore."

Chapter 33

GRADY ABADELLA WASN'T IN HIS OFFICE WHEN MR. ALBRIGHT ushered us in, so I had some breathing time to look around the room. It wasn't near as nice as Mr. Albright's office, and it was nearly as messy as our house. There were stacks of books, loose papers, files, and folders piled on the desk, the floor, and on top of the credenza beside a photograph of four little girls dressed in Halloween costumes. The princess looked to be about ten years old, the witch about eight, Red Riding Hood (I assumed as the hooded cape was red) was probably six, and the littlest one, around three years old, was a pumpkin.

Mama sat in the middle chair of the three chairs lined up in front of the cluttered desk. I sat on her right, Mr. Albright on her left. Mama kept tapping her purse as we waited, and I knew she wanted a cigarette. Mr. Albright tried to make light conversation to calm us. "Did you see in *The Lexie Journal* that a rodeo is coming to Magnolia? I was thinking of going. I haven't been to one since my grandfather took me when I was a little boy."

Mama stared at him as if he had been speaking in German or some other language she didn't know. It was up to me to fill the silence. "I like to watch the bull riders. It's so scary to see them fall off and run just before the bull's horns get them."

When the door banged open, all three of us jumped at the noise. "Good morning," Grady Abadella said, as he shook Mr. Albright's hand. Then he turned to Mama. "Mrs. Ebert, and"—he nodded at me as he walked around to his desk—"Layla Jay."

Mr. Abadella was fat. His stomach reminded me of Santa Claus's, but his smile was missing. He didn't waste any time at all. He shifted his glasses up on his bulbous nose and said, "I can impose a sentence of imprisonment for up to ten years. I'm offering five with the possibility of parole and time off for good behavior."

Five years! I'd be nineteen years old when Mama got out! I felt all the blood leaving my head; I was so weak I doubted I could stand up. I held on to the arms of my chair and stared straight ahead at the tiny window behind Mr. Abadella's head.

Mr. Albright cleared his throat. "We're asking for three months, probation with no time served."

Abadella reared back in his chair, the squeaking of its base sounding like a scream. "No way. Mrs. Ebert has recklessly caused a life to be taken. She has to serve some time for that. Voluntary manslaughter carries a mandatory sentence of incarceration in this state. My hands are tied."

Mr. Albright pulled his chair closer to the desk. "Grady, Frieda and Layla Jay are here to tell you what happened. I think once you hear the whole story, you're going to want to reduce the charges because you'll see that this woman doesn't belong in prison."

Mr. Abadella looked at Mama, who was gripping her purse like it was about to fly out of her hand if she didn't hold on to it. "Okay, let's hear it, Mrs. Ebert. What exactly went on in your bedroom that afternoon?"

Mama looked at Mr. Albright for support I guessed. He nodded his head. Mama licked her lips. "Well, can I start at the beginning?"

"Start anywhere you like, Mrs. Ebert. That's why we're here."

Mama talked for a long time. She began by describing Wallace when she first met him, recounting how he mesmerized the Pisgah Methodist congregation, how he professed to be a man of God, charged by the Lord Himself to save sinners and bring them to His fold. "I was one of those lost sheep. A sinner," Mama said, "and I thought that marrying

Wallace was going to change my life. I believed him when he said his love would save my soul."

I was glad I'd heard Mama practice her lines or I might have looked surprised that Mama hadn't been enjoying sinning when she met Wallace. Mama didn't look down even once like most liars do, and I shifted my eyes onto Mr. Abadella's face, but I couldn't read his reaction to Mama's story.

She went on telling about how Wallace had turned out to be a Jekyll and Hyde. "He made me do things I can't even say out loud." Mama bit her lip, looked down, and whispered, "Sexual things no woman should be asked to do, but I loved my husband and I thought God wanted me to please him." Wallace *had* said that. That loving him was like loving God. I looked back at Mr. Abadella, but his face was still as expressionless as Mervin's gnomes. Finally, Mama got around to my part. "Wallace was always wanting to take Layla Jay somewhere, be with her alone. I thought he was just trying to be a father to her. She'd never known her real father who died when she was a baby. I know you have little girls, so you understand how important a father figure is for them."

When Mr. Abadella glanced over at the photo of his girls, a little hope began to surface inside me. Mama had said his having all those girls was lucky. Maybe she was right.

Mama squared her shoulders and sat up straighter. "Can you imagine how I felt when I found out that Wallace had raped my baby girl?" She shook her head. "No, you can't. No one can know who hasn't had something so unthinkable happen to them." She opened her purse and withdrew a little embroidered handkerchief and daubed her eyes. "I felt like the worst mother in the world when I found out. Of course, I'd asked Layla Jay why she tried to avoid being with Wallace alone, but she was so scared of him, she couldn't tell me the truth." Mama looked over at me and squeezed my hand. "She wanted to tell, I know. Bless her heart. We'd never had any secrets between us before, and I know that it was just killing her to keep it all inside."

Mr. Abadella interrupted her. His double chin quivered as he turned his head toward me. "Layla Jay, maybe we need to hear what you have to say before your mother continues. What happened between you and your stepfather?"

My heart was on fire, flames roared up into my mouth and I couldn't speak. I gripped the chair harder. "Water," I finally managed to say. "Could I please have a glass of water?"

While Mr. Abadella yelled out the door to his secretary to bring water, Mr. Albright leaned over Mama and whispered, "You'll do fine, Layla Jay. Just tell him exactly what you told me."

After a few sips from the paper cup of cool water, I took a deep breath and began the tale I'd practiced so many times. "When my step-daddy married Mama, I was real happy to have a father at last. I talked to my daddy up in heaven all the time, wishing he hadn't died, wishing that I had a daddy like all my friends." These snippets of truth were easy to tell and gave me confidence to ramble on. I recited Wallace's interest in my underwear, the leering looks, the aftermath of my first date, which I said wasn't really a date since Mrs. Albright drove us to and from the dance. When I came to the made-up portion of my story, I hesitated, but Mama reached for my hand and squeezed her strength into me. "Then one Sunday on the way home after church, my stepdaddy pulled off the highway." I closed my eyes, not wanting to look at the man who held so much power over our lives. What if he didn't believe me? I imagined an antenna sitting on his head like the one on top of our TV set that could pick up the static of my lies.

"Take your time," Mr. Abadella said.

I was a little comforted by his saying that and the voice inside me whispered, "Thank you, Jesus. Give me courage." It flitted through my mind that I shouldn't ask for God's help to tell a lie, and quickly added, "And forgive me for what I'm about to do." I don't know if it was God who led me through the details, but it seemed almost as if someone else had taken over my mind and my mouth as it moved up and down telling about Wallace's threats, his overpowering me, my fear, which was real enough. I must have been speaking softly, because as I neared the final scene on the day of the real attempted rape, I noticed that Mr. Abadella and Mr. Albright were both leaning forward out of their chairs. And when Mama passed her handkerchief to me, I knew I'd begun to cry, whether from shame or true emotion I had no idea. I wiped my eyes. "On the last day, when my stepdaddy had a fever, Mama asked me to stay with him to be his nurse."

Mr. Abadella held up his hand. "And you didn't protest?"

This wasn't a question we had rehearsed, but the answer came easily.

"No, she would have asked me why I didn't want to be alone with him, and I couldn't tell her the truth. I was too scared of what my stepdaddy would do to me if I told."

He wrote a few words on the pad in front of him. "Okay, go on," he said, leaning back in his chair.

I related the events of the day in chronological order and came to the part where Wallace asked for the soup and 7-Up. "The soup was all gone, so I took him some crackers on a napkin and opened the bottle of Seven-Up, and he ate all of the crackers, but he didn't finish the Seven-Up and I put it on the table beside the bed."

"You put it there?"

"I . . . I think so. He may have. I don't remember for sure." Mr. Albright had said it was good not to know everything perfectly, that our memories were often faulty, and I didn't want to sound too rehearsed. I could feel Mama's body shifting beside me. She was remembering to follow the same advice. "Anyway, then he asked me to fluff his pillow like I had for Mama after her accident." Oh shit, I said to myself. I wasn't supposed to remind him of Mama's drunk-driving accident. I hurried on. "So when I reached behind him, he grabbed my arms and I fell on top of him, and then everything happened so fast, I don't remember exactly what all he was doing. His hands were on me. He pulled off my shorts and panties. I was fighting, and I think yelling at him to stop, and crying. I know I was crying. And then Mama came in and she was yelling at him, too. And I saw the bottle in her hand, and he wouldn't let go of me, and then he fell off of me, off the bed." I was shaking, my teeth chattering like I was freezing in the hot room. I was seeing it all again. Each time I'd practiced telling this, it had just been words, memorizing words like the poems we recited for English class. But this time, in this setting, it seemed like it was happening at this very moment, and I shook my head, "He was, he was, blood everywhere, his eyes staring at me, he was, he was dead, and Mama grabbed me and we rolled across the bed far away from him. I was so scared, I . . ."

Mama's arms were around me. "It's all right, honey. It's okay. It's all over. You're safe now."

I breathed in her perfume, burying my nose against her chest. "I know," I said. "But it, everything, just all came back like he was here."

Mr. Abadella wasn't at his desk anymore. He was back at the door, calling his secretary again for more water. "Let's take a minute," he said, as he handed me a new paper cup. I saw the crumpled one on my lap and offered it to him. He threw it in the trash can beside his desk and sat back down. "Maybe it's best for you to talk for a while, Mrs. Ebert. I think I've got a good picture of what happened from your daughter's point of view. Now I'd like to hear yours."

As Mama talked in a soft voice, my mind wandered away from the memory to June to Jehu to Grandma to Gaylord's dog. I couldn't remember her name, and then I thought of Mervin and me naming one of his dwarfs. Murphy. That was the name we gave the little figure with the pointed hat that drooped over the side of his head. I looked over at Mama; she was shaking her head like it was on a spring. "I didn't mean to kill him. I don't even remember sticking the glass in his throat. The only thought I remember having was that I had to protect my baby. Save her from this demon. We both were in shock. I don't even remember calling my father, and I don't know why I dialed his number instead of the police. I guess no matter how old a daughter gets, she always looks to her daddy when she's in trouble."

Mama hadn't practiced that last bit about Papaw, and I wondered if she really did think about him whenever she was upset.

Mr. Abadella asked her a few more questions about the party at Lake Dixie Springs. He read bits of Bonita Garza's statement out loud. "Did you say you'd shoot your husband, Mrs. Ebert?"

"Of course not! That's just ridiculous, and even if I had said such a thing, saying it and doing it are horses of two different colors. Bonita's always been jealous of me, but I can't believe she'd stoop so low to hurt me."

Mr. Albright cut in and said, "Grady, you've heard all the facts that matter. What do you say? Dismiss the charges. You know Frieda didn't mean to kill her husband. She and Layla Jay were Wallace Ebert's victims. If he hadn't died, he'd be the one you're prosecuting."

Mr. Abadella twirled his pen in his hand, looked down at his pad, then said, "I can't dismiss the charges. A man is dead and she is responsible for that death."

"No," I said.

"Shhhh." Mama laid her hand on my arm and pressed it against the chair.

"Tell you what I'll do. I'll reduce the charge to involuntary manslaughter, sentence of two years, eighteen months probation, serve six in the county jail."

"Three," Mr. Albright said. "She's got a daughter here with no other parent."

Mr. Abadella looked right into my terrified eyes. "Okay, three, but one slipup and she serves total time in prison. I'll draw up the papers. Send them over later today."

"She won't slip, and you'll sleep better tonight, Grady, knowing you did the right thing this morning."

Mr. Abadella grinned. "I sleep just fine. You're the one who's got to worry about all the criminals you've put back on the streets come Judgment Day."

Judgment Day for Mama was over, and Mama had won the day. Or had she? Three months living with criminals wasn't going to be easy. And where would I live now? What would happen to me?

Chapter 34

MAMA LIT UP A LUCKY AS WE WALKED TO THE GALAXIE, which bore a parking ticket on the windshield. "Crap," Mama cried. "I've already broken the law. Maybe Pop can get it fixed." She tossed her cigarette on the street. "Let's go home," she said. We were both so exhausted from lack of sleep and wrung out emotionally from the hour we'd spent in Mr. Abadella's office, we cried all the way back to the house. One minute Mama was crying, saying she was a convicted felon now, and the next she was laughing hysterically through her tears saying she wasn't going to prison after all.

"It could have been a lot worse, Layla Jay," she said, unbuttoning her dress as she headed down the hall to her room. "Three months isn't such a long time really. I'll be out before Christmas, maybe Thanksgiving. I've got so much to do. I'd better make a list," she said, disappearing into her room.

Mr. Albright had asked for three days' grace period for Mama to put her affairs in order before she had to report to the jail to begin serving her time. I was one of the affairs, and I waited to see what order she was going to make of my life. I wasn't her first priority. She phoned Mervin and Papaw and the bank before she finally called me into the kitchen, where she sat at the table in her best blue dress with the ruffle above her breasts. "Where you going all dressed up?"

Mama smiled. "Nowhere. I'm going to wear the prettiest things in my closet for the next three days. I'll be wearing prisoner's garb for three whole months." I looked down at her lavender-bordered stationery. My name was on the top of her list with a question mark behind it. "Right now, we've got to talk about you, not me. I was thinking you could stay with Pop and Louise until I come home. What do you think? Would you like to live with them while I'm gone?"

I thought of Jehu and June. I'd never see them stuck out in the country with Papaw's cows and pigs. "Sure," I said. "Whatever you want me to do is fine."

"Pop will love having you back, and think of how good you'll be eating with Louise cooking for you every night."

MAMA WAS RIGHT ABOUT THE FOOD. That night Miss Louise brought over a chicken casserole, snap beans, and corn on the cob, and Papaw carried in a sweet potato pie he said was the best we'd ever eat. Hugs, tears, and laughter multiplied around the kitchen table as we sat nibbling at our food. Mervin couldn't keep his hands off Mama. He'd take a bite of casserole and stroke her arm as he chewed. Papaw eyed the cigar lying beside his plate as though he'd much rather have it in his mouth than a forkful of beans.

They'd all three been shocked when Mama told them about our going to Mr. Abadella's office. When Mama explained that she did it because she didn't want me to testify, Papaw nodded his approval. "Your mother would be proud of you," he said. "And she'd have done the same for you."

"I know," Mama said. "I thought of her all morning."

When she fell silent, Papaw leaned over and kissed her cheek.

Then we all fell mute with our private worries and thoughts, and Miss Louise tried to lighten the heavy air lying like a cloak over our table. In a cheerful tone, she said, "Layla Jay, we'll go to Montgomery

Ward and pick out some pretty curtains and a bedspread to match for your room. We could even paint over that awful yellow on the walls. Maybe a soft pink. What do you think?"

I tried to act like I really cared what color the room I'd be sleeping in for three months was. "That'd be cool," I said. But I knew that nothing would be cool again until Mama got out of jail.

THE NEWS TRAVELED FAST. The sentence was printed in *The Lexie Journal* on page four, and anyone who didn't buy a paper received a phone call from someone who did. June called me first. She couldn't quite hide her relief that she wasn't going to have to testify, but her voice broke when she said how sorry she was that Mama was going to jail. "I don't know how I would feel if it was my mother. I can't imagine it."

"I don't know how I feel either," I said. "At least she's not going far off to prison. We can visit her in Magnolia, and she'll be home for Christmas anyway."

When I told her I'd be living with Papaw and Miss Louise, June said I could stay at her house as often as I wanted. "After school starts, you can come home with me whenever you want to."

"Thanks," I said. "But you'd better ask your mother first. She might not want the daughter of a criminal in her house."

"Layla Jay, what an awful thing to say. Your mother isn't a criminal. Your stepfather was the criminal, not her."

"I know. You're right. I'm just mad, so mad that this happened, that Mama and I will be branded like cattle for the rest of our lives. You know how mean people can be."

June's voice wavered. "I do know, and I'm going to be branded, too. For you know what."

She was right again. And when I hung up the phone, I thanked God that at least He hadn't made me a lesbian. I had Jehu's love. Or did I? He hadn't called, and now I worried that, after his dad told him about our meeting, he'd changed his mind about loving someone whose mother was going to jail.

Mervin brought over Murphy, the dwarf I'd help make. "Wanted you to have him," he said. "You can take him with you to your grandpa's and he'll keep you company."

"Thanks," I said. "I wish Murphy was a real flesh-and-blood dwarf, and I was in a fairy tale, and all of this was just pretend."

Mervin hugged me for the first time ever. "It is. The next three months don't exist. I'm pretending that your mother is just going on a long trip, and when she comes back to us, we're going to get married, build that house she wants, and the three of us will live happily ever after, just like in a fairy tale."

"Did you ask her to marry you?"

"Not yet, but tonight, after she gets back, I'm going to get down on my knees and beg her to have me. Bought the ring already. Think she'll say yes?"

I smiled. "I know she will. You're the only man she's ever loved since my daddy. She told me."

"She told me, too. I'm the luckiest man in the world. Just have to get through the next three months is all. And we'll do it together. I've promised your mama I'll take care of everything while she's gone, and that includes anything you need. Anything at all."

When he said that, I smiled for the first time since Mama and I had sat in Mr. Abadella's office. I held out my arms for a second hug, and as I laid my head against his chest, I knew that this feeling of comfortable love that was blooming inside me meant that God had sent me a real father at last.

MAMA TOLD ME that when Mervin asked her to marry him that night, she cried so hard, she couldn't say yes right away. On Sunday afternoon she asked me to keep her ring while she was serving her time. "They'll take it anyway, and I'd rather know it was here with you than in some envelope that says 'Personal Effects.'"

It was a small diamond, but it sparkled like the brightest star in the sky. "I'll take good care of it," I said.

"We'll celebrate our engagement with you tonight," Mama said. "Why don't you invite Jehu over?"

"I'm scared to. He hasn't called."

"Well then, you'll just have to call him, won't you? Tell him to come early, five. Mervin is bringing over barbecued ribs and we'll have a picnic in the backyard."

"You sure you want company? It being your last night and all."

"I wouldn't have said to call if I didn't. We'll have a little party." She pushed me toward the phone. "Now go pick up that phone."

My entire being filled with dread. I couldn't take any more bad news, and if Jehu didn't love me, I didn't see how I could survive the months that loomed ahead. I'd skipped church this morning, partly because I couldn't face the curious looks I imagined I'd see on the faces of the members of Pisgah Methodist Church, and partly because I was afraid that Jehu would be there. I imagined how he'd be embarrassed he'd fallen for a girl whose mother was going to jail. He'd be polite and say Hello, Layla Jay like I was someone he barely knew. My hands were sweating and I wiped them on my shorts before I lifted the receiver.

When he answered, I sank to the floor and pushed my back into the wall. "Hey, it's me," I said.

"Oh, thank God," he said. "When you didn't show up at church and I hadn't heard from you in so long, I was so worried."

"You were?" The gift of his worrying was the best present I'd ever gotten.

"Yeah, when my dad told me the news about your mother, I wanted to call you so bad, but I figured you might not feel like talking about it. I didn't know what to do or say."

"Come to me," I said. "Can you come over?"

"Faster than a speeding bullet. Open the door and I'll be there," he said.

IT WAS A PERFECT NIGHT for an outdoor picnic. There was a full moon, so many stars scattered across the clear sky, I wondered if God had sprinkled an extra few among the constellations just for us to admire on this our last night together. Fall hadn't quite arrived, but there was a hint of chill in the air that warded off the mosquitoes that usually plagued us after the sun set. We sat cross-legged on an old patchwork quilt Grandma had made years before, licking our fingers as we ate the barbecued ribs Mervin had brought. He'd also brought corn on the cob drenched in butter and cole slaw that tasted nearly as good as Miss Louise's. Every now and then one of us would remember that this was our last night together and a sadness would pass over our faces, but for most of the meal, we laughed and joked about what Mama would do in jail. "She'll have all the women doing the watusi in no time," Mervin said.

"I'll trade them lessons for cigarettes," Mama said, standing up and shimmying before she fell back on the quilt.

"I've got a surprise," Mervin said. He went into the house and brought out a tray that held four hot fudge sundaes. "Stopped by the Tastee-Freez after I picked up the barbecue," he said. "I snuck them into the freezer while you were bringing the food out."

"How did you know about our sundaes?" I asked.

"Frieda told me. She asked me to bring her one every time I came to visit her. I thought I'd get an early start."

Mama popped the cherry on top of her sundae into her mouth. "And Layla Jay, you're to bring one for both of us every time you visit, too. I can't stand the thought of my daughter having the blues while I'm gone. Promise?"

"I promise," I said.

Before the party ended, Mervin ran back into the house for another surprise. It was a bottle of champagne, and after he popped the cork with a lot of effort and much laughter from everyone, we toasted his and Mama's engagement and then we toasted the future. After clinking our glasses and taking a sip, Jehu leaned over and kissed me. Mama and Mervin didn't notice because they were kissing, too.

Around nine o'clock, Jehu said he had to leave. I walked with him as far as the corner of our block where he kissed me again. "I'll call you," he said. "I love you and I'll be here for you always."

When I returned to the backyard to help clean up, Mama stood up. "That can wait," she said. She leaned over, put her arms around Mervin, and kissed his nose. "Can you disappear for a little while? There's something Layla Jay and I have to do alone."

"Sure," he said. "I understand. "You need some time. I'll run down and get you some more cigarettes to take with you tomorrow."

Mama waited until we heard the Caddy's motor purring in the driveway, and then she grabbed my hand. "It's time," she said, pulling me back into the kitchen.

She pointed to the wall where the remnants of our life with Wallace were stacked. We lugged the garbage bags out into the backyard, to a spot Mama chose about ten feet to the right of the oak tree, and there we dumped everything into a pile as high as our waists. Mama doused it with the can of lighter fluid and struck a kitchen match. She held it above the pile and turned to me. "You ready?"

"Ready," I said.

She struck two more matches and tossed them onto the pile. Wallace's plaid shirt went up in flames, next a pair of undershorts, and then the navy blue nylon robe he never wore caught fire. After a few minutes the flames began to spread and in no time we had a huge bonfire going that shot sparks out into the darkness surrounding us.

Mama's face lit by the firelight wavered from one emotion to another. Sorrow, anger, and satisfaction, all that I was feeling, too. She squeezed her lips together and put her arm around my shoulders. As we stood watching the flames burning away our former lives, Mama whispered, "It's not exactly the celebration we'd planned, but it's still a fine way to say good riddance to our past." She kissed my forehead. "I love you. I'll miss you so much." She wiped her face with the back of her hand. "But you'll come visit. We Andrews women are tough; got Claude Whittington blood in us. We'll get through it, and we'll put all of this behind us. It'll be *c'est la vie* from then on."

"I don't know if I can *c'est la vie*. I don't feel so tough," I said. "I feel like a baby who needs her mama."

"You don't need me nearly as much as you think. You're just about all grown up now."

When we heard Mervin's car in the drive, she let go of me. "He's back. I'm going in. You coming?"

"No, I want to stay out here a little longer. You go ahead," I said.

As I stood alone in the backyard watching the fire slowly dying, I walked a full circle around it. With each step I heard Mama's words. "All grown up now, all grown up." And I had turned out to be a grown-up liar with secrets that would weigh heavily on my heart for the rest of my life. I vowed that night that I would return the things I'd taken from June's house one by one. I wouldn't be a thief after everything was back where it belonged, but I'd still be a liar, a sinner. I couldn't help wondering, if Mama hadn't accepted the plea bargain and gone to trial with a jury instead, if maybe they would have found her not guilty. But I also knew that they could have found her guilty and she'd be going to prison for a long time. What might have been? What would have happened? I'd never know, and I'll live out my life always wondering what might have been.

I looked over at the house just as the light in Mama's bedroom went out. I doubted Mama or Mervin would sleep tonight. They'd hold on to each other trying to make each minute memorable to carry them through the coming days. I knew that Mama was scared of what the morning would bring. Her hands had trembled earlier in the day when she crossed off the last item on her list. "Done," she'd said. "Everything's taken care of now."

Everything was done that needed to be done. My suitcase was packed. The phone would be disconnected tomorrow, and Papaw would come to return me to where I'd begun. But Grandma wouldn't be there and neither would Mama, nor was the girl who had left nearly a year ago coming back.

The fire had died down to embers now, small orange glows of light winked out of the burned circle of ashes. I knelt on the ground and bowed my head. "Please take care of Mama. Don't let anything happen to her in jail. Thank you for sending Mervin and Jehu to us and help June to find happiness, and bless Papaw and Miss Louise and Mr. Albright." I lifted my head. I knew there was more to say, but I couldn't form the words. Grandma said them for me. "That which you've been praying for all these months, you already had, Layla Jay. God answered your prayers long ago." I could feel her strength and her faith pouring into me, and a kind of serenity I'd never known settled deep inside me. I knew that tomorrow my fears would return, and God wouldn't answer all of my prayers. But some days He'd take away my fears and answer my prayers and on those days I'd have *c'est la vie* in my heart.

Hot
Fudge
Sundae
Blues

Bev Marshall

A Reader's Guide

A CONVERSATION WITH
BEV MARSHALL

Silas House and Bev Marshall met at a book signing in Jackson, Mississippi, in 2002 and instantly became friends and fans of each other's novels. Since that time, they've corresponded and occasionally had the opportunity to read and sign together across the South. Just after House's *The Coal Tattoo* was published, Bev completed the manuscript for *Hot Fudge Sundae Blues.* Now with three published novels each, Silas and Bev met again in Jackson at a favorite local watering hole to talk about their latest books. Here is a part of that lively conversation.

Silas House: Well, Bev, you know that I was one of your very first fans. I was lucky enough to be given an advance copy of your first novel, *Walking Through Shadows,* before it was even published, and fell in love with your writing immediately. What I love about all your work is how intimately we get to know the characters. We always leave your books feeling as if we've met a whole new bunch of people, made new friends. Layla Jay definitely joins that group of characters that I will forever think of as old friends. She's so endearing and complex and real. Was it hard to tell her good-bye when you finished the novel?

Bev Marshall: I can't think of a better friend for Layla Jay than you! Thanks for your kind words about her. As to saying good-bye, let me explain it this way. When I wrote the first draft of *Walking Through Shadows,* I wrote the entire novel from Annette's point of view. My agent suggested that the story would be stronger if I told it from several points of view in order to include the information that Annette wasn't privy to. As a result, I excised nearly two hundred pages of her thoughts, feelings, and voice. And although I knew the novel was better for that decision, I couldn't say good-bye to Annette. I knew that Annette's voice was going to resurface, and it did. Layla Jay is really Annette during puberty, and I was able to use some of Annette's story in *Hot Fudge Sundae Blues.* For example, the birthday party scene originally happened to Annette, and three years ago, Jehu was Annette's boyfriend. So now I'm saying good-bye to both girls and finding it difficult to let go of them. It just may happen that someday an adult Annette/Layla Jay will reappear.

SH: I love how you don't judge your characters. You just let them be and allow them to reveal themselves to the reader. I believe that's what makes your characters so real. They have plenty of faults. They're far from perfect, but still we love them. How do you accomplish this so seamlessly?

BM: I could say the same about your characters. I guess we both know that to be human means we're imperfect. And really perfect people—perfect characters—are just plain boring. I know a few individuals who seem saintly, but for most of us, making mistakes is a given. Our flaws are what make us unique, give roundness to our personalities and our lives. I love my friends' peccadilloes, their struggles, their bad choices, and I love that they know mine and love me anyway. So it's no different with my characters. Layla Jay loves her mother and June and forgives them when they hurt her because she is fully aware of her own capacity to do wrong. Writing the story was simply a matter of viewing each character holistically without judgment.

SH: I agree so much with that. I always say that nobody wants to read about saints. And really, readers don't want to read about happy people either. But I believe readers do want to read about people becoming happy.

BM: Well, maybe not all readers do, but I think that's true of the majority.

SH: One example of your nonjudgmental writing is Frieda. She'll surely never win "Mother of the Year," will she? However, she is a great mother in her own way. You want to tell us a little bit about the way you conceived her?

BM: [Laughter] Nope, Frieda will never wear a "Mother of the Year" button, but I doubt she'd want one anyway. Remember how horrified she is to think she looks like Donna Reed or Harriet Nelson. I'm happy to know you think she is a great mother in her own way because I was worried that my readers would judge her too harshly. She certainly makes plenty of mistakes to warrant criticism. I actually went back and added the scene with the dog and doll months after I had finished the novel, hoping to strengthen the readers' understanding of her love for Layla Jay. My conception of her was that, given her circumstances, she was doing the best she could, and I think that's all we can ask of people, whether it has to do with their parenting skills or any other role they find themselves in. I imagined that the early disappointments in Frieda's life affected her deeply. She lost the husband she loved, was a single parent of a two-year-old child, had no money, and was forced to return to her parents' farm. When that happened, under her mother's strict rule again, she lost her power and independence. And like an adolescent, she rebelled. After the deaths of her husband and her mother, Frieda was afraid of losing the people she loved, and her withdrawal, and sometimes harsh treatment of the people who loved her, probably seemed very cold and/or selfish. But I believed that Frieda was trying only to protect herself from future pain. When Mervin comes along and she finally realizes that he won't leave her, that she's safe in the relationship, she begins to trust and then allow herself to open her heart to him.

SH: You did a great job with all of that, then, because I understood everything you were trying to show with that character. Speaking of

Frieda, we both love to write about wild women. What is it that's so attractive about these characters to us?

BM: Well, in my case, I wanted to be one, but I doubt that's your motivation. Seriously, as we were both brought up in small towns with large rural communities, I think we, like everyone around us, knew someone like Frieda and Anneth in *The Coal Tattoo*. They are the women everyone loved to gossip about because they were more exciting and unpredictable than most women. In *Right as Rain*, Dimple is the wild woman, and you're right, I had a ball writing about her and Frieda's outrageous behavior. I think most women have a little Frieda in them, but most of us are too afraid of censure to let that part of us out into the world. I have to admit that the few times I've crossed the line of propriety I've enjoyed myself immensely.

SH: You know that you and I and Butch [Bev's husband] have been out to a few places and I've seen a bit of Frieda in you, Bev. [Laughter]

BM: Now, Silas, you don't want to tell secrets. Remember that I know a couple about you, too.

SH: Okay, I see your point, but you know people are going to ask you this, so let's go ahead and put it right here in print: How much of you is in Layla Jay?

BM: Since I just admitted to having a little Frieda inside me, I don't mind saying that Layla Jay resides within me, too. We have a lot in common, but there are huge differences as well. I knew what it felt like to be unpopular, to long for a boyfriend, to be wrongly accused, and to suffer guilt for sins, both real and imagined. But I had a great mother who would never have done any of the things Frieda did. And my father is very much joyfully alive at eighty-five. However, my model for Papaw was my maternal grandfather, and I borrowed many of his traits in the story. He chewed cigars and said "bullshit" all the time, and my relationship with him was very similar to that of Layla Jay and Papaw. He *was* a churchgoer though. I also cleaned the church with my maternal grandmother, who died when I was twelve, and on many a Saturday, just like

Layla Jay, I preached, played hymns, and confessed to all manner of sins in the church where I grew up.

SH: I loved all those facets of Layla Jay so much. You really got inside a teenager's head, too. I'm writing a book right now that's from a child's point of view and it's the hardest thing I've ever done, finding that balance of observing the world as a child but also being relatable to an adult reader. Did you find that difficult?

BM: No, actually, writing from a child's perspective is much easier for me than an adult's perspective. Maybe that's because I just haven't grown up yet myself, but if so, I hope I never do. The hardest task in writing in a child's point of view for me is remaining faithful to a young person's vocabulary. The temptation to use inappropriate language is always there, and oftentimes I go back and delete those ten-dollar words I'll find in a child's dialogue. But the thoughts, doubts, dreams, actions of my youthful characters, thankfully, come quite easily to me as I write the stories they tell me.

SH: You did a great job of it. Religion is a theme that runs throughout this book. Having grown up in the South, wouldn't you agree that even people who aren't "raised in church" have a profound respect for religion, and are constantly aware of it? Religion is obviously a part of Layla Jay's very culture. Was it the same for you, growing up?

BM: I definitely agree that in the South, religion has a great impact on our lives. Whether you are a churchgoer, a lapsed Christian, or even an atheist, you can't avoid the effects of religion on your culture and on those who live there. I mentioned earlier that I cleaned our church with my grandmother, and my brother and I took turns enacting the roles of preacher and sinner in made-up plays when we were children. But religion played a much larger part in my upbringing. Our social lives were entwined with the church. Family sing-alongs were generally hymns or gospel songs, and we went to church twice on Sunday, Wednesday nights, and never missed a day of revival. It seems quite feasible to me that Layla Jay's faking salvation weighs heavily on her, and her quest to understand her relationship to God is paramount.

SH: I could relate to that so much, because I grew up in a very religious family. I'm glad for it now, but back then it was sometimes difficult. I also related to the way Layla Jay interacted with her family. I love the way she relies on them, never turns against them no matter what. She loves her mother and grandparents and even her dead father with a vengeance. I remember you once telling me that you had a big party when your first book was released and I was amazed by all the cousins and family members you had. Do you have a large, tight family?

BM: Oh, yes! I grew up visiting every one of my twenty great-aunts and uncles, not including their spouses. I have no idea how many cousins I have today. Although we no longer visit often, we remain a very close-knit family. As you mentioned, many of them came down to my publication party, and the editor from the California publishing company, who met all of them there, said that every one of them was a novel in themselves. And that's so very true! They're the source of many of my stories. My dad in particular will trade a good tale, packed with wonderful detail, for a hot meal or a slice of cake.

SH: Lord, that sounds just like my family, the storytelling. Maybe that's why we get along so well. Remember that time we drove from Jackson up to Oxford together? I remember that we told stories the whole way. We barely took a breath, we were talking so much.

BM: Yes, that was so much fun. We do have a lot in common.

SH: I thought that one major theme in this book was judgment. Jehu believes that the people in Zebulon are so good-hearted they'd never sneer at Layla Jay or her mother, but Layla Jay knows better. Were you consciously making a statement about how judgmental our society is, how quick we are to jump to conclusions about our neighbors and decide to judge everyone as guilty before proven innocent?

BM: Absolutely not! I never write with an agenda. However, I have to admit that your assessment of my feelings about people judging others is accurate, and I'm sure that it's inevitable that my values oftentimes coincide with those of my characters. But it's not something I would ever consciously do, as I believe that a novel, once it is written, belongs to the reader, not the author. What conclusions someone wants to draw from a particular novel have to come from within them, not me. But you know, Silas, I do think one of the worst flaws of our society is that we judge others, and often we judge unfairly.

SH: Well, I do, too. And I think you make a very good point, that the author should never be present in the actual book, but should simply put everything on the page for the reader to come to his or her own conclusions. So it's only natural that that's one theme I took away from the book, since I do think a lot about how judgmental we are of one another, about how we jump to conclusions and see everything as being very simple, while everything is, in fact, very complex. But since you don't have any kind of agenda (and I'm glad you don't), I'm just curious what you want people to gain from your writing. What do you want them to feel once they've closed this book?

BM: I hope they feel that they've read a good tale about some people they like and can relate to on some level. Really, I don't have any expectations of my readers beyond that. Well, I guess, I also hope they feel they didn't waste their money or their time!

SH: I know, I always say that if someone's going to shell out money for my books, I want them to have a good time. And I want them to feel as if they've gone somewhere, escaped to a whole world. That's something that I completely feel when I'm reading a Bev Marshall book, and one way you do that is by all the quirky little details you supply. Tell me, do you secretly have a coffee table that's shaped like the state of Mississippi? I thought that was brilliant.

BM: No, my coffee table is very ordinary, but if you ever see one shaped like Mississippi, or Louisiana, let me know and I'll buy it. I grew up seeing all sorts of bizarre objects made out of wood, so Frieda's coffee table seemed even a bit mundane to me. And, by the way, all those little stone people I described? They live just about five miles down the road from me. I'm thinking of getting a couple for my back-yard someday.

SH: Get me one of those dwarfs. Before we go, I have to ask: Do you have a hot fudge sundae when you're having an especially bad day?

BM: You bet I do!

QUESTIONS AND TOPICS
FOR DISCUSSION

1. Layla Jay begins the book wishing to be like her mother in all respects: the way she looks, the way she is with men, etc. Do you think Layla Jay still feels that way by the end of the book? If not, what do you think changed, and why?

2. Frieda treats Layla Jay "like a girlfriend instead of a daughter." Do you think this is beneficial for Layla Jay? How do you think it shapes her relationship with her mother, and her relationship with the outside world?

3. Layla Jay has a very strong connection to her father even though she doesn't remember him. How accurate do you think her depictions of her father are? Do you have similar feelings about someone who passed away and you wish you could have talked to more?

4. When Layla Jay and Frieda move out of Grandma and Papaw's house in the country and into the city, Layla Jay frequently misses the house and the land. What effect do you think our environment has on us? Did you move as a child? How did the change affect you?

5. Why do you think Layla Jay feels pressured to get saved? What role does religion play in the lives of these characters? Did you ever ex-

perience this feeling of pressure by your church affiliation or its members? How did it affect you?

6. The way we view Wallace certainly changes throughout the novel. How did you feel about him when he was first introduced? What exactly do you think his intentions were when he married Frieda? How do you think they shifted, both before and after he was "saved" again?

7. Layla Jay and her mother have the tradition of getting hot fudge sundaes when they feel "as rotten and low and hopeless as you can be and you think the world's biggest sponge couldn't mop up all the tears inside of you." Why do we find comfort in rituals, and do you have any that you rely on to make you feel better when you're down?

8. Frieda tells Layla Jay that Jehu should make up his mind about his feelings for her. What do you think about Jehu's seeming ambivalence toward Layla Jay? Do you think he's a good choice for a boyfriend?

9. Some of the lies Layla Jay tells aren't as significant as others. Do you think the gravity of the lie makes a difference? Were any, or all, of Layla Jay's lies justified and okay to tell? When do you think it's okay to "stretch the truth"?

10. Layla Jay and June are bound by their sense of being outsiders. What criteria do you think is the basis for acceptance in a community? Does this vary if it's a small town or a city? Have you ever felt like an outsider, and if so, on what do you base your feeling?

11. The friendship between Layla Jay and June develops into a complex relationship. Many changes occur within the friendship, from the day Layla Jay fakes salvation until the last conversation between her and June just before the end of the novel. How did you perceive this relationship and does it seem plausible?

12. Why do you think Layla Jay thinks about commiting suicide? Do you think she seriously considered it? What do you think this indicates about her personality, if anything?

13. Do you think Frieda was justified in attacking Wallace? Do you think she intended to kill him? In your opinion, are crimes of passion more excusable than premeditated crimes?

PHOTO © CHRIS JOHN

BEV MARSHALL is the critically acclaimed author of *Walking Through Shadows* and *Right as Rain*. She grew up in McComb and Gulfport, Mississippi, and earned degrees from the University of Mississippi and Southeastern Louisiana University. After living as a nomadic military wife for many years, Marshall returned to her Southern roots and now lives with her husband in Ponchatoula, Louisiana. She is the visiting writer-in-residence at Southeastern Louisiana University.

About the Type

This book was set in Bembo, a typeface based on an old-style Roman face that was used for Cardinal Bembo's tract *De Aetna* in 1495. Bembo was cut by Francisco Griffo in the early sixteenth century. The Lanston Monotype Company of Philadelphia brought the well-proportioned letterforms of Bembo to the United States in the 1930s.